IAN THEWLIS taught at colleges and universities in the UK, Libya and Nigeria before joining the Middle East oil industry. *Arabian Night Patrol* draws on his experience of Saudi Arabia and Kuwait during the first Gulf War, the genesis of Al Qaeda and the subsequent invasion of Iraq.

After leaving the Arabian Gulf, Ian travelled the world as an oil industry training consultant. He returned periodically to the Gulf and also experienced the aftermath of the Soviet collapse in Russia, Kazakhstan, Azerbaijan and Georgia.

Ian has written several business books but now devotes his time to writing fiction. *Arabian Night Patrol* is the first novel in a trilogy tracing the genesis and development of the War on Terror.

G000056714

ARABIAN NIGHT PATROL

IAN THEWLIS

SilverWood

Published in 2019 by SilverWood Books

SilverWood Books Ltd
14 Small Street, Bristol, BS1 1DE, United Kingdom
www.silverwoodbooks.co.uk

ISBN 978-1-78132-819-4

British Library Cataloguing in Publication Data
A CIP catalogue record for this book is available from
the British Library

Page design and typesetting by SilverWood Books
Printed on responsibly sourced paper

*To Ann Marie, Ray and friends who lived through
the Gulf War and the genesis of the War on Terror*

Acknowledgements

Thanks to all who helped me through the research and writing of this novel. In particular, I appreciated reviews from Doug Johnstone and Thalia Suzuma of the Literary Consultancy who encouraged me with their comments. Thanks also to Patricia Duncker and Jenny Parrott, my tutors on the Arvon Foundation's editing course, and Catherine with the team at SilverWood who brought this novel to fruition.

Special thanks to my talented son, Alex, for his advice, suggestions, patience, and critical red pen.

1

Another Night in Paradise

Saudi Arabia *12 January 1991 / 26 Jumada 1411*   *21.00*

Nine o'clock and only three more nights before the war starts. Rob Watson urges Cilla, his black Labrador, into the back of the patrol car, settles her on an old yellow carpet, and drives out of Acacia Court for his first night back on patrol. Swinging right past Banyan and Cactus Courts, he turns onto Perimeter Road and cruises beside the high chain-link fence of the airbase, headlights searching for breaks in the wire. Even at this time, the oil camp's streets and courtyards are deserted, people huddled in their homes waiting for the next news bulletin, the first Scud alerts to start wailing out. But soon he's feeling comfortable inside the patrol car, with the company's Easy Listening music muttering over the radio and Cilla stretched out on the back seat, shifting occasionally to raise her head, look around, and settle back again.

As he left the house, CNN were reporting that James Baker, the US Secretary of State, was visiting the airbase, checking the preparations for war. Now, beyond the perimeter fence, the base lies waiting, brooding through this wintry night, and gathering itself to attack. On this side, the oil camp's courtyards are silent, oblivious to what Rob knows is the frenzied activity over there; trucks shuttling aviation fuel and supplies along the roads, the candy men loading planes and helicopter gunships with munitions, pilots being briefed for their reconnaissance flights over Iraq and occupied Kuwait. Yet despite the sharp silhouettes of hardened shelters, the pinpricks of light in the gloom marking the giant Galaxy transports, that feverish activity is difficult to imagine here, cruising slowly along by the perimeter fence.

He drives down towards the Utilities Department, its illuminated Pepsi vending machine standing guard outside the office building. Further along, the still waters of the sewage treatment ponds glisten under yellow sodium lights. The emerald grass around these ponds was recently mown and he remembers reading in the company newspaper about a crazy golf competition there, an event designed to publicize the company's new sanitation system.

Next stop, the camp garage. Old cars and trucks are parked haphazardly outside, abandoned when their owners fled after Saddam Hussein invaded Kuwait and threatened Saudi. Rob pulls into the space between a white Ford Transit and a Toyota pick-up with black garbage bags dumped in the back. Facing the padlocked gate, his headlights beam through the wire mesh onto the garage forecourt, the vehicles parked for repair and the inspection ramp curving up into the night sky. He gets out, scanning the area with his flashlight, checking for suspicious movements beyond the beam of his headlights. The smell of gasoline that always hangs over the camp is usually strongest here, but the chill wind from the sea is dispersing it, threatening more rain and discomfort for the troops camped up north near the Kuwaiti border. It's the coldest and wettest Saudi winter he can remember, and he zips up his Security windbreaker and pulls the baseball cap firmly down on his head.

No lights show in the garage workshops where the remaining Filipino mechanics devote evenings and weekends to their private business, repairing Westerners' cars and four-wheel drives. Behind the garage he can see the junk yard's piles of rusting parts, with two large metal containers parked up against the fence. 'It's a weak point,' warned Rick, the big American security boss, when he drove Rob around before Christmas. 'Better stay alert.'

But tonight there are no suspicious movements. He reverses back onto the road, driving down towards the grove of palm trees screening the agricultural research station. He cruises into the car park, headlights washing over the dimly lit plant nursery and greenhouses, where tomatoes and cucumbers grow in plastic tubes without soil, sustained only by running water enriched with plant food. The tops of the palm trees are swaying in the breeze. The car is warm and comfortable inside, and he winds down the driver's window. Already he's feeling tired, needing this blast of cold air.

Past the agricultural station, the road turns sharp right, heading towards the lights of the bachelor housing block. But he drives straight on, following the chain-link fence. With a bump, he leaves the tarmac and pulls onto an unlit dirt track used by garbage trucks going to the landfill site. He drives more cautiously, headlights scanning the rough track and manoeuvring between potholes. Before the invasion, this wasteland with its mounds of rubble was a testing ground for teenagers racing BMXs and dirt bikes. After the invasion, most kids were evacuated with their mothers, back to homes around the world. He wonders how many will return. And will Fiona, his wife, ever come back?

Headlights pierce the gloom and a US army Humvee, with a search-light and machine gun mounted on top, bounds along the track on the other side of the fence. Spotting the white patrol car, the base guards flash their lights, acknowledging their common purpose. They're heading to-wards the Patriot battery hidden among the small limestone *jebels* and waiting to shoot down missiles attacking the base. The Pentagon has spent billions of dollars on missile defence systems but will this Patriot work? At first the Americans and British said that Saddam's Scuds couldn't even fly this far, but now they say they'll shoot them down.

Rob parks and lets Cilla jump out to roam around while he walks up a small *jebel*, a rocky perch overlooking the airbase, where he can smoke a cigarette and perhaps spot James Baker's plane on the tarmac. Five years since he stopped smoking, but for this time and place he's awarded himself the luxury of just one Marlboro cigarette each night.

Lighting up, he savors the deliciously illicit taste, this moment saved for tranquillity, and looks across the base. The shapes of hardened shelters and barracks stretch into the distance, and the low moaning vibration of generators carries on the wind. It feels like he's living next door to a friendly giant who's kindly offered to take care of him. Or a mass murderer, whose surreptitious movements disturb him during the night, but when he sees him in the morning, he waves cheerfully on his way to work.

No sign of James Baker's plane. Perhaps he's already left. Rob wonders what he should think about tonight to while away the hours on patrol. Football? He and Chris, his student son, went to Anfield on New Year's Day to see the Reds beat Leeds. So, are Liverpool going to win the League this year?

Or maybe he should think about his family. Back in Southport, on his last night at home, his parents and some friends phoned asking if he was still going back to Saudi. It was obvious there was going to be war and maybe thousands killed. Not sure whether he sounded brave or just foolish, Rob told them he was returning and gave his usual reasons – he wouldn't be dictated to by Saddam Hussein, people at work depended on him, and he had to go back for Cilla, the family dog. But nobody seemed convinced.

After dinner he sat drinking coffee with Fiona and Chris round the kitchen table.

'So why are you really going back, Dad?' asked his son, more confident after his first term at university.

Again he began to rationalize but Chris broke in. 'Cut the bullshit, Dad. Is it the money?'

'Partly. I've got no pension and we need some savings.'

'What else then?'

'Well we've got Cilla and our things at the house.'

Their discussion dissipated over more coffee but Fiona hadn't joined in the questioning. He was conscious of her strained expression, her determination to let him make his own decision, no matter how ill she felt. But how ill was she? He'd been reluctant to inquire too deeply as she might flare up at him. She'd seen the doctor about headaches and depression and returned with some pills. Hopefully, they'd work.

In just a few months he'd complete ten years and qualify for full severance benefits. 'I'm coming back after ten,' he'd promised Fiona, as he nuzzled into her hair at Manchester airport. 'Only a few months to go.'

Now he crushes his cigarette into the sand, strolls down the bluff to the patrol car and opens the back door to let Cilla jump in. On the radio, Phil Collins is singing about something in the air tonight, as Rob checks in with the Big House.

'*Assalamu alikum.* Welcome back to Paradise, my friend.' Abdul Karim – Al to his Western colleagues – greets him through the crackling, his Texan accent a legacy of detective training in Dallas. 'How's the family? You have good Christmas?'

'Good. So how's your family, Al?'

'*Zain.* I take to Riyadh for safety. Only strong men stay for this war, *sideeki.*'

But Al's usual good humour sounds constrained. Is Rick, his American boss, listening in?

'You see Mr Baker?' Al asks. 'He's visiting the guys at the Base.'

'No, he's probably left. Nothing to report here. All's quiet.'

'*Alhamdullilah.* Good to know you're back, my friend. But be careful out there.' Al concludes with the familiar warning from the roll-call sergeant in *Hill Street Blues.*

Time now for Rob to drive to the small lake which drains off water from the camp's sewage ponds. Scrubby tamarisk trees and bushes screen this man-made oasis where, in the evening, amateur naturalists and photographers come to spy on migrating birds. After a day's work and in the cool of the jogging and dog walking hour, the lake seems a peaceful place, skirted by reeds and illuminated by the setting sun. But it's close to the Patriot missile base. Terrorists could attack from here.

He bumps along the dirt track towards the trees, parks and steps out into the whine of mosquitoes already gathering round his head. Snakes lurk in the long grass, so he puts Cilla on the lead and with his flashlight beaming the way ahead, walks down the sandy jogging track. Halfway round the lake, the shrubs grow dense, sheltering him from the cold wind. He halts and plays out the lead for Cilla to snuffle round and pee in the bushes. He listens to the sound of the reeds shifting with the breeze, testament to the sheer persistence of nature even in this barren place.

He pulls on the lead but Cilla resists, and giving way, he decides he's got time to think. Here, stranded in the middle of his life and facing this war, he should decide what he's going to do. He could go back home, and this Christmas Liverpool looked more prosperous after the unemployment, rioting and despair he fled in 1981. Maybe there are job opportunities like Fiona says. But he's almost ten years older and his CV shows he's been out of the country too long. So should he carry on working here?

This war might change his life, and if he's ever going to change, now's the time.

He pulls Cilla back from the bushes and follows the jogging track round the other side of the lake. It's usually brighter here with light from the bachelor housing block shining across the barren spray fields. But since the invasion, this apartment block's emptied out and tonight only a few isolated lights on the ground floor are visible.

The lights snap off, the road and housing block lost in blackness, as if someone's pulled a master switch. They said there'd be blackouts when the war started. But maybe this is a practice. Feeling vulnerable, he moves his flashlight round and pulls Cilla to him as he hurries back to the patrol car.

Next on his checklist is the derelict electricity substation, standing isolated in the wasteland. But he's only driven for a few minutes when a large boulder appears unexpectedly in the headlights, barring the way forward. Mounds of dirt and building rubble border the track, but this boulder seems deliberately placed to stop a car driving on. It looks too heavy to move so he edges his patrol car off the track onto the sand and dirt. Immediately he feels the vehicle sinking, the wheels slipping. He stops. There's been heavy rain over the last few days and he could get bogged down. Shifting into reverse, he struggles to back up onto more solid ground, sweat trickling down under his arms as the engine revs. At last, the wheels jerk back onto firmer ground and he can straighten up.

He decides to walk to the substation. Taking the flashlight from the passenger seat, he puts Cilla on the lead, and steps out of the car's warm security. His headlights shine ahead, picking out more rubble on the track, scraps of litter blown against the substation's wire fence.

But something shifts, a flicker of movement by the wire fence, and in the corner of his eye he sees something. He halts, shining his light around the substation. Everything seems still. He steps forward, scanning the area and giving an intruder the chance to run. Still nothing. Conscious of leaving the safety of his patrol car further behind, he advances. Cilla is barking, pulling him forward. Another flicker across his vision, and the flashlight almost catches a low shape fleeing across the wasteland, then lost behind mounds of rubble.

Shocked, he yanks Cilla back. A wild dog or maybe one of the desert foxes that scavenge round the dumps? Or a man? Could it have been a man crouching low as he ran for cover? A terrorist escaping from behind the substation? Cilla's still barking, rearing up on her back legs and straining to charge forward. Rob stays still, forcing himself to calm down, control his breathing and listen into the night sounds. But there's only the steady chirping of cicadas, and the wind's low moaning. Was it really someone running, hiding behind the mounds of rubble, and escaping across the spray fields?

He slowly walks round the substation, examining the chain-link fence and holding Cilla close, alert to any movement in the shadows. His flashlight shines through the wire, sweeping round to the grey metal door of the control building and a *DANGER* sign with a white skull-and-crossbones and electrical shocks radiating out. Below is *KEEP AWAY* in Arabic and English. More Arabic letters are scrawled in white paint on the door and a large rusty padlock hangs loosely in place. A polystyrene cup lies trapped under the fence, some flattened Pepsi and Dr Pepper cans gleam in the light and a Domino's pizza box has blown against the gate. People have eaten here. But recently? No damage to the wire, no sign of anyone breaking in. Maybe he's imagining things.

A last sweep of the area with his flashlight and all's clear. He walks back along the track to his patrol car, feeling like a returning hero bathed in the welcoming headlights. He opens the door for Cilla to jump inside and settles back into the warmth and Easy Listening sound of John Denver, taking him back where he belongs. Almost eleven o'clock and time to check in again with the Big House.

'*Assalamu alikum.*' Al greets him. 'Where are you, my friend? Anything to report?'

'I'm near the electrical substation. Think I saw a desert fox, something there.' He almost jokes about Cilla chasing it, but then remembers dogs aren't allowed on patrol. If Rick or Al found out...

'Sure it's an animal?' Al's on the alert. 'What did you see?'

Rob isn't sure but if he says so, they'll drive round and catch him with Cilla.

'OK Al. Calm down. An animal – four legs, not two.'

A sudden eruption. Cilla cowers on the back seat and even with his hands clasped over his ears, Rob recoils at the shriek and reverberation as four jets rise in formation over the perimeter fence and burst into the air. He watches the heavily laden planes climb and recede into the distance, the gold and purple flare of afterburners fading into the night sky.

Only three more nights before the war starts and who knows what will happen? Scuds could hit this area with nerve gas or chemical warheads, there's talk of Saddam having a 'dirty bomb' and hundreds could be killed. Terrorists might attack the camp and then what would he do? Now, Rob realizes, he's being put to the test.

2

The Brothers

12 January 1991 / 26 Jumada 1411   22.45

Ibrahim's heard that the Crusaders train their dogs to smell out and attack Arabs. Now this vicious creature is barking furiously, pulling on the security guard's chain and jumping towards his hiding place. Crouched behind a mound of rubble only a few yards away, he daren't move in case he's caught by the guard's flashlight and the animal sees him. Just one bite on his hands or legs and he could die from the deadly rabies this snarling black dog probably carries.

He holds his breath, fearing the animal might hear him, and presses his body into the rubble and dirt, his fingers wet with grime. His ankle is hurting from the fall when he ran to escape and he can feel wet mud sticking to the legs of his tracksuit. The black dog's still barking, straining to be released and attack him, but the guard's holding it back as he shines his flashlight around the electricity substation.

Ibrahim glances behind him into the surrounding darkness but there's no sign or sound of Majed, his older brother, or Saeed, his Saudi friend. They ran away when the security man and his animal appeared, and left him behind when he slipped and fell in the mud. They'd persuaded him to come over here on their reconnaissance of the airbase, but then deserted him. He's furious at Majed for leaving him behind, just like he used to when they were children.

Alhamdullilah. The black beast has stopped barking. Bending down and edging sideways, he risks peering round the mound and sees the security guard moving away to circle the substation. As he watches this figure in baseball cap and windcheater, his face illuminated by the flashlight, he sees that it's Rob, his British boss. He should have known, especially after hearing him boast to Patience, the Indian secretary, about his night patrol. Ibrahim feels strange as he secretly watches this British mercenary who he speaks to every day at work, this boss who listens too much to his secretary and his friend, a Lebanese Christian engineer. In the broad daylight of the company offices they're working together, pretending to be on the same side. But here in the dark of this wasteland he realizes he's watching a Western enemy who could ruin his life.

At last, Rob's walking away, back down the track and leading his dog towards the lights of the patrol car. Relieved, Ibrahim stands up, drawing back from the dirt and stink of the rubbish mound and waits until he hears the car drive off, headlights beaming towards the perimeter fence. With the patrol car gone, the blackness returns, but his eyes are growing used to the dark and he's got a small flashlight in his pocket. Now he needs to find a way back to his brother's apartment across the spray fields and rejoin Majed and Saeed.

The street lights switched off some time ago, as if for a power cut, and above him the night sky is grim with clouds obscuring the moon. He shades the flashlight with his hand, pointing it down at the rough ground in front as he hobbles with his aching ankle along a track, through the heaps of rubble and dirt. Wearing only a thin grey tracksuit, he feels chilled by the dampness and this cold breeze from the Gulf.

A great roar erupts behind him and he turns to see four planes rising up over the airbase fence. He switches off his light and shelters beside a pile of rubble topped by pieces of rusty corrugated iron. The Crusader jets are loaded down with bombs and missiles, and power up above him into the night sky, rehearsing for their onslaught on innocent Muslim women and children and young Iraqi conscripts in Kuwait. These planes will inflict the evil destruction that he and his brothers must try to stop.

As he reaches the flat expanse of the spray fields, the street lights click back on along the road and he can see the bachelor housing block. But he's out in the open now and feels exposed. Despite his aching ankle, he hurries across the hard flat ground. Almost there, but he can feel vibrations under his feet, hear the pressure of liquid growing, before tiny sprinklers in the earth begin to spray water round his legs. He hobbles on, trying to escape the polluted spray and heading for the housing block. At last with tracksuit legs and trainers drenched, he reaches the tarmac road. *Alhamdullilah.* No cars driving past and no one's around to see him limp across.

He parked his old Chevrolet in the shadows by the metal garbage bins. But Saeed's left his red sports car with its conspicuous *IROC–Z* sign below the doors, directly under the light outside Majed's ground floor apartment. How stupid, when neighbors might notice and security are patrolling the area. Ibrahim's suspicious of this rich young Saudi living at his father's villa in what people call the Golden Ghetto. But wealth is not a sin, Majed says. The noble Sheikh Osama is rich and could live the playboy life, but instead he's devoted his wealth to Muslim charities and the holy *jihad*.

Ibrahim limps across the parking lot to Majed's apartment and presses the electric bell.

His brother throws open the door. 'Where've you been? We thought they caught you.'

'I hurt my ankle.' He stumbles, almost falling through the door. 'And you left me behind.'

'Welcome, my brother!' Saeed calls from the galley kitchen and puts down the phone. Tall and athletic, he has a well-trimmed beard and is wearing a smart green tracksuit.

'You are too slow Ibrahim,' Majed says. '*Mujahid* must always keep fit and ready for action.'

'I twisted my ankle.' Ibrahim's furious at his brother's criticism – typical of this tubby middle-aged man who's jealous because his younger brother has a better paid job.

'Did the security man see you?' Majed demands. 'Anyone follow you?'

'No. But I didn't know where you'd gone. You deserted me.'

'*Khalas*. Stop complaining. You escaped. But you are too wet.' Majid hurries to spread newspaper over his couch and helps Ibrahim sit down. 'I'll bring a towel for you.'

'The sprinklers came on.' Ibrahim feels sorry for his soiled wet self and is about to describe his escape from the vicious dog when he realizes Majid will probably make jokes at his expense.

'No problem, my friend.' Saeed calls from the kitchen. 'You scared us but I'm making calls to reassure our brothers. Rest now.'

Pleased that at least Saeed sympathizes with him, Ibrahim pulls off his wet trainers and, weary from his trek across the wasteland, dries and gently massages his sore ankle with the old towel Majid's brought. When no one's looking, he bends his head to smell the wet tracksuit bottoms – only a faint unpleasant odour, and that might be from the drying mud. A few minutes rest and he'll drive home. Muna's expecting him and will be getting worried. He hopes there's been no more ringing of their doorbell, with the local Saudi kids shouting insults about the Sudanese. And tomorrow they must start packing for the trip to Khartoum. The roads west to Jeddah are crowded with people fleeing, and it's difficult to get tickets for the ferry across to Port Sudan.

Majid brings some coffee and having made his phone calls, Saeed joins them. Taking the remote, he switches on the TV and is angry to find only CNN's American propaganda, even on the Saudi channel. They have to watch *Headline News* from Atlanta, this previously unknown American city making itself the news centre of the world. A woman with strange eyes is reading the reports and struggling to pronounce names and places. After mangling the name of the UN Secretary General, who's on a peace mission to Baghdad, she announces that Saudi Arabia has pledged to pay half the costs for the foreign forces in the country.

'That's billions of dollars!' Saeed bangs the arms of his chair. 'For these Zionists and Christian invaders. The Sheikh promised that we'd defend the holy mosques with thousands of faithful brothers, veterans from *jihad* in Afghanistan. But instead the Al Saud bring these American invaders.'

The woman newsreader is gabbling about James Baker's tour of the Middle East. They watch film of him visiting the airbase, wearing desert camouflage uniform as he speaks to pilots and ground staff crowding round. He promises they won't have to wait much longer as they pass the brink at midnight, 15 January, in three days' time.

'We should have attacked while Baker was here,' Saeed says. 'With weapons, we could be on CNN tonight. We should be ready. Maybe George Bush will come...'

Next comes the international weather forecast and Ibrahim watches the temperatures and snow conditions at luxury ski resorts in Europe and America scrolling down the screen to Christmas music. While poor Muslims like the Palestinians and Sudanese suffer, these rich Westerners are enjoying themselves. But why should *they* be untouched?

'We learned something from our reconnaissance,' Saeed says. 'We know the times and weakness of enemy patrols.'

'But we need more support,' Majid says.

'OK. I have friends who can help,' Saeed says. 'Students who live near here.'

'Students?' Majid teaches at the training centre and knows students only too well. 'They talk too much and are unreliable. We shouldn't get mixed up with kids.'

'These are brave and enthusiastic brothers,' Saeed says. 'They want to attack the invaders.'

'OK,' Majid says. 'But don't tell your students about me and Ibrahim. We want brothers we can trust.'

Observing their discussion, Ibrahim realizes how well his older brother and Saeed know each other. But should he get involved? He's a married man, Muna is pregnant with their first child and he needs this oil company money to build his family house in Khartoum.

'We need to know where the Patriot batteries are,' Saeed says. 'When there's a Scud attack, we'll see where the Patriots are fired from.'

'But how can we attack them?' Majid asks. 'We need weapons.'

'No problem.' Saeed says. 'I know a pious and trustworthy contractor, who can help us.'

Ibrahim glances at his watch. 'I must go. They'll close the main gate soon.' He struggles up from the couch, and, putting weight on his sore ankle, thinks he can drive. 'Muna will be worried and we need to pack for our journey to Jeddah.'

'I'm visiting our *mujahid* brothers in Jeddah this week,' Saeed says. 'The noble Sheikh Osama is there and I can introduce you to him.'

'That's a great honour,' Majid tells his younger brother.

Ibrahim smiles, imagining himself meeting the famous Sheikh who fought so bravely in Afghanistan. But for now, as he steps out of the door, his aching ankle is enough to deal with. And tomorrow he must ask for extra leave days to take Muna back to his father's house in Khartoum.

'When Muna goes, you'll be free to help.' Majid holds Ibrahim's arm, as he hobbles across the parking lot to his old Chevrolet. 'Religion and duty require this my brother…'

3

The Emergency Plan

Next morning, Krieger, Rob's American boss, calls him into the office. At work Krieger's a ruthless perfectionist, whey-faced with the effort to control and make sure everything goes to plan. Prematurely bald and stooping like a praying mantis over his new computer, he briefs Rob on the company's plans for the war.

'We should be well organized,' he says, his voice low and fiercely logical, as if war can be controlled as systematically as the engineering department he's used to managing.

With only a few hours' sleep after last night's patrol, Rob's already tired. By the time he got home, he'd decided it must have been a dog or fox he'd glimpsed running from the substation. At night when you're on patrol, you start imagining things.

His gaze drifts beyond Krieger to the office window diagonally crossed by strips of broad masking tape. Through the X of the tape, he can see a Portakabin first aid station being assembled on the concourse in front of headquarters. A Red Crescent flag on top of the cabin flutters in the breeze, as if already greeting future casualties.

'You OK?' Krieger is staring at him. Startled, Rob forces himself to focus on his boss and the company's plans.

Yet, as he listens to Krieger's droning certainty that a company evacuation can follow the twenty-five page General Instruction 102.001 Emergency Plan, he grows more sceptical. This grandiose plan envisages a fleet of buses supported by fuel and water tankers travelling hundreds of miles south to Dubai, along dangerously congested roads and across barren wasteland and desert. What if the buses and trucks break down and people panic? What if the convoy's attacked and plundered by desperate refugees or fleeing soldiers?

As usual, they have to deal with two sets of rules: the Western oil company's, based on wishful thinking, which they have to be seen to follow, and the Middle East's unwritten rules enabling them to get things done. But soon they could face life or death situations.

'What if it doesn't work?' he asks, startling his boss.

'What doesn't work?' Krieger senses a challenge to his authority.

'This complicated evacuation plan.' Rob stops there, reluctant to pick holes in the company's grand plan, especially as he suspects Krieger helped to develop it.

'It's our job to make sure the company's plan works,' Krieger warns him.

Looking back into his boss's unyielding blue eyes, Rob realizes there's no give in him, no flexibility. This Emergency Plan could collapse into chaos and he'd break down.

'Make copies for your staff.' Krieger pushes the Emergency Plan package across his desk. 'And we'll brief our people at this afternoon's staff meeting.'

Lunchtime, and Rob drives to a warehouse near the British Consulate to pick up a gas mask. At first the British, like the Americans, claimed that Scud missiles couldn't reach the area and they didn't want to encourage panic. But finally the Consulate gave way and started distributing what the army called 'respirators' to British citizens.

Young soldiers direct him towards a long orderly queue, enjoying a holiday atmosphere as friends find each other and exchange news and gossip. Joining a small group, he watches a sergeant demonstrate how to put a respirator on correctly and explain what to do in a chemical attack. Families with young children are receiving instruction, and small boys chatter excitedly, proudly wearing *Desert Shield* T-shirts and military insignia donated by the troops. This might be a memorable family adventure for some but he's relieved that Fiona isn't here.

When he returns to headquarters carrying the black army-issue respirator, Patience, his Indian secretary, welcomes him back. Today she's dressed in an emerald green sari and he realizes she's been wearing more vivid saris recently, as if to strengthen her confidence.

'So what about *your* mask, Patience?' he asks, embarrassed that, as her boss, he hasn't checked she has one.

'My husband's gone to collect our company masks. But they say the British army ones are best.' She smiles, always ready to tease him about the Raj. 'The British are best, as usual.'

Later, at the afternoon staff meeting, Krieger explains the company's Emergency Plan. When he asks if there are any questions, a Geordie engineer speaks up.

'People keep phoning from home to see if I'm OK. It's costing a fortune to phone back. Can the company give us free phone calls? And is there any news about a war bonus?'

Interesting questions, and Rob notices Tony, his Lebanese colleague, suppressing a grin. They exchange a conspiratorial smile as Krieger makes notes and promises to raise these issues with upper management. Patience, sitting beside Rob, shifts unhappily in her chair and whispers to him about the rumours of an evacuation.

'Any news on evacuation flights?' he asks on her behalf.

A flicker of irritation crosses his boss's face, before he assumes a sympathetic expression and explains that the company has no plans for evacuation flights. Other people remain tight-lipped, but Ibrahim, a young Sudanese engineer in Rob's group, speaks up.

'I live in a flat outside this camp. My wife's pregnant with our first baby and she's afraid to go out. Saudi children keep knocking on my door, calling us bad names because we're Sudanese.'

'Sorry to hear that,' Krieger says. 'But if the situation deteriorates, we plan to move employees and their families into the camp.'

'But my wife's pregnant. It's dangerous for her to stay here.'

'Don't worry, Ibrahim.' The Geordie engineer speaks up. 'You can live in one o' them big tents on camp. It's close to a mosque so you'll be fine.'

But Ibrahim isn't laughing. 'I must take my wife back to Sudan.'

'We'll discuss your personal situation later,' Krieger decides and turns over the meeting to a burly Scotsman, an ex-sergeant major. He's prepared some overhead transparencies and revels in instructing the civilians on how to put on a respirator, set up a safe room, and survive a chemical or gas attack. He distributes a booklet – *Protection against Chemical Agents* – with envelopes containing strips of glossy green paper chemically treated to detect blistering and nerve agents. The ex-sergeant major makes it sound like a gas or chemical attack is imminent and Rob notices Patience's shoulders trembling beneath her sari as she holds the ominous green paper.

'Cut the chemical paper in half,' the Scotsman recites from the booklet. 'Then staple a piece to a windowsill on each side of the house. When you see pink or red spots, the area's contaminated.' He shows a transparency with blood-red spots spattered over it. 'When somebody's contaminated with blistering or nerve agents, carefully remove their clothing. Then wash their body with a neutralizing agent – something like Clorox bleach mixed with water.'

At this, Patience jumps up and hurries out of the door. Rob stands, feeling he should follow, but Krieger's warning look tells him to stay. Undeterred, the Scotsman moves on to his next slide showing a Clorox bottle.

'When you're washing a body, avoid getting bleach in your eyes. Then wash yourself with soap and water. Remember, the best place to decontaminate a body is at home in your bath.'

A stunned silence as people imagine a contaminated body in their bath, but Rob hears a snuffle. Someone is snoring gently behind him, and he turns to see Aziz, his plump Saudi clerk, snoozing through the lecture. As the meeting ends, Aziz wakes up and explains. 'Last night I take our maid to airport for flight to Bangkok. She's going crazy and will hurt my children if she stay.'

'Good you took her, Aziz.' Rob's pleased the war has released the Thai maid from household bondage and given her a ticket home.

'Yes, I'm very good boss,' Aziz says, as they walk back to the office. He nods towards a grey-haired moustachioed Palestinian, who usually wears Western clothes but has come into work wearing a Saudi *thawb* and red checked *keffiyeh.*

'He tries to look like Saudi, but *we* know these people,' Aziz says. 'The Kuwaiti were too soft with Palestinians. On TV, our government say we will execute terrorists. We'll watch them carefully.'

Rob fears for the moustachioed Palestinian darting around the office area, and hiding in his cubicle. A few months ago, he'd suffered a heart attack and major surgery. And now this.

Later, the Scotsman checks people's gas masks and ensures they can strap them on properly. First, he looks at Patience's company mask but it's too small. As she tries to squeeze it over her head, she cries out in fear and humiliation. The company's gas masks are a jumble of East German and Yugoslav models, Cold War army surplus that's reached Arabia through a chain of East European and Arab middlemen taking large commissions. Like Patience, some adults have been given children's masks and vice versa.

'Don't worry, Patience. I'll find a respirator for you,' the Scotsman says, and she rewards him with her warm smile, already recognizing him as a war hero.

After work, Rob leaves headquarters with the superior British respirator in his briefcase and feels a gentle rain spotting his shirt. In the community centre, his mailbox is full of Christmas cards from ex-colleagues wondering if he's still at Ground Zero for the coming war. There's also a postcard stuck at the back of his box: the Stars and Stripes with the legend *These Colors Don't Run* across it. On the back of the card, written in red ink, he reads, '*Assalamu alikum*. Murmurs of maternal lamentation. Falling towers. Kuwait City, Baghdad, Tehran. See you soon. Bill'. No stamp or postmark, so it must have been delivered by hand. The near quotation from T.S. Eliot's *The Waste Land* tells him it's from Bill Eliot and he remembers the lumbering American peering at him through granny glasses. He remembers too that sunny morning on North Camp several years ago when he'd been hurrying to breakfast in the mess hall and had seen security guards dragging a dead body out of the outdoor swimming pool. A slight figure, who he now knows as Al, was sitting on the low stone wall, watching as he smoked a cigarillo. Bill Eliot had left soon after what proved to be his neighbor's death, and Rob never heard whether it was murder or suicide. Now the postcard announces that Bill's back, but Rob isn't sure he wants to see him again.

Despite the rain, Rob decides to go downtown to buy additional war supplies and catches the shoppers' bus. As he boards the Greyhound, he sees June, Fiona's teacher from the art group, sitting near the front with a friend of Fiona's. Probably fearing the *mutawwa*, the religious police, Fiona's friend is wearing a long skirt and headscarf, but June's dressed in blue jeans and her short black hair is uncovered, shining as if she's just stepped out of the shower. Maybe she's only going to the Safeway supermarket, mainly used by Westerners, but Rob admires her defiance. He greets her and she smiles in recognition as he passes down the aisle.

Only a few empty seats but he can sit down just behind the two women. The bus is crowded and subdued, mostly carrying Western housewives, Filipino nurses, and Indian secretaries venturing out for last-minute shopping. Instead of the happy chatter of the usual weekend expedition, the atmosphere is gloomy and even the lights in the bus seem to dim with foreboding as they drive off.

June turns to him. 'Where's Fiona? Did she come back with you?'

'No, she's not very well and decided to stay in the UK.'

28

'What's wrong with her?' the other woman asks and he remembers she's a Canadian doctor's wife.

'We don't know. She keeps getting headaches.'

'She doesn't like it here, does she?' the doctor's wife says, adjusting her headscarf.

'Can't blame her, especially with this war,' June says. 'But it's a pity. She enjoyed our painting class. So you came back by yourself, Rob?'

'That's right.' He feels sorry for himself but then cheered by June's warm smile and interest. Hadn't Fiona made a joke about her liking his British accent and asking about him? Then he remembers she's married to Rick, the big American security boss.

'Did you pick up a gas mask from the British Consulate?' the doctor's wife asks. Unlike June, she's carrying a khaki gas-mask satchel over her shoulder.

'Yes, but I left it at home tonight,' he says.

'What beats me is the story they tell us keeps changing,' June says. 'First these Scuds can't reach us and we don't need gas masks. Now they tell us there might be chemicals or nerve gas and we've got to have masks.'

'The Iraqis have improved their Scuds.' Rob remembers the ex-sergeant major telling him. 'Now they can fly further and reach us.'

The bus passes through the main gate, driving down the highway towards town and June turns back to her friend to discuss some painting class. There's no patrol tonight so Rob can sleep at home, but after last night's alarms he's still tired. He closes his eyes, beginning to doze off.

The rain has ceased by the time the bus stops and he wakes up at Happy Corner, a block of electrical, clothes and audio cassette shops. While June stays on with the doctor's wife to shop at Safeway, he leaves the bus with a group of Filipino men.

Before Christmas, these streets were bustling with the downtrodden workers of the world – Filipinos, Pakistanis, Indians, Bangladeshis – inspecting Japanese TVs, listening to cassette tapes and milling around the stores searching for bargains and gifts to take home. But tonight Happy

Corner lies mournful and deserted, no lights showing in the shop windows. Eve's Jewellery still displays expensive gold trinkets, but this magnet for expat women appears empty, except for a few shop assistants clustered behind the counter.

At the staff meeting, the ex-sergeant major had warned that in an attack, flying window glass would injure many people and the camp's water supply and electricity could be switched off. Most shops are closed and although Rob buys an extra jerry can to store water, he can't find a back-up flashlight, additional batteries or masking tape for his windows. In the near-deserted Al Shula Centre, he walks the marble-floored corridors through the echoing mall. Most shops have metal shutters pulled down over their doors, but on the second floor he discovers a household goods store still open. Usually the Saudi proprietor sits at the cash register by the door, but tonight the two young Indian shop assistants are alone.

'Where's your boss?' Rob asks the teenagers as they show him different flashlights.

'Gone to Riyadh, sir,' one says. 'But we cannot leave. Boss take passports.'

The shop assistants gather round him, anxious for news, and several others wander in from neighboring stores. After the invasion of Kuwait, they'd watched on TV as tens of thousands of Indians and other Asian workers fled carrying their few possessions. The refugees trekked hundreds of miles north across a hostile Iraq, attacked by bandits, threatened and abused by police and soldiers, and then struggled to survive in hastily erected camps on the Jordanian border. The teenagers are desperate to know: will they have to flee and how can they get home?

'Will Saddam send Scuds?' one asks. 'We have no gas mask.'

Feeling guilty, Rob repeats the official assurances that Scuds can't reach this far and the teenagers pretend to believe him as he leaves with his flashlight, batteries, and rolls of masking tape.

The eeriness of this last-minute shopping is heightened by the town's deserted and drizzled streets as he walks back to Happy Corner to catch the bus returning from Safeway. When he boards it, June waves to him but there's no seat near her. He has to sit two rows behind, and staring out at the ebony shine of the wet road, he dozes off as the Greyhound carries them back through the damp evening.

He wakes up at the main gate when a tall Pakistani guard boards the bus to check IDs. Peering out at the guardhouse, Rob notices the casual young Saudis gossiping over their *chai* or *gawa* have been replaced by smartly uniformed and darker skinned officers methodically checking vehicles entering and leaving camp. A patrol car pulls up beside the Big House facing the main gate and, under the floodlights, he recognizes Rick, June's husband, getting out. Tall and powerfully built, wearing a windbreaker and jeans, the Security boss looms over Al, a slight figure in his grey winter *thawb*. Rick halts on the steps of the Big House to light a cigarette and Rob glances towards June, but she's talking to her friend and doesn't seem to have noticed her husband.

A yellow bus carrying Indian gardeners off camp is parked at the side of the road for inspection, and Rob watches the guards hauling a youth in green overalls down the steps.

'Look June!' The doctor's wife exclaims. 'They've got one of the gardeners.'

'What are they doing to the poor guy?' June peers out.

'Maybe he's stolen something,' her friend says. 'Ask Rick about it.'

'You think John Wayne will tell me? Everything's on a need-to-know basis now. Hey! They hit the poor guy.'

'ID!' a voice in Rob's ear demands. He looks up to the guard, shows his senior staff identity card, and feels grateful for its protection, a privilege denied the Indian gardener being dragged towards the Big House.

'What's that noise?' The Englishman beside Rob sits up.

Everyone's stopped talking to listen to a high-pitched whining, like a faulty amplifier, sounding from outside.

'Air-raid siren.' Rob's neighbor stands as passengers start scrambling up with their shopping bags. 'We'd better get out. Maybe it's Scuds.'

That one word is spreading fear and panic through the bus. The doctor's wife and others are pulling out gas-masks, people already struggling down the aisle with their shopping. Annoyed that he's forgotten his own mask, Rob stands and forces his way into the aisle. The guard checking IDs has disappeared and the bus door opens for the people in front shouting and crowding out. Panic, hysteria and Iraqi Scuds are only moments away.

4

Boy Scouts and Rattlesnakes

13 January 1991 / 27 Jumada 1411   20.35

Shit! Is this for real – a Scud attack already? Rick charges into the Big House where in the chaos guards are shouting to each other, pulling on gas-masks, and some guys escaping out of the back doors. Al's in his office already on the phone to Emergency Control.

'What's happening?' Rick shouts over the whine of the siren.

'Don't know yet,' Al yells back.

'What we do, Mr Rick?' It's Maria, the Security Chief's cute Filipino secretary, the only bright smile and trim figure in this all-male building.

'Just stay calm sweetheart.' He's tempted to put his arm round her slender shoulders. 'You're safe here.'

'It's OK, Rick.' Al turns to his boss. 'The contractors are testing the new sirens. See how many are working.'

'Testing – why didn't they fucking warn us?' Then conscious of the girl, he forces himself to calm down, be the big American security boss and in control. 'Tell them to cut the sirens and let us know next time.'

'Are we safe Mr Rick?' Maria asks.

'Sure, false alarm.' He smiles at the girl, smartly dressed in white high neck blouse and knee length black skirt – no wonder the guards keep hanging round this area. 'No problem. So where's the Chief?'

'He's still at the mosque, Mr Rick.'

'OK.' Typical Chief – never here when he's needed. 'I'd better get out there and bring some order to this chaos,' he says, though he'd like to stay and reassure her.

Outside by the main gate the guards are putting on gas masks and peering up into the night sky, while people are still shouting and struggling to get off the Greyhound with their shopping.

'OK folks. False alarm.' Rick yells and leaving Al to deal with the guards, starts shepherding passengers back onto the bus. Once satisfied everyone's back, he climbs up beside the Filipino driver.

'Relax, sit down, folks. False alarm. They were just trying out the new sirens.' He pauses, looking down the aisle to make sure everybody's sitting back down and avoiding eye contact with June, who's likely to make some wisecrack. At last the useless sirens cut out. Shit – only two days before this war starts, and they're still not working properly. They say no plan survives the battle but this war's about to kick off and these motherfuckers are still screwing round.

He turns to the bus driver. 'OK, my friend. Drive on to the ballpark.' He steps down off the Greyhound and watches it roar off before turning to deal with the next problem. Faisal, the big shift supervisor, and two of the guards are holding a young Indian gardener. The guy isn't resisting but Faisal's slapped him round the head and cuffed him to make sure.

'Look, he has video, boss.' Faisal's pasty face is flushed with anger as he holds up the cassette for Rick to see. An anonymous VHS cardboard cover with no title or label. Could be anything. Disney cartoons, some pirated film, home-made porn.

'Please, sir.' The young gardener appeals to Rick's white face. 'I find video in trash.'

'OK, take him for questioning,' Rick says. 'I'll check it out later, after

34

the Chief's briefing. And Faisal, keep things moving. Tell that driver to head out of here.'

Faisal waves towards the contractor's yellow bus and it drives off, the Indian gardeners peering out of the windows to watch one of their own being arrested. But Rick's happy enough with that – it's a warning that Security's running a tight ship.

Taking some time to de-stress, he lights a Marlboro and waits for the throbbing and tightness in his forehead to ease. Not a shriek when they first tested the sirens this afternoon and the contractor's men stood round like dickheads blaming each other. Now, after months of meetings, fooling around with the Chief's cousin and his half-assed company set up to milk the war, they end up with crappy sirens. And who's going to carry the can? Not the Chief or any Saudi bosses. Just Rick, the American. No wonder he's got this hypertension and high blood pressure, and has to keep popping different coloured pills every morning.

Al interrupts his thoughts. 'So what are we going to do about these sirens?' he asks and Rick realizes his Saudi deputy has been standing behind him on the steps, smoking a cigarillo and keeping his distance as usual. Al doesn't like to get his hands dirty – always washing them with anti-bacterial soap – and since he went on that security course in Dallas, he's been spouting all this bullshit about Values, Integrity and Respect. Values! They'd only make the job more difficult and the bad guys would take advantage.

'OK, let's decide about the sirens – see if the Chief's back.' Rick drops his cigarette into a sand bucket and he and Al walk back into the Big House.

But the Chief still hasn't returned and Maria is sitting at her desk flicking through *People* magazine with that actress from *Pretty Woman* pouting from the cover. The girl looks up, smiling at the American boss, and says she'll bring them some coffee in the Chief's office.

Sitting inside, Rick and Al discuss the screw-up with sirens and decide that when there's a Scud alert, the patrol cars will drive round camp using their own sirens. Good enough as a quick fix, and Rick grabs a handful of mini-Snickers from the glass bowl on the Chief's desk. Got to cut back on the cholesterol the doc keeps warning him. But with this war coming and June giving him more hassle, he deserves some sweet things in life. Like this cute girl bringing in the tray of coffee and Oreo cookies for them.

'OK guys, there's bad news and good news,' the Chief says as he sweeps in, wearing a heavy grey winter *thawb*. 'My cousin says some sirens aren't working.' He announces this as if it's some Big Surprise and plonks himself down behind his desk and the new Apple Mac he still can't figure out.

'Chief, *most* of these sirens aren't working,' Rick says. 'You heard. They just tested them. So we've decided when there's an alert, we'll use the patrol car sirens round camp. Quick and dirty until the new system's ready.'

'Smart one, Rick.' The Chief beams and leans back in his brown leather chair, hands folded over his paunch. 'Don't bring me problems, bring me solutions,' he tells Al, who's always walking in with difficulties and more headaches.

'OK, Chief,' Rick says, 'we'll let the guys know about using their sirens.' He remembers all his years in third-world places like Vietnam and Iran. Experience teaches you to expect screw-ups like this, to grin like you're used to stupidity, and still carry on with the job. 'So what's the good news, Chief?' he asks. 'We're getting a war bonus?'

'Not yet, *sideeki*.' The Chief smiles as if he's jolly old Santa about to deliver a great sack of goodies. 'Good news is we're getting guns for you guys. Al, you make a list of who needs training. But make sure it's guys we can trust.'

Al looks surprised, although it's no shock for Rick. He already knows about the guns and what they're getting. Bill Eliot's told him it's the Beretta M9, a replacement for the Colt they used all those years ago in Vietnam.

'Rick, you coordinate with this guy, Bill Eliot,' the Chief says. 'He'll be our contact with the airbase. Says he knows you.'

'Sure Chief. We've worked together before.' He's comfortable with Bill and the Base set-up, the guys he sees at the Mission Inn for Friday brunch, while the Chief and Al are just rookies learning about war.

The Chief picks up the only file in his in-tray and glances at a letter in Arabic pinned to the front of it.

'This is from the Ministry of Interior. We know Arafat and the Sudanese support Saddam. So what are we doing about the Palestinians and Sudanese here?'

'We need to do a lot more Chief,' Rick says. 'You know they used to tell us this rattlesnake story in the Scouts.'

'Let's hear it.' The Chief likes Rick's war stories and settles back in his chair to enjoy it.

'There's this Boy Scout sheltering in his tent on a mountainside during a terrific thunderstorm,' Rick begins. 'Before long he hears an old rattlesnake outside the tent crying out. *I'm cold and wet and I'll die if you don't let me inside.* The rattlesnake's pleading, but the scout says, *If I let you in, you'll bite me and I'll die.* But that old rattlesnake's still crying out. *Please. I'm old and I promise I won't bite you.* It keeps on whining, until the scout lets the snake into the tent and keeps it warm and dry with his blanket. At last, the storm ends, the rain stops and the sun comes out. But suddenly the rattlesnake bites the scout with its fatal venom. The scout cries out, *I saved you and you promised not to bite me.* But the snake says, *You knew I was a rattlesnake and I did what rattlesnakes do. It's my nature.*'

The men are silent with just the noise of phones ringing, people talking and moving round in the department cubicles outside.

'Great story.' The Chief slaps the arms of his chair. 'Especially that bit about keeping the snake warm with his blanket.'

'Sure, great.' Al keeps on smiling.

'We've got these Palestinians and Sudanese all round us,' Rick says. 'They smile to your face but maybe they'll turn like in Kuwait. We know this part of the world's a snake pit, so we can't be Boy Scouts when it comes to war.' He looks towards Al.

'Sure,' the Chief says. 'So we need to check out these Palestinians and Sudanese. Al, you speak to the *mabahith* and the police.'

'Yes, sir.' Al's keen to show he's not a Boy Scout.

'We'll coordinate with Personnel and set up a Watch List,' Rick says. 'Then we can identify and monitor these guys, get a grip on the situation.'

'But what about the Saudi Afghans?' the Chief asks.

Rick's confused. 'Who the hell hired Afghans? We've got enough problems.'

But the Chief's referring to his letter from the Interior Ministry and talking about the young Saudis who travelled to Afghanistan a few years ago to fight the Russians. Seems the returning heroes have become dangerous troublemakers hanging around coffee shops in Jeddah and Riyadh and talking about some crazy caliphate.

'But most of these kids went there to help religious charities,' Al says. 'A relative of mine worked for a charity in the refugee camps.'

'What relative?' the Chief demands and Rick knows Al's made his usual mistake of questioning the boss. No matter how stupid his ideas, just kiss up and make him believe he's some great thinker.

Al begins the excuses. 'He's the son of a cousin. He was only there a few weeks. It was too rough in the refugee camp, sleeping on the ground. He helped the wounded in the hospital.'

'What's his name?' the Chief insists.

Al gives way. 'Abdulla – he helped the doctors. He's very religious. An idealist.'

'Tell your relatives to be careful, especially at this time,' the Chief warns and Al nods in submission.

'If the kid wants a vacation, he should go to Dubai, grab a few beers,' Rick says.

The Chief laughs. 'OK, guys. These Saudi Afghans. Check them out.'

'*Mafi muskallah*,' Rick says, as he and Al leave the office. 'No problem Chief. We'll get onto these guys.'

While Al stays to talk to the Egyptian IT expert about setting up a Watch List of potential terrorists, Rick walks out through the back of the Big House and across the car park to a block of dirty-white Portakabins. The door to the first cabin is ajar, and he hears the amplified sound of whispering and sexy music as he enters this box room stinking of sweat and indolence.

Faisal's lounging in a ragged brown armchair with his bare feet up on a stool, hands folded over his paunch as he watches TV and a couple going at it, illuminated by candles on a fancy staircase. At least it's not home-made porn. Then they'd have to investigate expats living on camp, maybe open some stinking can of worms. He watches a few minutes of the couple grinding away in a movie he remembers falling asleep to with June. But he doesn't want to think about her now. She's wearing him down with feminist crap and bitching about being stuck here. Instead, he imagines Maria, the cute secretary, buck naked and squirming beneath him...

He watches more of the couple screwing, aware that Faisal, who keeps a stash of confiscated porn in the VCR cupboard, is enjoying it as well. Then the scene shifts to some dull lawyer's office and Rick picks up the remote to switch off.

'Where did the gardener pick up the video?' he asks Faisal.

'In the trash outside a house. Probably expats leaving, throwing stuff out.'

'Where's the guy now?'

'In the holding cell, boss. He fights too much and got hurt. But no need for doctor.' Rick nods. Maybe he should check on this. But he's got enough headaches already.

'Keep the gardener in for questioning. Maybe he'll tell us something useful. We gotta go now.'

'Right, boss.' Faisal shuffles his feet back into his sandals and levers himself up out of the armchair.

'Hey, what happened to the Indian gardener?' Al's standing in the Portakabin doorway. 'His mouth's bleeding and his arm's injured.'

'Guy probably fell over,' Rick says. 'This is war and accidents happen, Al.' He turns away from the Boy Scout. 'Time to check the back gates, Faisal. *Yalla*. Let's go catch some bad guys.'

Leaving, he thinks about the Maria, the cute Filipino. She lives in the ballpark flats. Maybe he'll call round to see her sometime – check on her safety, offer his protection.

5

The World Needs a Policeman

14 January 1991 / 28 Jumada 1411   *08.00*

Rob realizes that, as the deadline for war approaches, more people are disappearing. Some expats haven't returned from their Christmas holidays and a lot of Saudi managers have left on business trips, leaving their assistants in charge.

During his lunch hour, he shops at the company supermarket where the shelves are emptying with panic buying. Then when he walks through the community centre a crowd of Asian houseboys and gardeners are besieging the Travel Office. So many people are trying to escape but the company's still pretending *mafi muskallah*, no problem. Yet beneath the business-as-usual façade, Rob senses the welling up of uncertainty as people hesitate on the edge of panic.

When he returns to headquarters, Patience tells him that Krieger has designated his office as a Safe Room, an assembly point when there's a Scud attack. At the staff meeting, the ex-sergeant major warned that an explosion would shatter all the building's windows, and more people would be killed or injured by flying glass than anything else. Torn between this warning and fear of ridicule, Rob tapes health and safety posters over his office window. Just as he's admiring the photos of pipelines winding through sand dunes, a super-tanker being loaded at the sea island terminal, and technicians monitoring screens in the refinery, Krieger phones for him to come to his office

Rob's shocked to see Bill Eliot sitting there with a crew-cut middle-aged man in US Army uniform.

'We know each other.' Standing up, Bill claps Rob on the shoulder. 'We lived on North Camp in the good old days.'

Several years on from those 'good old days', Bill's shaven-headed, the granny glasses larger and his stomach bulges under a white shirt and tan cord jacket.

'Must have been fun,' says Krieger, who's always lived in the small-town American comfort of Main Camp.

'Sure was,' Bill says and Rob laughs with him, as if they had a great time sharing washrooms and showers, whiling away evenings in the Western Mess, and sleeping in long Portakabin dormitories.

'So what are you doing here, Bill?' Rob asks.

'Showing Colonel Parker round and touching base with old friends,' Bill says.

'Rob's been helping out with the night patrol.' Krieger smiles, keen to gain brownie points with his military visitors.

'That's one of Rick's operations,' Bill tells the Colonel. 'Company volunteers are helping out with security.'

'Good man.' The Colonel nods. 'Security cooperation between us and the company, that's what we need. Secretary Baker's put us on notice. We pass the brink at midnight, January fifteen. Any diplomatic efforts to extend or postpone the deadline will not succeed. As you know, gentlemen, we're responsible for this key strategic area so we need to stay on the alert.' He leans forward to shake Rob's hand. 'Glad to have you aboard, sir.'

'Hey, I heard about our old friend, Kamal,' Bill turns to Rob. 'He's done damn well, climbing the old company ladder.'

'Kamal Esayad,' Rob explains, realizing he's not told Krieger before.

'We knew him on North Camp when he first came to Saudi.'

Krieger contains his surprise. 'Kamal's our Department Head, Colonel,' he says, tight-lipped with corporate discretion. 'I've scheduled a meeting with him later.'

'Great!' the Colonel says. 'I need to touch base with all the key personnel, let them know what's happening. Make sure we're all singing from the same hymn sheet.'

'We knew Kamal when he was a rookie teacher,' Bill says. 'Seems he's a big shot in the company now. Shows what you can do by marrying the right woman eh?'

Ignoring that, Krieger stands up. 'Coffee, Colonel?' he offers and leads them out of his office towards the trolley by the elevators.

'So, Rob,' Bill says, as they walk along behind their bosses. 'Still sucking at Mother's old teat. Company treating you well?'

'Sure, the milk's still sweet. So what're you doing here, Bill?'

'Just helping out the guys at the base.' He extracts a card from his breast pocket – the military contractor's embossed name with *Major William Eliot BA, MBA. Military Training Task Force* beneath. Taking out his pen, Bill redlines one of the phone numbers.

'My direct line. I use the commissary at the Base, so anything special you need... We've got Jack Daniel's woodchips if you want to make some brown. Don't use it myself now, though.' He glances at Rob, his blue eyes sincere behind the granny glasses. 'Got sorted out through AA a few years ago.'

'Good.' Rob guesses the sorting-out came after Bill's abrupt expulsion from North Camp following the unexplained death of his neighbor.

'Yeah, haven't touched a drop for years.' The big American squeezes Rob's elbow.

'So, where you living, Bill? On the Base?'

'No, up in the Towers. Sharing with a bunch of pilots. It's crowded, unpleasant. Always having problems with the bathroom and damn shower.'

'You can use mine when you visit camp. We Brits have got this *Scrub a Squaddie* program for our troops.'

'Thanks, but you don't need to scrub me.' Bill grins. 'Unless you want to, my friend.' He glances over to where Krieger and the Colonel are talking beside the coffee trolley. 'So how is our old friend, Kamal?'

'Fine. But it's strange. He seemed more upset about Saudi women driving round Riyadh than with any Iraqi invasion.'

'He's probably listening to these religious nuts. Long-bearded guys with short *thawbs*. They're producing audio tapes you can buy downtown, attacking the Al Sauds and the Great Satan, the good old USA.' He glances round, checking there's no one nearby, and lowers his voice. 'We're expecting some kind of terrorist attack. Maybe from Palestinians. Some of these guys believe what Saddam says, that he'll attack Israel and liberate Palestine. And we've got these young Saudis back from the *jihad* in Afghanistan. Over forty thousand headed over there, so there's likely to be blowback. Saw these guys in the base camps round Peshawar learning how to fire RPGs and make IEDs.'

'So what's an IED?' Rob's irritated by Bill's love of military acronyms.

'Improvised explosive device. They use what's available. Plant fertilizer, Semtex, nails... The *jihadis* learned how to build and use them against the Soviets.' The Colonel and Krieger are returning with their coffees and Bill slaps Rob on the back. 'Stay safe, my friend, and see you later. Life's just got way more interesting.'

Rob returns to his office to start February's work scheduling and absorb the shock of Bill's reappearance. He remembers Al questioning him about Bill and his next door neighbor, the dead accountant. Now the big American's back with warnings about *jihadi* terrorists and IEDs. Rob had volunteered for the camp's night patrol as a change and diversion. But now, from what Bill says, it feels more dangerous.

'This looks very artistic.' Tony, Rob's Lebanese friend and colleague, steps into the office and admires the safety posters covering the window.

'An explosion would blow this window in,' Rob says. 'We could be injured by flying glass but these posters should help.'

'Good. So you learned something useful from our staff meeting.'

Tony closes the door gently, in conspiratorial style. 'I learned we've got to depend on ourselves.'

'But what about the company evacuation plan?' Rob keeps a straight face. 'Krieger says he wants us to follow that.'

'Let *him* follow the company's grand plan.' Tony smiles. 'I feel safer with my own plans. But I see we have important military visitors today.'

Rob explains, briefly telling him about Bill and his mysterious expulsion from North Camp and Saudi Arabia.

'Do you trust him?' Tony asks.

'Not really.' Rob's never heard a convincing explanation for the death of Bill's neighbor – not even whether it was suicide or murder.

'Your friend probably wanted to impress his Colonel,' Tony says. 'Bringing him here and showing how many company people he knows.'

'Maybe, but I'm surprised he's even allowed back in the country.'

'These good old boys.' Tony smiles. 'They always find jobs for each other. You'll see more of these re-treads, especially when there's a war bonus.'

'Re-treads? You mean like reconditioned tires.'

'Sure. Your friend Bill's probably back for one last big payday before retirement.'

'So what do *you* think about the situation?' Rob sits back, prompting the kind of political discussion they both enjoy.

Yet Tony remains bemused by events, still trying to puzzle things out. Like most Lebanese and others in the Middle East, he believes in the Great Conspiracy, the Plot that once revealed will explain everything. Having grown up in a Machiavellian world, amidst the betrayals of the Lebanese civil war, he respects the power of *realpolitik* and scorns Western idealists bleating about democracy and freedom. He keeps returning to the key questions. What's the war about? What are the deep-laid plans? Who stands to gain?

They discuss the possible conspirators. The US, which can now justify permanent bases in the Gulf, control the Strait of Hormuz and the vital oil supplies. The Pentagon, which, faced with the financial disaster of winning the Cold War, is desperate to retain its budget and resist military cuts as the

Soviet Union collapses. The Saudi Royal family and the Gulf sheikhdoms, who need the Americans to protect them, not only against Iraq and Iran but from their own people. The oil companies, who profit from price rises, and the construction giants who are already recruiting people to rebuild Kuwait. They all stand to gain.

Tony's conspiracy theories intrigue Rob but they seem too elegant in their clear-eyed cynicism, too neat for messy reality. He argues for the everyday muddle and misunderstandings, the sheer incompetence giving rise to war. Saddam Hussein misjudged the West's response to the invasion of Kuwait and handled the crisis with the arrogance and stupidity of an oriental despot. Given the American fear of another Vietnam and the democracies' distaste for war, Saddam doubted the West's willingness to risk bloodshed. Although Tony listens politely to Rob's arguments, he resolutely focuses on the money trail and the great conspiracy.

'Who benefits?' he persists. 'Who cares about these Saudi and Kuwaiti playboys? Bush says he wants to free Kuwait but what have the Al-Sabah got to do with freedom? Some people blame that stupid woman, the American ambassador. She told Saddam the US wouldn't interfere in his argument with Kuwait. So he took it as the go-ahead for invasion.'

'That's ridiculous,' Rob says, suspecting the Arab male's prejudice against a female ambassador.

'But perhaps she didn't make a mistake,' Tony adds, alert to another layer of deception. 'Now the Americans have the excuse to stay in the Gulf as long as they want. That's what our *jihadi* friends are protesting about.'

Rob remembers Bill's patriotic postcard: Kuwait City, Baghdad and Tehran. But wasn't that just American boasting?

'So, you're against this war?' Rob says.

'No.' Tony's shocked that his friend should reach such a simplistic conclusion. 'This war's necessary. The world needs a policeman, even if he's crude and stupid.'

Patience interrupts them, bringing in the daily press bulletin and beaming with her good news: the ex-sergeant major has found a gas mask that fits her and she's carrying it in a khaki satchel over her purple sari.

'Congratulations, Patience.' Tony glances through the press bulletin. 'And look, here's more good news. Oil's risen to over $37 a barrel. Enough to pay for all these soldiers. And who knows? Maybe there'll be some left over for us, for a well-deserved war bonus.'

They laugh but there's a knock on the office door, Ibrahim standing there.

'Krieger sent me to see you. I must take my wife to Khartoum. She's pregnant.'

Patience and Tony leave and Rob, feeling pressured by Ibrahim's aggressive tone, asks him to sit down so they can discuss the situation.

But Ibrahim remains standing. 'My wife and baby aren't safe. I need emergency leave to go home to Sudan.'

'So what did Krieger say?' Rob asks.

'He gives me only five days to drive my wife to Jeddah for the ferry to Sudan. Then he wants me to come back.'

'That's fair,' Rob says. 'When the war starts there'll be emergencies. We'll need safety engineers.'

'No, it's *not* fair.' Ibrahim is shouting back. 'You're against Sudanese people. I'm going to see Kamal, your manager. He will help me.' Banging the door, he storms out of the office – yet another person disappearing.

6

Tomorrow May Be Too Late

14 January 1991 / 28 Jumada 1411   *18.45*

Tomorrow May Be Too Late to Practice Safety is the slogan for January printed in Rob's company diary. Returning from work, he follows the ex-sergeant major's instructions by switching off the air conditioning and taping plastic sheeting over the air vents to prevent nerve or chemical gas seeping in. With Cilla following him around, he crosses the windows diagonally with wide masking tape and fixes plastic sheeting behind the doors and windows. The ex-sergeant major had told them to set up a Safe Room and he tests out the bathroom with Cilla. But even with the jerry cans of water and emergency supplies stored in the bath, there's not enough space to move around. He chooses his bedroom as less cramped for both of them to shelter in.

Finally, satisfied with his preparations, he bundles Cilla into the back of the old Range Rover and drives round to his friend Derek's house by the golf course. As he reaches the front door, left ajar for the cigarette smoke, he can hear his friend on the phone. He knocks but Cilla won't wait, nudging open the door to go inside where Derek lies reclining on the couch with two cushions behind his head. A pack of twenty Silk Cut, the large glass ashtray almost full, and a tumbler of *sid* and water are set beside him on the coffee table. As usual, he's speaking to his wife: one of those interminable conversations where she tries to persuade him to return to Hemel Hempstead, while he gently resists, promising he'll be back soon and indulging her with talk of a new bungalow. At last, after repeated assurances, he puts down the receiver.

'Costing a fortune in phone calls,' he says, with a sigh of resignation. 'Always has, but it's even worse now. She wants me to come home but also wants this new bungalow. I've told her ten years, and ten years it'll be. Saddam's not stopping me getting that full severance check and I've only a few months to go.'

Rob's tempted to raise his own worries about Fiona wanting him to return but avoids depressing the conversation. 'Speaking of money,' he says, 'have you heard from our friends at Berkeley Square Investments?'

'Yes.' With his wife's voice no longer in his ear, Derek revives. 'Curiously enough, their tour of the Gulf's been postponed.' He blows smoke up into the air. 'Seems it's too dangerous here for our brave financial advisors.'

He points the remote and increases the TV volume, the American reporters becoming more hysterical about *War in the Gulf.* Since the invasion of Kuwait, CNN has been relayed through Bahrain and now the world seems to be linked and only make sense through Atlanta, a bizarre hub for this global village, where the fast-talking Bobby Battista presides, like a spider pulling the news threads together. Rob's used to listening over his shortwave radio, to the BBC with its distant RP voices calmly reporting and analysing stories. But now he's confronted with dramatic events as they happen, in a continuous present tense. The French are presenting a peace plan, the Pentagon threatening military action at any time, the oil price jumping to $38 a barrel.

'Last night was quiet downtown,' Rob says. 'I went to buy some jerry cans and a flashlight.'

'Well, I hope you've got everything you need,' Derek says. 'Our bosses said the roads off camp will be closed when the war starts. We're not supposed to leave here.' He elbows himself up off the couch. 'Cup of tea or some *sidney?* Just to keep us going?'

'*Sid* and 7-Up,' Rob says, as his friend ambles through into the galley kitchen.

'Always good to get back after the Christmas holidays,' Derek decides. 'Back into the old routine.'

'Yes, and thanks for looking after Cilla while I was away.'

'No problem. We enjoyed it.' Returning from the kitchen, Derek hands him a sparkling *sid* and 7-Up. 'So, ready for action?'

'I've taped across the windows and put up some plastic sheeting…'

'Good.' Derek settles back to lie on his couch. 'To our finest hour.' He lifts his tumbler of *sid* and water and offers a toast: to Winston Churchill, themselves, and this exciting *War in the Gulf.*

Cilla shifts round beside Rob's armchair to catch the breeze from the doorway, but suddenly jumps up, barking and charging out through the open door. Another dog is barking and as Rob runs out shouting for Cilla, he sees June from the art group, hauling back a powerful brown mastiff on its chain.

Cilla's smaller than the mastiff but she's barking furiously as if about to attack. He hasn't brought a lead and leans down to grab his dog's collar and pull her back.

'What a ruckus. Jackson! Calm down.' June grins, relaxed in a green smock dress and a necklace of colorful stones round her neck. 'Don't worry, Rob. It's just the usual male macho stuff.'

Slowly, the dogs edge back and cease barking, while still eying each other warily.

'Now that's over, come in for a drink,' Derek says, observing the action as he leans against his doorway.

'Sure. Let's visit, eh, Jackson?' Following the men, June boldly steps over the threshold into their smoky British lads' domain, slipping off her cherry-red flip-flops by the door.

She glances towards their drinks. 'Looks like you Brits are enjoying yourselves.'

'Just trying to make the best of things.' Derek presses the remote to mute CNN's excitement. '*Sid* and tonic? Tea or coffee?'

'Never waste good alcohol. *Sid* and tonic, for me.' She offers her hand towards Derek. 'I'm June, a friend of Rob's wife.'

Rob offers his chair and moves to the other armchair while Derek slices a fresh lemon for the visitor and pours their drinks. June settles her dog beside her and looks up to meet Rob's gaze.

'Jackson's named after Jackson Pollock, the American painter,' she explains and nods towards his dog. 'So why Cilla?'

'She's a black lab,' Derek answers, returning with her drink. 'And Cilla Black's a screeching singer from Liverpool, the place where Scousers like the Beatles and Rob come from.'

June smiles at this display of British culture. 'So what are you guys doing here?'

'As little as possible.' Derek stretches back on the couch and lights another cigarette. 'I'm in Finance – basic bean counting.'

'And I'm in safety training and inspection,' Rob says. 'We try to make sure people don't fall into machinery or things blow up.'

'Safety.' June laughs. 'This company's always preaching health and safety. But what about living?'

Derek grins. 'So here's to more living,' he toasts, raising his glass. 'So what are you doing here, June?'

She settles back in the armchair, slightly plump Rob notices beneath the green smock dress. Her eyes and smile are teasing, challenging, like a mischievous child.

'I'm an artist and paint in oils and watercolors.' Her tone's firm and confident. 'I also make Native American pottery. But for the war effort, I'm helping out at the International Hotel. Working with the media guys in the Information Bureau.'

'Have you met Clive Fox?' Rob asks. 'Works for the *Guardian.*'

June considers. 'Yeah, tight-assed British guy. Keeps bugging us to let him go up to the frontline and catch some of the action. The Saudis took him out on a field trip to the camel market in Hofuf. But he complained about the smell and fell off his camel. So how do you know him?'

'Oh, we were at university together.' Rob hopes she doesn't think *he's* a tight-assed Brit who'd fall off camels.

'So what are you guys doing for the war effort?' June asks.

'Just observing the chaos.' Derek puffs smoke rings into the air.

'I'm helping out with the night patrol around camp,' Rob says.

'Good for you.' June smiles. 'Rick says you guys are doing a great job. So what do you think about Rob when you're out on patrol all night? Whiskey, pork chops, women?'

'All three I suppose.' He grins, wary of exposing his uncertainties to this confident woman.

'You live near here, June?' Derek asks

'No, I'm visiting friends and Jackson wanted a run out.' Hearing its name, the mastiff rises and barks towards Cilla, who shifts anxiously, eying the larger dog, as Rob grips her collar.

'Well, here's to the war and to us.' Derek lifts his glass towards the muted Bobbie Battista on CNN. 'And here's to our finest hour, as old Winnie used to say.'

'Sure. But who's Winnie?' June asks.

'Winston Churchill.' Derek puffs patriotic smoke rings into the air. 'His mother was American, so he was half yours as well.'

'To us, then. Brits and Americans together,' June says, and Rob leans over to chink glasses and meet her gaze, her smile illuminating Derek's sitting room and this familiar lads' evening.

'Well, excuse me. Got to visit what you guys call the restroom.' Derek struggles to his feet, hitches up his jeans, and they watch him slowly mount the brown-carpeted staircase.

'So, any more news on Fiona?' June asks. 'She coming back?'

'No, and for obvious reasons she didn't want *me* to come back this time.'

'What about your son?'

'Chris. He's gone back to university and Fiona's by herself at home.'

'So what are *you* going to do? Stay on or go back to England after the war?'

'Not sure.' He finds himself looking into her sympathetic brown eyes. 'I said I'd do ten years. That's up in August. After that, I don't know. What about you? You going back to the States?'

'I don't know, either.' She laughs. 'Sounds like we're both stuck. Waiting for this war to start and something to happen or change, something to make up our minds.'

They're smiling, leaning over towards each other, but upstairs the toilet flushes, the sound of running water. Derek's imminent return threatens their warming intimacy.

'I'm teaching at the art group tomorrow night,' June says. 'Why don't you drop by? Maybe sign up for a class? We've got all kinds of courses. You can touch base with your artistic side.'

Derek's coming downstairs towards them and June swallows the rest of her drink.

'OK guys. Gotta go before Jackson tries to jump your girl.' She stands up, pulling the mastiff back on his chain and slips on her red flip-flops. 'OK big boy. Let's hit the road.'

Polite goodbyes and June's gone, leaving them to their British lads' night, drinking *sid*, watching TV and grumbling about the company and the war.

'Another bloody Septic.' Derek dismisses their American visitor as he stretches back on the couch and increases the volume on CNN's *Headline News*. But Rob refuses to agree. Thoughts about seeing June, maybe tomorrow night, linger in his mind all the way home and through the long night's patrol of the camp perimeter.

7

The Manager's Corner Office

15 January 1991 / 29 Jumada 1411   *08.00*

'We pass the brink on the fifteenth,' the American Secretary of State had told the troops gathered round him at the airbase. The war could start anytime. When Rob arrives at his office in the headquarters building and looks around, more people seem to have disappeared. Ibrahim left yesterday, Patience hasn't come in this morning, and many of the other offices and cubicles are empty.

Almost immediately, Kamal, the department manager, phones, wanting to see him. Why? Is it because Ibrahim left in a temper, complaining about him and Krieger? As Rob enters the manager's spacious corner office, Kamal's on the phone, sitting back behind his desk in a dark grey *thawb* rather than his usual American business-casual clothes. Behind him, through the large glass windows, Rob can see across to the warehouse area, the shipping containers and stacks of steel pipe in the storage yard, and the continual flurry of vehicles around the camp entrance gates. But something important is missing.

After Kamal puts the phone down and they greet each other, Rob says,

'You've no masking tape on the windows.'

'No problem.' Kamal dismisses it. 'We'll only have to take it off again when the war's over.' For someone who's always criticizing the Americans, he seems a firm believer in their military power and a quick victory.

Instead of the chair in front of his desk, Kamal indicates a brown leather couch and plonks down there beside Rob. Over the years since they first met on North Camp, the lean clean-shaven Egyptian teacher has transformed himself, gaining weight, gravitas, and a fierce-looking beard, as he climbed the company's promotion ladder. The lively expression and youthful enthusiasm have slowed down into wary middle-aged maturity and now he sits leaning forward with his hands clasped in counselling mode: a technique he probably learned on some management course.

'Did Ibrahim come to see you?' Rob asks, taking the initiative.

'Yes, he wanted more leave days to take his wife to Khartoum. I told him he should have left her there in September when he took his vacation. Isn't that what you and Krieger said?'

Rob nods. 'When the war starts, we'll need him for emergencies.'

'Good. Anyway, he's taking his wife to Jeddah for the ferry to Sudan. Let's hope he comes back. But I wanted to speak to you about something else. Haven't you got a son at university?'

Rob's surprised at this topic. 'Yes. Chris is in his first year.'

'You know my eldest son, Hashim? He was with Chris in your youth soccer team a few years ago.'

Rob recalls a small curly-haired boy, nervous and seeming overwhelmed by the bigger lads on the team. But he was plucky and kept coming to practice sessions.

'He's done well,' Kamal continues. 'Good 'A' levels and he's been accepted for Physics at Imperial College, London. But he's delayed starting his course. Said he needed a gap year.'

Rob nods, thinking of Chris, who's also done well, despite their lack of time together. He's tried to use money to compensate, but the money still feels inadequate when he speaks to his son on the phone.

'Bright young people,' Kamal says. 'But in their teens, they can become too idealistic and want to change the world.'

Rob guesses he's probably remembering himself: the bright Egyptian student studying hard for success in Alexandria before he gained a well-paid job in Saudi Arabia. Then the years living on North Camp before he took a second wife, the daughter of a wealthy Saudi contractor, and the company elevated him to this prestigious corner office.

'Hashim's very idealistic.' Kamal seems uncertain whether to be proud or critical of his son. 'Some of his friends travelled to Afghanistan to help the *mujahedeen* fight the Russians. They went off like Boy Scouts on a camping trip, going to discover the world. But I stopped Hashim from joining them, and I think he blames me.' He pauses and looks Rob in the eye. 'So I agreed to this gap year. But that was before Kuwait. Now he's decided to stay here.'

'So what *is* he doing?'

'Wasting time.' The words are spat out by an exasperated father who struggled through *his* early life. 'He has friends living here. Basically they're good boys, but...'

Rob wonders why Kamal's telling him this. Surely he's strong and cunning enough to command his son's obedience. But as well as brains, perhaps Hashim has inherited his father's determination? Rob remembers one evening in Bill Eliot's box room on North Camp when Kamal opened his wallet to show a photo of his smiling Egyptian wife and his son standing proudly beside her. There's probably friction between Kamal and his son, maybe problems with the second wife, the Saudi stepmother.

'He needs careers advice.' Kamal takes refuge in educational platitudes. 'Some guidance for the future. Will you speak to him?'

'The university will have careers advisors.'

'But you know the British system and about the life here, about where he's coming from. You can give a fresh perspective, talk to him about life at university.'

Life at university? Does Kamal mean the college bar, drugs, maybe girls? From the secretary's office outside, Rob can hear Krieger's voice, cool and logical, amidst the laughter and joking of the Saudi superintendents waiting to come in for their weekly management meeting.

Hearing his subordinates, Kamal glances towards the half-open door. 'Come over to my house and meet Hashim. It'll be good to have a British visitor, someone new for him to talk to. This Thursday night?'

'OK. I'll check to see if I'm on patrol then.'

'Good. Did you see Bill Eliot when he came round?' Kamal asks as they shake hands. 'He seems to be looking forward to this war.'

Raised voices are coming from outside, and the door to the office opens wide. Khalid, the department's accountant, bursts in, his usually smiling face flushed and agitated as he explains to Kamal in Arabic, seeming to plead with his boss for help.

Before the invasion of Kuwait, Rob and Khalid had been friendly, but after the invasion, Rob had overheard Khalid joking about the British civilians Saddam was holding hostage and using as human shields.

Now Khalid turns on Rob. 'Aziz, your clerk, insults me. He insults the Palestinian people. He says Palestinians are traitors and help Saddam in this war.' He turns to his manager. 'Aziz says I'm terrorist and will blow up this building. He says he'll tell Security about me.'

'Don't worry,' Rob tells Kamal. 'I'll speak to Aziz.'

'You must control your clerk,' Khalid demands. 'Punish him for bad behaviour.'

When he gets outside, Rob asks Krieger what happened.

But it's one of the Saudi superintendents who explains. 'An argument at the coffee trolley. Your clerk said Palestinians were helping Iraqi soldiers in Kuwait. Khalid lost his temper.'

Glancing back into the manager's office, Rob can see that Kamal's persuaded his accountant to sit down on the leather couch. He's leaning forward with his hands clasped, listening to him in management counselling mode.

So Rob must speak to Aziz, reprimand him, and make sure it doesn't happen again. They'll probably have another argument about Palestinians, and Aziz will sulk and complain for the rest of the day.

It's a dreary prospect and tonight, at nine o'clock, he'll have to go out on patrol again, struggling to stay awake as he checks the camp perimeter. Maybe he could go round to Derek's for a drink before that... He needs something to look forward to.

8

Life Expands

15 January 1991 / 29 Jumada 1411   *19.30*

Brake. Peninsula road is deserted, the long highway leading straight ahead, and with his thoughts drifting back to Fiona's phone call earlier, Rob's been picking up speed. 'The doctor says it's depression – probably something to do with living in Saudi,' she told him. 'And he's given me a prescription.' When he asked if she was returning after the war, she'd cried out that he wasn't listening and they couldn't go on like this. Then she slammed down the phone. Tonight's patrol doesn't start until nine, and to get out of the house and away from Fiona's phone call, he set off in the patrol car, unsure yet of where to go.

Brake. He opens the driver's window to keep awake and, obeying the traffic sign, slows to forty kilometres per hour.

The Junior High school, where Chris had been a student, lay in darkness, but the floodlights illuminating the tennis courts and the emerald turf of the sports field create a bizarre country club appearance. Don't these lights make the camp an easier target? Should he report it to Al or Rick? But when he thinks of Rick, he remembers June teasing him at Derek's house.

He passes the blocked-off entrance to the riding stables where, before the invasion of Kuwait, some expats kept horses. Opposite the stables, large ghostly white tents bloom out in the wasteland. They were erected weeks ago for company workers and their families to come in from the surrounding area – people like Ibrahim and his pregnant wife who lived downtown – but no one's moved in yet and the jokes about *Carry on Camping* have grown stale. Yet what's going to happen when the war starts? If the Scuds start falling and there's a gas attack, thousands will be panicking and struggling to flee the area.

Picking up speed past more waste ground, Rob admires the rocky outcrops of sandstone *jebels*, rugged in the light from the road, yet so fragile when several were blown up for this new housing area. Derek's courtyard is fast approaching but he visited him last night and doesn't want to discuss Fiona's phone call. Passing the entrance to the courtyard, he feels a sudden jolt of energy as he remembers June's invitation to sign up for an art class. He needs petrol, anyway, and the filling station's near the art building.

Traffic lights, and he stops at the deserted junction of Peninsula and Golf Course Road, waiting for the red light to change. Nothing coming. He could drive straight through but still he refuses to break the rules. Following the rules to the letter might be a strength, but if the worst happens, it could be fatal. Just staying here on this camp could be fatal. Suddenly, his safe, no-risk taking life – like waiting for these traffic lights to change – feels absurd.

Green. He releases the clutch too quickly, jerks forward and stalls in the middle of the junction. Fortunately, nothing's coming and he starts up again, turning left by the golf course. *Caution Golfers Crossing* warns a sign and he winds down the window further to let in some cold air and stay awake. Passing the golf clubhouse he sees a few fanatics, wrapped up against the *shamal*, standing out on the driving range. Beneath the floodlights and as if on stage, they position their squares of green AstroTurf and hit balls out over the rough ground towards the filling station. He could drive into the club car park and here, from the top of the *jebel* overlooking the airbase, watch the planes taking off. But he needs petrol first, before the filling station closes.

A young Indian wrapped up in a shabby grey jacket and scarf, head covered by a brown Biggles helmet with ear muffs, runs from the shelter of his Portakabin. He hurries to fill the tank, anxious to regain the warmth of his hut and the radio playing country and western music.

'You have mask, sir?' The youth's peering in at the gas mask on the passenger seat.

'Yes,' Rob says.

'I have no mask, sir. You know where I find?'

'I'm sorry.' Embarrassed by his privilege, he doesn't know what else to say and finally just hands the young Indian some *riyals* for the petrol with enough for a generous tip.

As he drives out of the filling station, the traffic lights at the junction change to red. He could still turn back, drive home and watch CNN with Cilla until it's time to go out on patrol. Maybe he could phone Fiona back, sympathize more with her illness, and try to persuade her to return after the war. Or he could drive on through the intersection to the art building a few hundred yards away.

He drives to the traffic lights and stops for a gaggle of Indian house boys to walk across the zebra crossing. Out for an evening stroll, they chatter together, heading towards the guardhouse entrance to the domestic camp, a wire fence surrounding the long dormitories these men call home. But even the domestic camp is emptying as the cooks, cleaners and house boys flee, desperate to escape from Scuds and regain their homes and families thousands of miles away. The traffic lights stay red, but still nothing's coming. He drives through, turns right and parks outside a block of flats opposite the art building. He used to drop Fiona off here at this old bungalow for her painting class and has only occasionally gone inside. But tonight he's invited and a prospective art student.

Through the bungalow's screen door, light shines out onto the entrance steps, and large Texas beetles blunder around the lamp above the doorway. The beetles were stowaways on ships carrying military equipment from the US and with no natural predators have multiplied. As Rob walks up the steps, he can hear women's voices from inside and old Bobby Dylan crooning about staying forever young. Opening the screen door, he steps over the threshold into the spacious art studio.

June's standing behind the front bench, bare-armed in a striped butcher's apron. She's kneading a hunk of milky brown clay and talking to three other middle-aged women. As the screen door bangs behind Rob, she looks up, startled to see him.

'Hi'. He hesitates, wondering what else to say, with the women's faces looking towards him, especially Fiona's friend, the Canadian doctor's wife.

'Come in, Rob,' June calls. 'Want to sign up for a class?'

'Sure. Just thought I'd look at what's on offer.'

'Go through to the kitchen.' She indicates behind her. 'There's a list of courses on the board. We'll be taking a break soon. Why don't you put the kettle on for some nice English tea?'

Relieved she's found him something to do, he walks past the wooden benches with the women's gas mask satchels piled up beside freshly baked clay pots, warming the air with their scent of Mother Earth. Compared to most buildings on camp, this art group bungalow is old and dilapidated. Built by the oil pioneers in the late fifties, it's been converted into an art and craft studio with work benches, wooden cupboards and lockers, a kiln room, and a kitchen and bathroom at the back. There's a musty early sixties atmosphere: shabby and bohemian, like Greenwich Village in the era of Peter, Paul and Mary, mysteriously surviving on the edge of the Arabian Desert. Here, out of sight and ignored by the company's bureaucracy, aspiring artists feel free to indulge their imaginations and create something of their own.

He steps down into the kitchen, warmed by the large open pottery kiln he can see at the back. Company guidelines ban anything but health and safety posters on the walls, but here are Toulouse Lautrec prints of colourfully costumed women dancing at the Moulin Rouge and a poster of Picasso's *Guernica*. Pleased with his entry into June's bohemian world, he fills the kettle at the double sink and plugs it in. Lipton's English teabags and sugar are on a tray at the side, with milk in a small fridge and a stock of Pepsis, 7-Ups and Dr Peppers. A selection of mugs lie on the draining board and ignoring the company's gold-and-black fiftieth anniversary mugs, he chooses two Andy Warhol *Campbell's Soup*, two Jasper Johns *Three Flags* and for himself one chipped Roy Lichtenstein of an American jet zapping an enemy plane with an explosive crimson and yellow *Whaam!*

Waiting for the kettle to boil, he glances at the list of classes on the bulletin board: oil painting, watercolours, stained glass, and pottery. At school he was interested in art and a good painter. Maybe he could try again. Alongside the class listing are advertisements for Laguna Beach art supplies and a poster for a painting workshop on the Greek island of Santorini. The poster's photograph shows a clifftop village, whitewashed houses clustered round an Orthodox church, its cross gazing out over the cobalt blue Aegean. June's named as the organizer of this Easter trip and he picks up an information leaflet headed *Life Expands*. Above the workshop details there's a quotation: *Life shrinks or expands in proportion to one's courage – Anaïs Nin*. Sounds good and he folds the leaflet, putting it in his jeans pocket.

The women are leaving the studio, June stepping down into the kitchen with her students. 'So how's the gallant night patrol?' she asks.

'What's that?' The doctor's wife turns to Rob.

'We're volunteers helping out with security,' he says.

'A lot of our brave security guards have skedaddled,' June says. 'So expats like Rob are filling the breach. Thank you, sir, for keeping us safe.'

'You're welcome.' He feels flattered, yet slightly absurd, to be the heroic centre of attention. The kettle pipes up and a tall thin woman busies herself making tea.

'Did you look at the classes?' June asks. 'Thinking of joining our pottery class?'

'Not really. I'd probably make a mess of it. But maybe I could try painting.'

'Good. It would be interesting to have a man in the class.' June turns to her students. 'Don't you think so, ladies?'

Fortunately, the ladies are more interested in discussing the Easter workshop on Santorini and asking June how much it will cost. Rob takes his chipped *Whaam!* mug and stands in front of Picasso's *Guernica* trying to identify the surreal images: a mother holding what may be a dead child, her head screaming to the heavens, and what might be a light bulb or the evil eye blazing down over her.

'Is Fiona coming back after the war?' asks the doctor's wife. Startled, Rob turns to her. 'Only I thought she was enjoying our painting classes.'

'I don't know yet,' he says, as June comes over to join them.

'Tell her, I was asking after her.' The doctor's wife smiles brightly and re-joins the others to discuss the Santorini trip.

'So, Rob, are you interested in Santorini?' June asks.

'Maybe,' he says, but then realizes it would be stupid. He should be going home at Easter to see Fiona and Chris, maybe looking for a job in the UK.

'Why don't you sign up, then?' June says.

'I'll think about it,' he decides.

But doesn't he want his life to change and expand? A painting holiday with June on a romantic Greek island – it sounds and feels magical.

'Isn't *Guernica* powerful?' June says, looking towards the Picasso poster. 'I'm starting work on a Gulf war painting or collage – something abstract for the art show I'm organizing. But I wonder what symbols to use. Gas mask, some kind of shield for this Operation Desert Shield. Nothing too obvious like mosques or camels.'

'How about oil refineries, desert pipelines?' he says.

'Typical man's view. Technology and money.' She turns to her group. 'Ready, ladies? We'll walk through with our English tea and start the critique.'

The students follow June back into the studio to discuss their fired pottery: an assortment of clay vases, small bowls, and decorative tiles.

'Well, tell us what you think,' June begins as they inspect their work.

'I'm not happy with this.' The tall thin woman examines the bowl she's holding. 'The glaze has turned out all wrong.'

'You never know what's going to come out of the kiln,' June says. 'You try for something and maybe it works. Or maybe the fire and clay do their own thing. Sometimes it's great, sometimes a total disaster. What was the effect you wanted?'

'Not this.' The woman sounds unconvinced by June's philosophy, but the doctor's wife is pleased with the cobalt blue of her small bowl.

'That's art. Sometimes you do it and it works, and sometimes...' June grins. 'Well, shit just happens.'

'Like these Scuds.' The tall thin woman's voice is low, her pale face strained with keeping things in. 'We don't know what's going to happen.'

No one risks speaking until June says, 'We've got the Patriot missiles to protect us.'

'How do we know they'll work?' The thin woman's voice is rising, on the edge of hysteria. 'We could all be killed.'

Rob speaks up in what he hopes is a voice of authority. 'You're more likely to get killed or injured in a car going down town.' For a moment the words sound hollow in his own mouth but looking at the women's faces, they seem to be convinced.

The pager on his belt is beeping. Looks like a security number and he'll have to go to the patrol car.

'I'd better get this, June. I'm on patrol tonight.'

As they walk to the door, he asks, 'Going to one of these eve-of-the-war parties?'

'Sure. Dave, our *sid* supplier's invited us to his party.'

'Good.' He can't keep the pleasure out of his voice. 'I'm going too.'

'Dave's got lots of thirsty customers to satisfy. But Rick might not make it with this war starting.'

'Good.' He'd said it without thinking. 'But don't worry about the war, June. We'll be fine.'

'I'm not worried, sweetheart. This could be fun. *Carpe diem,* baby. Seize the day and all that.'

Cheered by her 'sweetheart', he wants to kiss her, but June's already returning to her students while the early sixties Bobby Dylan's singing now about God being on our side.

9

The Tank Farm

15 January 1991 / 29 Jumada 1411   21.10

As soon as Rob's in the patrol car, Rick's shouting over the radio, 'Get your ass over here. We're at the Golden Ghetto.'

He drives past the fire station with its two fire trucks parked on the forecourt ready for action, through the camp security gate, then uphill towards the lights of the Golden Ghetto. The Saudi senior managers live here, overlooking the camp in their two-storey mansions with their Asian servants and heated swimming pools. Rounding a bend, he spots two patrol cars parked at the side of the road. A small group of men are standing there, headlights trained on the high chain-link fence protecting the tank farm further down the *jebel*, where petrol tankers fill up with fuel for the jets flying over Iraq and occupied Kuwait.

He parks behind the other cars and steps out with his flashlight, leaving the warmth for the chill wind blowing in from the Gulf. Rick in his Army windbreaker towers over the two security guards and Al, his deputy in a grey winter *thawb*.

'Some bastard's cut the wire.' Rick's voice rises above the shrill Arabic music from the patrol cars. 'We gotta search the area.'

In the headlights, Rob can see the break, the wiring peeled back. Beyond that, the sand and rocks of the *jebel* fall steeply down towards the silvery tops of fuel storage tanks lying below like giant metal draughts illuminated by floodlights. Rick speaks into his radio, giving instructions.

'*Assalamu alikum.*' Al shakes Rob's hand vigorously, peering up into his face. 'How you doin', my friend?'

'*Walaikum assalam.* How are you, Al?' Their conversations always run like this: following the courtesies but superficial and avoiding any sensitive issues. Rob feels they have much more to say to each other, but with no chance of drinking alcohol together, he suspects they'll never get round to it.

'So, where's Faisal?' Rick asks his deputy.

'He's off duty tonight,' Al says. 'He's taking his family to Hofuf for safety.'

'Shit. You should have told me.' Rick turns to the others. 'Listen up guys. We don't want sirens going off all over camp, management shitting themselves. Gotta get down there and check things out. But I've contacted the base and they're sending some of their people.'

'Rick, we need more guards to secure the area,' Al says. 'I spoke to the Big House and they're on their way.'

'Can't wait,' Rick decides. 'If this tank farm blows, our jets won't fly and Saddam will be laughing at us. Let's catch these terrorists before they blow us all sky high.'

Rob follows the others, crouching and scrambling through the gap in the wire. Rick leads, scanning the ground with his flashlight as they move slowly down the *jebel*, trudging through sand and gravel. As they advance on the floodlit metal tanks below, Rob realizes he doesn't need to be here. He could easily be somewhere else, drinking a *sid* and tonic with Derek as they follow *War in the Gulf* on CNN, maybe watching June teach her pottery class. But instead he's here, dragging his feet through *jebel* dust, descending towards this tank farm where terrorists are hiding and these giant fuel tanks can explode into hell fire.

Rick turns, keeping his voice low. 'You guys, spread out. Al, Rob, you circle anti-clockwise. Aziz and Hassan – follow me. Yell if you see anything. Christ, we need some guns…'

Rick and the guards move off, veering to the left of the tank farm. 'OK?' Rob looks to Al and is glad to stay with him rather than June's husband. And Al's probably right: they should be waiting for more help. There must be better ways of doing this, or is he just making excuses to hang back by the patrol cars?

'*Yalla.*' Al nods and they move ahead towards the right, a giant storage tank beginning to loom over them, the stink of petrol in the breeze.

The floodlights snap out and with the instant blackness, Rob trips up, drops his flashlight and falls on his knees. He grits his teeth to stop himself shouting out with the pain shooting up his left leg. He can't see the flashlight and feels around the sandy gravel with his hands. Someone's just switched off the floodlights so the intruders must still be here. But how many and what are they doing? And where's Al now? He peers round into the darkness, but maybe Al's already moved behind the fuel storage tank. On his knees, he waits for the pain in his leg to ease and forces himself to be patient until his eyes adjust and refocus to the night.

He still can't see Al. He must be on the other side of the tank. Should he stay here, kneeling in the dust, waiting to see what happens? Or should he try to stand up and move on round the storage tanks towards the unknown intruders? It feels more tempting, more sensible, to retreat back towards the lights of the Golden Ghetto shining down from the crest of the *jebel* behind him.

Gradually he can see a little in front of him and struggles to his feet, hobbling towards the storage tank until it's towering above. A stronger smell of petrol and moving forward, he realizes this could be suicidal. But, afraid to stop and lose his nerve, he presses on. At the foot of the tank, he turns round, but there's still no sign of Al or any flashlight beams. He listens to the night surrounding him – the rhythmic chorus of cicadas, the growl of a lorry travelling along the road below the tank farm. He looks back again towards the lights of the Golden Ghetto where the Saudi managers are sleeping, oblivious to danger and cocooned with their families and servants. Slowly he begins to move round the metal tank, his feet firmer on the flattened ground and his body leaning in close to the cold metal skin.

Crash. A body bangs down on him, crushing his face into the dirt. He panics, fighting for breath under the man's weight, his ribs pressed tight. His arms are pinned to the ground, his body struggling, nose and mouth gagging for breath out of the dirt. He can't move. Somebody is trying to crush him. The big man on top grunts, his hand pushing Rob's face down again into the dirt. Sand's being forced into his mouth, grinding against his nose and cheeks. He's fighting for breath, suffocating.

A light shines out and instantly everything's illuminated.

'Hey. Break it up you guys.' Al's standing there, shining his flashlight towards them. *'Khalas.'*

His whole body trembling, Rob staggers to his feet, holding onto somebody muscular and powerful in the light.

'Shit.' Rick pushes Rob in the chest, away from him. 'Shit!' The two men step back, exposed like boys caught fighting by the teacher.

'Christ! What the hell?' Rob's words escape in short bursts, his body shaking and bruised. 'What the hell were you doing?'

'OK guys, cool it,' Al says.

'Shit. I thought it was…' Rick protests. 'Why didn't you yell?'

'I couldn't. You were on top.' Humiliated, Rob can't stop shaking as he faces the Security boss.

Now the Saudi guards are laughing, their fears relieved by white faces making fools of themselves. More flashlights are approaching, American voices climbing uphill from the fuel tankers' parking area.

'Hey, guys. We're over here,' Rick calls out. 'And for Christ's sake, don't shoot.' He glares at Rob. 'We've had enough screw-ups already.'

More security guards are scrambling down the *jebel* and Rick takes charge, giving instructions. He turns to Al and Rob. 'OK, we'll take care of this. But before these terrorists get away, you guys drive round the Golden Ghetto. See if anybody's hanging round.'

'But why break in up there?' Al asks. 'Why drive through security gates and an ID check? It's easier to park down there, off the main road, and then cut through the camp fence.'

'The bastards might have broken in there as well,' Rick says. 'We'll check.'

But Al's looking up towards the lights of the Golden Ghetto. 'Could be somebody living up there. Maybe listening to these religious tapes.'

'What tapes?' Rick's impatient to join his buddies from the airbase.

'The police found religious tapes on sale downtown, in the *souks*,' Al says. 'Tapes of preachers attacking the Western crusaders.'

'Crusaders?' Rick scoffs. 'You guys are obsessed with religion. No, this is probably Palestinians or Sudanese terrorists. Call our IT guy, and tell him to print out a list of Palestinians and Sudanese working in this area. Then drive round the Ghetto, see if anybody's still moving about. Now I gotta see Bill Eliot and the guys from the Base. Probably bitching already about our security set-up.' He spits into the dust and walks downhill to supervise the search around the tank farm.

'Did he say Bill Eliot?' Al turns to Rob.

'Yes, you remember? He lived on North Camp a few years ago.' Rob wipes blood from his nose with a scrap of tissue from his pocket. 'Bill's back. Seems a lot of these contractors are returning.'

Rob recovers his flashlight and they trudge back up the *jebel* towards the patrol cars. 'We investigated Eliot,' Al says finally. 'On that murder case. The guy we found dead in the camp swimming pool.'

'Did you find out who did it?' Rob halts, breathless and needing to ease the pain in his ribs. He massages them gently.

'No, and in the end we arrested some Filipinos. They were gambling and making *sideeki* on the side.'

Such a banal outcome, Rob thinks as he struggles uphill. As people predicted at the time, some Filipinos had been arrested, imprisoned, and hopefully deported in one of the annual Ramadan amnesties.

Back at the patrol cars, Al offers to drive and Rob gingerly moves into the passenger seat, his face, ribs and lower back still aching. Al radios the Big House for the IT specialist to print out names of Palestinians and Sudanese working in the Golden Ghetto.

'Hey, what's that smell?' Al sniffs again.

'My dog,' Rob admits. 'She tried to get in the back when I was leaving home.'

'*Haram*. No dogs allowed.' Al wrinkles his nose in disgust and winds down the window.

'Sorry.' Rob changes the subject. 'You think the guys breaking in were house boys or chauffeurs?'

'No, but Rick wants easy answers. The usual suspects. Doesn't want any trouble with his bosses.'

'Do you?' With his body aching so much, Rob's annoyed with the interminable office politics.

'No, I don't want trouble,' Al says. 'I'm Shia, one of Saudi's ten per cent, with my family to worry about.'

'OK.' Rob massages his arm muscles, relieving the soreness, and eases back in the seat to reduce the pain from his ribs.

'You're injured, my friend. After we look round, I'll drive you home. Better rest tonight.'

Rick's voice breaks through on the radio – no sign of explosives at the tank farm, and it looks like the terrorists were scared off.

'No problem, Rick,' Al says. 'We'll catch these guys *inshallah*.'

'No more *inshallah*,' Rick demands. 'We got terrorists on the loose and gotta catch them. You hear that, Al? No more excuses and God willing.'

'Sure, Rick. We're on the job,' Al says as they drive off to search round the management villas of the Golden Ghetto.

10

Sahwa / The Awakening

16 January 1991 / 01 Rajab 1411   *19.20*

Following *maghrib* prayer, Ibrahim sits with Saeed and his brothers in a coffee shop on the Jeddah Corniche. While Saeed and his *mujahid* friends reminisce about Afghanistan and exchange their news, he thinks about what the enthusiastic young preacher said. He'd reminded the faithful of the Prophet's words 'Let there not be two religions in Arabia.' And it was a great sin to allow these Crusader armies – Christians, Jews and even women – to invade this land of the two holy mosques where the Prophet received and recited the message of Allah. They should resist this infidel occupation. But what should *he* do? Still weary from two days driving across Arabia, Ibrahim sips the thick sweet *gawa* and gazes out onto a near-deserted Corniche, the calm sea beyond and this chilly evening darkening towards war.

When he and Muna escaped from their small apartment in Dammam, he was relieved to be leaving behind the rising fear and hysteria at the threat of Iraqi Scuds. But it had been a long exhausting drive to Jeddah and he'd battled with police checkpoints and hundreds of reckless drivers, desperate to flee what they thought were imminent missile attacks. Now he's relaxing against the soft cushions of a couch in this open air coffee shop with Saeed and his comrades. He rests back, lulled towards sleep by the chatter of friends, the sweet smoke of a man nearby puffing at a *shisha* pipe and the rich aroma of freshly ground coffee. As a child, he remembers visiting the Mahdi's tomb in Omdurman – its silver dome glinting in the wintery sunshine as his father told him about the great hero who defeated General Gordon and the British at Khartoum and liberated his country for Islam.

Ibrahim's startled and awake. Something brushed against his leg and he glances under the table to see a skinny black cat scavenging for scraps of food. The cat meows, looking up to appeal to him but he knocks the creature away with his shoe. Tonight his friend, Saeed, is wearing his lucky *pakol*, a black woollen beret he brought back from Afghanistan, and is reminiscing with his two *mujahid* companions from Riyadh. One sacrificed his arm for the *jihad* and is heavily built and shaggy bearded; the other, a quiet, mild looking man, had fired a Stinger missile and shot down a Russian helicopter. They're remembering their days of glory, fighting the atheist army, while several students listen in, admiring their elders. The *mujahid* fought for their religion and the students are growing excited about the opportunities this new war might bring: a chance to redeem this land of the two holy mosques and become heroes in their own lives.

He wonders – isn't it his religious duty to help this great awakening? But he has family responsibilities, and his thoughts shift back to Muna waiting for him at his uncle's house nearby. She's pregnant and he wants to take her all the way back to Khartoum. But Rob and Krieger tried to stop him. With that false sympathy on his face, the American boss said he 'understood' Ibrahim's situation, but his hand was twitching, anxious to get back to his new Apple Mac. Ibrahim had emphasized it was Muna's first pregnancy and asked for additional leave days to escort her respectably on the crowded ferry to Port Sudan and onto Khartoum. But Krieger said that upper management had made a decision: he could take five days to travel to Jeddah and back, but if he took more time he'd have to resign. *Resign?* For a moment, he'd been tempted to shout and insult the arrogant imperialist, but he needed this well paid job for his family and to build a new modern house.

This morning he'd bought two ferry tickets for tomorrow but should he risk his job and its benefits? He'd worked hard to pass school and university exams and to gain this position in the oil company. Why should he throw it all away? Saeed suggested he send Muna back with his uncle's family. They'd take good care of her on the ferry and her older brother could pick her up at Port Sudan. But still, this is his first child, maybe a son. What if the rough journey made Muna miscarry?

Shouts are coming from a crowd on the pavement outside the coffee shop. A grey Land Cruiser has pulled up, and there's a stir around the entrance.

Saeed turns to him. 'Look, the Sheikh is here like I promised.' Under the Afghan *pakol*, his face brightens with expectation as they stand up to watch the Lion of Jaji arrive. Here is the brave Sheikh, his turbaned head prominent above the bodyguards and disciples crowding around him. Here is the great Arab leader who brought down the mighty Russian bear. He's shaking hands, exchanging greetings, and being escorted to sit with his followers at a long, reserved table at the back of this coffee house.

Ibrahim sits down again, feeling the atmosphere quickening, the talk growing louder and more excited. He'd been distracted with thoughts of Muna and the baby but now listens to Saeed and his brothers discussing the Sheikh and their plans for resisting the Crusaders invading this holy land. They order more *gawa* and talk about some new ideas, enthusing and exciting each other with righteous zeal. Maybe the American aircraft carriers standing offshore in the Red Sea could be attacked before they bombard Iraq with missiles. Maybe students could demonstrate and take over the American Consulate like in Tehran in 1979.

'Maybe we can bomb McDonalds,' one of the students says, trying to impress his *mujahid* elders. But they laugh and tell him that's crazy as too many Muslims, especially children, would be killed.

'What about the buses carrying American soldiers?' Ibrahim says. 'I saw two of them passing as I drove to the mosque tonight.'

The brothers turn to the Sudanese stranger. Saeed had introduced him as a disciple of Dr al-Turabi, the Sudanese religious leader, and reminded them of Sudan's support for Iraq. Yet still Ibrahim senses they suspect him. Earlier, someone had warned that the Saudi monarchy were not happy with the Sheikh and his plans – so the *mabahith*, the secret police, or government informers might be here tonight.

'Buses carrying soldiers,' Saeed says. 'Good idea. We need these practical ideas, not big Mac ones,' he jokes with his friends.

Ibrahim glances surreptitiously at his watch – almost eight o'clock and Muna is waiting for him. He'd better leave. They need to be awake early in the morning for the ferry to Port Sudan.

But the famous Sheikh has left his reserved table and is walking towards them. Still in his thirties, his posture is upright despite walking with a cane, the mark of his heroism in the Afghan *jihad*. Dressed in a plain white robe, he carries a pistol in the leather holster on his belt, but the kindly expression on his long ascetic face makes the gun seem more like decoration than a deadly weapon. After joking with the two *mujahid* from Riyadh, he speaks to the students at their table but is so softly spoken that Ibrahim has to lean forward to hear him urge the young men to work hard at their studies. The Sheikh reminds them that he attended the same university, and was taught by the martyred Abdullah Azzam, killed by a car bomb in Peshawar on his way to Friday prayers. The Sheikh turns to Saeed, inquiring about his family, his father, and particularly his uncle, the pious government contractor.

'I hear he has good contracts with the Americans.' The Sheikh laughs, covering his mouth with one hand. 'I hope they pay him well for his services.'

'Very well, sir.' Saeed returns the thin smile. 'But he is ready to use these American dollars to support our cause.'

'Good. We will need his help when this war starts.' The Sheikh glances towards Ibrahim. 'Your friend is Sudani?'

'Yes, I'm from Khartoum sir,' Ibrahim says, looking into that noble face, with its sympathetic eyes and aquiline nose above the long greying beard. The great Mahdi, the lion of Khartoum, probably looked like this in his days of glory.

'I like Sudanese people,' the Sheikh says. 'I like their food and righteous fighting spirit. Our company have some important business building a new airport in Port Sudan, and I will travel there soon. You live in Jeddah, my friend?'

'I drove from Dammam with my wife sir. She's pregnant and returning on the ferry, to be safe with my family in Khartoum.'

'Very good. But please don't say you are abandoning us, my brother, in our hour of need, when this sacred land is occupied and reduced to an American colony.'

Ibrahim feels himself wilting under the Sheikh's gaze, as if he's being accused of betraying the holy mosques and his brothers to the Christian and Jewish invaders. But Saeed intervenes, explaining that they both work in the Eastern Province, the centre of the oil and gas industry.

'Very good,' the Sheikh says. 'My father worked and helped build this great oil industry before he started his contracting business. But these Americans and the Al Saud have stolen Allah's great blessings, our precious oil and gas, and are using our natural wealth to fight this war.'

'We want to do something for *jihad*, sir,' Saeed says.

The Sheikh lowers his voice, glancing again at Ibrahim, as if wondering if he can be trusted. 'There are many things we must do to resist these Crusaders and their invasion of Arab lands. They have bases everywhere and want to control the oil fields of the Eastern Province.'

'I can help sir,' Ibrahim says. 'But what should I do?'

For a moment, Muna's face intrudes, waiting for him at his uncle's house. But he pushes it aside.

'We must do whatever Allah commands,' the Sheikh says. '*Inshallah* you can work together with Saeed and our brothers?'

A bodyguard has touched him on the arm. The noble Sheikh has stayed with them too long. Ibrahim shakes the surprisingly soft, almost girlish hand, and the Lion of Jaji moves on, exchanging greetings with the students at the next table.

Ibrahim feels honoured and ennobled to have spoken with the famous Sheikh for so long, when there are so many experienced *mujahid* here and important matters on the great man's mind. The other brothers in the coffee house would have seen the Sheikh conferring with him and Saeed, and he feels the warmth of acceptance and comradeship around him.

The Sheikh and his bodyguards are leaving and the energy seems to drain from the coffee house atmosphere. Ibrahim realizes he has to go back to Muna at his uncle's house and make his decision. After saying goodbye to their comrades, he and Saeed walk out onto the Corniche, the sea breeze blowing into their faces and carrying the faint odour of rotting sewage. In the distance, across the bay, searchlights are illuminating a great gusher of water soaring up into the night sky.

'What's that for?' Ibrahim asks.

Saeed smiles. 'That's the King's Fountain and they boast that it's the highest fountain in the world. It's just more waste, like these hundreds of royal palaces and thousands of princes. But now things can change here, my friend. This war will begin soon and who knows what will happen. Maybe we'll start a revolution in this land.' He turns to Ibrahim and squeezes his arm. 'Your wife can travel safely with your uncle's family. Like the Sheikh said, stay and help us, my brother against these Western Crusaders.'

11

The Eve of Destruction

16 January 1991 / 01 Rajab 1411   *18.30*

The United Nations and White House deadlines for Saddam Hussein to withdraw from Kuwait have passed. The war is due to start tonight and home after work, Rob watches *War in the Gulf,* the rising hysteria of American voices resounding through the empty house. At times like this, he wishes Fiona was here to talk to, and when the phone rings, thinks it might be her. But instead it's one of his squash partners who's driving his family south to stay in Hofuf as his apartment downtown seems too vulnerable to Scud attack.

Yet another friend leaving, and Rob feels increasingly deserted as he sits down again to watch television, with Cilla stretched out at his feet. He remembers a story from a management course about a frog living in a warm pond that's gradually heating up. The frog feels comfortable, at home, and reluctant to leave its pond. But eventually, it loses consciousness before it's finally boiled alive. The message was that to survive, you need to respond to change and danger. Other people, like his squash partner, recognize the situation's becoming more dangerous.

Should *he* be leaving as well, maybe jumping out of the warm water? Or has he left it too late?

From CNN Centre in Atlanta, Bobbie Battista reports there are six US aircraft carriers in the Red Sea and the Gulf preparing to launch planes and Tomahawk missiles against Iraq. The White House announces that President Bush is 'ready to make the tough decisions ahead' and in Baghdad, thousands of demonstrators are crowding the streets in a show of defiance, some waving placards proclaiming *Saddam We Love You* towards the Western TV cameras. *Love*! A surreal word to use, and Rob wonders at millions of Russians still saying they love Stalin, Saddam's own hero. Many Iraqi families have fled Baghdad, shops have pulled down their shutters and at the Al Rashid Hotel, Western journalists are gathering, eagerly anticipating their front page world exclusives.

Weary and still bruised from his fight at the tank farm, he falls asleep to dream of the Greek island of Santorini, an artist's studio overlooking the blue Aegean, and June… He wakes to find himself still in CNN Centre, Atlanta, with the commentators growing more hysterical about the war. Switching off the TV, he checks his watch. Time to shower for the Sidman's eve-of-war party and he's going to see June tonight.

The hot shower revives and reminds him to shave off his beard so the gas mask fits more closely. He's delayed long enough and this afternoon Krieger criticized him for not setting an example. Finding some large scissors, he sits in front of the mirror above the sink in the bedroom, the small light bulbs which illuminated Fiona as she put on her make-up. Laying sheets of kitchen roll in the sink to collect the hair, he begins to snip off his beard. He shaves several times, gradually exposing the tender white skin. He peers at himself in the mirror, noticing the slight cuts and abrasions from his fight with Rick. But the real shock is his new face, without a beard for the first time in years. He assesses himself from different angles, hoping his looks might improve, that he'll soon get used to more prominent ears, a weak white chin, and a scalp which seems even balder. But he's grown bored with himself and his life and this change in appearance could mark a fresh start, transforming him from an over-cautious safety supervisor to a younger spirited, more spontaneous man, ready to take risks.

But he's arrived too early at the party. June isn't in the crush round the ornate wooden bar where the tubby Sidman presides, resplendent in his black and white-striped Newcastle shirt. Derek's there drinking with the Geordies in their Toon Army replica shirts and winding them up about Gazza, their ex-star, now playing for his beloved Spurs. Rob walks through and looks in the sitting room, but June's not there. It's just Phil Collins, warning that you can't hurry love.

Maggie, the Sidman's middle-aged girlfriend, pours Rob a large *sid* and 7-Up and commiserates over his lost beard. She's nervous, speaking rapidly and determined to be bubbly on the eve of war, but her joking about frightened girlfriends driving west to Jeddah or south to Dubai sounds brittle, on the edge of hysteria. Avoiding the Geordie bar huggers, Rob wanders out into the small patio garden. Several groups are sitting round plastic tables with coloured lamps illuminating the white and pink blossomed bougainvillea climbing the garden walls and evoking a twilight serenity. Standing in the patio doorway, with the sweet scent of flowers in the air, he feels the scene's set as the guests wait expectantly like actors for their first read-through, ready to play their part when this Gulf war starts.

'OK, listen to this, guys,' Jerry, the radio station DJ, announces with his sunshine smile and laid-back 'California Dreaming' voice. Wearing a Grateful Dead T-shirt and sitting at the centre table with guests clustered round, he starts a small tape recorder.

'This is the Voice of Peace from Baghdad.' An angry Iraqi voice crashes the party, brutalizing the atmosphere. 'To the American soldiers in the Arabian Desert, you must know Iraq has the strongest army in the Middle East and experience of eight years of war. Iraqi soldiers are the bravest in the world and ready to sacrifice their lives for their land and their glorious leader, Saddam Hussein. So American soldiers, what is your interest? Why are you here?'

That question hangs in the silence of the garden, intimidating any immediate response. The Voice of Peace dedicates Barry McGuire's 'The Eve of Destruction' to the American soldiers in the desert, and overwhelming the crooning of Phil Collins from the house, McGuire's rasping voice resounds like an Old Testament prophet, foreseeing world- wide death and destruction. Rob knows that Saddam Hussein has already used chemical and biological weapons against the Kurds and Iranians, and some experts say he might have a 'dirty bomb'. And what if Israel intervenes and uses its nuclear weapons? Last summer, like most people, Rob had assumed Saddam was bluffing and wouldn't invade Kuwait. He'd been wrong then, and could be wrong again. Some anti-war politicians are predicting a Middle East Armageddon and tonight, at the Sidman's party, they could be on the eve of destruction.

DJ Jerry speaks into his tape recorder. 'I'm here tonight at an eve-of-war party. It's the sixteenth of January, 1991. The UN ultimatum has run out, and tonight the Gulf War is due to start. Catch the vibe – I'm recording this from a garden by the main Coalition airbase. Soon we'll be listening to the F111s and F15s taking off on their first sorties over Iraq and occupied Kuwait. I've got some guests here'. He waves over his red-haired English girlfriend. 'Angela, can you tell us what your feelings are?'

Sitting down beside him, she edges up to the tape recorder. 'To be honest, Jerry, I'm scared. We don't know what'll happen. But I'm still going to enjoy the party.'

'So you'll stay and defy Saddam's Scuds. Good for you, Angela. Going to be an exciting night, memorable for all of us'. Jerry stops the tape. 'Here I'm going to play a counterblast to Saddam – Bruce, the Boss, Springsteen singing about the chimes of freedom.'

Rob wanders back to the sitting room and is delighted to see that June's arrived wearing a loose red dress with her long jangly necklace of colourful stones. She's leaning against the ornate Thai bar talking to the Sidman. But where's Rick?

In pride of place, behind his bar, the paunchy Sidman's boasting about how this valuable mahogany wood was carved by Thai craftsmen, and shipped over to Saudi. As June admires the decorative carvings of elephants, snakes, and what might be gods or lovers intertwined, he describes how he smuggled his bar through Customs at the port.

'Listed it on the inventory as an oriental table. But still the bastards wouldn't let me have it. Had to speak to our Saudi friends.' He nods towards two young men in casual Western clothes loitering by the patio door as they drink their illicit *sid* and appraise the expat women.

'That's great, Dave.' Wide-eyed June's flattering him and having gone to stand beside her, Rob feels neglected.

'This is the best bar on camp, probably in all Saudi,' the Sidman says. 'When I leave, I'll ship it out, put it in the place I'm buying in Phuket.' He lifts his drink towards a photograph pinned up behind the bar, and takes it down for June to admire.

'The Beach Club.' She reads the sign above a wooden shack with rickety looking tables and chairs on the veranda. 'Looks great.'

'I'm crossing off the days.' He gestures towards the 1991 company calendar, taped up next to where the photograph was. 'Only three months to go, and my ten years are up. Full severance and it's *ma'assalama* and good riddance to Saudi.'

Maggie, his girlfriend, appears beside June. 'The Saudis want more drinks. And they want to take a bottle of *sid* with them.'

Cursing, the Sidman leaves to attend to his thirsty guests, while June squeezes Rob's arm and whispers. 'I'm trying to get hold of some hash for us.'

'Hash!' Shocked, he remembers *Death to Drug Trafficker* in red lettering on the Saudi immigration card. But she'd said 'for us' and the thought of smoking hash together excites him.

'I think Dave's got some stashed away.' Her eyes shine. She's like a mischievous child searching for sweets. 'Hey, what happened to your face, and the beard?'

He explains, blaming Rick for his cuts and bruises from the tank farm and appealing for her sympathy.

'Sure, but you're very white. Here…' She raises her hand, stroking his jaw with her fingers. 'Feels soft as a baby's.'

Conscious of Derek and the Geordie lads at the bar observing them, Rob glances round. 'So, where's Rick?'

'It's a big night for Security. He told me to stay home. But how could I miss the big event?'

The Sidman returns, complaining under his breath about 'ragheads' drinking his *sid*, how they're not used to it and can't hold their booze.

'It's too good to waste on them,' he says. 'I run this mash three times so there's no impurities. No headaches in the morning. It's even purer than Scotch whiskey.'

'So, Rob, what do you think about Dave's bar in Phuket?' June passes over the Beach Club photograph.

'Check it out on your next vacation,' the Sidman says.' Enjoy yourself and forget about Old Blighty. Nothing there but whinging wives and the dole. Treat yourself. There's some good-looking women over there.'

'So what about it, Rob?' June teases. 'Imagine the beach at Phuket with all the beautiful Thai girls. If you were free to go anyplace, where would you go?'

But right now, he only wants to be with her and says, 'Painting in Santorini sounds great to me.'

'Sounds great to me, too,' she says.

'Hey, Rick.' The Sidman calls across the room, towards the security boss in his Army windbreaker heading towards them. 'What are you drinking?'

'Straight Pepsi. Hell, what're *they* doing here?' Rick stops at the bar to stare at the two young Saudis drinking by the patio door. 'Get those guys outta here Dave. For Christ's sake, there's a war starting.'

Retreating from Rick's arrival, Rob joins the other partygoers drinking and gossiping as the smooth *sid* and soothing sounds of Phil Collins and Chris Rea anaesthetize their eve-of-war jitters. He returns to the patio garden and finds Bill Eliot in his tan cord jacket, observing the group gathered round DJ Jerry and his tape recording.

'I dropped by with some Jack Daniel's wood chips for your Sidman,' Bill says. 'Can bring some for you as well, Rob. Add chips to your *sid* and you get super smooth whisky with no hangover in the morning.'

'But aren't you AA?' Rob nods towards Bill's glass of black liquid.

'Sure, this is straight Pepsi, my friend.'

'Major Bill.' DJ Jerry looks up from his tape recorder. 'You know all about this stuff. Come over and tell us about these Scuds.'

'Sure, Jerry.' Bill stiffens to attention, becoming the military expert, and takes a seat beside his interviewer. 'Basically these Scud missiles are just primitive Soviet hardware. We guess Saddam's got maybe a hundred fixed and mobile launchers, and some Scuds might carry chemical warheads. But the weather's going to be critical. If it stays clear, our AWACs flights will spot the missile launchers and we can knock them out as soon as they open their hatches.'

'So what else do the AWACS planes do?' the DJ asks.

'Airborne warning and surveillance.' Bill smiles, explaining the technology. 'Basically, they give us eyes in the sky. Early warning of Iraqi attacks, all-weather surveillance, command and control. Pretty well everything we need for air supremacy.'

'But what if it's cloudy or there's a *shamal*?'

'It'll be harder for us to see the launchers and there might be more incoming missiles, here and in Israel. Then we'll depend on the Patriot missiles doing their job and shooting the Scuds down.'

Jerry nods. 'So isn't this Patriot a spin-off from Reagan's Star Wars?'

'Sure. The SDI, the Strategic Defence Initiative.' Bill corrects him. SDI sounds less glamorous but more reassuringly scientific than the Hollywood version.

'So how does this Patriot work, Major Bill?'

'It's a very impressive system. Each launcher holds four missiles and behind them is the high-tech nerve centre, a mobile control station that identifies incoming missiles or aircraft. We've got batteries, Alpha and Bravo, on opposite sides of the airfield. Don't worry, ladies and gentlemen, we'll shoot down anything headed this way.'

Murmurs of satisfaction around the group. This sounds like high-tech protection.

'But what about evacuation flights?' one girl asks. Bill looks at her as if he doesn't understand.

'Aren't there evacuation flights?' The girl's voice grows shrill and the chatter round the patio stills. 'I've heard about these flights,' she says, her voice weakening with her confidence.

'Don't you worry, little lady,' Bill says. 'These Scuds are very inaccurate. Primitive Warsaw Pact weapons. They're not a credible military threat.'

'Not a threat?' June's voice breaks in from behind Rob. 'For months you guys have been saying these Scuds can't reach us. Now, suddenly they can. Why should we believe you this time? So you military types aren't worried. Scuds aren't smart enough to hit *you*. But sounds like they could be dumb enough to hit *us*.'

Bill shrugs. 'When the AWACs spot the launchers, our pilots will destroy them. If they don't, the Patriots will shoot the Scuds down. Double insurance.'

'But these Scuds are likely to be aimed at the airbase,' June persists. 'So when a Patriot shoots them down, they'll fall on us.'

'Enough of this peacenik stuff, June.' Bill stands up. 'Believe me, we've got double insurance. They won't get through.'

'Don't bet your life on it,' she says, and looking round at the suddenly sober faces Rob senses the partygoers, maybe for the first time, imagining casualties. Real people like themselves.

Jerry intervenes, encouraging Major Bill to tell everybody about the high-tech Stealth Nighthawks that can't be tracked by Iraqi radar and will lead tonight's Desert Storm offensive. Rob goes to the bar for another *sid* and 7-Up and returns to the patio garden, standing close to where Maggie's sitting at a table with Rick and June.

'Call of duty.' Rick eventually stands up. 'We gotta go. Time to check the main gates, make sure everything's nailed down. At midnight, we're going to seal off the camp. Nobody comes in or leaves.'

'OK big guy. I'll hang on a while.' June clasps Maggie's hand. 'Maggie says she'll give me a lift home.'

'No, I'll drop you home first,' Rick insists, looming over her. 'We've heard enough from you tonight.'

'It's OK. I'll come later, sweetheart. Maggie needs help with her party.'

'Now, babe.' Rick leans down, grabbing his wife's bare arm, but she pulls free, confronting him. 'OK I'm not fighting you here, kid. We'll settle this later.' He strides off into the house.

Rob takes his place at the table and listens in to the talk in the garden: DJ Jerry recording his girlfriend and others; Maggie gushing to June about Princess Diana visiting military families in Germany; Phil Collins on a continuous loop, rhapsodizing over another day in paradise. Maggie glances towards Rob, who's quietly waiting.

'I want to dance,' June says, and Rob follows her inside, appreciating the sway of her body inside the loose red dress.

'Hey, this sounds like funeral music,' she calls over to the Sidman huddled at the bar with his Geordie mates. 'How about something more lively, Dave?'

'Help yourself from the CDs,' he calls back. Derek seems to have left, and at last Rob feels free to slip his arm round June's waist, his fingers pressing into the red fabric and softness of her flesh. The war's starting tonight, Scuds might be falling soon, and who knows how things are going to end?

On the bookshelves, below Maggie's shelf of glossy Royal Wedding and Delia Smith cookery books is a pile of CDs, mainly Genesis and romantic ballads sung by Chris Rea. Searching through, June picks up Tina Turner's *Private Dancer* and Rob puts it on the CD player. They start to dance, his excitement growing as he responds to June's mischievous smile and feels her soft body beneath the red dress. Dancing only inches apart, she's mouthing the words – she'll do what he wants her to do.

*

86

Past one o'clock and the Sidman's Geordie mates have left, staggering home or to someone else's place, and their host is curled up on the carpet, snoring beside his Thai bar. Maggie has wedged a cushion under his head and is wearily clearing away the glasses.

Collapsed in front of the Home Cinema, Rob and the few remaining guests watch the opening of *War in the Gulf.* It's a high-tech TV spectacular and the first war in history to be shown live for a global audience watching from home. Half-drunk, half-dozing, they listen to the CNN reporters sheltering at the Al Rashid Hotel as they describe the early morning fireworks over Baghdad. The city's blacked out but the skies are lit up by bright flashes. A bomb explodes near the hotel and shakes the whole building. A bright flash illuminates an oil refinery and parts of the city seem on fire. As Bill predicted, the Stealth Nighthawks have dropped laser-guided bombs through the roof of the Air Force headquarters, and British Tornadoes are bombing Iraqi airfields in low-level strikes. US Navy vessels in the Gulf are firing Tomahawk cruise missiles and planes are scouring the Iraqi desert for mobile Scud launchers. And while CNN's Holliman, Shaw, and Arnett are recording history, and making their names as war reporters, DJ Jerry lies on the carpet recording extracts for his Gulf War audio cassette.

'So this is the way we were on the first night of the Gulf war,' he concludes, stopping the tape. 'That's a wrap.'

'Sweet. Sounds great, Jerry.' June stretches out on the couch, drowsily watching TV and stroking the back of Rob's neck as he sits beneath her, his head propped up against the couch, pressing against her leg through the fabric of the dress. Reciprocating her stroke, he finds his hand moving over her dangling foot, her toes and the soft instep, bent and curved for his touch. The slow caressing movements so drowsily begun are becoming more intense, bolder, and demanding.

CNN's Wolf Blitzer, his beard tailored for authority, reports from the Pentagon on the night's military strikes, unable to restrain his exhilaration and the thrill of triumph in his voice. Like the other reporters he's waiting for 'the other shoe to drop', for Saddam to respond to the bombing offensive, but it sounds like he's just covering himself against being too gung-ho.

Now only Maggie and DJ Jerry remain as Rob caresses the soft inner sole of June's dangling foot. Losing interest in the war, his eyes and body are directed towards this woman stretched out above him on the couch. She mutters something about going to the bathroom and holds her hand out for him to help her up. She staggers against his body, then rights herself while he holds onto her small hand, releasing it to watch her going up the stairs.

A long moment while he surveys the Sidman lying unconscious on the floor, DJ Jerry fiddling with his tape recorder and Maggie clinking more glasses as she fills the dishwasher in the kitchen. Abandoning caution on this eve of war, he follows June up the stairs. The bathroom door's shut and he waits outside on the landing. The toilet's flushing and he prepares himself. But when she opens the door, she's not surprised to see him and steps back into the bathroom, illuminated only by the yellow glow of a small lamp.

He closes and locks the door behind him and at last wraps his arms around her body, kissing her on the mouth.

'Hey, you're squeezing me to death,' she whispers, and he eases his grip, feeling her warm and still tight against him.

'Here?' she asks, and he nods, speechless with desire, as she turns and lifts off the red smock revealing her cream bra and pants. She glances into the bathroom mirror to check herself, shrugs, and unfastens her bra, releasing her breasts for his hands to grasp. His mouth tastes the sweet perspiration as he buries his face between her breasts. The stones of her jangly necklace shifting in his hair as he licks at her skin.

But now there's a caterwauling coming from somewhere, from outside the bathroom, outside the house, as if someone's set off air raid sirens.

'We're under attack,' he mutters into her warm shoulder and the curve of her neck. But with his hands moving freely over her, it's too late to pay attention to anything else.

Yet someone's banging on the bathroom door. Maggie shouting out.

'June! We're under attack.'

He feels her body withdrawing away from him.

'OK. Coming.' June calls and squeezes his hand. 'I'll go down first,' she whispers and he has to watch her refasten the bra, lift the dress back over her body and leave, closing the door on him.

12

Good Morning Again in America

17 January 1991 / 02 Rajab, 1411   *07.50*

Rick savours peace, perfect peace under a cloudless blue sky, as he strolls back from the mail centre leading Jackson, his loyal mastiff. Friday morning at about eight o'clock in the middle of camp, and nobody around – people lying in after last night's excitement. This morning, with his mind and body so tired, yet relaxed, he feels like he's walking through that old Reagan election commercial. It's Good Morning Again in America – the sun beaming down on neat pioneer bungalows behind white picket fences, and front lawns with kids' toys and the occasional trampoline left outside. He's slept only a few hours. Not just because of the Alert sirens and false alarms, but because of June. As she lay, warm and gently snoring beside him, his anger and suspicions about last night grew and festered until he had to get up.

He waits under a palm tree, letting out Jackson's chain for him to snaffle for fallen dates around the tree's base. The poor mutt's not as lively as usual, moving about lethargically in tune with Rick's weariness. But it had been a successful first night of the war. As he predicted, the new alert sirens mostly failed, but they'd saved the situation by using the patrol car sirens. 'Keep up the good work,' the Chief said when he called as Rick was leaving the house. But he wasn't calling just to congratulate his main man. He wanted to know why nobody had been arrested yet for the break-in at the tank farm. Had Rick checked out these Palestinians and Sudanese? And what about the Afghans? For a moment, Rick had been confused, but then remembered the Saudi Afghans, the *jihadi* blowback from Afghanistan.

'You want me to arrest a bunch of Saudis?' he'd asked. 'Their families will be all over us, threatening to see some Prince.'

The Chief retreated. 'Speak to Al. He'll know what to do.'

'I'll get onto it.' Rick reassured him and after calling Al for a status report, left the house.

Jackson's still mooching round the palm tree, gobbling dates, and Rick's mind returns to June and last night's party. She should have come home when he told her. But she'd been high on her usual bullshit, laughing with that Brit at the bar when he arrived, arguing with Bill Eliot, and treating him, her husband, like some Texan hick. No way he can trust the bitch. No way. But he needs to calm down and take the blood pressure pills when he gets home.

He glances through the letters he's picked up from the mail centre. Money first and a statement of his company pension. The bottom line figure looks good. More reason to stay on with Mother, despite June bitching about ten years being more than enough. Maybe enough for her, but not much hope for him of a job back in the States, especially at his age. And he'll never have another chance to pay off the house and stash away so much drop-dead retirement money. No, he's determined to stay, to stick it out, even if it kills him.

Next, he scans through his son's weekly letter from the military academy. Danny's OK with the discipline – sports are great, but the usual problems in academic subjects. Complaints about the school food, of course, but at his age, Rick was just grateful to escape from his parents and the claustrophobia of this small-town America on the edge of the Rub al Kali desert.

He pulls on the dog's chain and Jackson glances up to his master, ready to move on. Such trusting, pleading eyes like his old man's towards the end and Rick realizes his dog's over seven years old. Seems that mastiffs only live to eight or so and already the vet bills are adding up. As they carry on walking, he watches Jackson's movements from behind. The vet said mastiffs usually have hip and joint problems and often die of heart conditions. June should take him to the Kennel Club for a check-up.

Depressing to think about death, even a dog's death, and he glances up into this cloudless blue sky. The AWACs and Patriot early warning systems should detect any incoming Scuds, but Vietnam taught him one big lesson – in these third-world places, detailed planning and fancy technology don't count for much. They usually don't work and crazy things keep coming out of left field when you least expect it.

Jackson's walking better now, head up and livelier. When he and June escaped from Tehran in '79, he had to shoot Bandit, his last dog, a wonderful white-and-grey St Bernard. Anything to save the poor mutt from the local kids who hated dogs and threw rocks at them. And last August, if Saddam's tanks had kept on rolling down the coast highway from Kuwait, he'd have had to kill Jackson before they could be evacuated. Yet again – Vietnam, Iran and now Saudi. One long retreat. But Uncle Sam's not going to lose here. He can't afford to.

Passing the Dining Hall, he can smell brunch – sausages and bacon. A tantalizing scent even if it's only beef and turkey sausage and bacon. So, no pork. Maybe he'll have steak and French fries when he and June meet up with Bill for brunch at the Dining Hall. Now he notices the executive banqueting suite has a new sign outside – *Crisis Cafe (Open all Night)*. Some touchy-feely guy in Personnel had this bright idea to give free coffee and cookies to people who were too frightened to sleep and might panic at an alert. The guys at work said it was a good place to meet secretaries and nurses from the hospital. Maybe he should try that. He could do with some nursing. Anything's better than this feminist aggro he's always getting from June.

At the ball field, a bunch of Flip drivers are chattering by the bus shelters, while their Greyhounds purr with the air conditioning on, waiting to set off for the other oil camps. He waves to the drivers and they smile and greet him, cheerful and appreciative of last night's bombing. He's always liked Flips – good mechanics and technicians, and he worked with a lot in Vietnam. They even dress and play baseball like real Americans. And then there are the Flip girls like Maria, the Chief's secretary – cute and cheerful, happy to look after a big guy like him.

Maybe he could get together with her – she lives in one of the ballpark apartments. Second floor, Flat 212 it said in the staff listing. Maybe she's feeling lonely and is frightened after last night. He glances across at the apartment block, imagining himself looking down from the window of her bedroom at this ballpark and the bleachers where now he only stands with Jackson. Maybe he should call round tonight and check on her.

At the entrance to the recreation area, the Saudi guard salutes the big American security boss and without needing to show ID, Rick leads Jackson along to the Snack Bar. Back in the Sixties, he used to hang out here with his Junior High buddies drinking Coke and listening to the Everly Brothers and Johnny Cash. But no country music this morning as he walks in – just the TV in the corner panicking about *War in the Gulf.* Sitting by the Snack Bar window, a middle-aged American couple with three small children are huddled around the table finishing breakfast. They look nervous, whispering to each other, their faces grey and washed out as if they haven't slept. CNN doesn't help. It's enough to give anybody the shakes and make them run for evacuation flights.

But the young Flip behind the counter is cheerful and welcomes the Security boss, waving aside any payment for his Diet Pepsi.

'You look after us, sir,' he says and warming to the recognition, Rick gives a wave as he leaves.

Outside the movie theatre, a poster's advertising that pretty boy Kevin Costner in *Dances with Wolves.* June's keen to see it and he'll probably tag along, even though it's about some wimpy US cavalryman going native and joining the Sioux Indians. June's a sucker for what she calls Native American culture. She's always bragging about being part-Indian herself, as if these guys just sat around worshipping Mother Nature, making clay pots all day, and not really scalping people. June's first husband was a no-good Indian, who left her penniless, but still she's filled Kate, her own daughter, with this liberal bullshit that's made the poor kid go off to find herself in San Francisco. At his expense, of course. At least his boy Danny at the military academy hasn't been infected.

The smell of chlorine drifts out from the swimming pool entrance. June's started to go there in the afternoons as one of her New Year dieting resolutions. He passes the gym's blacked-out windows. This new Nautilus equipment has arrived and he should get back to lifting weights. Glancing down at his stomach, there's too much flab. Need to cut back on the pizza and the sticky Arab cookies Al's started bringing into the office. Funny that Al never gets fat but stays thin and wiry, like the desert foxes you sometimes see round the spray fields. Not a bad guy, but he's getting to be a pain with this Boy Scout horseshit.

In the community centre window, a poster's advertising the *Arabian Pioneers* exhibit. Personnel have organized it as a morale booster and June with her Saudi girlfriend, the General Manager's daughter, is setting up an art exhibit as well. Rick's already looked round at the pioneers' photography – mainly black and white prints of old Ford trucks trundling through the sand dunes, the first discovery wells, and American geologists in Arab robes drinking *gawa* with the *bedu* round a desert campfire. Pity there's only a few photos of the small dusty town he grew up in – a dyed-in-the-bone Republican place where Americans could still wave the flag and be can-do pioneers. Dad had been a lowly craft teacher at the Junior High, Mum a proper housewife who ran a tight budget and never got over him marrying a loudmouth Berkeley peacenik with one kid already.

So why the hell had he done that? Married June in the spring of '73 soon after he got back from Vietnam? Easy answer – the bitch seduced him, not just with her tits bouncing free under a Grateful Dead T-shirt, but with her spiel about modern art and freedom. After Vietnam, he'd been ready to try something different, discover a new life and arriving by himself at his cousin's party, he'd been easy meat, a poor grunt for the slaughter. Then the security job in Iran had gone belly up and the escape from there made returning here necessary and almost inevitable. Where else could somebody like him with no fancy degrees find a good job and enough money to keep June quiet? He knew this place and was known here, so the job interview was just a few middle-aged guys reminiscing about the good old days.

At the gate in the fence, a dark-skinned guard – one of the Pakistanis brought in to replace the motherfuckers who'd gone AWOL – sits in his sentry box listening to Urdu music on his cassette player. He jumps up, standing erect to his full six feet and salutes the Security boss. Rick salutes back to his British 'Good morning, sir' and strolls along by the ball field fence.

Still too early to head home and June won't have surfaced yet. With Jackson stretching out on the ground below him, he sits up on the metal bleachers to finish drinking his Pepsi and read Danny's letter more carefully. The boy's always had trouble with school exams, like he did. But thank God he likes being in uniform and is good at sports. Rick remembers sitting here on the bleachers and watching his son play baseball for the All Stars one Friday morning – remembers Danny swinging with his good strong arm, and the joy of the All Stars' winning home run. That time when he'd jumped up from his seat among the other fathers and hollered with pride as the fly ball soared majestically through the air, everyone gazing up towards this white spot flying so high he had to shade his eyes from the sun, before the ball began dropping into the emerald green outfield.

Voices are shouting out. The Flip bus drivers have seen something and are pointing up in the air. Two F15s are flying high above camp, performing victory rolls as they tumble through a blue sky delicately laced with grey contrails from returning jets. Mission accomplished and the Flips are clapping and laughing together, releasing all the anxieties and tensions of the last few months. They can phone home and send letters to their families that all's well and they'll soon be returning. The planes are rising again, sunshine glinting on their million-dollar bodies, and for this moment all seems right in the world.

But Rick corrects himself. After this bombing, a lot of civilians back home will think the war's as good as over. Yet he knows better. Vietnam's made him cagey, wary of armchair generals and bullshit artists like Bill Eliot who talk like they know everything. Saddam's bound to fight back dirty and like invading Kuwait, he'll probably do something Schwarzkopf and the big shots in Riyadh don't expect. Maybe poison gas or chemical weapons, and some experts on CNN think he could have a dirty bomb. If he does, he might use it. Sounds crazy, but this is a crazy part of the world. And if the Israelis decide to use the nuclear weapons they say they haven't got…

He glances at his TAG Heuer watch, Mother's ten-year service award. Almost eight thirty and the Flip drivers are climbing into their Greyhound buses ready to set off north and south for the other oil camps. June's probably still lying semi-conscious in bed. He can guess what she's thinking. It's happened before – she takes a fancy to some guy and plays the Great Artist in Love. But no way she'll make a fool of him again. Yesterday he picked up some book she was reading about flaky American artists and writers wandering round Paris and New York in the Twenties and Thirties. Drop-outs like Henry Miller and this Nin woman, living off other people's money, parasites with no regular jobs and too much time to screw around. June says there's some sexy new film about these deadbeats, even sexier than the video they took from the gardener who Faisal knocked around. Al said there was some complaint from a doctor about that Indian kid. As if they haven't got enough shit to deal with.

But despite all the crap, Rick's glad he's got this big job to do. He stands up on the metal bleachers and looks out over the rust brown baseball diamond, and the meadow-green outfield beyond, the scene of Danny's All Star triumph. He can see across to the Snack Bar, the movie theatre, swimming pool, gym and the community centre with its white banner announcing *Arabian Pioneer Days*. He's responsible for looking after all this, for the safety of this small-town America set down in the desert over fifty years ago, when the first oil well was spudded and the black gold flowed. This is his territory and as its guardian angel he stands up on the bleachers determined to protect and take good care of it.

13

The Other Shoe Drops

17 January 1991 / 02 Rajab 1411   *09.10*

The phone's ringing and from watching CNN, Rob rushes into the kitchen. Might be June. But the woman's voice on the line is distant: Fiona's just got up and is breathless with relief at the morning's good news.

'It looks like the Scud launchers have been destroyed,' he tells her and can hear the elation in his own voice. 'But we're waiting for the other shoe to drop.'

'What shoe?' Across this gulf, he realizes her incomprehension. Far from gas masks, air raid sirens and CNN's Breaking News, she's standing in the kitchen and looking out over the garden of their semi-detached in Southport, Lancashire.

'It's a phrase they keep using on CNN. General Schwarzkopf used it. We're waiting to see what Saddam's going to do next.'

'CNN?' Again he has to explain, but losing interest, she asks, 'How's Cilla?'

'She's fine.' He glances through into the sitting room where Cilla, after slopping down a few gulps of water from her bowl, is settling under the dining table. 'I've just taken her for a walk.'

'Good. And how's Derek?'

'Excited. The war reminds him of National Service. He lies on the couch, criticizing everybody, especially the Americans. How's Chris?'

'He's gone back to Uni. Worrying about some girlfriend and his exams. So what are you doing, apart from watching this CNN? Have you been to mass yet?'

'No, I don't really feel up to going by myself and I'm tired most of the time. We're trying to work as usual during the day. Then at night I'm helping security on the camp patrol.'

'But isn't this patrol dangerous?'

'Not really.' Yet after the break-in at the tank farm, he's not so sure. 'But it means I don't get much sleep,' he says, wanting her to admire or at least sympathize with him.

Instead, she's annoyed. 'So why are *you* doing it? You're not a security man. Is Derek doing this patrol?'

'No,' he says, recalling his friend's sarcastic comments.

'It's not your job,' Fiona decides and moves on to another subject. 'Laura, the doctor's wife, phoned me yesterday. She saw you at the art group, at June's pottery class.'

Suspicion in Fiona's voice? But he stays calm. 'I just went to see if there were any interesting courses. I'm trying to take my mind off the war, expand my horizons.'

'So did you choose anything? I bet June wants you in one of her classes.'

Silence as he hesitates, wondering what else the doctor's wife might have said. 'No. I decided I'm doing enough with this patrol. I've hardly got time to sleep.'

'OK. Well, I'd better make some breakfast,' she says brightly. 'I'll ring you tomorrow.'

'Good,' he says, like a dutiful husband looking forward to his wife's next call.

*

Through Friday afternoon, he lies on the couch with Cilla stretched out on the carpet beneath him, watching the global spectacle of *War in the Gulf*. Still centre stage are last night's scenes of the sky over Baghdad: a black canvas stitched by tracer as the Iraqi gunners fire vainly at planes so remote they seem to fly in a parallel universe. Shaky handheld film of rooms and corridors at the Al Rashid Hotel, where the reporters are holed up, is framed by a succession of military experts urging caution, stock market analysts worrying over the war's economic impact, and journalists thrilled at being in the front line. CNN flits through a variety of locations – the Pentagon, the New York Stock Exchange, the White House, an aircraft carrier in the Gulf, even the nearby International Hotel beside the airport. An American reporter broadcasts from the hotel roof and Rob feels thrilled to be part of the world's top story, stoically soldiering on in the centre of the action.

The generals and military experts are still waiting for that other shoe to drop. Saddam's forces are taking all this punishment, but when are they going to fight back? *Can* they fight back? A giant Uncle Sam seems to be battering a cowering Iraqi pigmy into submission. After months of tension and military build-up, Rob begins to feel regret, as if he might be cheated of his finest hour.

Between more updates from Atlanta and constant repeats of *War in the Gulf*, other-worldly advertisements appear. Jet-setting businessmen present their American Express or Diner's Club cards and gain instant attention at international hotels and restaurants. Power-suited mums and dads phone expectant children at home in the US to fulfil AT&T's slogan: 'A Promise is a Promise'. Smiling tourists check in at Holiday Inns around the world to enjoy a 'Home from Home', and in dark-panelled London clubs, sharp-suited Far Eastern businessmen settle into deep leather armchairs and sample single malt whiskies that make them irresistible to smouldering long-haired blondes.

Momentous events and trivialities, life and death struggles and fashion tips succeed each other in rolling twenty-four-hour news. Yet everything is linked and only seems to make sense through Atlanta, a bizarre hub for this global village, where the fast-talking Bobby Battista presides, pulling the threads together. At the end of each half-hour segment, Valerie Voss, CNN's weather girl, forecasts the global weather and the snow conditions at international ski resorts. Gstaad, St Moritz, Innsbruck: names redolent of wealth and luxury scroll up the screen to Christmas muzak as Rob slips back into dreaming about the island of Santorini, an artist's studio overlooking the blue Aegean, and making love to June through a drowsy afternoon *siesta*.

Cilla's barking at something and he wakes up to *The Hollywood Minute*, a man gabbling through the latest film star gossip in no more than sixty seconds. The phone's ringing in the kitchen. June calling? Or maybe Fiona again? But it's Bill Eliot, flush with the joys of victory, coming to Rob's house tomorrow evening for a shower and to deliver some Jack Daniel's wood chips.

On The Road Again. Rob scans the high chain-link fence as he cruises down Perimeter Road and sings along with Willie Nelson on the Easy Listening station. He pulls in at the camp garage, sliding into his usual space in front of the entrance gate. But there's more space than before – a gap where the white Ford Transit had been rusting away. His car headlights beam through the gate's wire mesh and across the forecourt towards the inspection ramp curving up into the sky. But the steel padlock on the gate is hanging loose and unfastened.

Grabbing his flashlight, he steps out of the patrol car, pushes against the gate and forces it open. A light's showing through the far window of the mechanics' workshop. Should he call the Big House for back-up? The mechanics were supposed to finish at five but this might be an American or Brit, high on a dose of *Top Gear*, working on his car. Or maybe somebody just left a light on. Yet the heavy padlock's hanging loose and open. He's got to investigate.

He pushes the gate further back, deliberately making more noise and encouraging any intruder to escape. Then, with the flashlight guiding him across the forecourt he advances past the inspection ramp, the car wash he used this morning, and towards the mechanics' workshop. Reaching the far window, he peers in through the glass but all he can see in the dim light are the cars waiting for repair. No sound of equipment or anyone working.

The door to the workshop's not locked and gently he turns the handle, gradually opening to see the missing Ford Transit, the light beneath coming from the inspection pit. Is someone hiding there? With his flashlight, he nervously scans the workshop, the vehicles and garage equipment. Nobody and nothing moving. Yet with the smell of oil and petrol there's something else in the air. A vibration. As if someone's just left, the rush of flight lingering in the atmosphere.

'Anybody here?' His voice echoes around the workshop. He shouts again, staying by the door and gripping his flashlight like a club. This might be the same men who broke into the tank farm – he should have called Al when he spotted the light. Now he wishes he'd brought Cilla to bark and frighten away any intruders.

He can't find the light switches. They must be on the other side of the workshop. Slowly he advances towards the Transit van perched over the inspection pit, and scans the nearby vehicles with his flashlight – a red sports car with an *IROC-Z* sign below the doors, a heavy grey Suburban, and an old blue Chevrolet. Still fearful of someone hiding, he bends down, looking for feet lurking behind or underneath a vehicle. Two strides forward to the inspection pit and he peers down. No one inside but there's a blue toolbox, oily rags and spanners, beside a can of Pepsi on the cement floor.

'Security. Anybody here?' he shouts again, glancing round.

At once, resounding through the workshop, there's a flush of running water and he sees the door of what must be a restroom open up, under the wall clock at the back. A stocky Filipino wearing a faded *People Power* T-shirt and dirty jeans faces him, caught like a guilty child in the beam of his flashlight.

'What're you doing?' Rob demands with all the authority of company security.

'Very sorry, sir,' the Filipino calls. 'I have rush job.'

'But why are you working so late? Have you got special permission?'

'Soon I go home to Philippines, sir.' The mechanic threads his way through the vehicles. 'My daughter will be married and we need money for beautiful wedding, sir.' Rob realizes the Filipino's appealing to him as a fellow foreigner, another family man far from home.

'But you shouldn't be here.' He keeps the flashlight beam on the mechanic's face, this frightened father with dark bags under his eyes. 'What's your name?'

But the Filipino's expression has changed as he realizes something. 'I am Rody, sir. And I think you go to my church.' He smiles, anxious to placate authority. 'Friday at the school. I am in the church choir and see you with your good wife at mass.'

Rob nods. Many Filipinos sing in the church choir and he thinks he recognizes Rody.

'We listen to same Father, sir. Father Peanuts, we call him.'

Facing each other the two men smile, united through listening to the comic book tales of good old Charlie Brown, which the diminutive American priest translates into simple Christian messages.

'You'd better finish,' Rob orders. 'We need to lock up.'

Rody scrambles down into the inspection pit beneath the Transit van and starts to return the tools to his box. He looks up. 'Please, sir. I don't want to lose my job. Please don't report.'

'You shouldn't be here this late at night.' But if Rob does report Rody, the mechanic *will* lose his job, be deported or could even go to prison. He might spend months in one of the large communal cells, where thieves, illicit *sid* distillers, Christians caught evangelizing, and other unfortunates are thrown together. Rody would have to sleep on the floor and depend on his friends to visit the prison and feed him. Maybe the guards would abuse him.

'Hurry up.' Rob lights the way for Rody to clamber out of the inspection pit.

The clock on the back wall of the workshop shows almost ten o'clock, the second hand jerking round, and he has to check in with Al soon. Rody locks the workshop door, no lights showing now, and they hurry across the forecourt into the headlights of Rob's patrol car. As they're passing the inspection ramp, there's a roar and they halt to watch four giant planes rising up into the air before them. Bomb-heavy and only narrowly clearing the perimeter fence, they expose their broad underbellies before powering upwards into the night sky heading for Iraq and Kuwait.

'When will the war be over, sir?' Rody asks. 'My daughter's wedding is in April.'

'Should be over by then, Rody. And the flights home will start up again.'

They've reached the garage gate, the large padlock hanging loose. 'This should be locked,' says Rob. 'Where did you get the key?'

'The foreman help me, sir. He knows about my daughter's wedding and is my good friend.'

And Rob knows friendship is everything in this place. That's what foreigners depend on to survive, just as he depends on visiting Derek and talking to Tony and Patience at work. But he and Rody must hurry and padlock the gate before another patrol car, maybe Rick or Al on one of their random checks, sees them.

Rody walks to his scooter concealed among the abandoned cars. 'God bless you, sir.' He shakes Rob's hand vigorously, almost bowing in gratitude. 'Please don't report.'

Rob hesitates, looking into the Filipino's eyes pleading with him. He wants to reassure the man in the church choir, the father of the bride, and send him happy on his way.

'I'll do my best. But this is war, Rody. And don't work late again.'

'No, sir. Please no report.' The Filipino's desperate for reassurance, for the British man to give his word before he leaves.

'Good luck with the wedding,' Rob calls as he gets into the patrol car.

He reverses and drives away down Perimeter Road, with Rody perched on his scooter, disappearing in the rear view mirror.

Past ten o'clock and soon he has to check in with Al. Should he tell him about Rody? The Filipino shouldn't have been working so late without permission, and now Rob realizes he should have asked more questions: about the key to the padlock and the foreman who'd allowed Rody to stay late. Like Fiona said, he's not a security man, but he has to decide on the Filipino mechanic and his family's fate.

Before reporting to Al, Rob savours his ritual Marlboro cigarette on the small bluff overlooking the base. Up north towards the Kuwaiti border it's raining, and here the sky's thunderous and overcast, obscuring the stars. According to CNN, there's enough cloud cover tonight for Saddam's mobile missile launchers to move around freely.

He watches another squadron of jets taking off – this relentless conveyer belt of destruction – and pities the young Iraqi conscripts in their trenches and the civilians trying to shelter from this bombing. These same people suffered for years under Saddam and his thugs and were forced to surrender their sons to a long, futile war with Iran. That war ended less than three years ago, after eight years of trench warfare. A battle of attrition which consumed half a million soldiers and civilians, and inflicted countless casualties. But, he reassures himself, this war is one of technology and should be over soon. Maybe it will topple Saddam and give the Iraqi people the chance of a fresh start.

Alert sirens start up, whooping over the airbase and Rob hurries down the bluff to his patrol car. He opens the driver's door and on the radio, DJ Jerry's voice is coolly reciting, 'Put on your gas mask, stay in a safe place and stay tuned.'

A safe place? Rob wonders what to do. The patrol car isn't safe but where could he hide? Should he put on his gas mask? It's probably another false alarm. The sirens settle into their chorus of dismal wailing as he peers out of the car window.

Whoosh! A crack like a giant bullet being fired. A missile's soaring up like a bonfire rocket from behind the perimeter fence, a plume of smoke streaming behind as it weaves through the night sky. It seems to adjust in flight, flattening out its trajectory to seek the target, until high over the spray fields comes the interception – an explosion with flares of fire and sparks illuminating the wasteland like something out of a Hollywood movie. The Patriot's scored a direct hit.

The sky and everything's lit up, but now fragments are falling on the roof above Rob's head and he starts the patrol car. Bits of missile are raining down, clattering and tapping against the car roof as he drives away, bumping along the track by the fence. Burning debris is dropping from the sky and in the rear view mirror he can see the bluff where he was standing billowing with smoke, flames flaring up from blazing petrol. Another cigarette and he would still have been standing there.

At last the tapping on the car's stopped. He's clear of most of the smoke and gets out to see what's happening. Sirens are still wailing over the base, but now he can hear soldiers yelling and whooping from the Patriot battery beyond the fence and behind a low *jebel*. The first Iraqi Scud's been shot down and he can't resist joining in, cheering and clapping with relief. Like June, he'd had doubts and suspected Bill was bullshitting, but now they know. The Patriot's found its target like in a giant video game.

He switches on the car radio and the intercom crackles with Al's voice. *'Alhamdullilah.* This Patriot works, my friend.' Watching from the Big House, Al had seen the missile strike, the explosion over the spray fields, and they share their relief and excitement. But still the debris was close. It could have dropped on the airbase, houses on camp or the head-quarters buildings. It had almost fallen on Rob.

Looking for more success, Rob asks, 'So, what's happening about the tank farm, Al?'

'We're questioning Palestinians and Sudanese, like Rick said. And it looks like the break-in was a reconnaissance for something bigger. Anything else to report, my friend?'

Rob hesitates, but after his narrow escape and such celebration, he isn't going to betray a poor Filipino working late to pay for his daughter's marriage.

'*Mafi muskallah.* No problem, Al.' So that's settled: instead of languishing in prison, Rody can travel home to pay for and enjoy his daughter's wedding.

14

You Are a Refugee

18 January 1991 / 03 Rajab 1411   *16.45*

Al has translated into Arabic the three Security values he learned from his training course in Texas: integrity (*keyam, al nazaha*); vigilance (*al ista'dad* or *al hudoor*); helpfulness (*al musanada*). But will these values work in their security department, he wonders as he and Faisal leave the Big House and drive onto the residential camp. When he returned from Texas and talked about the training to the Chief's boss, he seemed interested. But the Chief himself was unimpressed and as usual, Rick dismissed Al's new ideas as bullshit.

Thinking about integrity, Al's frustrated that he's wasted most of the day questioning the usual scapegoats – the poor Palestinians and Sudanese working as chauffeurs or maintenance men in the Golden Ghetto – while Faisal stood behind them threatening the violence he'd seen on TV cop shows. But no actual violence was needed. Al made sure of that, especially after a Canadian doctor had complained about Faisal's 'accident' with the Indian gardener. Today they played good cop/bad cop to extort extravagant condemnations of Saddam Hussein and some trivial gossip, but Al knew they were only going through the motions to satisfy Rick and the Chief. These poor workers wouldn't dare cut through a high chain-link fence and threaten aviation fuel tanks. They desperately wanted to stay out of trouble and keep earning enough money for their families back home.

Content to let Faisal drive the patrol car, Al relaxes back in the passenger seat, resting before what might be a difficult interview with a senior Palestinian. Looking out of the car window, he enjoys these visits to the residential camp, appreciating the order and cleanliness of the company's well-maintained houses, children's playgrounds and small parks. He'd like to move here with his own family, away from the untidiness and litter around his neighborhood, but this small-town America was built for expats: a place where foreigners were free to go to the company's cinema, swimming pools, and community centre. Here, the expat tribe could enjoy their own culture and lifestyle, without conflict or arguments with the Saudi world outside.

'See the satellite.' Faisal points towards a large metal dish fixed to the side of a house. Before the invasion of Kuwait, they could only watch Saudi TV or the company's TV channel starting at five o'clock with children's programs and finishing after the Saudi news at ten. But with thousands of foreign soldiers arriving, the doors to the outside world had been thrown open to CNN, the American Forces Network, and other broadcasters. Now, satellite TV dishes were sprouting up like giant ears all over camp, people listening in to programs from all over the world. Al watches the international news and sports reports, but there are bad things like Madonna and MTV videos, which provoke the Wahhabi preachers and the *muttawa,* and that he wants to keep away from his sons. This openness to the world can be good, but also very dangerous.

Faisal turns into an avenue of sand-brown two-storey houses with islands of palm trees running along the centre.

'Nice area.' The young man sneers. 'What's a Palestinian doing here?'

'He's worked here for over twenty years.' Al's irritated by these ignorant young guys like Faisal who dismiss their elders' years of service and expect Palestinians to stay in refugee camps. For their minimal effort, they expect a lifetime of rewards: free health care and education, home loans, and effortless promotion. He always reminds his two sons about the company's first Saudi CEO starting as a tea boy and working his way up.

The Palestinian's house is halfway along the avenue, with a basketball hoop over the garage door. On the fenced balcony a teenager's sitting back, sunbathing with his shirt off, baseball cap on backwards.

'Somebody's expecting us,' Al says, as the youth jumps up and goes inside.

Wary of having his freshly cleaned white patrol car marked by falling dates, he stops Faisal from parking under the palm trees and they walk back along the avenue. Even in this cool weather, the heavily built young man struggles to keep up with his wiry boss, and Al takes some pleasure in that.

He presses the doorbell and waits. There's a moment when he knows he's being inspected through the tiny spy hole, until the door opens onto a stocky middle-aged man, smiling broadly and wearing a starched white *jalabiya*.

'*Assalamu alikum.*' Al shows his ID. 'We're from Security. Mr Khalid Shehata?'

The Palestinian's shocked by the Security ID. He holds the door open but doesn't invite them inside.

'We need to speak to you, sir.' Al steps forward, forcing their host to retreat into the cool, carpeted hallway.

'Please. You're very welcome.' Recovering himself, the Palestinian smiles, almost bowing in the effort to ingratiate. 'We don't expect visitors.'

'Don't worry, sir. If you've nothing to hide, you've nothing to fear. We'll take our shoes off to save your beautiful carpets.'

As they place their shoes on a *Welcome* mat, Al notices one of Faisal's grey socks has a hole in it, with a big yellow toenail protruding. It's yet another fault they should discuss, but the list is getting too long. He'd suggested a transfer for Faisal but Rick dismissed it. Maybe the Chief might help.

The Palestinian leads the way into a bright, spacious sitting room with French windows looking out onto a walled back garden.

'We saw a young man on the balcony,' Al says.

'My son, Mohammed. He's on vacation from college in the States.'

'But vacation's over. My sons went back to school two weeks ago.'

'My wife's not well and she wanted Mohammed to stay longer.' The Palestinian smiles nervously. 'But with the airport closed because of this war—'

'We knew when the war was starting, sir. OK. We'll speak to him later.'

Al hadn't expected the son. Mohammed isn't on the database listing, probably because he's a visiting student. They need to check – maybe other students are staying over because of the war.

He glances towards the sitting room couch and armchairs. 'We'll sit down, sir.'

Khalid's flustered to be reminded of his host's duties. 'Please make yourselves comfortable, gentlemen. I'll see that my wife makes *chai* for us.'

While the Palestinian hurries to the kitchen, Faisal plonks himself down with a sigh into an armchair. Al takes the other armchair and picks up the *Arab News* from the coffee table. Headlines celebrate the Coalition's round-the-clock bombing and the Patriot battery shooting down a Scud heading for the airbase. *Alhamdullilah!* He recalls his and Rob's excitement, but lack of sleep and today's interrogations have drained away that exhilaration. He's ready to go back to bed and sleep for a long, long time.

He glances into his notebook. According to Khalid's security file, he attends Palestinian social gatherings and donates to Arafat's PLO. But so what? Might be a crime in Rick's book, but a man should help his people. Al sympathizes with the cause, but experience has taught him to distrust some of the Palestinians he's worked with. When people feel insecure and are struggling to survive, they'll say and do anything. But after twenty years of pleasing his Saudi and American bosses, Khalid must be skilled at surviving. Why suddenly flip and lose his temper with a young Saudi clerk? Understandable maybe, considering his own irritations with Faisal. But still he can't see this stocky middle-aged man scrambling down a rocky *jebel* to break into the tank farm. An athletic Palestinian student, though?

A bookcase fills the alcove facing them. Al remembers that a man's books are windows into his soul, and he walks over to see what Khalid's books reveal. There's a top shelf of green World Book encyclopaedias, probably for the student; Colonel Gadaffi's Green Book preaching universal revolution; several paperbacks on Palestine by Edward Said, and Mahmoud Darwish's poetry lamenting the loss of his homeland. He remembers a Palestinian friend at university reading out a poem by Darwish. What was it? He takes out the poetry book, glancing through the list of contents and starts to search the pages.

'My apologies, gentlemen.' Khalid returns with glasses of *chai* and water on a tray which he sets on the coffee table. He offers a plate of sweet *baklava* to his two guests. Al politely declines but despite his growing paunch, Faisal leans forward to grab one in each hand.

'How can I help you gentlemen?' The Palestinian looks to Al, who's remained standing at the bookcase with the poetry book.

'I was admiring your library, sir. Mahmoud Darwish.' Al holds up the book, conscious that Palestinians consider Saudis uncultured. 'I remember his poems from university. There's a line about people refusing to help Palestinians.' Leafing through the pages, he finds the poem and recites. 'They threw him out of every port... And then they said: You're a refugee.'

'Yes. Darwish is our national poet.' Khalid speaks with a rueful smile. 'That's his most famous poem – the Identity Card. We are refugees but we've lived happily here for many years. *Alhamdullilah.*'

Al slips the book back into its place. 'We have a disturbing report, sir. Some things you said at a meeting a few days ago.'

'Let me explain.' Khalid leans forward on the edge of the couch as if anxious to put matters right. 'We were drinking coffee and this young clerk insulted Palestinians. I was upset and said some things. But I apologized and told my manager about it.'

'Your manager?' Khalid's boss hadn't reported this. An Egyptian subordinate of Khalid's, probably keen to take his job, had informed Security about the incident.

'My manager is Kamal Esayed, an Egyptian. He's head of my department and understands our problems. That day I was very upset to hear a young clerk blaming Palestinians for the troubles in Kuwait.'

Al makes a mental note to check on this manager's background and remains silent, sipping hot *chai* and allowing the Palestinian to say more. With his fixed smile and anxious eyes, Khalid seems nervous enough to reveal something. Al remains standing to command the situation and takes out his notebook to find one of the incriminating quotations. 'You said that everybody comes to help the Kuwaiti but nobody helps Palestinians to take back *their* homeland.'

'I was very emotional,' Khalid says. 'Our land's been occupied for forty years and the world does nothing. All we hear is talk, while the Zionists keep building settlements. But when Kuwait is occupied, all the world comes to fight for *their* freedom.'

Al reads again from his notebook. 'You criticized Saudi Arabia for helping Kuwait.'

'But I was very tired, sir. No sleep with these sirens and my wife's nerves are not good.' Khalid rubs his hand over his stomach. 'And I suffer from this acid in here. It keeps bubbling up because of stress and I have to go to the clinic.'

Al reads on. 'You talked about Kuwaiti playboys running to Saudi Arabia and living in luxury hotels. You criticized the United Nations…'

'They pass resolutions,' Khalid says. 'But they do nothing to help us. I was upset. You understand our frustration?'

Al does, but doubts whether Rick or the Chief will understand. They want some terrorists arrested for the tank farm break-in. ASAP, as soon as possible, Rick demanded, and chauffeurs, gardeners, and house boys aren't good enough. A Palestinian mastermind would be ideal.

'We have a problem sir,' Al says. 'Your Chairman, Yasser Arafat, supports Saddam Hussein. And some Palestinians in Kuwait are helping the Iraqi invaders.'

'It's only rumours. People always blame us. I work here for twenty years with no trouble. I know many Saudi and American managers – they give me good reference. I can give you their names.'

A cough as the young man from the balcony enters. He's probably been listening in and wants to help his father.

'Come in, Mohammed,' Khalid says. 'We have guests from Security.'

The boy tries to smile, only to be met with Faisal's scowl, and sits down on the couch beside his father. He's taken off the American baseball cap and put on a blue college T-shirt and long khaki shorts. Al considers this teenager with his black curly hair and marks of acne on his face. These innocents often make mistakes, do stupid things and endanger themselves and others. Al's thinking of his own teenage sons, two Shia young men in a Sunni-dominated society. Injustice and slights rankle over time, especially when you're young and haven't been tied down yet by family and jobs.

'So, Mohammed, what were you doing last Tuesday night?' Al asks.

'I'm sorry. I can't remember, sir.' Father and son sit closer together on the couch, facing the investigator.

'No answer is still an answer,' Al says quoting the proverb. 'But not a very good one. Think again, Mohammed. Where were you last Tuesday night?'

'I usually hang out with my friends, sir.'

'So, tell us. Who are your friends?'

Khalid intervenes. 'Mohammed thinks it's too boring here. One day is like another. He'll be glad to get back to college in the States.'

'Sorry, sir. But I need to hear Mohammed's story.' Al moves forward, focusing on the youth. 'What happened last Tuesday night? Your friends. Give us their names. OK, Faisal you make notes.' He turns to his assistant, who's been yawning, and watches as he fumbles a notebook from his *thawb*. 'Mohammed, we want your friends' names so they can help us.'

'My friends have done nothing.' The boy turns, appealing to his father.

But Faisal intervenes. 'Security will decide this. Give us their names, my friend, or it will go very hard for you.'

'Mohammed,' Khalid pleads, 'we must help Security people.' He nods to Al, assuring him of cooperation.

'We've done nothing wrong.' The boy's face is set in obstinacy.

'Good. So, no problem giving your friends' names.' Al tries another way. 'Where do you guys hang out?'

'Sometimes the snack bar or youth centre. We practice throwing baskets.'

Al smiles, trying to relax the boy. 'Expect you're good at that. Tall guy like you.'

'Sure.' Mohammed returns the smile. 'I play for the college team.'

'*Mabrouk*. So who did you see at the snack bar and youth centre on Tuesday night?'

Reluctantly, the teenager surrenders a few Saudi and other Arab names for Faisal to repeat and scrawl down. But not much seems to have happened: the friends threw baskets, wandered up to the ball field and hung around the snack bar. They didn't drive up to the senior management compound and Mohammed doesn't seem to know what a tank farm is. Something military or to do with growing stuff?

'Anything more you can tell us?' Al lets the silence settle, observing the boy's face and Khalid's nervous clasping and unclasping of his hands. 'Anything you can do to help us? And to help yourself, of course.'

Father and son look to each other and seem to decide they've said enough.

'Can I go now?' The young man glances towards the door and begins to stand.

'No. Stay here.' Al prolongs the silence, observing this student who should have returned to college and the father who should have kept on swallowing the insults and held his tongue.

Khalid speaks up. 'I'm sorry, sir. Mohammed has a lot of college work to do.' He sees that Al's angry. 'But he can do it later.'

'*Khalas*. That's enough.' Al notes the smile of relief spreading across Khalid's face. 'But Mohamed must come to answer more questions.'

Shocked, the father doesn't know what to do. He probably thought the worst was over, he'd protected himself and his son, and family life could continue as before.

'My boss has some questions of his own,' Al says. 'And Mohammed can help us with more information.'

'But it's very late,' the father says. 'We can see you in the morning. I will bring Mohammed to your office.'

'He's coming now,' Faisal says, standing up to move behind the student.

'Your son must come for further questioning.' Al puts out his hand to Faisal. 'You got those names?' He checks his assistant's notebook and is irritated with the lazy, near illegible, scrawl. '*Yalla*. Let's go.'

Faisal grabs hold of Mohammed's arm and they hustle the son of the house down the carpeted hallway. The Palestinian mother appears from the kitchen and starts crying out, appealing to Allah to save her family.

'Wait.' Faisal takes some plastic handcuffs from his pocket. 'We'll cuff him. Hold out your hands my friend.'

But the mother's stricken face is appealing to Al for mercy.

'No. Not yet, Faisal.' He tries to reassure her. 'Don't worry. We won't hurt him or keep your son for long.'

Just long enough to exert some pressure, he decides, as they slip their shoes back on and try to ignore the mother's entreaties.

They escape out into the early evening sunshine, hurrying Mohammed back along the street towards the patrol car. Al feels the student tensing up with fear as he grips his arm, and to relax him, he asks about college and basketball. Only monosyllabic replies and the boy keeps glancing back for his father, who said he'd follow them to the Big House. Fear's not a bad thing, though. They'll probably get the information they need more quickly. While Faisal pushes the student into the back of the car and sits with him, Al takes the driver's seat and reports to Rick that they're bringing in a Palestinian student for further questioning.

'Good,' Rick says. 'Our IT guy's produced a new Watch List. You'd better work on it when you get back.'

'OK, we're on our way. But there's a manager we need information on.'

'Manager?' Rick doesn't sound happy with that. He's probably worried about *wasta,* this manager's contacts and influence, and whether he's one of the Chief's cronies.

'I'll explain when we get back,' says Al starting the car.

As they cruise through the camp's residential streets, they pass gangs of Asian gardeners in green overalls sitting beside the road, waiting for the yellow buses back to their contractor's dormitories. Many are desperate to leave, frightened by tales of what happened to their compatriots on the long trek from Kuwait through Iraq and into Jordan. But with the airport closed, they are trapped here far from their families and homes.

As Al drives along, he glances through the rear view mirror at the two young men on the back seat: Faisal sitting there, heavyweight and aggressive in his white *thawb,* beside the athletic Palestinian student. One destined through birth for a home life of ease and authority, the other a stateless refugee destined to struggle in the world for citizenship, security and a career somewhere.

At the intersection, the traffic lights switch to red and Al pulls up behind a yellow bus carrying more gardeners. Exhausted from two nights of alarms and little sleep, his mind begins to drift back to alert sirens starting up and wailing, the Scud and Patriot exploding together in mid-air, the security guards at the main gate cheering the miraculous interception.

But there's noise and a scuffle behind him, the car door opening and Mohammed jumps out. Faisal's shouting, holding his stomach where the student's hit him. The teenager's escaping, running across the sand towards the *jebels,* as Al gets out of the patrol car and belatedly gives chase.

He runs across the fitness trail round the golf course and almost collides with a man staggering along in a sweat stained T-shirt. Stumbling, Al recovers to chase after the student, but his feet are sinking deeper into the sand, slowing him down as Mohammed in his blue T-shirt races far ahead, disappearing behind a rocky *jebel.* Al's panting and with a stitch in his side has to halt, catch his breath and look round for help. But Faisal's nowhere in sight and the patrol car's still parked on the road at the traffic lights.

Mohamed will be well away by now. Resigned to failure, Al jogs on to the *jebel* and turning the corner, sees no sign of the student among the sandy hillocks. He calls out the boy's name once, and then again, shouting it louder. Doesn't Mohammed know this makes things worse, makes him more of a suspect? But he's no longer there to be persuaded, and now Al has to return to the patrol car to report the escape to Rick and the Chief. He trudges back towards the road, furious with himself for not anticipating trouble, and with Faisal who was too lazy to join the chase.

Al halts. He'd been too kind to Mohammed's mother when he told Faisal not to cuff the teenager. He'd been too trusting, like the Boy Scout in Rick's story. Now he'll have to alert the guards at the gates to arrest Mohammed if he tries to leave camp. They'll need a recent photograph and he'll have to question Khalid again about the boys' friends, where he might go and hide. But there could be one positive from this: Mohamed might lead them to the others involved in the tank farm break-in. He could unravel the whole plot. But Rick and the Chief are still going to be furious about the student's escape and blame him.

As Al nears the road, he can see Faisal speaking into the car radio, probably reporting to the Big House that his boss has screwed up, failed to cuff a suspect, and a Palestinian terrorist's on the loose. They'll have to catch him before this whole thing and Al's career prospects blow up.

15

The Golden Ghetto

18 January 1991 / 03 Rajab 1411   16.30

Rob's relieved to leave work after another day of uncertainty and mounting hysteria. More people are fleeing by road for Jeddah or Dubai, and Krieger's allowed an American engineer in Rob's group to leave on the first evacuation flight. In the afternoon, there's another Scud alert and when Rob hears Aziz arguing with an elderly Palestinian, he has to warn his clerk again about blaming Palestinians.

'But these devils are our enemy,' Aziz protests and flounces off to complain to his friends in the Mail Room. The company which appeared so strong and substantial is, like Saudi Arabia, proving fragile when threatened by a few primitive missiles.

At home, after taking Cilla for a walk, Rob treats himself to a reviving double *sid* and tonic. But as he's leaving to visit Kamal's villa in the Golden Ghetto, the phone rings.

'Hi Rob.' June's voice. 'Bill Eliot's got a new Land Cruiser and we're heading off on a desert trip to some ancient city. Bill wants you to come.'

'Great.' He feels better just hearing her voice. 'When are you going?'

'Next Friday. We're leaving our place around eight.'

'Friday. That's my birthday.'

'Congratulations, sweetheart. Is it a big one?'

'Forty,' he says and feels the inadequacy of a life that, speaking to June, feels only half lived. But next Friday he'll be spending his birthday with her.

'Forty – the big Four Zero! We'll have to celebrate. Let's make it a party.'

'Sure. Let's celebrate.' While Fiona weighs him down when she phones, June's picked him up, making him look forward to his one and only fortieth birthday.

'See you Thursday, sweetheart.' She's put down the phone but 'sweetheart'… Her voice saying that word lingers, warming him as he leaves the house to visit Kamal and his student son in the Golden Ghetto.

'We'd better go to our safe room,' Kamal says. An alert siren's shrieking from nearby, forcing them to abandon their half-eaten lamb *kapsa* and hurry down the marble-floored hallway, its walls lined with Egyptian prints and decorative copper plates.

Kamal opens the door into a palatial bathroom complete with a walk-in shower, whirlpool bath, Western lavatory, and Eastern *hammam*. Rob notes that Kamal's following company instructions with a red fire extinguisher and first aid box beside the shower, a flashlight and shortwave radio on top of the lavatory cistern. Two blue jerry cans with plastic cups stand in the corner in case the water's cut off during an attack. Rob also notices the company checklist of supplies taped on the back of the door, together with the letter on 'Air Requirements in Safe Rooms' which Krieger wrote for Kamal's signature. Someone's marked with a yellow highlighter: *Physical activities in the safe room should be minimal to conserve oxygen*, as well as Krieger's mysterious equation (*Hours in Safe Room = Length x Width x Height divided by 39 x Number of Adults*). Rob remembers listening to *The Hitchhiker's Guide to the Galaxy* and supercomputer Deep Thought's answer to the great question of Life, the Universe and Everything. A simple answer

– forty-two. So where the hell did Krieger's thirty-nine come from?

While Rob and Hashim perch on the edge of the whirlpool bath, Kamal sits on the Western toilet seat in his grey wool *thawb*. He tunes in the shortwave radio until they hear DJ Jerry's cool 'California Dreamin' voice once again reciting, 'Put on your gas mask, stay in a safe place, and stay tuned.'

'*Alhamdullilah*. We're organized.' Kamal takes the khaki satchel from round his shoulder. 'Where's *your* gas mask?' he asks his son.

'Sorry, Dad. Left it upstairs.' Hashim offers a placatory smile, but Rob guesses he's left his 'uncool' gas mask behind on purpose. He's about the same age as Chris, Rob's son, but remains slightly built in his student garb of jeans and black Jimi Hendrix T-shirt. Security at the airport gave him some hassle when he returned from the UK but he's kept his glossy black hair subversively long, almost touching his shoulders.

Rob puts down his satchel on the tiled floor. He'd pulled on the British army mask during the first alerts but it felt suffocating and his resolve has been weakened by false alarms and a sense of the absurd when he saw a goggle-eyed alien in the mirror.

Kamal shrugs. He's shaved off his beard to wear an elephant-grey company mask, and dutifully pulls it on as DJ Jerry's voice calmly repeats the official warning.

'Where is everybody?' Rob asks, wondering about Kamal's wife and other people in the house.

'The women and servants have their own safe rooms,' Kamal says. There's been no sign of his Saudi wife except for a knock at the *majlis* door when the food was left outside, and Rob wonders what she looks like. Young and attractive? Or is this daughter of a wealthy contractor merely a tool of Kamal's ambition?

The sirens are wailing on in chorus but it could be a false alarm with the Scuds heading elsewhere – to Riyadh, Bahrain, or even Israel. Bill says the AWACS trigger the alarm as soon as Iraqi missiles are launched and before they know which way they're heading. So millions of people all over the Middle East are being terrorized by a few primitive and relatively cheap missiles.

Rob looks across to his department manager wearing the elephant-grey mask and listening to the sirens. He recalls the enthusiastic young teacher he met in his first weeks on North Camp – their meals together in the Mess Hall, conversations enlivened by discussions about Arab culture and politics. He remembers their trip to Al Hasa with Bill Eliot when they were shocked to hear President Sadat had been assassinated in Cairo. Kamal had praised the noble assassins while Bill was furious and quarrelled with him. Now, almost ten years later, Kamal's a prosperous senior manager living in the Golden Ghetto. His life's been transformed but have his opinions?

'This is boring.' Hashim stands up. 'Let's go outside and see what's happening.'

'No.' Kamal's raised his mask. 'The company wants us to stay in our safe room and not leave until the alert's over. There might be chemicals or nerve gas.'

'But it must be safer outside, Dad. We can see if a missile's coming. And the house won't collapse on us.'

Rob glances up at the bathroom ceiling. Would it hold if the house was hit? Very unlikely. And what if a Scud or part of one fell and they died here in a fire? A blaze like the one he'd just escaped by the airbase. Kamal and Hashim, father and son together, made sense, like in a family cremation. But he'd die bizarrely out of place – a stranger thousands of miles from Fiona and Chris and away from his homeland.

'We've got to stay inside,' Kamal says, exasperated with his son's resistance. 'At our management meeting, they said these Scuds can carry chemical warheads.'

Rob tries to prevent further argument by resuming the football discussion they were having before the alert. 'So what do you think about Gazza, Hashim? He's very popular in England after the World Cup.'

'Because he cries like a girl?' The young man scoffs at such weakness.

'Hashim likes this Italian.' Kamal joins in. 'Roberto Baggio. The man with the famous ponytail. If I was his manager—'

'But you're not, Dad.' Irritated, Hashim turns on his father. 'Baggio's his own man. No big company or manager can force him to cut his hair. Rob, did you see his goal against Czechoslovakia?'

'Agreed. Baggio's a great player.' Rob offers his approval. 'The Italians call him the Divine Ponytail.'

'Divine!' Kamal protests. 'Instead of worshipping footballers, young men should admire our *mujahid* in Afghanistan who gave their lives for their religion. These footballers spend all their money on sports cars, drugs and gambling.'

A loud explosion like a shot fired outside, and the bathroom shakes. Startled, Rob ducks, kneeling on the tiled floor and facing Hashim who's also dropped down.

'What's that?' Kamal grasps his gas mask and pulls it back over his head as the bathroom shakes again. More explosions, as if giant bullets are being fired up into the sky, the house reverberating.

'Patriot missiles,' Rob says to reassure them.

The fluorescent lights in the ceiling flicker, steady momentarily, and flicker again along their length. Kamal grabs his flashlight, switching it on before the tubes die and they're in darkness. A woman's scream pierces the air, echoing through the house. Rob looks to Kamal and Hashim as the woman cries out again, driving a shudder of fear through his body.

'That's our Thai maid,' Hashim says. 'She gets hysterical, frightening everybody. Dad should send her home. She's making things worse.'

Enduring the woman's screaming, Rob remembers the fuel storage tanks only a short distance away. As he drove to Kamal's, he'd glanced down the *jebel* to the silvery tanks illuminated in the floodlights and spotted two Humvees like desert beetles squatting nearby in the sand. If a Scud fell and the tank farm exploded, the firestorm could sweep back up the *jebel*, maybe even reach here. He feels dangerously confined in this gloom with Kamal in his grey mask shining the flashlight around on their faces. The air conditioning's been switched off in case of a gas attack and the bathroom's growing warmer.

Like Hashim said, if they were outside in the fresh air, at least they'd see the missiles or an approaching firestorm and be able to escape.

Hashim resumes their conversation, almost shouting through the maid's screaming. 'Dad says you're helping security with something.'

'The camp night patrol. We drive round checking buildings and the perimeter fence.'

'What's it like?'

'Very boring and hard to stay awake. But last week we had a break-in at the tank farm down the *jebel* from here. You can see the tops of the storage tanks from this house. The aviation fuel's highly explosive.'

'This is too warm.' Kamal puts his flashlight on the floor and peels off the gas mask.

'Somebody cut a hole in the fence between here and the storage tanks,' Rob says. He finds himself observing Hashim's reactions, but the boy, with his long hair and black Jimi Hendrix T-shirt, seems just like other students – bright and probably angry about the mess the older generation have made. 'We searched the area but couldn't find anybody and no sign of explosives. Strange thing is they cut through the fence on this side.'

'Why's that strange?' Kamal asks.

'It's easier to break in from the main road. To get up here you need to go through the security gates and an ID check. Doesn't make sense.'

'We should have more men guarding these tanks.' Kamal assumes his managerial role. 'I'll speak to the Security chief. He's our neighbor here.'

'It's secure now,' Rob says. 'Soldiers from the base are guarding the tank farm. They're armed, of course. And they've also strengthened patrols around the airbase.'

'These Americans are taking over everything,' Hashim says. 'And now they're going to stay here to control the Gulf and our oilfields.'

'Who do you think broke in?' Kamal asks, ignoring his son's outburst.

'Maybe supporters of Saddam Hussein,' Rob says. 'Or maybe Palestinians, Sudanese…'

'We've a lot of Palestinians working for the company,' Kamal says.

'Arafat was stupid, standing shoulder to shoulder with Saddam. And they say the Palestinians in Kuwait are helping the Iraqi army—'

'It's not true, Dad,' Hashim objects. 'People always blame the Palestinians.'

They've been speaking through a pause in the wailing and when the sirens resume, they sound less frantic. On the radio DJ Jerry's reciting, 'Civil Defence has sounded the All Clear.'

The fluorescent light surges back on and, relieved, they stand up, almost sheepishly leaving the forced intimacy of the bathroom, and returning along the brightly lit hallway.

'OK. The power's back on so let's see what's happening.' Kamal leads them into his study where a large screen TV is showing *War in the Gulf* and Wolf Blitzer reporting on some captured Coalition pilots.

'Dad, CNN is just propaganda,' Hashim says. 'These Americans boasting about smart weapons and bombing poor Iraqis. CNN's worried about these captured pilots and a few cuts on their faces but they're lucky not to be executed for what they've done.'

'They're prisoners of war,' Rob says. 'And the Iraqis shouldn't use them as human shields. There's the Geneva Convention—'

'Geneva! They're bombing and killing thousands of people.' Hashim remains standing near the door, as if about to leave. 'And now they complain because of a few cuts and bruises. Anyway, they probably got hurt when their planes were shot down.'

'Hashim, let's just listen to the news,' his father demands.

Rob and Kamal settle into black leather armchairs facing the TV, where a middle-aged woman in Atlanta, sounding like she's never left the Deep South, is reading the Gulf War headlines. No news yet about the Scud attacks and Patriot missiles but more Iraqi pilots have flown their planes to Iran. Saddam's army are blowing up Kuwaiti oil wells, releasing oil into the Gulf and creating a slick over twenty miles wide that's slowly drifting south. Western environmentalists are being interviewed about the coastal pollution, the effect on birds and other marine life, and sound like they're blaming the Coalition.

'This oil slick could damage the desalinization plants,' Rob realizes. 'And pollute our drinking water.'

'It's OK,' Kamal says. 'We're sending clean-up teams to protect the plants. The guys are setting up booms round the seawater intakes. And we're getting skimmers flown in from the States so we can install them on our vessels. You might have to take a trip up north yourself.'

'Good,' Rob says but then realizes he doesn't want to miss the desert trip with June on his suddenly important fortieth birthday.

CNN shifts to Tel Aviv with news that Scuds fired at Israel have killed one person and injured several others. The Israelis claim seven Scuds have been shot down by the Patriot missiles the Americans shipped to them.

'Attacking Israel makes Saddam more popular,' Kamal says. 'Especially with the Palestinians.'

'But it's always the same.' Hashim is still standing as if impatient to leave. 'America protects the Zionists. They wouldn't survive without the Americans.'

Abruptly, CNN switches to a live report from the airbase. A young Saudi pilot, surrounded by security guards and reporters, is being interviewed. Flying a high-tech F-15, he's shot down two Iraqi Mirage jets over the Gulf. Yet despite the media adulation, his speech is modest and he sounds apologetic towards the Iraqis, who he says are flying older, less sophisticated planes.

'The Americans probably forced him to shoot down the Mirage,' Hashim says. 'To save the face of the regime.'

'People say the Saudi pilots are forced to join in the bombing,' Kamal explains. 'But they keep returning with their bombs. They don't want to drop them on fellow Muslims. You know, some stupid American general said they would bomb Iraq back to the Stone Age. That shows the mentality.'

The phone's ringing beside the computer on Kamal's desk. Hashim quickly picks it up. 'My friends want me to come over,' he tells his father.

'Remember, we have a guest,' Kamal says.

'Don't mind me.' Rob rises from the chair. 'I need to go home, catch up on some sleep.'

'Stay for coffee,' Kamal says and turns to his son. 'You're not going out tonight. It's too dangerous.'

'Dad, my friends are expecting me.'

'They can do without you. As soon as the airport opens, you go back to London. I asked Rob here to discuss your future, your university course—'

'There are bigger and more important things than university, Dad. In Cairo, the students are demonstrating against Mubarak for sending his soldiers here. They want to stop the war—'

'That's enough!' Kamal glares at his son. 'Don't tell me about students in Cairo. I was a student there.'

'Sorry Dad. It's *my* life and I need to make my own decisions, like you did.' With a nod to Rob, Hashim leaves.

Embarrassed for Kamal, Rob carries on watching CNN and news of the Americans bombing what they claim are nuclear installations, chemical and biological weapons facilities.

'So what would you do?' Kamal asks when the commercials for international banks and luxury hotels begin. 'How would you deal with Hashim?'

'Try to keep him out of trouble. I know it's difficult.' Wary of giving bad advice, Rob asks, 'So what do *you* think about this war?'

'The Americans say they're fighting because Saddam invaded Kuwait but what's Kuwait? You British drew the borders and created it, and you created Iraq as well. Then they say it's because of democracy but the Al Sabah are not democratic.' He shrugs. 'My friend, we know this war's about oil.'

'That's part of it,' Rob says, wondering where Kamal's loyalties really lie. 'But Saddam is a tyrant, Kuwait's a small country that's been invaded, and there's the brutality...'

He stops, listening to what sounds like a doorbell. A delay before it rings again.

'I hope it's not Hashim's friends.' Angry at the intrusion, Kamal gets up.

'OK, I'd better go now.' Rob's decided that when he returns home he'll ring Chris, speak to his own student son, and make sure he's OK. He follows his host down the hallway, Kamal opening the front door.

'*Assalamu alikum.*' Al is standing there, wrapped up in a grey winter *thawb*, his thin face stern in the entrance light. A heavy-shouldered young man in white *thawb* and jacket looms beside him, and behind them are uniformed guards and the headlights of patrol cars parked outside.

Kamal and Al exchange frigid greetings and, shocked by Al's arrival, Rob wonders what to do. He wants to leave, but Kamal's looking to him as if for help. Should he stay?

A shout and he glances back down the hallway, the noise seeming to come from inside the house. More shouting and what sounds like Hashim's voice.

'*Yalla,* Faisal.' Al indicates to the guards and they are moving round the side of the house, through the garden. Rob looks to Kamal but he seems bewildered, still standing in the doorway as Rob follows Al and the guards across the freshly turfed lawn and through a hedge of newly planted shrubs.

'What are you doing here?' Al turns to Rob.

'Visiting my department manager.'

'You know he was in the Muslim Brotherhood?'

They've blundered on through into a back garden illuminated by patio lights and bordering a swimming pool. At the end is a changing hut, and a teenager in blue T-shirt and long khaki shorts standing outside, with a blanket round his shoulders. For a moment, Rob thinks it's Hashim, but Al calls towards the youth. 'OK, Mohammed. No problem. We just want to talk.'

House lights switch on behind Rob and he can hear men's voices arguing with each other. He glances round into the open doorway of a kitchen where Kamal's shouting and gesturing to his son, furious at his disobedience.

The heavily built Saudi and two security guards are moving round the pool towards the young man by the changing hut. He panics, dropping the blanket and running towards the garden wall to climb the red-and-white flowering shrubs. He jumps, scrabbling with his hands and feet to clamber up the branches and over the wall. But fear and his momentum aren't enough. He struggles and falls back onto the big Saudi who's grabbed him by the leg. They're shouting and rolling together over the grass verge beside the pool, one struggling on top of the other. The uniformed guards are standing back, and Al shouts, running forward to intervene. But it's too late. A loud splash and the two young men are in the water. The T-shirted youth is swimming away to the centre of the pool while Al's assistant is crying out, desperately floundering in his voluminous white *thawb* and jacket. He can't swim and his clothes are weighing him down.

Rob sees the guards are hesitating at the poolside and glances round, grabbing a long cane pole with a cleaning net at the end. Standing at the side, he calls to Al's assistant, still splashing and shouting out in the water. He holds out the pole and the young man grabs it. Rob pulls him towards the side and guides him to the pool steps where Al and the guards haul him out, dripping and raging at the teenager still floating and watching from the middle of the pool.

'Take Faisal into the house,' Al tells the guards as they help his assistant inside away from the pool.

'He can use our bathroom and towels,' Kamal says, anxious to please. 'But I swear, I know nothing about this.'

Once again the centre of attention, the teenager's treading water in the pool. Kamal switches on the underwater spotlights, illuminating the young man in his blue T-shirt. Al shouts out something in Arabic, which the teenager seems to consider as he splashes about with his arms. Hashim goes to the side of the pool and calls for Mohammed to come to him. Eventually, he swims towards his friend and allows himself to be helped up out of the water, dripping and dejected with his head down.

'Hashim was trying to help his friend,' Kamal is telling Al. 'They're just kids. Idealistic students upset about this war. Don't worry, I'll explain everything to your chief. He's a good neighbor of mine.'

16

The Beautiful Voice

20 January 1991 / 05 Rajab 1411   *17.00*

Wasta! Al's furious at the Egyptian manager using his friends and influence
to save his son. And now he and Faisal are being treated like chauffeurs
driving these students – not even in handcuffs – to the coach station for
the overnight journey to Dubai and flights back to their US colleges.
Al wanted some time to interrogate them, especially after he'd been
reprimanded for not cuffing Mohammed and allowing him to escape. But
the Chief warned that top management was concerned and he and Rick
would question the students privately.

So what did they say? Why did they break into the tank farm? The
Egyptian manager and the Chief claimed that the teenagers meant no harm
and felt sympathy for the poor Iraqi people being bombed. Khalid, the
Palestinian, said his son had been brainwashed by Dr Eissa, the local imam,
whose subversive audio tapes Al found in Hashim's bedroom. Of course the
Egyptian manager denied all knowledge of the tapes and their revolutionary
messages.

Not enough information, Al realizes, but as usual the power of *wasta*, of influence and connections, reigned. Kamal's security file showed he'd been active in the Muslim Brotherhood many years ago, but then he was a student in Cairo. Now he's too important to the company and his second wife's father, a wealthy contractor, has even more *wasta*. Al also suspects the Chief and Personnel want to avoid further problems, and delaying any longer will attract attention from the *mabahith*. No damage was done to the tank farm and no one wants these kids to be interrogated by the secret police. Who knows what they might say and what that could lead to?

They drive into the coach station but there's no thanks, of course, or apologies from the students. Only a sullen resignation as they get out of the car, and for a moment Al wishes Faisal had dealt with them. After his near drowning, he'd have given them a more aggressive interrogation. The boys' fathers are waiting to embrace their sons and, as the students climb onto the crowded long-distance coach, the two men are visibly relieved to see them escape. They briefly thank the security men but pretend as if nothing too serious has happened, aside from some temporary embarrassment. As Al watches the students waving and peering out through the coach window, he fears vital information might be disappearing with them.

'They should go to prison,' Faisal says as they drive away. 'For severe punishment.' If he'd interrogated Mohammed, the Palestinian would have ended up in hospital like the Indian gardener.

'Drive to the Home Loan estate,' Al says. 'The Chief wants us to deliver a message to Dr Eissa, our famous imam.'

The company's Home Loan estate lies opposite the desert *jebel* where North Camp's Portakabins once stood. A vanished and long-forgotten world Al thought, until looking down towards the tank farm he'd seen Rick talking to Bill Eliot under the floodlights. Was the American a murderer who'd escaped and now returned?

'Dr Eissa has a beautiful voice for Ramadan prayer,' Faisal says, as they turn into an estate of dusty two-storey houses. 'Everybody knows he fought bravely with the *mujahid* in Afghanistan.'

Al nods in agreement. But Afghanistan is the reason for Dr Eissa being on the Watch List which the IT expert's produced. In just a few years, the thousands of returning heroes trained to fight and use modern weapons have become a threat to the regime and their American friends. Dr Eissa, the imam who leads the faithful in prayer at the beautiful new mosque, travelled to the Afghan camps and needs to be interviewed. Especially after Mohammed and Hashim praised him as their inspiration.

There are no well-watered palm trees or manicured lawns on this dusty estate dozing in the late afternoon sunshine. Just sandy streets of villas with flat, stony waste ground between them. Al instructs Faisal to park the patrol car in the shade, outside a shuttered grocery store. An old dust-covered white Mercedes stands outside the imam's villa, a child's Chopper bicycle carelessly leaning against it. The database listed Dr Eissa as having four children, including two boys aged twelve and eighteen, and as they walk past, Al notices the litter of chocolate wrappers and children's toys scattered over the Mercedes' back seat. The Prophet said, 'Cleanliness is part of faith', and Al would never have allowed such a mess in his regularly cleaned Honda.

The imam's voice is renowned for its beauty but the stocky grandfather figure opening the door is shabby and dishevelled. Wearing a rumpled white *jalabiya*, thick-lensed glasses and bushy grey beard he welcomes them in the name of God, the Merciful, the Compassionate. But when Al shows his Security ID and introduces himself and Faisal, the imam's expression becomes suspicious and they exchange frigid greetings.

'I have no business with security or secret police,' the imam says, moving to close the door.

'We need your help, sir.' Al steps forward, almost forcing his way in through the doorway. Dr Eissa gives way and they enter a sitting room crowded with dark, heavy furniture and colourful children's toys.

'You want help? What help can I give to the *mabahith*?'

'I'm sorry, sir, but we are not the *mabahith* or *mubarakat*,' Faisal says, showing his respect for the noble imam.

Al keeps his face expressionless, but he hates words like *mabahith* and *mubarakat* evoking dark, ugly deeds and the torture cells used against his own Shia people. Suddenly, a pounding on the stairs and a tubby young boy wearing a yellow Brazil football shirt – number eleven, Romario – charges down the green-carpeted staircase towards them.

'Abdullah is practising,' the imam says. 'Keeping fit for football.' This must be the twelve-year-old, but where's the eighteen-year-old, the one most likely to be involved in trouble? The boy halts, puffing and blowing, glancing at his father with the two strangers.

'Well done, Abdullah.' Dr Eissa pats his son on the head. 'Some day you will score goals like Romario.'

The boy beams and his chubby face sets in determination as he begins running back up the staircase, showing off his stamina to his father and the visitors.

'He wants to play well for his team,' the imam says, with that warm smile and velvet voice which draw so many people in. Al sees Faisal is impressed, ready to sit at the Afghan veteran's feet, and he can imagine student disciples like Mohammed and Hashim gathering round to listen to the imam after Friday prayers.

'We want to speak in a quiet place, sir,' Al says, as Abdullah reaches the top of the stairs and turns to charge down again.

'We'll go to my study. But I don't have much time and must prepare for *isha* prayer.' Dr Eissa leads them into a small office. A large map of the Middle East and a company calendar are taped to the wall above an antique-looking wooden desk littered with papers. Next to it is a small book-case containing religious texts with *The Noble Qur'an* in Arabic and English, an Arabic/English Dictionary, and an Egyptian book by Sayyid Qutb called *Milestones along the Way,* which was said to be an inspiration for *jihadis.*

Al approaches the Middle East map, marked with coloured pins in places like Jalalabad, Quetta and Peshawar. 'So you were in Afghanistan with the *mujahid,* sir?' he says. 'You must know these places well.' He touches a red pin set in the mountains near the border with Pakistan. 'Where is this?'

'That is Jaji, the Lion's Den, where there was a great battle between our *mujahid* and the Communist airborne soldiers. The sky was raining bombs and the earth was shaking under our feet. The famous Sheikh was wounded there.'

'Did you fight in this great battle, sir?' Faisal asks, his face bright with admiration.

'Unfortunately, I missed that honour and the martyr's crown. Yet none can die except in the moment decreed by the Lord of the Worlds. No, I helped our charities give medical assistance to the holy warriors fighting the Russian atheists. Later, my noble friend, Dr Abdullah Azzam, my teacher at King Abdel Aziz University, was killed with his two sons. A car bomb in Peshawar on their way to Friday prayers. Maybe you have seen the film of his burial? It was only a year ago.'

'But who did that dreadful thing, sir?' Faisal asks.

Dr Eissa shrugs. 'Maybe CIA mercenaries, the Zionist Mossad. They have their agents everywhere. But why are *you* here?' He turns to Al, his tone becoming hostile. 'Who sent you to me?'

Still angry about the students and the Egyptian manager's *wasta*, Al's tempted to reply: a security chief who keeps an American as his deputy rather than promote a Shia, and Rick, a big Texan who knows nothing about Islam. But although Al distrusts his bosses, he distrusts Dr Eissa even more.

'So what do *you* think about this war, sir?' he asks, making his tone and expression sound sceptical.

'I'm a good Muslim. What do you expect me to think?' The imam's words are controlled but angry. 'On his deathbed, the Prophet, *Peace be upon him*, commanded, 'Let there not be two religions in Arabia.' Now our sacred soil, this land of the two holy mosques, has been invaded and defiled by Western Crusaders. Christians and Zionists and even women soldiers. Defending Muslim lands is every man's sacred duty and our holy shrines should be defended by faithful Muslim brothers. The Sheikh and his comrades told the Al Saud we were ready with our experience of the Afghan *jihad* to defend this holy land. But instead they chose the Americans and made this land an American colony. And these hypocrite religious scholars like Bin Baz approved the Crusader invasion. Now we have this filthy war and our Muslim brothers in Iraq, and poor women and children are slaughtered by the Crusaders' bombs.' The imam stops himself, and turns on Al. 'So who sent you to me?'

'We're investigating a break-in at the tank farm near the highway. Your name was mentioned, sir.'

'Tank farm!' The imam looks mystified. 'What's this? I'm a religious man, not one of your oil sheikhs or rich contractors.'

'We have information from the local police—'

'The *mabahith*.' He spits out the name. 'The dawn visitors. They come to my house early in the morning and search for religious tapes, for my righteous warnings against this corrupt regime and the Western Crusaders. They look everywhere and upset my family. But *alhamdullilah*, they find nothing. And I know nothing of your tanks and farms.'

'I'm talking about the aviation fuel tanks near the main highway,' Al says. 'We caught two of your young followers breaking into the restricted area. They had audio tapes of your preaching hidden in their rooms.'

'I'm not afraid to preach the truth and can't be blamed for what others do with that truth. Tell your chief I won't stop speaking against this war and the Crusaders. I have no time for this.'

'If you've nothing to hide, you've nothing to fear sir.' Al takes the notebook from his breast pocket. 'You are blessed with four children, sir. Where's Hussein, your eldest son?'

'Why do you ask? I sent him to the south, away from this war. He's staying at my brother's house in Hofuf.'

Al asks for the brother's address and Dr Eissa surprises him by giving it easily, as if he's prepared for this visit.

'Do you know any of these men?' Al reads from a list of the imam's known disciples who meet after Friday prayers – Palestinians, Sudanese and Egyptians as well as Saudis.

'These men are my brothers,' Dr Eissa says. 'Some travelled to Pakistan and Afghanistan with me. They are true Muslims. Why do you ask me about them? Is it a crime to be a good Muslim now? Are you a good Muslim?' The imam looks directly into Al's eyes, challenging his heretic soul, and Al looks back, refusing to be intimidated. These 'righteous' men hate the Shia as much as the Crusaders. They complain about the regime but with power, they'd be worse.

'Do you know the Palestinian, Khalid Shehata, and his son Mohammed?' Al persists. 'Or Hashim El Sayed, the son of the Egyptian manager, Kamal El Sayed?'

'Many of the righteous come to our mosque and I speak with lots of good men. But enough. Now I must prepare for *isha* prayer.'

Abdullah's sitting on the bottom stair, catching his breath, but when he sees the visitors he stands up as if to start running again.

'Rest now, Abdullah,' his father says. 'Football is over and now we must study.'

'Is there anything you'd like to tell us, sir?' Al asks. 'Something we might discover later?' Refusing to be hustled from the house, he faces Dr Eissa.

'No. I have nothing more for you people.'

'Thank you for your help, sir.' Faisal apologizes to the velvet-voiced imam.

'But we'll probably need to speak to you again,' Al says and allows the imam to escort them to the door and close it with a bang behind them.

Faisal remains silent as they drive away, leaving the Home Loan estate and heading back along the highway to the Big House.

'So what do you think?' Al settles back into the passenger seat, still smarting from the imam's question. *Are you a good Muslim?* He'd not answered. This schism between Sunni and Shia is too dangerous to argue.

'Dr Eissa is a noble and pious man,' Faisal says, sounding annoyed about Al even questioning him. 'Like Mr Rick says, it's obvious the Palestinians and Sudanese are to blame. We give these foreigners jobs and money but they stab us in the back. Everybody knows the Kuwaiti were too soft with Palestinians.'

Rick's voice comes over the radio and Al reports, concluding, 'He's a popular imam. If we arrest him, there'll be trouble.'

'Sure,' Rick says. 'You've given the guy a warning like the Chief said. Now he knows we're watching him and his buddies. But you guys better get over to the training centre. There's a Sudanese teacher called Majid shooting his mouth off about the war. Bring him into the Big House. And I want Faisal to deal with him. Understand?'

'OK, Rick,' Al says. After the fiasco with the Palestinian student, his boss obviously doesn't trust him.

'Good. Let's see this *Sudani.*' Faisal's happy they're no longer suspecting the noble imam and that Rick's chosen him specially to deal with the Sudanese troublemaker. 'These black men come here from Africa to steal our money and betray us. *Yalla.* Let's go,' he says, accelerating along the main road towards the company training centre.

17

A Target-Rich Environment

23 January 1991 / 08 Rajab 1411   18.15

One hour in the path of jihad is worth more than seventy years of praying.
Ibrahim listens to Dr Eissa's beautiful voice calling him to righteous action,
as he cruises back along the highway and through the early evening towards
the distant lights of company headquarters. The imam describes a world
divided between light and darkness, belief and unbelief, justice and tyranny,
virtue and vice, purity and corruption. And Ibrahim feels excited to be
joining the noble Sheikh, Saeed and his *mujahid* brothers in fighting the
unbelievers and for the way of Allah.

Past six o'clock and he's picked this time to drive back into camp.
The guards have their evening meal after *maghrib* prayer, and won't search
a company car returning from a gas oil separation plant in the desert.
Vehicle inspection takes too long, they're tired and the hot food's ready.
Even if they do stop him, the inspection equipment and tools in the boot
will be enough to confuse them. They won't look in the toolbox or the
spare tire compartment and discover the gifts he's collected from the pious
contractor's warehouse.

Majid, his elder brother, was supposed to collect these things. But after Security interrogated him about what he'd said to his students and a big Saudi knocked him around, he took fright. When Ibrahim left the apartment early this morning, his brother was still afraid that the big security man, built like a wrestler, might come to arrest him again.

Ibrahim's tired after his long journey there and back to the separation plant. One of the American engineers was supposed to do this month's plant inspections but when Ibrahim returned from Jeddah, he found out Krieger had let this American leave on an evacuation flight. Even Rob could see the unfairness when he asked Ibrahim to take over the inspections. Such injustice! But a Sudanese was expected to keep quiet and swallow it.

He cruises down the slip road off the main highway and onto the road leading to camp. Last night, he watched the military briefing on CNN and a stupid American general boasted that Iraq and Kuwait still offered 'a target-rich environment'. Yet this area is even richer in targets. He passes the radar station, perched high on a rocky *jebel*, with a supply road from the airbase winding round and up to the giant dish. Then further along, to his left, appears another rich target – the floodlit tank farm with a line of petrol tankers parked and waiting to be filled with aviation fuel for Crusader jets. But now, under the lights, he can see two armoured Humvees with GIs standing round them, guarding the entrance.

These soldiers were not there before and he can still hardly believe the stupidity – Saeed's student friends breaking in with no explosives and doing no damage to the fuel tanks. They were scouts on a reconnaissance, Saeed said, claiming the break-in had nothing to do with him. Reconnaissance? What was needed was righteous action. Fortunately, the students didn't seem to have mentioned Saeed, and anyway the rich young Saudi said he had friends in Security. They'd look after him.

But why ignore such an important target? These fuel storage tanks keep the Crusaders' planes in the air and with the pious contractor's gifts they could attack the petrol tankers. Explosions and a fire storm would close this road, confuse security and give the brothers time to hit other targets like the IT Centre with its famous supercomputers. Saeed works at the centre and is always saying how vital it is to the country's oil and gas production.

Ibrahim joins the line of vehicles edging towards the floodlit gateway and is pleased there's a Greyhound bus in front of him – a useful distraction with at least two guards needed to check passenger IDs and the baggage hold. Should he hide the banned religious tapes he's been listening to in the car? Dr Eissa's speeches denounce this corrupt regime, and the decadent American world that young people see on TV, where loose women flaunt themselves and the highest virtue is making money as fast as Jewish bankers. Only the rule of the righteous and strict *sharia* can save the faithful. So why should he hide the imam's speeches? These ignorant *bedu* guards aren't looking for religious tapes, anyway.

Good that Saeed's uncle has bought weapons and explosives and stored them in his warehouse for the coming *jihad*. They cost thousands of US dollars – enough to persuade and transform the lives of the Bangladeshi drivers and security guards working at the port. But they aren't too expensive for Saeed's pious uncle, blessed with oil company contracts, the respect of the noble Sheikh, and the protection of Allah.

Last Friday, after prayer time, Dr Eissa had reminisced about his time with the *mujahid* in Afghanistan. He'd inspired his disciples with tales of the Sheikh's Lion's Den, and how Afghan fighters—brothers without any technical training—had shot down Russian helicopter gunships. Here, just a few successful strikes could inspire the faithful to recover this sacred land from the Christian and Jewish crusaders.

Ibrahim looks towards the guardhouse, between the two lanes of vehicles. Usually there's a lazy air about the place with the guards drinking *chai* and gossiping while some Bangladeshi kids sweep up round their feet and clean the windows. But tonight the atmosphere is brisk. A tall uniformed officer, probably a Pakistani, is directing operations as he stands erect, surveying the traffic. The Greyhound bus pulls out of the line and into the parking area for inspection, and Ibrahim drives forward. A bearded guard trundles a mirror at the end of a pole under his car, checking for explosives, and another guard advances towards him out of the floodlights.

Usually company vehicles are waved through, but the guard's directing Ibrahim to pull in behind the bus for inspection. Anxious to drive on, Ibrahim looks at the guard again, but the youth impatiently waves him towards the inspection area. Why him? Obviously because he's Sudanese, a black African. These guards don't stop and inspect cars driven by white faces, the privileged Americans and British. Controlling his anger, he lowers the car window, and respectfully greets the young Saudi.

'ID,' the youth demands and Ibrahim hands over his card. This *bedu* kid can't be more than twenty and should show more respect to his seniors.

'*Sudani?*' The kid looks into his face, a sly suspicious glance. He probably believes everything he hears on TV about the Sudanese leaders' support for Saddam Hussein, the wild accusations of betrayal and foreign spies helping the Iraqi enemy.

'Only company tools and technical equipment in the boot,' Ibrahim says. He hands over a transmittal slip listing everything he took with him this morning on his inspection trip. But the *bedu* kid's still keeping hold of his ID as he scans the flimsy paper slip, pretending he can understand it.

'Company technical equipment,' Ibrahim repeats, unable to keep the irritation out of his voice.

The kid looks up, reacting to the tone. 'You go to inspection,' he commands. Weary after his long journey, Ibrahim's about to object but realizes that if there's any argument, the Pakistani officer will come over and make sure it's a thorough inspection. Exasperated, he pulls out of the line of traffic and drives in behind the Greyhound bus in the inspection area.

The young *bedu* walks to the back of the company car. After releasing the catch for the boot, Ibrahim takes his ebony prayer beads hanging from the rear view mirror. He reminds himself that a strong Muslim shows self-control, and he must stay patient, not antagonize this kid. He fingers the beads but is too nervous to pray and glances across to the guardhouse where the Pakistani officer's talking to a slightly built Saudi in a grey *thawb*. A clatter from behind where the *bedu* kid's moving tools and equipment around in the boot. Some of the gifts from the contractor's warehouse are hidden among the inspection tools and might be damaged. Should he get out and tell the kid to be careful? But that would start an argument and attract attention. More clatter forces him to open the car door and standing in the floodlights' glare, he watches the young *bedu* trying to match the equipment with the transmittal slip.

'What's this?' the kid demands, holding up a hydrogen sulphide gas detector. Ibrahim takes a breath and patiently explains that he's an engineer with vital work to do for the company. This technical equipment is used for safety inspections and is very important for oil and gas production. But watching this *bedu* carelessly move things around, he struggles to control his temper as he fingers the ebony prayer beads. Last week, returning from Jeddah, he'd argued with the police at checkpoints when they kept stopping and questioning him as if he were a foreign agent. Had they reported him to company security? Is his name on a list? He needs to be quiet and patient with this kid.

'Hey!' A loud American voice behind him, and he turns to see a heavily built man wearing a tan cord jacket squeezing out from the back of a taxi. He's waving an ID card and protesting to the guard who's pulled the taxi over. The Pakistani officer and the Saudi in the grey *thawb* are hurrying over from the guardhouse to deal with the commotion.

'Sir, you phone sponsor on camp,' the officer tells the American.

'I'm visiting Rick, your security boss. I got military ID,' the big man protests. 'You should be checking for terrorists, not guys like me.'

'Sorry, sir, but we gotta check everybody.' The slightly built Saudi speaks up and Ibrahim bridles at the Texan accent, the voice of a collaborator. This sounds like one of the security men who questioned Majid and made him so frightened.

'Come to the office and you can call your sponsor, sir,' the Saudi says and leads the arrogant American towards the guardhouse. Now the Pakistani officer's looking towards Ibrahim and his company car, the young *bedu* still holding his ID. The guards are stepping down from the Greyhound in front and with a roar from its exhaust, it starts forward. The Pakistani officer starts walking towards Ibrahim and signals to the young guard.

'OK. *Yalla.*' he calls over and the *bedu* kid gives up, banging the car boot closed.

Ibrahim takes his ID and transmittal slip and slowly, with dignity, gets back into the car. Released, and with fresh confidence, he drives through the camp entrance and on towards the illuminated towers of what the Americans call Houston East – this centre of Western imperialism and source of the cancer spreading through the Muslim world. Allah had blessed the faithful with oil and gas worth billions of dollars, sufficient to support them all their lives, not to enrich these foreign infidels. Attacks and explosions here could demolish these arrogant towers, halt oil and gas production all over Arabia and stop the Crusader war machine.

At last Ibrahim's cruising past the fire station, the company training centre where Majid works, and the floodlit ball field, the beating heart of this American colony on the edge of the desert. The floodlights are beaming down on this oasis of peace and security, a still point in the midst of a chaotic war. He's seen little boys here in smart white uniforms playing baseball, while Muslim children are dying in the brutal bombing of Baghdad and Basra. Why should only the children of these infidels remain safe?

He turns down past the golf clubhouse. Beyond, there's a glow in the night sky from the runway lights of the airbase, the Crusader jets taking off and heading for Iraq and Kuwait. Since the tank farm incident, patrols around the airbase have been strengthened, but *inshallah* with these instruments of justice in the car, they can attack other targets.

Weary after the gas plant inspection and long day's travelling, he accelerates down the road and eases back in his seat, looking forward to arriving back at Majid's apartment. He's glad to be carrying these weapons that will give the Crusaders – the fat Generals in Riyadh, and Bush in the White House – a mighty shock. In this target-rich environment, they can attack the IT Centre, the tank farm, maybe even this camp. He can imagine film of the destruction as dramatic breaking news on CNN and being endlessly replayed to the watching world. Evidence that Muslims are fighting back against the invaders and the corrupt regime who've allowed this holy land to become an American colony.

As Ibrahim turns into the parking lot beside the bachelor housing block, he's pleased to see a light in Majid's ground floor apartment and Saeed's red Camara outside. He parks and rushes through the door into the apartment to celebrate the wealthy contractor's gifts. But only Saeed is sitting there on the couch, watching CNN and loaded with bad news. The Security interrogation and threats frightened Majid too much and, terrified of being arrested again, he's left for Jeddah and the ferry home to his wife and children in Khartoum.

'He's gone?' Ibrahim can hardly believe it. Wasn't Majid the one who wanted to attack the invaders?

'Yes, but let's not despair.' Saeed embraces his brother-in-arms. 'Now we stand before Allah together.'

They clasp each other tightly, united against this decadent imperialist world, this vast polluted ocean of *jahiliyya*. And, as they separate, Ibrahim realizes he's not unhappy that his older and hyper-critical brother has left. At least there'll be no more sneers and joking at his expense.

'So let's see what gifts you've got in the car.' Saeed claps his brother on the back. 'The Sheikh wants us to hit a very important target. We're going to make it onto Headline News, my friend.'

18

Lines in the Sand

31 January 1991 / 16 Rajab 1411   *08.45*

'Free at last!' June's exultant. 'Been going stir crazy, stuck on this camp.'

'Put your seat belt on,' Rob says, sitting with her in the back of Bill's Land Cruiser. 'We're coming to the main gate.'

'Rob, you're so buttoned up. These guards don't care about all your health and safety stuff.'

'They should. Just put the belt on,' he tells her, not sure whether to be amused or exasperated by her resistance.

'Do what he says,' Bill yells from the driving seat. 'Put the fucking belt on, June.'

'OK, Captain Kirk.' June's belt clicks in place and, as the guards wave them through, she slips her hand onto Rob's knee. 'But if we're stopped, who am I married to, Bill? You know I'm not allowed out without a husband.'

'I'll volunteer,' Bill says. 'So long as it's only for today.'

They're cruising downhill past the National Guard barracks with its armoured cars and jeeps coated in sand and rusting away, waiting to be replaced by more high-tech weaponry from another multi-million-dollar arms deal.

June settles back beside Rob, with only her black and white striped shoulder bag between them. 'Rick had to go to some meeting up north,' she tells him, her hand still on his knee. 'Won't be back until tomorrow.'

'What happens if the police stop us at a checkpoint?' asks Fahad, Bill's young Kuwaiti interpreter, sitting in front with a map of Saudi Arabia.

'That's why you're here,' says Bill. 'To explain stuff. But I've got military ID. That's enough for these guys.'

Now they're travelling along the old coastal road, past a clutter of garages, lorry parks, and shabby roadside cafes. Off to the left is a long stretch of wasteland with several military helicopters flying low under the power lines.

'See the Apaches over there?' Bill says. 'Tank busters with Hellfire missiles and rockets. They're training to fly in low, ready for the big push into Kuwait.'

'So when do you think the ground war will start?' Rob asks.

Bill shrugs. 'Soon as we're ready. We're preparing the battlefield.'

The old road joins a deserted and newly built highway with fresh green signs at the junctions to Hofuf, Riyadh, and north to Kuwait. Below the signs, crude wooden signposts mark the deployment routes taken by the American Big Red One and the British Desert Rats. Occasional military vehicles pass by on the road, but the Coalition armies drove through here months ago, leaving just these reminders of the half a million men entrenched near the Kuwaiti border and awaiting the order to attack.

While Bill drives and Fahad studies his map, June and Rob luxuriate on the back seat. They skim through guidebooks from the camp library and glance outside at the desert wasteland, the rust-brown pipeline beside the road, sometimes concealed under banks of oiled sand and dirt, sometimes emerging on metal stilts, exposed to the elements.

The whining sounds of the company's Country and Western programme gradually fade from the car radio and Bill slots in a cassette tape. 'Soundtrack from *Platoon*,' he says. 'Great film.'

But melancholy music. Rob remembers a night on North Camp with Bill drinking *sid* and 7-Up and listening to Vaughan Williams' 'Tallis Fantasia', the music Bill said he'd played in Iran after he heard his father had died in Houston.

'Sounds like a funeral,' June protests but Bill ignores her and soon the mournful 'Adagio for Strings' gives way to Smokey Robinson cheerfully tracking his tears and Jim Morrison yelling 'Hello I Love You'. Bill's waved through a police checkpoint beside a busy mini-market and, following Fahad's directions, he turns off before a motorway bridge and drives down a gravel track, bumping along for several kilometres before striking off towards the sand dunes.

'Hold on,' he calls and, exhilarated at this chance to go dune bashing, he accelerates towards the sands. Thrown about in the back, Rob leans in against June, holding her hand as they climb the sand dunes hardened by rain and cold winds, then plough back down again, shouting and laughing with each other like giddy teenagers.

'Gotta keep the speed up or we'll get stuck,' Bill yells, pausing on the crest of another dune. The truck sways in the balance, as they look out over successive waves of the sand sea, before plunging down the other side.

But they've ploughed deep into wet sand and Bill struggles with the wheel to drive out. The Land Cruiser roars and roars again before stuttering to a halt, the engine revving uselessly. Cursing, Bill jerks the gear stick into reverse, slipping back, then drives forward again. But the wheels are digging deeper into wet sand.

'No panic, guys,' Bill says. 'There's some gear in the back. We'll soon get outta here.'

They scramble out of the truck but, opening the back, find only a rusty shovel, a length of rope, and several short planks among a jumble of barbecue gear and collapsible picnic chairs. While June volunteers to walk up the sand dune and wave for help, Rob and Fahad shovel out damp sand and wedge planks under the Land Cruiser's back wheels to increase traction. Bill sits revving the engine while, with their shoulders braced behind the truck, Rob and Fahad heave and push forward, their feet sinking deeper and wet sand spurting from the tires up into their clothes and faces. The back wheels slip off the planks, dig deeper into sand, and Bill jumps out.

'Try again,' he shouts. 'This time, let's use the planks under the front wheels.'

'Did you leave a message?' Fahad demands. 'Let people know where we were going?' His denim shirt and cream chinos are gritted with wet sand. Furious, he brushes them down with his hands.

'No.' Bill stands with his feet apart, confronting his interpreter. 'Did you?'

Fahad's outraged. 'It's basic desert safety. You're the driver. You should have left a message.'

'Why didn't you?' Bill bangs his fist against the truck door, the thump resounding in the desert air. 'You're the navigator. I'm sick of you guys. Anything goes wrong and you blame the nearest American.'

'Americans are to blame,' Fahad shouts back. 'You take all the decisions. You think Arabs are too stupid.'

'Let's stop arguing and check our supplies,' Rob says, intervening before the argument worsens. He opens the back of the Land Cruiser and lifts out the basket of food and the cold box. But, hurrying round the company supermarket before leaving, he and June had bought only enough for an afternoon picnic – *pitta* bread, feta cheese, tomatoes and olives, biscuits and chocolate, and cans of cold Sprite and Pepsi. While June's brought a chocolate cake in the cold box and some sparking apple juice to celebrate Rob's birthday, there's only a litre bottle of water. They should be better prepared for the desert.

Almost noon and glancing up towards the warming sun, Rob remembers a report at the last Safety Coordinators meeting. Two Filipinos, new to the country, had driven out in their truck and broken down in the desert. Instead of waiting for rescue in the shelter of their vehicle, they'd set off walking. Several days later when they were found, the sun had blackened their faces so much, they were mistaken for Africans. That was in summer. This is winter, but it's still too easy to get lost and die out here in the Empty Quarter.

'Let's stay close to the truck,' Bill tells them. 'Then it's easier for a search party and planes to find us.'

'But you didn't leave a message.' Fahad's still furious. 'Nobody knows we're here.'

'Let's try the planks again,' Bill says. 'Under the front wheels this time.'

'You try.' Fahad steps back and flicks more grit from his chinos.

But June's shouting and waving from the crest of the dune as an engine's roar erupts through the desert air. Two Toyota trucks appear and stand poised on top of the dune as if observing them. Bill yells and waves towards the trucks, but Rob senses their vulnerability as Westerners un-armed and exposed here to bandits or terrorists. The men in the trucks still seem to be deciding, until finally they start forward, barrelling down the sand dune. Two young Saudis with rifles slung over their shoulders and an older grey-bearded driver are sitting in front of the first truck, while sheep are crowded into the back of the vehicle. The second pick-up is driven by another young Saudi and carrying several bags of what looks like animal feed or fertilizer.

'*Asalaamu aleikum*,' Bill calls to the Saudis. '*Alhamdullilah.* Welcome, *sideeki.*'

After exchanging courtesies, Fahad explains, and the young Saudis tie a rope from the Land Cruiser to the back of their half-empty pick-up truck. Reluctantly Bill gives up his driver's seat and the old Saudi takes the wheel. With furious engine-revving and sand-blasting, the men heave with their shoulders behind the Land Cruiser until, with shouts of *Alhamdullilah!* they manhandle it onto firmer ground.

Past noon and while June lunches inside the Land Cruiser, Rob eats with the other men beside the Toyota trucks, accompanied by piteous bleating from the sheep crowded in together. The Saudis and Bill dig into the picnic food and eat quickly using their hands, but Fahad, sitting beside Rob, eats fastidiously with his own plastic knife and fork, as if he were in a Kuwait City restaurant.

The young Saudis glance across, suspicious of the smart Kuwaiti in Western clothes, and seem reluctant to speak to him, but Bill makes them laugh with his attempts at Arabic conversation.

'He's swearing in Arabic,' Fahad tells Rob, not amused by such coarseness. 'You know Bill a long time?'

'Not really.' Rob realizes he hardly knows the big American. About six months together on North Camp, sharing interests in politics, archaeology, and TS Eliot. But that was years ago. Then there'd been their trip with Kamal to the desert caves near Al Hasa, where they'd wandered through the narrow passages, admiring the limestone stalactites and stalagmites of the Judas Cave. A welcome relief from the weekend routines of camp life, until Bill turned on Kamal for praising the 'noble' assassins of President Sadat. A nasty argument had broken out with Bill accusing the Egyptian of being a Muslim Brother and anti-American.

'Strange how these Americans and Saudis make friends,' Fahad says, glancing towards Bill and the Saudis laughing together. 'They think Allah watches over them and they are his *special* people.'

'Hey! *Shufti*' The grizzled Saudi patriarch struggles to his feet, brandishing his rifle. 'We are the Kink's tribe. If Shia in Qatif make trouble, if Khomeini come, we fight him to death.'

'*Wajid zain*, very good.' Bill applauds the old man. 'Khomeini, very bad. And Saddam Hussein, too.'

'Saddam?' The patriarch glances round, bewildered. Maybe he thinks Iraq and Iran are still at war. Maybe his sons haven't told him that Saddam, once praised as the modern Saladin, has become the new Satan. Reluctant to argue with an honoured guest, the old man sits down.

Lunch over, the brothers are keen to show their Western friends the family farm and their scientific irrigation system, a gift from 'the Kink'.

The patriarch also has a surprise. 'You are officer, Mr Bill. You come see my farm, and you know Stinger?' He grins, exposing his remaining yellow teeth. 'I have Stinger in my house. You come see.'

Bill's shocked. 'You mean Stinger missile?'

The patriarch smiles. 'We have new Stinger for safety. For when that devil Khomeini come.'

Surprised, Rob and Fahad look to each other, but the young Saudis are beaming with pride. Their father takes his old walking stick and holds it to his shoulder, aiming it towards the sand dunes across the horizon. 'Whoosh!' he calls and cackles with joy.

'You come to farm and see famous Stinger,' one of the sons says. 'Very beautiful.'

'But where did you guys get it?' Bill demands, standing up. 'Stingers are only for the US military.'

Shocked, the brothers exchange glances. The big American's voice was too loud, and their hospitality and friendship are cooling fast.

'Stinger is not for civilians,' Bill says. 'You must return it, to the Americans or the Saudi military.'

Fahad intervenes. '*Mafi muskallah*. No problem, my friends.' He touches Bill's elbow. 'We need to go.'

'No. These guys should know.' Bill turns again to the Saudis. 'If you return this Stinger to the military, they will reward you.'

The young Saudis say something to each other, which makes Fahad look concerned. 'OK, we go now,' he tells Rob and June. 'Let's get in the truck.'

'Let's go, Bill,' Rob repeats, clapping the American on the shoulder.

Fahad leads them in saying a brief, rather frigid farewell to the old Saudi and his sons and they get back into the Land Cruiser.

'These guys are angry with you Bill,' June says. 'Let's skedaddle.'

'*Yalla*. Let's go,' Fahad demands, and, still grumbling about Stingers, Bill starts off.

'But how did they get one of our Stingers?' he asks. 'They must have stolen it.'

'Are they following us?' Fahad turns to Rob who glances back towards the Saudis getting into their pick-up trucks.

'You can't trust these *bedu*,' Fahad says. 'They are uncivilized.'

'Didn't like the way the old guy kept looking at me,' June says. 'Like he wanted to add me to his harem.'

'They're driving off now,' Rob reports. 'But one of the trucks is following us.'

'I'll drive faster,' Bill says.

'No, keep a steady speed,' Fahad orders. 'And stay on the track. No more accidents.'

They reach the relative safety of a firm gravel track through the dunes and follow it until they come to a rusty oil drum like a roundabout marking the junction of several dirt tracks.

'Straight on,' Fahad says, and after a few kilometres, Rob's relieved to see that the truck following them has disappeared.

'Looks like they've gone in the other direction,' he says, and turns to Bill. 'So, what happened with your Stingers?'

'Some have gone missing. Problem is, we shipped in too much stuff, too quickly. Couldn't keep track of it all. Seems these desert sheikhs like to have one of these missiles as a fancy toy, a status symbol. We're offering rewards for the missing Stingers.'

'You'll be lucky,' June says. 'These guys will want to keep them. But what if they decide to fire them at us?'

'You heard them,' Bill says. 'They're King's people. They support us.'

'For now,' Rob adds. 'But what if terrorists get hold of these missiles?'

'They'd need special training.' Bill peers at the track ahead, but even he doesn't sound convinced.

Eventually they join a wider track leading through the sand dunes and drive across a barren salt flat towards a large mud brick fort surrounded by a chain-link fence and looking out over the lagoon. They park beside the fence and walk around, looking for a way in to explore the fort, but the gate's padlocked and barbed wire tops the fence.

'In Jordan and Egypt, they have museums and places for tourists,' Fahad says. 'They don't lock everything up and make fences like these Saudi.'

He still seems annoyed with Bill and lags behind as Rob reads aloud from the guidebook he borrowed from the library. 'Over two thousand years ago, this was the trading port for the lost city of Gerrha. It traded in spices and incense, frankincense and myrrh from Yemen and Oman. Pliny, the Roman historian, described Gerrha as five miles in circumference with towers built of square blocks of salt...'

'So, where is it now?' Bill turns to survey the salt flats and the sand dunes beyond. 'Like old Percy Bysshe Shelley says, 'Nothing remains. Boundless and bare, the sands stretch far away.' You guys know I studied English literature at college?'

'So that's why you're so sensitive, Bill,' June says.

'Sure. But look around you folks.' He moves his arm to encompass the barren landscape. 'The whole country would be like this if we hadn't come. No oil wells or shopping malls, no Mercedes. Just sand dunes and these salt flats, with the Bedouin jumping off their camels to pray five times a day. Nothing would ever happen, if we hadn't come with our old Yankee pioneer spirit. There'd just be archaeology, buried under the sand. So what's it say about this fort, Rob?'

'It was built by the Ottoman Turks.' He reads aloud from the guidebook: 'In 1922 King Saud, who'd recently unified Saudi Arabia, met the British here to negotiate the boundaries of his kingdom. They made an agreement defining the borders of Saudi Arabia with Kuwait and Iraq. The head of the British delegation, Sir Percy Cox, was advised by Gertrude Bell, the famous Arabist.'

'A woman!' June laughs. 'Thought we weren't allowed to do anything here, except have babies and look after you guys.'

'She worked with Lawrence of Arabia,' Rob says. 'And helped create Iraq, after the First World War.'

'A woman with *cojones*,' Bill says. 'Like your Mrs T, the Iron Lady.'

'They drew a line on the map.' Rob continues reading. 'From Kuwait and Iraq at the head of the Gulf, across to the Jordanian border with Saudi Arabia in the west. They also created a large neutral zone on the border with Kuwait to allow the Bedouin to move more easily with their sheep and camels.'

'You Brits sure knew how to get things done in those days,' Bill says. 'Draw a few lines on the map, some lines in the sand and leave the locals to get on with it.'

'So is that what we're fighting about?' June asks. 'Saddam doesn't agree with what you Brits decided years ago at this place in the middle of nowhere that nobody knows about. Well, excuse me. I gotta find the restroom.'

While she wanders off to find somewhere private, the men unload the Land Cruiser and collect firewood from the scattering of thorn bushes clinging to the salt flat.

'Seen your old friend Kamal recently?' Bill asks, as if in passing. 'Rick said they had to let his kid go because of heat from upstairs. But this tank farm break-in puts your old buddy back in the frame. He was in the Muslim Brotherhood and these guys are creating hell in Cairo right now. So what does Kamal have to say?'

For some reason, Rob feels obliged to defend himself. 'He just asked me for advice on his son's education.'

'Sure. But maybe you should advise him some more. Maybe to keep out of trouble. We need to drain this swamp of religious crazies with their audio tapes and troublemakers in Jeddah.'

June reappears and she and Rob stroll round the perimeter fence protecting the mud brick fort. June's looking for 'found objects' she can use for her *Desert Storm* picture and they scan the ground, picking up shells, fragments of pottery, and a small desert sand rose she slips into her shoulder bag. Then, standing together on the deserted beach and struck by the romantic setting, they gaze out across the lagoon, trying to imagine the clamour of this harbour as camel caravans were loaded and unloaded, and wooden dhows prepared to sail north to Mesopotamia or east to Persia and India.

'I'm leaving Rick,' June says at last. 'As soon as this war's over.'

Rob's startled. 'So what will you do?'

'Probably go to Santa Fe or Taos in New Mexico – I've got friends there and can work as an artist…maybe I'll go back to college as well. Hell, I'd even work in a bar just so I'm free to do my own thing.'

'But don't you have kids?' Rob says, thinking of Chris, his own son.

'Sure, but Kate's twenty three now and as grown-up as she'll ever be. And Rick will look after Danny who's going through military school.' She turns to Rob. 'Isn't there something you want to do in life? Instead of just working for the Man?'

He looks out across the shallow lagoon as if for inspiration, but nothing as romantic as June's artistic ambitions comes to mind. He feels condemned to be practical.

'Working for the Man has benefits, June. It's got us here to this place.'

'Sure, but we're in our forties, in our prime now…we've got to take our chances.' June squeezes his arm. 'Nothing to fear but fear itself, sweetheart.'

She turns to look back towards Bill and Fahad standing by the Land Cruiser. They seem to be arguing with each other.

'Better head back before Bill gets suspicious,' she says, hitching the bag of 'found objects' over her shoulder. 'He's Rick's best buddy.'

When they re-join the others, June presents Rob with an Elvis Presley musical Happy Birthday card and *Biograph*, a Bob Dylan compilation CD.

'Better not play this for Bill,' she tells Rob. 'He loves 'Masters of War.'

'Just more hippie bullshit,' Bill says but smiles as they celebrate Rob's fortieth with fizzy apple juice they pretend is champagne and the chocolate birthday cake that June swears she baked herself.

Fahad walks out into the wasteland for *maghrib* prayer and with the atmosphere chilling, darkness falls like a camera shutter. Rob lights the brush wood fire and, sitting beside June on her Navajo blanket and gazing into the flames, he begins to feel like they're children peering into the blaze whilst ghosts slowly rise up from the ruins beneath the salt flats and hover about them. Bill takes the flashlight, disappearing into the darkness for a pee, and at last they're alone.

'Do you think Bill's coming back soon?' Rob puts his arm round her waist.

'You mean is he making up with his boyfriend?' She bursts out laughing at his shock. 'Didn't you know sweetheart? Bill's gay.'

Rob realizes his naivety when June leans in to whisper. 'It's Bill's big secret. He'd kill me if he knew I'd told you.'

Embarrassed, Rob recalls the lingering touches on his shoulder and goodbye hugs when he and Bill finished playing squash together. He remembers the body of Bill's neighbor floating in the outdoor swimming pool one morning on North Camp. Was that it? Some gay argument?

'Bill loves you Brits. Fancy English poetry, tweed jackets and British Empire. He wants the US to have an empire as well, and play the hero. But you're shocked. OK, sweetheart?'

'OK.' He embraces her, feeling the length of her body against his, the dress rising up her olive-brown legs as he reasserts his masculinity, stroking his hand down her back.

She pulls away. 'No rush, sweetheart. We've got time. John Wayne's not coming home tonight.'

'Let's go for a walk, take the blanket,' he says.

She considers, playing with his hand in her lap. 'Bill would guess, and I don't know what he'd do. Rick's his old buddy...'

A light flashes from outside, beyond the fire circle and pointing towards them.

'You guys OK?' Bill calls from the darkness, lumbering back into the campfire light. How long has he been there, spying on them?

Frustrated, Rob takes the flashlight and goes for a pee himself. A hundred yards into the wasteland and he pauses but, challenged by the silence and sheer emptiness, the magnetic power of solitude, he walks further. He steps into a slight depression and puts down the flashlight to pee from its beam out into the darkness. Beneath his feet, he senses the weight of past civilizations, all those ancient lives and anxieties buried thousands of years ago under these salt flats and sand dunes encircling them. And all this too would pass – his fortieth birthday, this journey into the desert and a war that seemed so important and a turning point in his life. It would soon be over and forgotten. He can go forward, perhaps to a new life, or back to Fiona and Chris and carry on with his old life. It's getting time to decide.

He walks back towards the blazing fire, returning to Bill and June's voices in conversation. But before entering the firelight, he switches off his flashlight and lingers inside the darkness, eavesdropping on what sounds like an argument. He hears Rick's name but what are they arguing about? Is Bill warning June, threatening to tell Rick about them?

'You there, Rob?' Bill's standing up, looking out to see him, and Rob re-enters the campfire circle. He reclaims his seat on the blanket beside June and places his hand beside hers, fingers touching to regain contact.

A crackling sound, and Fahad's returned from prayer with his shortwave radio, adjusting the antennae for a clearer sound. Strangers' voices speaking Arabic intrude into the desert silence, and the young Kuwaiti announces, 'The Iraqi are attacking across the border. Their tanks are driving south.'

'Shit.' Bill says. 'The Arab radio's got it wrong as usual.'

'It's the BBC Arabic Service,' Fahad retorts. 'There's an armoured column. Sixty thousand Iraqis attacking near Khafji. *Yalla*. Let's go.'

'Sixty thousand!' Bill's incredulous. 'Bullshit. It's just enemy propaganda. What we call the fog of war.'

June scrambles to her feet. 'Some fog. It's on the BBC, Bill. We'd better hightail it out of here.'

Despite Bill's protests, they hurriedly pack and drive back, following the gravel track across the salt flats and through the high dunes, headlights beaming along their lifeline to the main highway.

19

Don't Get Mad, Get Even

31 January 1991 / 16 Rajab 1411   *19.50*

'Shit! What's this?' Light floods the Land Cruiser, forcing Bill to brake hard. A white jeep with searchlights on the roof is blocking the track onto the main highway.

'Police,' says Fahad. 'No problem, I'll speak to them.'

He jumps out and, following a brief animated conversation with two policemen in the glare of the jeep's headlights, he climbs back into the passenger seat.

'The *bedu* told the police about us. You shouldn't have threatened them, Bill. They said we were spies.'

'But I'm American and you're Kuwaiti.'

'They don't like Kuwaitis. We've got to follow the jeep to the police checkpoint.'

'And keep it shut Bill,' June says. 'That way we'll get out of this.'

'Hey, these guys stole one of our Stingers. What do you expect me to say? Help yourself?'

'Leave the talking to Fahad,' Rob says. 'We want to get home tonight.'

The white jeep turns back onto the highway and they follow it to the checkpoint they passed through in the morning: a scruffy one-storey police station beside a shuttered mini-market. As Fahad strides ahead leading them inside, Rob's surprised to hear an Englishman's voice. A lean bespectacled man wearing British army uniform is arguing with the sergeant sitting behind a desk.

'Hey, Clive. How you doin'?' June calls and she and the Englishman embrace, warmly and too long for Rob's comfort. Two Europeans in military uniform, who are playing cards on a wooden bench, stand up to kiss her on both cheeks. 'So here's the French Foreign Legion as well. What are you guys doin'?'

'We're heading north for the front line,' Clive says. 'Want to find out what's happening. But the police stopped us.' He shakes hands with Rob. 'Clive Fox, Middle East correspondent.'

'Rob Watson. I'm working for the oil company.'

'Hey, don't you guys know each other from university?' June says and the two men consider each other, Englishmen evaluating class and potential usefulness. Rob recalls the pushy student journalist reporting on Vietnam protests and university scandals for Fleet Street tabloids, a face still youthful and enthusiastic but now weathered under thinning grey hair.

'Your British accent,' says June. 'It's different from Rob's.' And the inferiority Rob felt at university beside the public schoolboy's confident drawl is fleetingly revived.

'Well,' says Clive, 'he's from Liverpool. A Scouser.' He makes partial amends by adding, 'Like the Beatles.'

'This sounds like an Old Boys' Reunion.' Bill turns from the police desk where he and Fahad are impressing the sergeant with their military importance. 'But what are you guys doin' dressed up like you're in the Service? The Iraqis might think you're real soldiers and shoot you.'

'We can't do our jobs properly with this pool system your military's set up,' Clive says. 'We're like hotel journalists hunting for scraps. So we're heading north for the front line. See what's really happening.'

'So you guys are going AWOL?' Bill says. 'I guess you journalists have to write your stories, but you get in the way of the war effort, let the enemy know what we're doing. Like all the smartass reporters we had in Vietnam.'

'So what are *you* doing here?' Clive asks. 'Charity work?'

'Sure, but the best kind of charity. We're helping the Saudis help themselves, with military OJT and mentoring programs.'

'OJT? Mentoring?' Clive raises his eyebrows at more American military bullshit.

'On-the-job training and coaching,' Rob says, irritated with Bill's addiction to acronyms and the Englishman's patronising sarcasm.

'So what are you training the Saudis for?' Clive asks. 'Bombing Iraq back to the Stone Age, interrogating prisoners…'

'We're trying to win this war, buddy.' Bill raises his voice. 'And we don't want wise-guy reporters shooting off their mouths, second-guessing and tying one hand behind our backs. The Cold War's over. We won it, despite you peaceniks and naysayers. And Eastern Europe's glad to be free. Don't you want the Arabs to be free?'

'Freedom!' The journalist sneers. 'Let's not kid ourselves. This war's all about oil, and you guys controlling the Gulf.'

'No, you listen, my friend.' Fahad turns from the desk sergeant. 'You people have your freedom but you don't respect it – you take it for granted. *Your* country hasn't been invaded and made into a prison. My family are still in Kuwait City hiding in their houses. We're a small country and all these years we give millions of dollars, jobs and big contracts to Palestinians and other Arab countries. Then Saddam invades and Arab leaders do nothing, except talk and think about what more they can steal from us. Only the Americans and British come to help. So we are thankful.'

'Look!' Rob points to the small TV perched on a shelf behind the police desk. 'The battle's going on for Khafji.'

The French journalists stop playing cards and everybody peers up at the screen to see a Marine officer break off his interview with CNN and run towards an artillery piece dug in behind sandbags and firing out over the wasteland.

'Looks like Saddam's caught you guys with your pants down,' Clive tells Bill.

'Hell, it's only a small border town. We abandoned the place and left it for the Saudis to take care of. It's got no military importance.'

Clive smiles. 'Maybe not to you guys. But it's important to the Saudis. It's their land. If they lose Khafji, the regime will be shamed in front of their own people and the whole Arab world.'

The phone's ringing on the sergeant's desk. He speaks to someone and then to Fahad who interprets. 'The police chief says that everybody go home. The journalists return to the International Hotel with a police escort.'

'For your safety,' the sergeant adds in English with a grin towards Clive.

'What if we don't want to go back,' Clive says. 'We're heading for the border.'

'OK.' Bill turns towards the police sergeant. 'Maybe our Saudi friends should take away your press cards and keep you safe in the cells tonight. How's about that buddy? Your choice.'

At last, they turn the corner by the floodlit ball field. But Rob's shocked to see a tall figure in uniform standing on the garden path outside June's bungalow. Rick's back. Did he know Rob was going on Bill's desert trip? Probably not, and the security boss looks surprised and then angry when Rob follows June down from the Land Cruiser's back seat, carrying the picnic basket in front of him as if for protection.

'Our meetings were cancelled with this attack along the border,' Rick tells Bill. 'Come in for a drink, buddy.'

'A quick one, Rick. But then we gotta get back to base, find out what's happening in Khafji.'

'I'd better go,' Rob tells June as he lays the picnic basket down inside the doorway.

'Just come in for a birthday drink,' she says.

Frustrated at the night ending this way, he follows her inside and fending off the mastiff's slobbering welcome, sits on the couch. CNN is reporting that thousands of Iraqis led by Soviet-built tanks are attacking along a twenty-five mile front. They've captured Khafji in a surprise attack and are fighting to hold onto it. Eleven US Marines are reported killed so far.

As Rob watches a succession of confusing reports and talking heads trying to make sense of them, he relaxes back on the couch, drinking a strong *sid* and Pepsi, and wondering how he and June can get together now. Maybe Rick will go back up north once this fighting's over. He and Bill are talking about weapons training for the security guards and June's showing Fahad her half-finished *Desert Storm* painting set up on an easel. She's put Rob's birthday present, Dylan's *Biograph*, on the CD player and, weary from today's journey and last night's patrol, he rests back listening to Old Bob moaning through 'Lay, Lady, Lay' and 'I'll Be Your Baby Tonight'. For a moment, closing his eyes, he drifts off back into the desert, dreaming of making love to June by the light of the wood fire, his gaze slowly zooming out until they become sand-blasted ancient lovers half-buried in the desert.

Startled, he wakes to silence. No music. Bill and Fahad have gone, and he's lying on the couch, with a heavy red blanket over him. June's stretched out on the couch opposite with her bare feet propped up on the arm, toenails varnished a flaming red. Rick's sitting beside her in a brown leather recliner, and watching him. Has Bill said something?

June notices he's awake. 'You were exhausted Rob. Snoring fit to blow the roof off. But we didn't want to disturb you.'

'Thanks.' He pushes aside the blanket and struggles to rise up from the deep-cushioned couch. 'Better go home.'

'How about a nightcap, birthday boy? Why don't you fix us another drink, honey?' June coaxes her husband, and drains her glass of green liquid.

'Okey dokey.' Clasping the arms of his recliner, Rick levers himself up, steadying as he looms above them in his blue security uniform, before heading into the kitchen.

June shifts, stretching out her bare legs along the couch. Even separated by this space, he feels her body taunting him. 'I want to sleep with you,' she slurs, whispering across.

'I do,' he mouths back but fearful of Rick hearing, glances towards the kitchen, listening for the clinking of ice into glasses.

'Tomorrow afternoon, sweetheart,' she slurs. 'Come for some nice English tea.' Rick reappears through the kitchen doorway. Did he hear?

But his face is set, handing Rob a fresh tumbler of *sid* and Pepsi. Straightening up on the couch, his back against a cushion, Rob takes a gulp of the black stuff. There's a rough metallic taste beneath the sweetness, but he's past caring. June settles back with a fresh glass of green liquid and Rob swallows more black stuff, before realizing he needs to piss. Must go to the bathroom. Yet somehow he can't get up. Another gulp and he makes a massive effort, pushing down with his hands and arms as they sink into the cushions, swinging his legs round, trying to straighten his back and heaving himself forward off the couch. At once he's falling as if in slow motion, his arm knocking magazines off the coffee table as he sprawls over the carpet. His head's whirling, the room dizzying around him. On his knees, he tries to crawl towards the door.

'I'll drive him home.' Rick's voice above and he feels himself being grabbed and dragged helplessly away from June, her face receding out of focus as his feet trail across the sitting room floor.

The screen door slams and he's bumped down a stone step into the chill evening air, the chirping chorus of cicadas in the garden. Beyond the white picket fence, he can see the floodlit ball field, the brown earth of the diamond, a meadow-green outfield – a vision of peace and tranquillity. But he can only stare across, his body feeling paralyzed, powerless to do anything. Rick grunts, lifting him up and manhandling him into the back of the truck, his head knocking against a metal jerry can stinking of petrol.

Rick's face peers down at him. 'I don't get mad, I get even. Stay away from my bitch, motherfucker.'

The back doors slam shut and Rob's in darkness. The engine cranks into life, the truck jerks forward and they roar off, banging over speed bumps as he rolls about the ridged metal floor, against the jerry can and bags of what smells like barbecue charcoal.

The truck pauses, then starts again, bounding over more speed bumps and along the road. He struggles to sit up, his hands grasping the wooden handle of something that feels like a spade. He must fight back, but fighting feels useless and if he fights, Rick will hurt him more. A screech of brakes and the truck halts. Rob pulls himself up onto his knees and grasps the handle of the spade with both hands. The back doors are opening and in the light Rick's leaning in to grab him. Rob swings the spade but too slowly and Rick grabs it, drags him out and dumps him onto hard tarmac. Bruised and winded, he looks up to find himself lying beside a traffic island of palm trees shifting against the night sky. Rick's looking down at him as if deciding what more punishment to inflict. A boot's placed against his chest and he curls up in anticipation. Rick steps back and waits so Rob thinks he's leaving, but then the kick doubles him up with a crushing pain in the ribs. Rick kicks him again and he cries out, pain shuddering through his body. He wriggles on the tarmac, desperate to escape the punisher.

But there's noise of another car coming, headlights sweeping across the courtyard. He must get up and defend himself, not just lie here. But now he hears doors slamming, Rick's truck roaring off and echoing into the distance.

Rob lies rigid with shock. Is something broken? His ribs? He moves his hands over his body and tries to soothe away the aching in his chest, waiting for it to subside. Slowly, gently he massages and struggles to recover his whole body and move with less pain. A few more minutes lying here and he'll get up, but when he tries, he crumples back onto the tarmac. He blacks out.

A large beetle's whirring around his ear and he wakes up, sick in his stomach. He's lying in front of what he realizes is his own house. Relieved, he wants to lie here longer and recover his strength but he's going to wet himself. Gritting his teeth to control the pain, he crawls on hands and knees towards the front door, the big Texas beetles blundering around the outside light.

The front door's locked and he fumbles in his pockets for the house key. It's gone. Probably dropped at June's or in the truck. But with the pressure in his stomach he can hear Cilla barking from inside the house, urging him on. He tries the side door to the garage, turning the handle. Miraculously, it opens, and Cilla's jumping up at him, licking his face, slavering her wet love over him as he stumbles through the garage and into the house. On his knees, he manoeuvres his body to crawl step by excruciating step, up the stairs.

The phone's ringing downstairs in the kitchen, but he can't answer it. At last, inside the bathroom he can sit down to piss and then spew into the lavatory bowl. Black sweet Pepsi, bits of chocolate cake and red tomato from the picnic, until he starts coughing out thin yellow bile. Rick must have given him undiluted *sid*, raw alcohol with impurities. Kneeling at the bowl to spit out the last dregs of bile, Rob knows two things for sure: Rick could have kicked him to death, and he'd better keep away from June before worse happens.

The phone's still ringing from downstairs and he realizes. It's probably Fiona calling to wish him a happy fortieth birthday.

20

The Firing Line

02 February 1991 / 18 Rajab 1411   05.15

Allahu Akbar, God is Great. Through the gloom, Al's peering into the community centre. Green emergency lights shine above the fire exit doors and onto Faisal and his *mujahid* brothers wearing dark *thawbs* and pointing their pistols at a crowd of people crying out and panicking. In the confined space, Faisal fires his gun, shots reverberating through the exhibition as people shout out, bodies falling beside the arts and craft display tables. People are trying to escape but their way's blocked by the *mujahid* at the exit doors. Faisal walks forward and kicks each body in turn to see if it moves. A teenage girl groans and he leans down to shoot her in the head, while Al can only watch, a powerless observer with his body leaden and paralyzed. What can *he* do?

He shifts and, with a start, wakes to find himself scrunched in the armchair where he fell asleep last night, watching television for news from Khafji. It's early morning and the shooting he can hear is from the TV: the National Guard crowding round Prince Sultan, their commander, and firing into the air to celebrate the town's recapture.

Al goes for a shower, gradually recovering from his bad night and nightmare about Faisal. It's too early to phone his wife and sons in Riyadh and he wishes they were here and rejoicing with him, jubilant that the battle for Khafji has ended with the National Guard victorious. Scores of Iraqi soldiers are kneeling down beside the main road with their hands on their heads, before waving and grinning with relief towards the camera as they're led away to POW camps. They've escaped death and injury and know they'll be fed in the camps.

TV film of the town shows a tall water tower pitted with bullet holes, shops in ruins from the artillery fire, and dead camels lying in the streets among the rubble. Burned out Iraqi tanks and armoured personnel carriers lie abandoned on the highway from Kuwait, remnants of what Saddam had called his great victory. The Americans supported the National Guard with helicopter gunships and artillery, but Saudi soldiers had fought house-to-house in defence of their own soil, defying the Iraqi invaders and Westerners like Rick who thought the Saudis wouldn't fight.

On his drive into work, Al sees men waving Saudi flags from their trucks and cars, other drivers honking their support. For this moment it feels like the country is united and this war could change everything. Some newspapers think there will be a *majlis*, a consultative council, women will have more freedom, and Shia like him, who've been loyal and withstood the Scud missiles, will have more chance of a good job and a better life for their families.

But at the Big House, the Security Chief is depressed at the abrupt departure of Maria, his Filipino secretary. She's fled to Jeddah with some girlfriends and it looks like he'll have to accept a male secretary in her place. Al tries to cheer him up with the recapture of Khafji and they look forward to the end of the war when the Chief promises they'll get back to normal. Despite his hopes for a *majlis* and more opportunities for the Shia, Al doesn't argue with the Chief's 'normal'. But he has to speak when his boss mentions Faisal's request for promotion.

'He still hasn't passed his exams or completed on-the-job training,'

Al says. 'And a doctor at the clinic is complaining. Faisal injured an Indian gardener when he questioned him.'

'An Indian gardener?' The Chief waves that aside. 'Who cares about gardeners? Maybe Faisal's too enthusiastic sometimes. Like Rick says, he's not a Boy Scout. But he didn't run away after the invasion and stayed with us. Faisal's done his duty.'

Al nods, recognizing that since the war started, the Chief and Rick have changed their minds about the previously 'stupid' Faisal.

'We'll see how he does,' the Chief decides as Rick comes into the office for the daily eight o'clock meeting. But it's a different-looking Rick this morning.

'What happened to your face?' The Chief indicates the long plaster under his deputy's eye. 'Looks like *you* were in Khafji.'

'Got into a fight with my old dog.' Rick sits down and dips his hand into the Chief's glass bowl of mini-Snickers. 'Tripped up over the old mutt.'

'An old dog?' the Chief says. 'My advice is get rid of it. Dogs are unclean and carry diseases. You checked your wound with the clinic?'

'Sure. It's OK.' Rick glances back through the door to the outer office. 'Hey, what's happened to Maria – where's the coffee?'

'She left yesterday for Jeddah. I couldn't stop her, Rick. She was too frightened of these Scuds.'

'So no coffee.' Disappointed, Rick grabs another mini-Snickers. 'Just got a call from the firearms instructor. He's on his way from the base. Class starts at nine so we'd better head over to the Training Centre.'

'But Rick, can we trust these guys with guns?' the Chief asks yet again. Al gave him the list of security guards for training over a week ago, but even now the Chief's having second thoughts. 'What if they shoot the wrong guys?'

'We picked the most reliable guards,' Al says. 'Men with experience, who we can trust.'

But the Chief remains unconvinced. 'Do we need to give them live ammunition?'

'Chief, we've got to train these guys,' Rick says. 'Unless you want the US army to take over security, like they've taken over the tank farm. Maybe they should guard the Main Gate, as well.'

'No, we don't want that,' the Chief decides. He couldn't face the shame of Americans taking over the main gate and his empire diminishing any further. 'Go ahead with this training. But be careful, Rick. You stay with these guys and make sure there's no accidents.'

In the Training Centre's classroom, Al helps out with translation as a stocky middle-aged Texan, gives the firearms orientation. He uses the overhead projector, monotonously reading out from a stack of old black-and-white transparencies listing Colonel Cooper's and NRA rules for shooting, the features of the Beretta M9 semi-automatic, and the Weaver shooting position. To keep the guards interested, Al tries to make his own voice and translation lively. But he wonders – how could this Texan expert make something so dangerous sound so boring?

The range master's a Vietnam vet like Rick and they speak the same language, occasionally livening up the presentation with jokey references to grunt life in Saigon and knowing comments about the army's switch to this new Beretta pistol. According to the Texan, some of the Marines don't want to replace their old Colts with the Beretta, and he and Rick argue the pros and cons of the change. Faisal and the guards look confused but impressed at the same time by the veterans' experience and the technicalities.

After the classroom session and coffee break, the Texan leads his class out to the shooting range for gun familiarization and shooting practice. The guards are nervous and excited by the victory at Khafji, and the war seems much closer now they're putting on shooting glasses and ear defenders and handling their new Beretta pistols. Standing under a canvas shelter on the shooting range, they gather in a circle round the Texan for the gun safety briefing. Using Rick as a model, the range master describes how to hold, grip and point the Beretta.

'Wait for the perfect moment,' he says. 'That moment when you've lined up the cross hairs. Let the gun tell you when to pull the trigger. And aim for your target's head, the head of that black silhouette over there with the red dot in the centre.'

As Al translates, Rick and the range master demonstrate, step by step, the Weaver position shown on the orientation transparencies.

'Stand with your feet a shoulder width apart,' the Texan says. 'The leg on your strong side should be slightly back, like you're a boxer. Then angle your support arm's shoulder towards the target. Bend your knees like this. Keep your body weight slightly forward and hold the gun using both hands. And remember – keep your elbows bent with the support elbow pointing downward. Got it?' Al translates and checks the nods of understanding around the group.

'I can shoot with one hand,' Faisal boasts.

'No,' the Texan says. 'When you use two hands you keep your balance and stability. You increase your speed and accuracy.'

Usually, Faisal argues with trainers, especially Americans. But today, possibly thinking of promotion, he nods as the instructor continues his demonstration.

'Whatever you do,' the Texan says, 'don't stand sideways, and try shooting with one hand like in the old cowboy films. Don't try to look like John Wayne.'

As Al translates and explains about the veteran film star, he looks towards Rick, tempted to point out similarities of physique and movement. But he can't risk the guards laughing at their boss. Rick's already looking injured and weakened with the plaster on his face, and could easily get angry.

'Hold your steady position and keep a good sight picture,' the Texan says. 'Control your breathing and squeeze the trigger firmly. Like this.' He fires towards the distant target and scores a near bullseye in the black silhouette's head.

'OK.' Encouraged by the success, he warns them. 'Practicing just once or twice on this range isn't enough. You need to practice, practice, and practice some more. Because what you do in your training and on the range is what you'll do when you're in action. When the adrenaline starts flowing and you aren't thinking clearly, you need what we call muscle memory. They're the habits we've drilled into your body and mind on the firing range. OK, guys, now it's your turn.'

Moving from lane to lane, Rick and the range master coach each guard in turn, before they shoot at the black enemy silhouettes about a hundred yards away. Finally, the Texan declares the firing line hot and the whole class, kitted up with ear defenders and shooting glasses, shoots towards the targets.

Through his glasses, Al focuses on the black silhouette, with scoring rings circling it. He holds the Beretta with both hands, squeezes the trigger and feels the recoil shudder down his arms and through his shoulders. But the bullet hole's too far from the red dot at the centre of the head. He practiced a lot on the training program and knows he's good enough, but still he feels rusty and under pressure from the Texan's critical eye as he walks past. Aim, and Al fires again, the shot closer. Next shot and he opens his mouth in a whoop as he hits the red dot and attracts the Texan's appreciation.

He's shooting well now with a tight grouping round the head, but who's he really shooting at? The Iraqis if they break through and drive south? But that's unlikely. Terrorists? But who are they? These Palestinians, Sudanese and Saudi Afghans the Chief keeps talking about? Who *should* he really be shooting at? Maybe the royal princes jetting round Europe and America from one nightclub and casino to another? The Chief, who seems to have forgotten about *his* promotion? Still, since the invasion, he's become friendly, sometimes asking for advice. Maybe, after the war, he'll get promotion and more money to educate his sons.

Al glances at Rick shooting in the lane beside him, the long plaster on his face covering the injury from his dog. His gaze is fixed on the target as he shoots, and Al senses that John Wayne's absorbed in his own world. So who's he shooting at? Saddam Hussein and the Iraqis? Boy Scouts like Jimmy Carter who lost Iran and Rick's good job there? Or maybe the Mexican 'illegals' he complains are invading Texas? He's often an angry man but he's smiling now, enjoying this shooting practice.

In the lane on Al's other side, Faisal, paunchy in white shirt and denim jeans, is correctly using his two hands and firing confidently. Unlike his other training, it doesn't look like he'll fail and have to repeat this. For now he's disciplined, his face grim with determination as he scores hits around the silhouette's head. Walking past, the Texan range master calls Faisal a sharpshooter and offers more expert suggestions.

But who is Faisal firing at? The Indian gardener injured during his interrogation? The Canadian doctor who complained, or Al who reported it to Rick and the Chief? Nothing's happened yet, except Faisal keeps scowling at Al and avoids speaking to him. After his nightmare, Al realizes that Faisal's a very dangerous man.

Further along the firing line, the other security guards are following the Texan's instructions and shooting well. Who might *they* be firing at? The Iraqi invaders in Khafji? Maybe their new Pakistani boss, who's imposing strict timekeeping and discipline at the gates? But they admire their new boss as a very austere and religious man.

The guards are solid enough, Al decides, but what happens if there's a major terrorist attack? Will they stand or run? And what will he do?

The Texan halts, removes his ear defenders and waves his arms, signalling everybody to stop firing. Alert sirens are wailing out across from the Big House and the nearby hospital.

'Scud Alert. Remove the magazines. Unload your guns. Open the action. Place your weapons on the table behind you for me to collect.'

Al shouts out a translation and the guards rush to obey, with a flurry of unloading, and a clatter of weapons on the wooden trestle table.

'Hands in the air!' the Texan shouts and glances round to check. 'OK. The line's cold. Now let's get outta here. Back to the training centre.'

The sirens are still wailing but there's no real urgency. No one wants to look frightened and there've been too many false alarms recently. Glancing up at the sky for signs of a Scud, they hurry away from the range towards the shelter of the Portakabin training centre where the Indian clerk is shouting to Rick about a message to call the airbase. Back in the classroom, the guards follow the Texan's instructions to put on their respirators, but it's a false alarm and soon the sirens are sounding the All Clear. The Texan decides they might as well eat before the afternoon practice session.

'What do we eat?' Faisal asks.

'We've got some delicious MREs specially for you guys.' The Texan grins. 'We'll heat 'em up in the microwave. Then get back to practice.'

'We have our own food' Faisal says. 'And it's *salah*. Prayer time.' He glances round to the other guards.

'Sure, but we gotta get on with shooting practice.' The Texan assumes his officer's tone. 'We've lost too much time already.'

'We have prayer time now,' Faisal says, as if reprimanding an irreligious Muslim or atheist. 'We go for *salah*.'

Recently, Al's noticed that Faisal's become more publicly religious, strictly adhering to prayer times, telling the guards to follow him, and always accompanying the Chief to the mosque. Is that Dr Eissa's influence?

'But we're wasting practice time.' Exasperated, the Texan looks to Al for support.

'No, we go for prayer.' Faisal glances round, ensuring the guards will follow him.

'It's OK,' Al tells the Texan. 'They can go now.' He turns to the guards. 'Come back at one o'clock.'

As the men leave, Rick returns from his phone call. 'That was Bill Eliot at the base. There's been a terrorist attack on an army bus in Jeddah. Shooting and some casualties. Not clear yet if anybody's killed.'

'Did they catch the terrorists?' Al asks.

'Zilch. But Bill reckons there'll be more attacks – maybe something here. We need to give weapons training to more of our guys.' As if this is good news, he claps Al and the Texan range master on the shoulder. 'Hey, looks like we'll be using these new Berettas after all.'

21

Ashes

08 February 1991 / 24 Rajab 1411   11.25

Friday morning and Rob's returned from cleaning his car at the camp garage when Al phones.

'I've recommended you for special weapons training,' he says. '*Inshallah*, you'll learn to use this new Beretta.'

'I don't want a gun,' Rob says, feeling virtuously British.

'There was a shooting in Jeddah *sideeki*. Terrorists might attack the camp.'

'I don't want a gun. There are too many accidents.'

'But you'll be safer. Think about it, my friend.' Al rings off. Soon after, Bill Eliot calls, wanting to come over for 'a decent shower' and to visit the Big Man. Who's that Rob asks, and the American mentions the 'RC meeting' – code for Friday evening's Catholic Mass.

'I'm looking for some old-style purification,' Bill says when he arrives, carrying a bag of Jack Daniel's wood chips. 'These will turn your *sid* into good old American whiskey.'

'Thanks, Bill. But why purification? What have you done?' Rob asks.

He suspects that Bill told Rick something about him and June after their desert trip, but doesn't expect him to admit it. While he's recovered from Rick's beating that night, Rob still doesn't know what happened to June.

'Speak to you after my shower.' Bill says, warding off Cilla's affectionate jumping up at him, as he heads upstairs to the bathroom.

While he's waiting for his visitor, Rob phones Fiona. She's delighted with the early Valentine's Day bouquet he sent her, but frightened by news of Saddam's threat to use a 'dirty bomb'. Rob tells her not to take it too seriously. It's just a bluff, but secretly he wonders: wasn't that what the Japanese thought in 1945?

Fiona's looking forward to him coming home after the war and for once he doesn't argue but listens to her worrying about Chris at university and some decorating that needs to be done in the house. She's reminding him that ordinary life is going on in the world outside. People hear about Scuds and bombing on the radio or TV, but now it's several weeks old, the war seems to have faded into the background. There's an occasional flurry of excitement when British pilots are shot down and captured, Iraqi civilians are accidentally killed, or seabirds get caught up in the oil spill. But *Coronation Street* and *EastEnders* probably seem more relevant to most people. He's not sure whether to be amused or angry at being largely forgotten.

'I've got to go and get ready for church,' he says, knowing that will please her.

'Oh, good. But promise you'll start looking for jobs here. I think it's living in Saudi that's made me depressed. Are you still going out on that night patrol?'

'Yes,' he has to admit.

'You should stop. It's too dangerous. You're not a security man.'

The sound of showering stopped some time ago and he can hear Bill coming downstairs and into the sitting room to be enthusiastically welcomed by Cilla.

'OK. I'll start applying for jobs in the UK,' Rob promises, and puts down the phone.

'What's that I hear?' Bill asks. 'You quitting? Don't desert us now, buddy. Can't leave us in our hour of need.' Wearing a fresh white shirt under his cord jacket, he sits down on the couch and Cilla pushes up to his knees to be stroked.

'I'm not leaving yet. Just looking around,' says Rob, joining them in the sitting room. 'But I want to quit these night patrols. I'm not really a security man and don't want to learn how to use a gun. I just need a few good nights' sleep.'

Bill rubs Cilla's ears. 'Hey, we're all security now. Better get used to it, buddy. And it's good to get yourself some weapons training. Could be a terrorist attack any time.'

Rob feels too tired to argue. 'OK. I'll think about it.' He wonders when and how he can ask Bill about June, find out how she is.

'So, had a good shower?' he asks.

'Great. Makes a difference when the shower's powerful and you don't have to share a bathroom with all these other guys. So that's my physical purification before the battle.'

'Battle? You going somewhere?'

'Sure. The AWACS guys have invited me along for a ride over the Gulf.' Bill can't keep the excitement out of his voice, at getting into the action and putting his life on the line.

'So you made your will?' Rob says jokingly, but then realizes how crass that sounds.

'Sure.' Bill's matter of fact. 'I keep it up to date, my friend. Don't you?'

Embarrassed, Rob realizes that he doesn't. Why? Carelessness. He didn't have much time when he was home. Or was it fear? What if a Scud dropped or someone shot him? What would happen to Fiona and Chris?

But now Bill's turned to the TV muttering in the background. 'Hey, look at this.'

Rob increases the volume as CNN shows London under a Christmas-card covering of snow, the stately Houses of Parliament overlooking the

Thames. This morning the IRA fired a mortar from a Transit van parked on the Embankment, and almost hit 10 Downing Street where John Major, the new Prime Minister, and his Cabinet were meeting to discuss the Gulf war. One shell exploded in the back garden, making a crater several feet deep. The Cabinet ducked for cover beneath a heavy wooden conference table and from there, Major had suggested, 'I think we'd better start again somewhere else.'

Bill bursts out laughing. 'I think we'd better start again. Love that British *sangfroid*. Churchill would have been proud.'

Rob laughs, too, but he's shocked. Preoccupied with this war, he'd forgotten about the IRA and Northern Ireland. Terrorists could strike and kill when you least expected it.

CNN's report ends with a military expert judging the attack as a near miss. Even a slight change in the mortar's trajectory and the shells could have destroyed Downing Street and wiped out the British Cabinet.

'Sure, a near miss,' Bill says. 'Baghdad Radio's broadcasting coded messages asking terrorists all over the world to attack us. And more stuff's gone missing from the port. A bunch of Bangladeshi drivers and guards have gone AWOL. They're probably back home now, setting up businesses with the proceeds.'

'What kind of stuff's missing?' Rob asks.

'Weapons, munitions. The guys are checking and double-checking.' Bill glances at his watch. 'OK. Time for us to go see the Big Man. See what He has to say.'

They're in church, or what's officially known as the 'RC morale group', meeting in the Junior High School gym. The wooden floor's marked out as a basketball court with rows of raised wooden benches along one side and a giant electronic scoreboard overhead. The mainly Filipino choir with Rody the garage mechanic, prominent in the front row, are practicing the hymns before Mass.

Bill glances back towards the gym's entrance doors. 'I keep thinking the *muttawa* will break in and drag us off to jail.'

'Don't worry,' Rob says. 'You've got military ID and the company will protect us.'

Gradually, the congregation carrying their gas mask satchels are trickling in for the Ash Wednesday Mass: Filipino technicians and nurses, a few Christian Arab and Indian families, a sprinkling of Europeans and Americans. Rob notices his secretary Patience with her husband and two sons, and raises his hand in greeting. She's probably noticed his absence from church since Fiona left, but hasn't mentioned it at work. She's still fearful of a Scud attack and upset by Krieger's refusal to give her extra leave days to return to India with the children. Yet like most people she knows that she and her husband can't afford to resign. What would happen to their sons' education and job prospects?

Bill's kneeling on the wooden floor to pray and Rob kneels down beside him and closes his eyes. He tries to focus on Fiona and her phone call, to look forward to being at home and going with Chris to see the Reds play at Anfield. But the anxieties of trying to find another job in Liverpool and signing on at the dreaded Job Centre keep intervening. He opens his eyes and sees that Bill's sitting back on his chair and looking to him.

'So how's our old friend Kamal?' he asks, as if continuing a conversation.

'He's tied up with this oil spill response and the clean-up on the coast.' Rob's wary. 'I haven't seen much of him recently.'

Bill lowers his head and tone. 'You advised him on his son's education and were there when they arrested his kid. Aren't you still buddies?'

'I told you. He's busy with the oil slick up north and I've got my own job to do, Bill. As well as another bloody patrol tonight.'

'Swearing in church?' The American smiles but persists. 'See if Kamal needs more advice. Find out what's he thinking, who his friends are. His father-in-law's a big contractor. He's tendering for some important contracts with us and we need to check.'

His remaining words and the choir's hymn are drowned out by the roar of jets flying low overhead and making the gym building tremble.

'Onward, Christian soldiers,' Bill says as the roar recedes and the choir resume practising.

Reluctant to respond on Kamal, Rob asks, 'So how long do you think this bombing's going to last?'

'As long as it takes to shape the battlefield.' Bill repeats the official line but then confides. 'Cheney and Powell are visiting Riyadh this weekend, deciding what to do next. It's probably too early for the ground offensive into Kuwait.'

'But this bombing's destroying the Iraqi bridges and electricity system,' Rob says. 'Too many civilians are being killed and injured.'

'Better than hundreds of our guys finishing up in body bags,' Bill says. 'This is war, my friend. Shit happens. We can't avoid collateral damage when we're fighting the bad guys.'

The choir start singing the entrance hymn and the priest, an Irish-American leprechaun of a man who the Filipinos call Father Peanuts, begins the Ash Wednesday Mass. For security reasons, no Mass or hymn books are distributed and the congregation follow the service on a projector screen. Rob joins in the opening prayer with its statement that 'our struggle is against the forces of evil'. But who are the forces of evil? Saddam Hussein, of course, and the Iraqi soldiers terrorizing Kuwait. But there's also this bombing with its civilian 'collateral damage'. He avoids joining in the chorus to the psalm: 'O wash me from my guilt and cleanse me from my sin'. Guilt and sin make him think too much about June.

Father Peanuts introduces the homily by telling a Charlie Brown comic story. This chirpy, upbeat approach leads him into the particularly American theme of self-improvement rather than the traditional British gloom of Ash Wednesday. Rob drifts into thinking more about going home and where he can get a job, until it's time to put money into the collection, join in the Lord's Prayer and shake hands with Bill and the people around them.

As the choir sing 'One Bread, One Body', Bill steps out to join the procession trooping forward to receive the Eucharist of pitta bread pieces and grape juice. Rob watches the Filipinos, Westerners, Arabs and Indians moving forward as the choir sing, 'we are one body in this one Lord'. The priest is blessing and tracing a cross of ash on the back of each hand while Rob remains rooted to his chair. It's been a long time since he's made confession and he doesn't want to think about June. He tries to focus only on Fiona and Chris, but finds it too difficult. Rick's beating should have taught him a lesson but he can't go up until he's sorted himself out. Yet maybe this might help him. Patience and her husband are passing with their sons, and she smiles towards Rob, making space for him, and at the last minute he joins them, walking forward together as one body.

'Remember, man, you are dust and to dust you will return.' The priest draws the cross of ashes on the back of Rob's hand before he returns and kneels down beside Bill. Finally, at the end of Mass, Father Peanuts warns everyone not to display the cross on their hands if they go downtown in case they attract the attention of the *muttawa*. Christian soldiers might be defending Saudi Arabia but religious intolerance must still be appeased.

'*I'm* not wiping *my* hand,' Bill says, sitting back up beside Rob who feels the same defiance at being dictated to by *muttawa*. 'The church is too passive, too goody-goody. We need to deal with evil and the bad guys – give them hell-fire. And in this war, we need a clear winner and a clear loser.'

Rob waves goodbye to Patience and her family and as they crowd out of the gym, Bill spots the taxi waiting in the car park.

'That's mine,' he says, shaking hands. 'But remember what I said about Kamal. Check how he is and give me a call.'

'OK. So have you seen anything of Rick and June?'

'No, but things aren't great between them,' Bill says. 'June quit her job at the Information Bureau and Rick's pissed off with her. She's a loose cannon, my friend, and needs to be tied down before she does more damage.' He nods, reinforcing the point and looks at Rob as if daring him to say something.

But Rob switches the subject. 'So when are you flying in the AWACS?'

'Very soon. Wish me luck.' Bill embraces his friend and marches over to the waiting taxi.

'Good luck,' Rob calls out and suddenly wonders if he'll see Bill again. The AWACS should be safe enough but as Bill says, shit happens like that IRA attack, usually when you least expect it.

Ten thirty and his cigarette break over, Rob walks down the bluff overlooking the base. He skirts the shallow crater in the ground where the flaming Scud and Patriot fragments fell early in the war. If he'd stayed here longer that night, maybe for a second cigarette, he'd have been incinerated by burning fuel.

It's time now to check in with Al, tell him Fiona's worried about his safety, and that he's leaving the night patrol. He calls Al, but before he can speak about quitting, Al asks, 'Have you changed your mind on the weapons training?'

'Sorry, Al. I've thought about it and now I want to quit the patrol.'

'Why? What's wrong, *sideeki*? Maybe we can help? Change your schedule.'

'Sorry, Al. My wife's very worried and I just want a few good nights' sleep.'

'But we need guys like you, *sideeki*. Men we can trust.' Al's exasperated. 'And your department sponsored you.'

'That's news to me.' Rob's surprised. He'd volunteered out of some sense of patriotism and company loyalty, but now Al's saying his department (Kamal, Krieger?) wanted him to do this job. If so, they hadn't bothered to tell him or given him time off.

'You'll have to speak to your management, my friend.' Al's tone has become official. 'Maybe they'll give you some days off. But if you leave us now, they'll have to find a replacement. We don't have enough people and after this IRA mortar attack, Rick says we could get copycat attacks.'

'OK, I'll speak to my boss.' Rob's angry and frustrated with himself for having volunteered so easily and with more hours of patrolling tonight, he wants to go home to bed. He switches on the car radio, tuning into the comfort of the Easy Listening station with DJ Jerry reviewing the pop charts and Elton John gently warbling about sacrifice.

Rob drives to the lake, around the electrical substation, and along the track to the perimeter fence and the road. The alert sirens start up, wailing across from the airbase, and on the radio DJ Jerry's reciting civil defence instructions. Rob drives up towards the camp garage but ahead, under the streetlights, he sees two track-suited figures emerging from beside the building. Have they broken in? Now they are jogging down towards him. It's past eleven o'clock. There's no official curfew but people shouldn't be around at this time.

He stops the patrol car at the side of the road and watches the two runners caught in his headlights and coming closer. Should he tell Al over the radio? But as they approach, he recognizes the shorter one in a grey tracksuit – it's Ibrahim, the Sudanese engineer in his department. Relieved, he gets out of the car.

'Hi, Ibrahim. What are *you* doing here?'

The Sudanese slows to a halt. 'We're keeping fit,' he says. 'Can't sleep with these sirens. But it's easier after a good run.'

'I didn't know you'd moved onto camp.' As Ibrahim's boss, Rob should have known or been informed. Why hadn't Ibrahim told him?

'I moved into a friend's place for safety,' the Sudanese says. 'Remember, my wife went back to Khartoum to have our baby. And Krieger stopped me going home with her.'

Rob turns to Ibrahim's bearded companion who's wearing a smart green tracksuit and running on the spot as if determined not to miss a moment's exercise. The young man steps forward, extending his hand. 'Hi, I'm Saeed. Good to meet you, sir. You're with the Security department?'

'Not really.' Rob warms to the young Saudi's good English and friendly smile. 'I work with Ibrahim. But I volunteered to help Security.'

'I'm sure the company appreciates it, sir. We all have to help when we suffer with these big oil spills and Scud attacks.'

A roar and they turn towards the airbase as a formation of four planes rises up over the perimeter fence. Rob stands beside the two joggers watching the fighter jets climb, the gold and purple flare of afterburners blazing behind

182

them, and gradually receding into the night sky.

'These bombers are killing too many people,' Ibrahim says, and Rob's tempted to agree.

'They should bomb this devil Saddam,' Saeed says, taking his friend's arm. 'But we know the devil only dies at his appointed hour.'

The wailing from the base pauses, before the sirens start up again with a calmer tone.

'That's the All Clear,' Rob says. 'The Scuds are probably heading somewhere else, maybe for Riyadh or Israel.' He takes out his notebook. 'What's your new address and telephone number, Ibrahim?'

'Why do you want to know?' The young Sudanese is annoyed, probably still upset about his pregnant wife having to leave.

'*Mafi muskallah*. No problem, Ibrahim.' Saeed puts an arm round his friend's shoulder, smoothing things over. 'Your boss needs to know so he can contact you in an emergency.'

Reluctantly Ibrahim gives the information for Rob to write down in the light from his patrol car.

'OK. We're heading straight home. Nice to meet you, sir.' Saeed waves cheerfully and the two joggers start off again, running down towards the wasteland.

Rob watches in his rear view mirror as they turn the bend in the road, jogging back towards the illuminated block of bachelor housing. For a few moments before he'd recognized Ibrahim, he'd felt isolated and vulnerable on tonight's patrol. Maybe he'd rejected Al's weapons training too quickly. Maybe he needs to think about a gun.

22

Fire and Forget

15 February 1991 / 01 Sha'ban 1411   16.50

Subha Allah. Glory to God, Ibrahim repeats, fingering his ebony prayer beads and trying to calm himself before he has to ask again. 'When are the brothers coming?'

'I told you.' Saeed's irritated. 'Before *maghrib* prayer. It's a long drive from Riyadh. They might be delayed at a checkpoint.'

That's what Ibrahim's worried about, as they wait in the white Transit van directly beneath the aircraft flight path and concealed among the trucks parked outside the vehicle workshop and transport café. Friday evening and the gates of the workshop are padlocked, metal shutters down over the café's doors and windows.

'We needed only two things to beat the Russians,' Saeed reminisces. 'The holy Koran and these Stingers.' He flicks through the manual's pages. 'And now we've got our own Stinger.' He's wearing his lucky *pakol*, the black woollen beret he brought back from Afghanistan.

'You sure our brothers know the way?' Ibrahim asks.

'They have a map. And I met them here once when they came to visit Dr Eissa.'

Ibrahim wasn't at that meeting but he remembers the evening in Jeddah, only a month ago, sitting in the coffee house on the Corniche with the two Afghan veterans. The heavy and shaggy bearded man who sacrificed his arm for the *jihad* had looked as if nothing but death could stop him. The quiet, mild-looking one, who'd fired a Stinger and shot down a Russian helicopter, looked similarly determined. They would get here if they could.

Five o'clock and the afternoon sun's still shining outside as the news comes on the car radio giving more horrific details about the Baghdad shelter bombing. This morning Ibrahim had witnessed the nightmare on TV – women's voices wailing through the dawn as stretcher parties stumbled across smoking ruins, the desolation dimly lit by showers of sparks from firemen's blow-torches cutting through tangled metal to reach the bodies. Over four hundred women and children sheltering from Crusader air strikes had been slaughtered, their bodies torn apart and incinerated with arms, legs and even heads scattered like lumps of charcoal in the ruins.

Yet in Riyadh, the American generals are still claiming the shelter was a military command and control centre, nuclear-bomb proof with its reinforced concrete walls. They showed video of a laser-guided smart bomb homing in on the shelter's weak point and snaking down through a ventilation shaft to explode in the crowded bunker below. The generals kept repeating 'command and control centre', saying that civilians shouldn't have been sleeping there, and maybe they were being used as human shields.

From the beginning, the Crusaders have pretended this is a clean hygienic war with few human casualties or messy deaths. Yet this massacre of innocents is too bloody for the world to ignore and at last people are waking up. The radio news reports that King Hussein of Jordan has condemned the bombing and announced several days of national mourning. Hundreds of demonstrators have marched on the American embassy in Amman and Egyptian students are protesting in Cairo against

Mubarak's support for the Americans. There are even more anti-war demonstrations in Europe and America.

Sickened by the massacre, Ibrahim switches over from the news but there's stupid Country and Western music – some bitch singing about DIVORCE – and he switches the radio off. Saeed sometimes listens to this American trash, a reminder of his time at university in Texas, but now he's busy studying the Stinger manual.

Ibrahim keeps fingering through his prayer beads. *Alhamdullilah.* Praise to God, he repeats. There's nothing to do but pray and wait until the *mujahid* arrive from Riyadh to fire this Stinger missile.

Earlier, he felt the lorry park was deserted, but with the window slightly open and evening drawing in, he's beginning to hear noises. The drone of traffic from the airport highway has diminished to a steady hum, but now he can hear sounds closer and beneath the van. As the light fades, rats are emerging, scuttling around under the trucks and vans. A rusty oil drum overflowing with food waste and white Styrofoam cups stands beside the café veranda and through the gloom, he can see a rat emerging and jumping down with something in its mouth.

Droning overhead and he glances up. Crusader jets returning from raids over Iraq and Kuwait are descending to land at the airbase. He's heard that the pilots call themselves 'Top Guns' after some Hollywood movie, and the bomber that killed the innocents in Baghdad probably flew from here. These young men taking off in their multi-million-dollar planes to kill poor Muslims probably return to gorge on Big Macs and French fries, cheesecake and endless varieties of ice-cream. They listen to that obscene prostitute, Madonna, and prancing creatures like Michael Jackson, lost in the pagan and corrupt world of *jahiliyya.*

But he must think of less depressing things. At least Muna and his own family are safe at home in Khartoum. In the office yesterday, he heard Rob telling Patience he'd sent flowers home to his wife, and the Westerners were talking stupidly and joking about Valentine's Day. Despite his scorn, he thought of phoning Muna, so they could talk together and plan for their baby son. But Security are probably listening for calls to the Sudan and he decided not to risk it. Majid had fled after being taken in for questioning, and Ibrahim's still afraid Security might come for him, too. Yet Saeed had reassured him. He'd spoken to a friend in Security and Ibrahim's name had been deleted from what they call the Watch List.

So what are Muna and his family doing tonight? It's the same time, past five o'clock in Khartoum, and Muna and his mother should be preparing dinner in the kitchen. Do they talk about him, or is his absence taken for granted now? The baby's due in April, and he's determined to go home for his first son's birth and the Eid celebrations.

He glances over towards the airport highway. A continuous flow of headlights, but still no car, no lights turning off down this track to the lorry park.

'What time did the brothers leave Riyadh?' he asks Saeed.

'They called about nine o'clock this morning. They should be here by now.'

'What if they don't come?' Ibrahim raises the difficult question. 'Shall we take the Stinger back to your uncle's warehouse? We can use it later. Maybe our brothers have an accident?' He knows these Saudis, like Saeed, drive too fast and are always killing themselves and other people in road crashes.

'OK...' Saeed glances at his watch. 'If they don't come, *I* could fire this Stinger. The Afghans were just simple peasants without our technical training. And even they learned how to fire Stingers.'

'But they had *some* training.' As a technical instructor and safety engineer, Ibrahim's sceptical. He's seen too many careless mistakes, too many stupid accidents in gas plants and refineries because people hadn't done the training.

'I had special weapons training in the camps,' Saeed says. 'The Stinger's a simple fire and forget weapon. You just need to aim and fire, and it locks onto the heat from the plane's exhaust.'

Sounds simple, but Ibrahim's not sure. Yet how can he argue with this veteran *mujahid?*

'Let's wait,' he says. 'Our brothers should come soon and you said one of them is an expert.'

'He shot down a Hind,' Saeed says. 'A Russian helicopter gunship. But I'll check through the instructions again.'

He turns back to the manual while Ibrahim gazes towards the airport highway, willing the two brothers to arrive from Riyadh. There's a constant hum of traffic and headlights beaming along the road, but still no vehicle bumping down the track towards them.

Daylight's fading and he can hear the muezzin calling for *maghrib* prayer. The coloured fairy lights strung above the café veranda have lit up, twinkling above the Pepsi and Lipton Tea signs, and onto some battered wooden tables and chairs. This waiting's beginning to unnerve him. Maybe the brothers have been arrested at a checkpoint and they're telling the police about him and Saeed and where they're meeting. But then he calms himself, remembering the determined faces of the two men in the coffee shop and what they'd done in Afghanistan. They were seasoned *mujahid* and wouldn't surrender information easily.

A car's turned off the highway, its headlights beaming across the wasteland as it moves slowly along the pot-holed track.

'This will be them,' Saeed says. 'Didn't I tell you?'

'You said they'd signal, flash their headlights three times…'

But Saeed grabs the flashlight. 'They probably forgot. I'll go and meet them.'

Ibrahim watches his friend hurry through the trucks and across the darkening lorry park. He's waving to the car and it slows down, illuminating Saeed in its headlights, and stops beside him. He's speaking to the men inside, but then the car starts off again, driving towards the industrial estate. Maybe there's a change of plan. Saeed's walking slowly back.

Ibrahim opens the van door, anxious for good news. 'Who was it?'

'I don't know. They said they were looking for a furniture warehouse.' Saeed glances back to the car, its tail lights disappearing towards the industrial area. 'I don't trust them. They sound like Shia from Qatif, maybe agents of Khomeini.'

'What did you tell them?'

'Nothing,' Saeed assures him. 'I just said we were waiting for some friends.'

'OK. So what are we going to do?' Ibrahim's question hangs between them. It's a simple question of fact, but threatens to become an accusation. While the brothers in Jeddah have followed his good idea and attacked a military bus, he and Saeed have done nothing yet to halt this Crusader bombing. Tonight, over four hundred dead Muslim women and children are crying out for revenge.

Saeed peers at his watch. 'OK. We've waited long enough. If they're not coming, I'll try. Back up to the cafe and we'll unload the Stinger.'

Relieved that at last they are doing something, Ibrahim reverses the Transit van up to the café. Illuminated, by the string of fairy lights, they lift out the heavy metal box and lower it behind the veranda wall. Ibrahim holds the flashlight so Saeed can see as he snaps open the metal clasps and checks the Stinger parts, identifying them, as he places each piece onto a brown *bedu* blanket: the Gripstock firing unit with its telescopic scope, the Battery Coolant Unit to fire up the electronics, and the launcher tube with the missile inside. Ibrahim tries to check with him but can't help glancing along the veranda towards the rusty oil drum stinking of food waste and the filthy rats darting round it.

'The IFF unit,' Saeed says. 'We don't need it.' He separates out the piece.

'Why not?' Ibrahim fears any deviation from the checklist and what seems the standard operating procedure.

'It transmits a signal, and friendly aircraft send a signal back that stops the Stinger firing.'

'OK.' Ibrahim realizes he has to trust Saeed and now the *mujahid's* preparing for action he moves briskly, appearing more confident as he attaches the scope on top of the launcher and peers through it.

'OK. I'll use this as the firing line.' He shoulders the assembled Stinger and stands against the low veranda wall.

'Make sure you follow the instructions.' Ibrahim takes the manual, peering at it in the light from the flashlight.

'I lived with the *mujahid*,' Saeed tells him. 'No more questions, teacher. Just help me.'

'It says fast jets are difficult.' Ibrahim quotes from the manual. 'But these planes taking off are weighed down with bombs and should be easy to hit. Remember, you've got to fire at where you expect the plane to be when the missile arrives.'

'I know.' Saeed pushes a round cylinder into the base of the handgrip. 'This BCU powers up the electronics.'

They wait until Saeed announces, '*Alhamdullilah*. We got power. It's working.'

Ibrahim turns his flashlight back to the manual. 'Remember to hit the switch that arms the missile's heat seeker.'

'OK, I remember. And I'm ready, *inshallah*.'

The holy warriors bow their heads. They recite beneath the flickering green-and-red fairy lights. 'In the name of Allah, the supreme and almighty. *Allahu Akbar.*'

Four jets are taking off from the base, heavily laden with bombs and missiles, exposing their wide underbellies as they climb up over the highway, the glow of vehicle headlights illuminating them in the sky above. So close and so easy to shoot down. Standing up against the veranda wall, Saeed shoulders the launcher, shifts on his feet to line up the planes, and presses the side of his face against the firing unit.

'Can you hear this special noise, feel the vibration?' Ibrahim shouts over the noise of jets.

'Be quiet. I'm trying to listen. Locking on.' Saeed raises the launcher further up onto his shoulder, pointing towards the planes overhead.

But Ibrahim can see a car approaching, headlights beaming along the rough track from the industrial park. Is this the *mujahid* brothers who've lost their way or the strangers from Qatif returning? Maybe the police. He mustn't distract Saeed who's ready to fire, but the car's headlights are glancing across the café veranda.

'What's that?' Saeed turns to the lights.

'Nothing. Fire!' Ibrahim shouts and Saeed recoils as the launch engine flies up. Moments later it's zooming across the wasteland, then firing off the Stinger missile.

'Alhamdullilah!' Ibrahim cries out as the magnificent Stinger soars up into the night, smoke trailing behind like a fireworks rocket, seeking the heat of a Crusader plane.

Yet now it's disappeared and Saeed's shouting something. The noise of the planes drowns out his voice as what looks like the strangers' car drives past, heading towards the highway where the Afghan veterans should have come.

'What happened?' Ibrahim yells.

'No acquired tone.' Saeed yells back, furious with himself and flings down the launcher like so much useless trash.

Silence as they watch the Crusader planes disappearing into the night sky, the diminishing yellow flares of afterburners taunting their failure.

'What was it?' Ibrahim says. 'You said you knew this Stinger.'

'I was nervous. Then the car came and the headlights.' Saeed's crying with humiliation. 'I fired too soon. Before the acquired tone. Maybe it's the software.'

Ibrahim struggles to control his temper and stay calm. 'We can't leave this behind.' He lifts up the launcher. 'They'll find it.'

The famous Stinger's missed its target and search helicopters will be coming soon from the airbase. He and Saeed have to escape but they can't take the missile into camp – the van will be searched at the main gate.

'Let's take the Stinger back to your uncle's warehouse,' Ibrahim says. 'We can use it again when our brothers come.' He's trying to keep Saeed calm as they hurry to disassemble the launcher, pack it inside the metal box and lug it back into the Transit van.

Afterwards, the *mujahid* slumps back in the passenger seat, furious and defeated. 'No acquired tone,' he keeps repeating. 'Must be the software.'

Ibrahim dims the van's headlights and, bumping along the pot-holed track, drives away from the lorry park and across the wasteland, heading back to the industrial estate and the shelter of the pious contractor's warehouse.

'Don't worry. We'll try again,' he reassures the failed *mujahid*. But next time he's determined to complete the mission himself and make sure it's a success. Religion and duty require it.

23

The Smog of War

24 February 1991 / 10 Sha'ban 1411   04.50

Sirens wake Rob around five o'clock and Krieger phones to say the ground war's started – he should let his staff know. After calling round to the few people left, Rob switches on CNN to find that Coalition forces have secretly driven hundreds of kilometres west along the old Trans-Arabian Pipeline tracks through the northern desert. They've broken through into southwestern Iraq, and are threatening to cut off Saddam's army in Kuwait. Now the Iraqis have retaliated by setting fire to hundreds more Kuwaiti oil wells to thwart the Coalition aircraft and conceal their headlong retreat.

Weary after another night on patrol, Rob drives into work through a dark grey fog of smoke blown south from Kuwait. He's falling asleep scheduling April's training and field visits, when Krieger phones for him to come to his office. As Rob enters, his boss is on the phone and indicates for him to sit. Through the *X* of masking tape across the office window he can usually see a queue of middle-aged men outside the First Aid Portakabin, where a gaggle of Filipino nurses take blood pressures and recommend low fat diets. But today smog from the burning oil wells obscures everything, except for the blurred shapes of palm trees and concrete barriers topped by metal fencing.

Krieger puts down the phone and glances at his computer, locating something on his To Do list. 'There's an Emergency Response exercise for headquarters this Friday morning. The Medical department's organizing it but your group should help. They need volunteers to play the dead and wounded.'

'Isn't it a bit late for all this?' Rob says. 'The Scuds have stopped coming.'

'There could be more,' Krieger says. 'Especially when Saddam's desperate. And there's still a terrorist threat. Last week a Stinger was fired near the airbase but the Saudis are keeping it quiet. Don't want people to think there's internal opposition.'

'What happened?' Rob remembers the desert trip with June, the old Bedouin raising his walking stick and Bill arguing with him. And he hasn't heard from Bill since he got to fly in the AWACS.

'Fortunately, nothing was hit. These guys usually mess up. But we've got to stay alert. Back to this Emergency exercise...'

Rob makes a note in his Day-Timer. 'OK, I'll check with Medical and see what help they need.'

Krieger peers down to his computer calendar for the next item, but then pauses to listen. The Alert sirens are sounding outside. 'We'd better go to the Safe Room. Your office.'

Returning to his own office, Rob finds himself playing host to a diminished band. Two engineers still haven't returned from their medical leave in the UK and several men are up north working on the oil spill response. Only Tony, Ibrahim, and Patience, who's wearing a defiantly crimson sari, gather round the table with Krieger and Rob. The war has tested everyone's endurance and loyalty, and Rob feels proud to have remained with his small band facing this test which could soon be ending. Tony has persuaded the Saudi coffee man to shelter with them and he hesitates on entering this senior staff office, only taking a seat when Krieger invites him. Rob places his shortwave radio on the desk and switches on, listening to DJ Jerry's familiar instructions.

'We should put on our respirators,' Krieger says.

The coffee man glances round, bewildered as the foreigners pull rubber gas masks over their heads.

'Ask him if he's got a respirator,' Krieger tells Ibrahim, who enquires in Arabic.

'He says he trusts in God,' the Sudanese responds. 'No man can bring forward or delay the day of his death. These Scuds will miss us *inshallah*.'

'OK. His responsibility,' Krieger says. 'But put *your* mask on, Ibrahim. God helps those who help themselves.'

The Sudanese obeys and, caught between the coffee man's religious fatalism and Krieger's bureaucratic rationalism, they sit, waiting and listening for something: the drone of a Scud, the crack of Patriots, or worse, an explosion smashing the building's huge plate glass windows. Rob glances at the colourful safety posters covering his window. How much could they slow the shards of glass blowing in on them?

His phone starts ringing and, slipping off the mask, he picks it up. A long distance ping and the American engineer who fled soon after the war began is speaking from Texas, nine hours and thousands of miles away.

'What's happening there?' he demands, as if he should be kept informed.

'We're on the alert.' Rob tries to contain his annoyance. 'We're here in the department's Safe Room.'

'What's that noise?' Even at this distance from Scuds, the man sounds jittery.

'It's the Alert siren for a Scud attack.' Rob offers the phone to Krieger, who'd approved the engineer leaving on the first American evacuation flight. But he shakes his head, and Rob holds the receiver back to his ear.

'I want to know about timekeeping,' the man says. 'Is Patience still marking me down for X days, approved days without pay? How many X days have I got left?'

No questions about the Alert or how his colleagues are coping. He's just checking that company personnel procedures are being followed, and when he'll need to return to his job with its generous salary, children's college fees, and company pension.

'Aziz is responsible for timekeeping now.' Rob relishes the consternation that will cause. 'We're on the Alert so why don't you phone back tomorrow and speak to Aziz? He's not here at the moment.' He replaces the receiver and returns Tony's smile of satisfaction.

'Is he coming back soon?' the Lebanese asks mischievously.

'When the war's over, I suppose.' Rob looks to Krieger but he ignores him. The wailing sirens have paused and resume with a lighter tone before DJ Jerry announces the All Clear over the radio.

Krieger picks up his Executive Day-Timer diary. 'OK,' he tells Rob. 'Let's go ahead and coordinate with Medical on this Emergency Response exercise.' He turns to the others. 'Any volunteers for this exercise besides Rob?'

'I'll help,' Tony says. 'As long as the nurses are good looking.'

While the others leave, Ibrahim stays behind to discuss his summer training course in London. Several weeks ago, he applied to the British Embassy for a visa and is annoyed nothing's come back yet. Rob appreciates that Ibrahim stayed for the war instead of travelling on to the Sudan with his pregnant wife, and phones the Embassy visa office. He gives Ibrahim's name to the female receptionist and waits through a long period of hanging on until a man's voice comes on the line. It's a low, dull voice, as if the official is sitting in a windowless back office hidden away somewhere. Rob asks for the man's name but the voice tells him he doesn't need to know that.

'I'm phoning about Ibrahim's visa application,' Rob begins. 'We want to send him to the UK for a safety training course.'

'And who are you?' the voice demands.

'I'm his supervisor. Ibrahim works in my department.'

Silence, before the voice asks, 'Can you vouch for this man?'

Rob's taken aback. 'What do you mean?' Across the desk, Ibrahim's sitting up, nervous and on the alert.

'Can you give this man a character reference? For example, do you trust him?'

Rob takes a breath, facing this Sudanese engineer he's worked with for the past few years. 'Ibrahim's a good employee. He's worked for the company for more than five years.'

'So, remind me,' the voice says. 'Why does he need a UK visa?'

'We want him to attend a training course on safety and inspection in oil and gas plants. We'll be paying tuition fees, food and accommodation—'

'There's a problem. I'm afraid your man is mixing with the wrong people.'

Rob's shocked. What people? Where are they? In the Sudan, with its long-running civil war between the Muslim north and the Christian south? Or are these wrong people here in Saudi? Or in London?

'Did you know about that?' the voice demands.

'No, I didn't know anything about it.'

'But *you* gave him a personal reference for his visa application. You signed his form.'

Although Rob's sitting behind his familiar supervisor's desk with framed photos of Fiona and Chris beside the phone, he senses that something unexpected and ominous has crept in and is darkening his office. This dull voice in his ear seems to be accusing him.

'What's wrong?' Ibrahim leans further forward across the desk, but Rob ignores him and asks the official, 'What about his visa?'

'Application denied,' the voice says, followed by a click as the receiver's put down.

'What happened?' Ibrahim's smile can't hide his anxiety.

Too shocked to think of anything else, Rob simply repeats, 'Application denied.' He faces the Sudanese engineer, not knowing what to say. 'It's probably the war,' he adds, attempting to cushion the blow.

Ibrahim hesitates, as if about to speak out and denounce the British Embassy, but he stands up and leaves the office without a word.

Feeling nervous, Rob tries to calm himself through routine office work. Following Krieger's instructions, he phones the Medical Department, arranges to meet the Emergency Response Coordinator, and volunteers himself for the exercise. He calls Tony into his office and they discuss the plan for April's training and field visits before at last they feel free to talk about the war.

'So have you decided what this war's about yet?' Rob asks.

'Well, we have different views depending on where we're sitting, our nationality and background.' Tony smiles. 'You're British and—'

'Have the British imperialist view. You're Lebanese and—'

'Christian,' Tony says. 'So I don't trust Muslim dictators.' He's smiling at the complexity and turns in his swivel chair to survey the Safety posters Rob taped up to reinforce the window glass. 'We've been wondering what this war's about. But maybe the answer's in plain sight, here in front of us. We're living in it. It's not just the trillion-dollar oil and gas fields. We've got modern refineries, pipelines, gas oil separation plants. This is one of the world's great prizes. The Americans built it and will stay here and do what's necessary to control it. On behalf of the Free World, of course. And they're right. Who wants Saddam Hussein, the Russians, the mullahs across the Gulf, or the *jihadis* to have all this power?'

'But that's a justification for Western imperialism,' Rob says.

'Sure.' Tony grins. 'Maybe you guys left these places too soon, left a power vacuum for thugs like Saddam to move in… You know I had a bet with one of the American engineers on how long this ground war will last. I bet fifty *riyals* on less than two weeks. He said a month. For some reason, he thinks these Republican Guards will fight.'

'Looks like you'll win, then.' But Rob's uneasy with the morality of this gamble. 'Too many innocent Iraqis are being killed.'

Tony shrugs. 'That's war. We worry and feel guilty about it, but men like Saddam don't care how many thousands die. For them, the people are a zero. They don't matter.'

Desperate for advice, Rob confides about the British Embassy refusing a visa for Ibrahim.

'I'm not surprised. Some of the things he says. But what are you going to do?'

'I don't know.' Rob realizes he doesn't know very much about Ibrahim. Tony isn't surprised about the Embassy refusing the Sudanese a visa and has heard his colleague say some 'things'. But Rob's heard nothing.

'What about your friends in Security?' Tony says. 'Tell them what the Embassy said.'

'They'll think the worst.' He can imagine Rick's reaction, especially when he knows Ibrahim's in Rob's group and under his 'supervision'. And these are only suspicions. After all, the voice at the Embassy didn't accuse Ibrahim of being a terrorist. Innocent until proved guilty. But isn't that naïve and dangerous in wartime?

'You should tell Krieger,' Tony says.

'But Ibrahim's a good worker. He could have travelled to Khartoum with his pregnant wife. Instead he put her on the ferry and drove back from Jeddah.'

'So why *did* he come back?'

Rob's startled. 'Probably because Krieger told him to.'

'OK, but he could still have left. You'd better be safe. Tell Krieger and let Security know'.

'But Ibrahim will know it came from me.' Rob's unhappy at the thought of betrayal, making a terrible mistake, and having to work with Ibrahim after an investigation. Yet he must do something.

Sunday evening and *Match of the Day* is on Bahrain TV. Tonight it's the all-important Liverpool derby and Rob drives round to Derek's house with Cilla. Stretched out on the sitting room couch, his friend ignores CNN's trumpeting of Desert Storm victories to greet Rob with some shockingly bad news.

'Your King Kenny's resigned as manager,' Derek announces. 'Dalglish has left Liverpool.'

'Resigned? Why?' Rob was looking forward to yesterday's highlights of the Merseyside derby, an exciting 4-4 FA Cup draw with Everton.

'Kenny says he's leaving because of the terrible stress of the job.' Derek rises from his couch to prepare their drinks. 'He should try the stress here in the war zone. So what's it like outside?'

'Still foggy but I can't keep Cilla in all the time.'

'Saddam's set fire to more wells, so it'll be like this for days. Like the dear old London pea-soupers when I was a kid.'

With Cilla lying at his feet, Rob settles to watch the Six O'clock Follies, the daily military briefing from Riyadh. Standing at the lectern, General Schwarzkopf is bullish, boasting that Coalition casualties are light and the ground offensive into Kuwait is going to plan. There's minimal resistance and thousands of Iraqi soldiers are desperate to surrender. Chemical weapons haven't been used so far, but Saddam's Special Forces are rounding up hundreds of people in Kuwait City and executing them at random.

Derek returns with their drinks and lies back on the couch. 'Guess what I discovered today.' He lights another Silk Cut and coolly blows smoke rings up into the air. 'Our ten years' service aren't Gregorian. They're *Hijri* years with only three hundred and fifty-four or three hundred and fifty-five days. I checked with Personnel – so we can get full severance and leave here at the end of next month. The end of March and *ma'assalama*, Saudi.'

Shocked, Rob doesn't know what to say. For years they've talked about hanging on for the ten years and full severance: one month's pay for each year of service. He promised Fiona he'd leave after ten and assumed that was at the end of July. Yet tonight it seems that time, which often passed so slowly here, has collapsed in on him. The fabled ten years are nearly over and soon it'll be mission accomplished as the generals in Riyadh keep saying.

But this abrupt ending is coming too soon. He's not prepared. Derek's smiling and delighted with his discovery, but is he actually going to leave in a few weeks? They've been friends since they arrived: supporting each other in the Portakabin world of North Camp, making fun of the company's American follies, and often sitting together in the evenings to drink *sid* and 7-Up and sympathize with each other's family and financial problems. As Rob watches his friend sipping on a large *sid* and water and congratulating himself on completing ten years, he realizes he doesn't want Derek to leave. And he's not sure he wants to go home yet.

Maybe it's lack of sleep, but weariness and a sense of desertion are creeping over him, and he doesn't want to make any decisions now. While the war continued, life felt on hold as he concentrated on day to day survival. Yet the time for decisions has been stealthily advancing. He's tried to ignore it but tonight choices seem to be hurtling towards him. Should he return to take care of Fiona and search for a job in Liverpool? But he'd be giving up on June and any chance of a new life.

He tries to persuade Derek. 'You don't have to resign immediately, just because your ten years are up. Why don't you take a few months to relax and prepare to leave?'

'No.' His friend is cheerfully adamant. 'I told my wife ten years, and ten it'll be. Ten *Hijri* years and I'll collect full severance.'

'But what are you going to do?' That same question keeps echoing in Rob's head.

'Nothing much. Don't need to.' Derek sips on his *sid*.

'You'll get bored hanging round at home. At least here you're paid for being bored.'

Derek considers. 'Bloke in the pub was telling me about classic cars – buying them cheap and doing them up. I might try that.'

But it sounds to Rob like his friend's deliberately giving up on life. And isn't that what he'd be doing if *he* left? Driving into a cul-de-sac with a high stone wall at the end and no space to turn around. In a few weeks' time, he could be looking after Fiona, doing the supermarket shopping, and watching *EastEnders*. And soon enough he'd have to start searching for a new job and going to the Job Centre. He dreads the indignity of 'signing on'.

He turns again to Derek. 'Have you told Berkeley Square Investments you're leaving?' He assumes the financial advisors will argue strongly against their client fleeing this honeypot.

But Derek's undaunted. 'Phoned them this evening. They've moved my money into emerging markets. They're the place to invest. You've got to move quickly, they said. Be agile. That's the word.'

But the word which occurs to Rob is 'churning', where the advisor keeps switching investments to skim off commissions. Yet while his friend's exhilarated with good news, he doesn't want to disillusion him. Derek sounds very optimistic and cheerful about flying home to his wife and early retirement, but Rob senses his confidence is fragile.

'Now *you* can leave as well,' Derek says. 'You'll have done ten years. And didn't *you* say ten years to Fiona? We arrived the same day and could leave on the same BA flight for Blighty. Mission accomplished.'

'But the job situation in the UK's still bad,' Rob says. 'There's the mortgage and I'll have to start digging into our savings.' He isn't sure whether he's making excuses or just recognizing the financial truth. And he'd never see June again...

'Well, if you only want money, you'll never leave,' Derek concludes, lighting another Silk Cut.

'But I like my job as well,' Rob says. It doesn't feel British to say so but he enjoys taking responsibility for safety training and inspections, working with a variety of nationalities and learning new things. He won't get as good a job back in the UK. He'd probably have to take whatever's available.

'Your choice,' Derek says. 'But doesn't Fiona expect you back soon?'

'Yes... OK, I'll think about it.' As Cilla stirs beside his chair, he recalls yet another reason for not leaving. 'I've got to think about quarantine for Cilla, as well.'

'More excuses.' Celebrating his earlier than expected departure, Derek drinks up and returns to the kitchen.

As his friend mixes more drinks, Rob recalls the night they first landed in Saudi, struggling through hostile immigration and customs inspections to a mini-bus bathed in cold air-conditioning and Country and Western music. As they were driven through a wasteland of building sites to the Portakabin dormitories of North Camp, Tammy Wynette stood by her man and Kenny Rogers played poker with a gambler who finally broke even. Nearly ten years later, he and Derek had more than broken even on the money, but on other things? Marriage, family, friends?

'So, what do you think?' Derek says, returning with fresh drinks.

'About what?' Rob needs more time and glances towards the TV. 'Better switch over to Bahrain. The Liverpool derby will be coming on.'

Derek presses the remote, extinguishing CNN's *War in the Gulf* in favour of English FA Cup football. 'King Kenny's last game as manager,' he says, settling back on the couch. 'And in a few weeks I'll be watching Gazza at White Hart Lane. Come on ye Spurs!' he calls out as *Match of the Day* begins.

Rob joins in with his friend's football banter, but in the morning he'll have to tell Krieger about Ibrahim and his conversation with the Embassy. And should he follow Derek in abandoning his job and his life here?

24

Scuds

25 February 1991 / 11 Sha'ban 1411   06.10

When Rob takes Cilla for her early morning walk, the sun's shrouded, the sky grim with smoke from hundreds of burning Kuwaiti oil wells. It's the second day of the ground offensive and while the military and TV reporters are proclaiming victory, here it looks and smells like the end of the world. Krieger's travelled south for a management field visit and, relieved from telling his boss about Ibrahim's visa, Rob works quietly in his office on a new Safety Leadership program.

He's interrupted by a phone call from Bill Eliot announcing he's moved into an apartment behind the Souks supermarket. His building has a squash court and Bill suggests they play tonight. He's exhilarated after his AWACS flight over the Gulf but furious about an abortive Stinger attack from near the airbase and the failures of Saudi security.

'They think it's some *jihadis* from Riyadh, but want to keep things quiet,' he says. 'Anything to stop the world knowing there's trouble in paradise. Thank God, these crazies don't know what they're doing – couldn't find their own ass.'

Rob wants to ask him about June, but how? Maybe Bill will say something tonight after their squash game.

When he returns home from work, Rob phones Fiona. But she isn't interested in the liberation of Kuwait and flying back to Saudi after the war. She wants to know if he's made any progress on looking for a job in the UK.

'No.' He's annoyed with her forcing him to leave. 'I'm just trying to get through this war in one piece.'

'Well, I'm not coming back to that prison. I'm seeing a lawyer about a divorce.'

He's astounded, not knowing what to say. As he stands in this kitchen thousands of miles away from her and gripping the phone, he feels ignored and neglected. At this moment, when the war's almost over, she's threatening to overturn their lives.

'Are you still there?' she asks. 'I've been with Jane to a lawyer's office in Liverpool.'

So that's it. Fiona's recently divorced friend is behind this initiative.

'Jane's lawyer is very good. A feminist. She arranged Jane's divorce and made sure it was a clean break. But first we have to get a separation. It costs about three hundred pounds to draw up the papers.'

So he's expected to pay for this, as well. Should he protest about the need for divorce, the lack of warning, the price of it all? It seems he's expected to just smile and pay up.

'Do you really want to get divorced?' he asks. Despite his anger, he's not sure he does – not yet anyway. Over twenty years of marriage and he still feels attached to the passionate young woman he met at university, the mother of his student son, and the life they've shared together.

'We can't go on like this,' she says. 'And I don't think you really care, anymore.'

'That's not true,' he says, but doesn't even convince himself. Then he realizes: unknown to her, Fiona's offering him a way out, the chance of a new life. Derek's retiring and going back to his wife, but *he* could be free to do anything, go anywhere. Not that he wants to hang out around Thailand's beaches and bars like the Sidman, but he could travel, settle somewhere else, maybe with June.

'So I'll ask Jane's lawyer to draw up the papers,' Fiona says.

'OK, if that's what you want.' He's furious at being forced into this corner.

'I'll send you the papers,' she says and slams down the phone.

The guards at the main gate are wearing white masks over their noses and mouths as they wave through Rob's old Land Rover. He feels his neck and shoulders loosening, the tension from Fiona's phone call easing away, as he accelerates downhill past the National Guard barracks. Maybe she's only threatening him and won't do anything in the end. But her friend, Jane is encouraging her...On the Easy Listening channel, DJ Jerry's playing upbeat war-winning rock music and as Rob drives through the fog and up onto the main highway, he joins Bob Dylan and the Grateful Dead in celebrating the chimes of freedom flashing.

He stops at the Souks supermarket to buy the English language *Arab News*. The front page trumpets *Desert Storm strikes deep into Kuwait* and so far Coalition casualties are light, with thousands of Iraqi troops surrendering. The predicted amphibious assault on the Kuwaiti coast proved to have been a deception tying the Iraqis down while the main Coalition forces secretly drove west along the oil pipeline tracks through the desert. They've outflanked the Iraqis, and are threatening to cut off Saddam's army in Kuwait. A diagram in the newspaper shows what Schwarzkopf, in the language of American football, calls his 'Hail Mary' play. It's a bizarre Christian reference for this Muslim country, but soldiers aren't known for cultural sensitivity.

The ground war's obviously been timed for Kuwait's Independence Day and the *Arab News* proclaims this thirtieth anniversary as a glorious new dawn. Further down the page, a photograph shows thick columns of smoke rising above burning oil wells. Hundreds of fires are still blowing out smog, and the temperature has fallen by several degrees. Western environmentalists are protesting about these black clouds creating poisonous acid rain, and climatic disruption over the whole Gulf. But that seems more reason to get the war over quickly.

To celebrate the success of the ground offensive, Rob buys some Desert Storm postcards to send home to Chris and some traditional British comfort food for himself: Captain Birdseye fish fingers and frozen chips, a box of Baxter's shortbread, and a large bottle of Sprite to mix with his 'brown' whisky from the Jack Daniel's wood chips. This kind of traditional British food and drink will be good for Derek's leaving party as well, in a few weeks' time. But he's not looking forward to that farewell, the door closing on a friendship which has sustained them through a decade.

As Rob wanders round the supermarket, bands of cheerful fresh-faced GIs – young women as well as men – liven up the food aisles with their joking and chatter. Like Bill, many are probably living in the nearby blocks of flats and warehouses converted into temporary barracks. They're shopping for treats and Arabian souvenirs to take home now this war seems almost over. Some are probably disappointed about missing the battle for Kuwait, but at least they can look forward to the yellow ribbons and family reunions. No one will know they were stationed far away from the action.

An Alert siren begins wailing from nearby and the soldiers browsing the aisles glance round apprehensively and up at the supermarket ceiling. Across in the toy section, Saudi parents are herding their children away from Lego boxes and GI Joe figures towards the exit doors. But there's no panic and no one is putting on a gas mask. Too many false alarms recently and isn't the war ending soon? At the checkout, he pays a smiling Indian cashier, and watches a mother in her black *burqa* struggle to persuade a small boy bouncing up and down in a yellow car to leave with her. Ignoring the Alert himself, Rob strolls back out into the smoky evening to drive to Bill's nearby apartment.

'I'm heading for Kuwait City tonight,' Fahad announces from Bill's armchair. Still in their sweaty squash clothes, Bill and Rob had no time to shower or talk about Bill's AWACS flight, before Fahad arrived, smartly dressed in his Kuwaiti air force uniform.

'One of my cousins has been arrested. The Iraqis are picking up these young guys from the street, torturing and executing them.'

'You got permission to leave?' Bill asks.

'No, but I'm going,' Fahad insists. 'Permission can come later. They're taking hostages like my cousin to Iraq. Probably for ransom.'

'OK, but how many cousins you got?' Bill's tone is sceptical.

'A lot,' Fahad retorts. 'But each one is important to me. Not like in the West where you guys only care for yourself.'

'Sure, you Kuwaitis are one big happy family,' Bill says. 'You head off when you feel like it, while us grunts gotta stay and follow orders. We've got families too.'

Irritated by the bickering, Rob stands up to go for his shower. But the Alert sirens are sounding again.

'Put your respirators on.' Bill grabs his satchel from beside the chair.

'It's another false alarm,' Fahad says. 'The war's over.'

'You wouldn't say that if you'd almost got a Stinger up your ass. Put the fucking thing on!' Bill's already pulling his gas mask down over his head. Rob hesitates, preferring to go for a shower, but to satisfy his host, pulls the mask on and watches Fahad reluctantly putting on his own.

They wait, listening to the sirens' familiar wailing, and what might be the last Alert before the war ends. Through his goggles, Rob glances round the small sitting room. Bill's put up some flowery curtains at the window: an effeminate touch for such a Spartan room. But Rob's still annoyed by the sweaty warmth of Bill's embrace when they finished their squash game.

Looking round, he sees the room is dominated by service photographs. Official portraits of Stealth jets and Apache helicopters line the walls and one in a gilt frame shows some General pinning a medal on a younger Bill's uniformed chest. On top of the small desk and bookcase beneath the window are photos of Major Bill's classes, the military trainer surrounded by groups of smiling young men in uniform:

Vietnamese officers before Saigon fell and they fled or were sent to re-education camps; proud young Iranians scattered after Khomeini's revolution; robed Afghans loosely gathered round their trainer at what looks like a students' country picnic; and now young Saudi officers lined up in front of a Tornado jet in its desert camouflage. But there's nothing of Bill's family: the difficult wife he once mentioned and the son who'd been studying at Berkley and maybe getting into drugs. These gallant young men in uniform look like what's left of Major Bill's family.

But what about his own family? Rob realizes there won't be anything left of his family if he and Fiona get divorced. And how would Chris react?

The Alert sirens are still sounding outside but Fahad's restless, standing up and moving towards Bill's desk and the window looking out on the street.

Thud! The room quakes from floor to ceiling, about to collapse in on them. The lights go out and the window glass crashes in, through the curtains. Rob's thrown down, hitting his head against the glass-topped coffee table. Sickened, he feels his head reverberating, blood trickling from his scalp onto the mask and goggles. Crouched on the floor, he cradles his head in his hands, holding it together and feels blood sticking to his fingers. Everything outside sounds muffled and distant, and he has to stop the bleeding.

Holding onto the coffee table, he levers himself to his feet, looking for his squash towel, and in the dim light from the window sees Bill helping Fahad up from the floor strewn with papers, smashed photo frames and shards of glass.

Muffled by the mask, Bill's calling out something and heading for the door that's fallen ajar. Rob staggers after him, out into the corridor lit by a ghostly green light in the ceiling. No smoke yet but he can hear the shouting and yelling of people trying to escape.

The building is still quaking, the ground shifting under his feet, but then he realizes – it's him, shaking and quivering with shock. Stumbling after Bill, he holds onto the big man's arm as if his life depends on this figure lumbering forward in sweaty Army T-shirt and long khaki shorts. No time to think, just to stay close behind the American.

Rob uses his wrist band to wipe blood from his goggles and sees at the end of the corridor a doorway with another green emergency light above it and a crowd of Filipino and other men in shorts and T-shirts shouting and struggling with each other to escape outside. He glances behind to see Fahad limping along without a gas mask and trying to catch up with them. But Rob's staying with Bill, who barges into the crowd round the doorway. Like joining a rugby scrum, Rob leans forward and pushes the American with his shoulder from behind and, straining against the mass of bodies, they force their way forward, squeezing through the doorway until they stumble out into the night's disaster.

A hundred yards down the street, a warehouse is on fire, smoke billowing out with people screaming and yelling above the wail of sirens. Young men and women – fresh-faced kids like the ones in the supermarket – are crying for help and scrambling to escape the blazing warehouse and falling debris. There's a stink of burning fuel and materials, maybe bodies, and without moving towards the fire, Rob feels a wall of heat pressing up against his face and body. He retreats down the street, away from the heat and smoke, and crouches in the shelter of a yellow contractor's bus. His face is wet with sweat and it's difficult to breathe so he peels off his mask and head down, stares at the sandy earth, gulping in cooler air. His head's still aching from hitting the table and he doesn't want to look up and face this chaos, the responsibility of having to do something. Sirens are howling as police cars and a fire truck force their way through the billowing smoke and confusion of people.

Shouldn't he do something? At least try to help? He feels like a voyeur observing this horror through the acrid fog. But he's still in squash clothes and bleeding from his head. The sounds of crackling and explosions are coming from down the street, the blazing warehouse. 'Ammunition!' someone yells. 'Stay clear!' People rush back down the street towards him and he retreats further behind the yellow bus. From this distance, he can see the firemen spraying the burning building and the military police starting to command some order. A helicopter's clattering overhead, and with its searchlight sweeping the ground it descends onto waste ground behind the warehouse.

'More ambulances!' a man shouts. Beside a nearby ambulance, two Filipino medics are wrapping a screaming soldier in an emergency foil blanket. Now Rob sees Major Bill and a military policeman hurrying down the street towards him. Do they want his help? But Bill doesn't see him as he climbs up the steps into the yellow bus and swings what looks like a metal truncheon at a window, shattering the glass and roughly clearing the frame. It looks like vandalism and Rob steps back to avoid glass fragments as Bill and the military policeman walk along the bus methodically smashing out windows. Only when the medics start carrying people on stretchers towards the bus does Rob realize: they're hoisting the stretchers up through the windows to Bill and the policeman who lay them onto the bus seats. While he's standing there feeling sick and bewildered, they're taking responsibility and saving people's lives. Major Bill's shouting instructions and the medics are lifting other stretchers, other bodies wrapped in shiny foil, into the bus.

But where's Fahad? Rob can't see him through the smoke and people struggling to get away. Maybe the Kuwaiti passed him in the confusion and got back to his car. But he'd been limping and looked injured following them down the corridor. In the rush to escape, Rob had ignored that and left him behind. Did Fahad even get out of the apartment building?

He retraces a few steps back into the heat and smoke, towards the doorway of Bill's building. He still can't see Fahad but about to retreat again, he spots him sitting on the ground with his back against the building wall.

'You OK?' Rob puts his hand on the Kuwaiti's uniformed shoulder.

'Where's Bill?' Fahad asks, as if in a daze. 'He doesn't care. He left me behind in that place.'

'He's helping the wounded soldiers… I'll help you stand up.'

'I hurt my ankle. I can't walk properly.'

'Here, hold onto me.' He helps Fahad stumble to his feet and with the Kuwaiti's arm round his shoulder, leads him hopping and hobbling through the crowd and away from the fire. Rob stops beside an ambulance, pausing so they can catch their breath.

'Do you want to go to hospital?'

'I must go to Kuwait to save my cousin. The Iraqis have taken him.'

'But you can't drive with your ankle like this.'

'The car's automatic. My right leg's OK.' Fahad grimaces with pain but is impatient to leave. '*Yalla*. Let's go, please. My car is down here.'

They hobble further down the street, out of the smoke and away from the cacophony of police sirens and ambulances with their flashing lights driving off to the hospital.

'There.' Fahad indicates a side street and what seems like an apparition: an immaculately white Mercedes parked under a streetlight behind the Toys R Us store. Fahad opens the car door and Rob eases him down onto the front seat. There's Kleenex in a large box on the dashboard and a plastic Evian bottle on the back seat. Rob helps Fahad take off his shoe and sock and with a wet Kleenex gently wipes over the red swollen ankle.

'Painkillers in the glove compartment,' Fahad says and Rob finds a pack of paracetamol, giving two to Fahad and taking two himself to swig down with the Evian water. While Fahad rests back in the seat, he wipes his own head and face clear of blood, closes his eyes for a few moments and savours his escape. His face and spirits feel refreshed by the water and the realization he's narrowly escaped death in this place. So much pain, injury, and death around. But he's survived. He opens his eyes again to see Fahad's found a clothes brush and is brushing the dust from his Air Force uniform.

'You OK?' He holds Fahad by the shoulders, peering into his eyes. 'Can you drive?'

'OK. I'm going for my cousin.' Fahad shakes Rob's hand. '*Alhamdullilah*. Thanks to God we're alive my friend. We meet again in Kuwait. *Inshallah*.'

'In Kuwait, *inshallah*', Rob says, guessing that will never happen. No matter, he's helped Fahad to escape.

The young Kuwaiti starts his white Mercedes and drives slowly down the deserted street, heading for the main road and Rob glances round.

Where's he left his own car? He walks to the end of the street and recognizes a grocer's shop with its metal shutters down, the street where he turned into the parking area behind Bill's apartment block. A nearby car shelter has collapsed onto the vehicles beneath, but fortunately his Land Rover's standing in the open and undamaged with only a light sprinkling of grit and dust over it.

Rob clambers up into the driver's seat and rests behind the steering wheel. But it's too soon to drive. He's still trembling with the randomness of the young soldiers' deaths, and the realization he's lucky to be alive. He switches on the car radio to hear DJ Jerry reciting the All Clear. To drown out the sirens, the cacophony of disaster around him, he turns up the volume of Easy Listening music singing about love and enjoying life. He's lucky. That Scud could have carried chemicals or nerve gas and fallen just as easily on Bill's apartment block – just as easily on them. He peers at himself in the rear view mirror. The cut in his forehead's no longer bleeding. His eyes are reddened by smoke but are more confidently gazing back at him.

Phil Collins is singing 'Take Me Home': ironic after his phone call with Fiona. But now he feels ready to drive off. The military police wave him through their road block and he re-joins the highway, heading down to the traffic lights at the airport road. A red light and he stops behind a lorry while two helicopters clatter high over the crossroads. On the other side of the road, more police cars and ambulances speed past towards the random death and destruction he's only just escaped.

The traffic lights change, he turns right and is clear of congestion, heading back towards town and then home. The town centre's crowded with weekend traffic, and the shoppers filling the pavements seem oblivious to the Scud attack less than two miles away. Halted at the traffic lights, he sees the windows in Eve's Jewellery shining bright and at Happy Corner the electrical stores and clothes shops are still crowded with gangs of GIs eager to spend dollars on their Arabian adventure. He's stopped behind what looks like an Indian family crammed into an old saloon car and he leans forward, trying to see if it's Patience and her family escaping their apartment for an evening's drive. Two young boys like hers wave through the rear window and he waves back. Waiting for the red light to change, he can see through his rear view mirror that the Saudi in the car behind is edging forward, leaning over the steering wheel for a racing start. Horns start beeping, demanding the traffic lights change, and at amber, they all charge through the intersection.

At last, joining a queue at the main gate, Rob feels his body reviving, adrenalin surging through his veins and bringing him back to life. No sign of Rick but a cluster of security men stand by the guardhouse gathered round the tall Pakistani supervisor. The sirens start up again and two ambulances from the hospital race out on the other side of the road, speeding to pick up more casualties.

No hesitation, no more self-questioning, and he heads straight for the ballpark. Curtains are drawn and lights dimmed in the other bungalows but there's a lamp in June's sitting room window shining out onto the tranquillity of the front lawn and white picket fence. Rick's patrol car is missing but his old Land Cruiser's there. The security boss might still be home. Rob circles the ballpark again, slowing past the bungalow, and parks behind the community centre, concealed among the other vehicles. Examining his face in the mirror, he spits on some paper towel and wipes away more blood, carefully circling the cut on his scalp.

No time to think, just to do. The night air tastes delicious, despite its smoky tang, as he walks up towards June's house, his body trembling at the fire and explosions he's only just survived. Younger people have died but he's alive enough to be walking past the community centre, opening June's garden gate, and advancing up the path. Under the light above the door, he feels conspicuous in his bloody Desert Shield T-shirt and shorts. But he's escaped a nightmare to be ringing this doorbell and may never feel so alive again. He can hear Bob Dylan, probably his birthday CD, croaking about being forever young but there's no sound of anyone coming to the door. Can June hear the bell? And what if Rick appears?

Barking comes from the side of the house, and Jackson limps round to stand beside him, slobbering over and licking his bare legs, tasting the salty sweat, and making the hairs stick together. The dog must have come from the back garden. Rob rings again but the front door's not locked and he pushes it open, advancing into the sitting room. He walks across the floor Rick dragged him along, past June's *Desert Storm* picture on its easel, and the couch where she stretched out, waggling her red varnished toes. Old Bobby Dylan's still longing to stay forever young as Jackson leads him through the bungalow to find his mistress.

Walking into the kitchen, Rob doesn't call out but pushes open the screen door, hinges squeaking as he peers out across the garden patio. Under the lights and wearing her striped butcher's apron, June's standing at a table wedging a wet mound of clay. Startled, she looks up, staring across at him.

'Hey, you look terrible. What's up, sweetheart?'

He feels his face screwed up, the blood streaked over his T-shirt, his voice croaking with disaster as he stares back at her.

'A Scud…exploded by the Souks. A lot of kids were killed.' He realizes again. 'I got away.'

'Good. Good, sweetheart.' June's coming towards him, opening wide her arms.

But now he can see under the patio lights the ragged cut from nose to lip. 'But what happened to you?'

'I accidentally fell over Jackson,' she says. 'After the desert trip.'

'The same night I got a kicking.' But holding her tight now seems to compensate for that humiliation. 'Where's Rick?'

'Up north sweetheart – he won't be back before tomorrow night… But your head's cut, you're shocked. Come to June, baby.' She lowers his injured head down to her breast, the wet clay smell and warmth of her body rising to enfold him.

'We've all the time in the world. So let's just clean off this blood and rest, sweetheart.'

25

Santorini

26 February 1991 / 12 Sha'ban 1411   07.25

'So was Cilla pleased to see you?' June is sitting up in bed with her glasses on, like a studious art mistress as she reads one of her glossy books of Native American art.

'Sure.' Rob sits down on the bed to take his shoes off. 'I fed and watered her and took her for a walk. Then I rushed back here like you told me.'

'Good boy. And did you call your office like a dutiful employee?'

'Yes. I told Patience I was close to the Scud attack and she said I should go to hospital for a check-up. But I think they've got enough with all these wounded GIs.'

'So did she think you were very brave?'

'Probably.' Patience did sound impressed and concerned he wasn't taking his health seriously enough.

'So duty done sweetheart.' June puts her book on the bedside table, slips off her glasses and pulls back the sheet. 'Now you've more work to do. Come in. I've been keeping everything warm for you.'

Later, Jackson is scratching at the bedroom door, whimpering for attention. What time is it? Rob glances at his watch – nearly nine o'clock and the morning sunlight is flooding around the sides of the window blind. Jackson barks and barks again.

'She wants more food and attention,' June says. 'I'd better get up.'

'No, you stay there. I'll go.' Rob swings out of bed. Such a narrow escape from death has energized him, made him want to keep moving and enjoy this body while he can.

As he opens the bedroom door, Jackson jumps up, almost knocking him over, before pursuing him into the kitchen. Some dog food under the sink and he fills Jackson's dish, puts water into a bowl, and opens the back door to release him into the garden's bright sunshine. For a moment, standing in the doorway looking out at the powerful mastiff peeing onto the grass by the picket fence, it feels like he's standing in for Rick. June said he wouldn't be back until tomorrow, but what if he's early?

He returns to find June reading about the artists' workshop on the island of Santorini. 'They sent us more information about the Easter painting workshop,' she says as he gets back in beside her. Beneath the headline, *Life Expands*, is a photograph of a clifftop village and whitewashed houses clustered round an Orthodox church, its cross gazing out over the blue Aegean.

'OK. Tell me all about it.' He gets into bed and lies back luxuriating in her warmth and accessibility.

'First day sweetheart, we've a romantic ferry trip from Piraeus to Santorini and the Artists' Lodge overlooking the harbour. Next day is our first painting workshop and demonstration of techniques. Third day, we've got a beach trip with individual coaching, and a focus on local atmosphere and colour. Day four and we'll be walking and sketching the island's landscape, using pencils and watercolours. Last day is painting what we eat and drink, and celebrating our week's work.' She strokes her hand over his bare shoulder. 'Party time, sweetheart. Imagine! Lots of Greek food and wine. Better than flying home to…what do you Brits call it?'

'Blighty,' he says. But what would he say to Fiona about not coming home? Yet now she's talking about divorce, why should he even bother? Time to start his new life.

'Listen to this,' June says. 'Partners who are not artists can spend quality time reading, swimming or enjoying the local *tavernas*.'

'OK, but I'll be joining the course myself,' Rob says. 'I used to be a good painter at school. Maybe I can get back to it. And when the war's over I'll join your painting class – be one of your best students.'

'Great.' June passes him the leaflet. 'See what it says. Life shrinks or expands in proportion to your courage. So it's time to be courageous, sweetheart. You're lucky to be alive, so lighten up and start enjoying life.'

'Too right.' He puts his arm round her. Isn't this the big change, the fresh start he's looking for? Maybe that Scud was the wake-up call he needed.

But the doorbell's ringing. It pauses a few moments before ringing again, demanding attention.

'Wait.' June puts a finger to her lips, but there's more ringing. 'Christ!' She grabs what looks like Rick's blue towelling dressing gown from a chair and pads out to the sitting room. Naked, Rob eavesdrops behind the door, relishing the cool air against his body and bare skin, a physical reminder of last night's escape from death and injury.

June's explaining that she's trying to get over a cold and the other woman's voice sounds like her friend, the Canadian doctor's wife, who's arrived with her paintings for the Art Show.

She's telling June about the Scud attack and her husband being called into the hospital last night to treat the victims. Almost thirty GIs have been killed and about a hundred wounded. How terrible for the parents who probably thought the war was ending and expected their sons and daughters to be flying home soon. At last, the sound of goodbyes, the screen door slamming and June's returning to him.

At this moment he could be lying injured in hospital or freezing cold in the morgue like those young soldiers. But *alleluia*, he's alive, as June walks in and he unfastens the belt of Rick's dressing gown, opening it wide and burrowing his head into her warm flesh.

*

Lunchtime, and while June's showering, Rob drives home to phone Fiona – let her know he's OK after the Souks bombing – and for a few hours' sleep. Fortunately, he's not on patrol tonight, but there's the emergency response exercise at headquarters tomorrow morning. He'd told Patience that he'd be along for that.

Nervous about speaking to Fiona, he delays and goes to bed but almost immediately the phone rings. It's Chris, not speaking from university where he should be, but from home. Fiona's got bronchitis and Dad should come home as soon as flights start up again. Rob asks questions – how serious is the bronchitis, what does the doctor say? But Chris is adamant. Rob starts to tell him about the Scud attack, his narrow escape and that he's lucky to be alive, but he might as well be telling his son about some Second World War film. Chris is speaking to him as if he's an irresponsible parent who needs to be recalled to duty.

'But why do you want to stay there, Dad?' he asks. 'Why don't you just resign?'

'Because it'll be difficult getting a new job at my age. Never mind a good job.'

'At least you can come back and start looking after Mum.'

'OK, but who's going to pay for everything?' Rob's growing angry. 'Are *you* going to pay?'

'Pay for what?' His son's taken by surprise.

'For the mortgage, for you to go to university…'

'Dad, you're always talking about money.'

'*Somebody* needs to. Or are you going to leave university and get a job yourself?'

'Dad!' Chris's turn to bang down the phone.

Standing in the kitchen, Rob feels like he's been shouting vainly across thousands of miles to a separate and alien world. Instead of Easter and an artist's life in Santorini, now he's faced with springtime in Southport – foreign language students, holidaymakers and retired couples wandering down Lord Street, round the Edwardian shopping arcades and sitting in cosy tearooms. Chris says he should be returning to look after Fiona but *she* said she wanted a clean break. Has she told him about that?

So what should he do? Cilla's jumping up at him, needing to go for a walk but suddenly Rob's tired of responsibility. Before finding the dog's lead, he decides to pours himself a generous 'brown' with 7-Up and think about what to do. He stretches out on the couch watching CNN – a long procession of Iraqi prisoners trudging along the road under smoke-black skies, commentators growing more excited about victory in Kuwait, interrupted only by advertisements for American Express, Holiday Inn and Diners Club. This is the triumph of what President Bush is calling the New World Order.

Rob lets Cilla out into the back garden, pours himself another drink, and as the 'brown' from the Jack Daniel's woodchips slips down so smoothly, he decides to visit June who's setting up her Art Show in the community centre this evening. Then he'll make up his mind what to do.

26

An American Colony

26 February 1991 / 12 Sha'ban 1411   13.10

'Master of the Day of Judgement. Guide us to the straight way.' The words of the prayer resound in Ibrahim's head, as he and Saeed stroll back from the mosque to the headquarters entrance gates. CNN are reporting almost thirty Crusaders killed and many more wounded when a Scud fell on the American barracks near the Souks supermarket. That's Judgement, Ibrahim believes – divine vengeance for the hundreds killed in Baghdad and Basra. If only this missile had struck earlier in the war, these arrogant Crusaders might have been stopped.

The atmosphere's still foggy with smoke blown south from the burning oil wells and masking the sun. This near darkness at noon and chilled atmosphere feels ominous and this morning Ibrahim noticed the crowd of Westerners going into work was smaller and more subdued than usual. No one was talking, as if they were on edge and fearful of another Scud attack, maybe on the headquarters buildings where they were going into work.

Now Ibrahim notices a Western woman looking at Saeed. 'You should take that *pakol* off,' he tells his friend. He's spoken to Saeed before about wearing the black Afghan beret. 'It attracts too much attention.'

'It's good luck,' Saeed says. 'And reminds me of brave times with the *mujahid*.'

'But the guards are more likely to stop and search you.' Since the Stinger failure, Ibrahim's grown annoyed with Saeed's reckless self-confidence. The brothers from Riyadh have gone into hiding to escape the *mabahith* and Saeed's pious uncle has moved his household to Hofuf until after the war. All because Saeed messed up with the Stinger.

'*Mafi muskallah*. No problem. Look, nothing to hide.' Saeed opens his hands as if for inspection as they pass the guards at the security gate and click through the turnstile. And of course, the guards, who know Saeed as a joker, smile and don't question him.

Ibrahim begins to feel less anxious as they cross the paved concourse towards the headquarters building. Rob isn't at work today and Patience said he'd been close to and shaken up by the Scud attack. Krieger's still down south on a management trip and it doesn't look like Rob's told his boss about the visa problem.

Yet the British Embassy suspect him. He could see that from Rob's shocked expression and reluctance to talk after his phone conversation. They know something – maybe about Majid, his brother, helping the militia in southern Sudan, or maybe something he said on the Hajj when he sat by the campfire praising the virtues of strict *sharia* with some Pakistani students from Bradford. But they supported *sharia*, as well, and boasted of demonstrating against Salman Rushdie, the Indian apostate, and burning his blasphemous *Satanic Verses*.

Outside the headquarters building, the two young men embrace and Saeed walks on to the IT Centre, while Ibrahim enters and takes an elevator to the seventh floor. As the doors open, he feels a shiver of apprehension from last night's dream about being arrested and almost expects to see security guards waiting for him. But only the coffee man with his trolley is there and, relieved, Ibrahim returns to his office cubicle. An American engineer and Tony, the Christian Lebanese, are joking in the next cubicle about their bet on how long the war will last. Not much longer, Tony says. The Iraqis are rushing to surrender and Saddam will save his Republican Guards to protect him against the Shia and Kurds after the war.

Ignoring the laughter of these Christian mercenaries, Ibrahim mentally rehearses the plan for tomorrow. Last night, they finished preparing the mortar and the Transit van before driving the vehicle from behind the camp garage to the bachelor apartment block. Early tomorrow morning they'll drive to the mosque to pray for success and say farewell to Dr Eissa. They'll park the Transit by the fence around headquarters and fire their mortar at the IT Centre. Saeed says the technicians change shifts at seven o'clock and they'll inflict most damage by attacking then. That way they'll halt oil and gas production all over the country and if the IT technicians are killed, it will take a long time to start up again. The West and its Crusader war machine will be paralysed and brought to a standstill.

In the panic and confusion of the attack, they'll escape in Saeed's sports car, drive out through the camp's back gate and onto the main highway heading for Jeddah, the ferry to Port Sudan and Khartoum. He'll be home at last with Muna and his family. He imagines their Eid celebrations with everybody happy together and decides to go downtown after work to buy homecoming gifts for the family.

Through his last afternoon, Ibrahim tears up papers, packs a few personal things in his briefcase and grows lightheaded with the knowledge that he'll never again have to return to this blue-walled cubicle. He won't have to see any more Saudis, like Aziz, lazing around, hear the British like Rob lamenting their lost Empire, and the American cowboys giving stupid orders while their women secretaries run everything. When he leaves, Ibrahim takes his family photographs from the desk and packs them in his briefcase. Then he hurries to the lifts without saying goodbye to the Western crusaders and unbelievers he's had to work with here for over five years.

Once outside and clear of the security gates, he turns to look back at company headquarters, these imperial towers waiting, on the edge of destruction and condemned to become history. He remembers a cartoon Saeed showed him of an old *bedu* standing in front of bombed out office blocks and telling his small grandson, 'This is where the imperialist oil company used to be.' *Inshallah,* this sacred land will soon be cleansed and purified of the invaders.

He catches the early evening Shoppers Bus outside the mail centre. As usual, most passengers are female – nurses, secretaries, and middle-aged housewives – and he's glad to find a seat beside an Egyptian teacher from the training centre. He's also going to buy presents to take home, and they discuss the various gift stores and compare prices. But as they travel downtown, the teacher asks Ibrahim about his plans now the war seems to be ending. Is he going to leave the company or stay? Ibrahim gives nothing away but all the man wants to talk about are *his* plans for extending his house and sending his three sons to the American University of Cairo. He'll stay with the company so he can afford to do that, and his sons will study accountancy and apply for jobs with good Western companies. While the teacher boasts about his sons and their glittering prospects, Ibrahim nurses the secret of his own big plan for tomorrow – the explosions that will shatter the Crusaders' IT Centre and scatter their camp followers like this treacherous Egyptian teacher.

They step off the bus at a brightly lit and busy Happy Corner, the pavements round the electrical and clothes stores crowded with mainly Asian and African shoppers. Ibrahim leaves the Egyptian teacher and as he walks through the side streets, realizes he's one of the few men tonight who's not celebrating Victory. The wartime atmosphere of darkened windows and shuttered or near empty shops has dissolved to be replaced by a rowdy drunken spirit, a great upwelling of pagan *jahiliyya.* In swaggering gangs, young Crusaders crowd the pavements shopping for Japanese TVs and sound systems, Arabian souvenirs and fake Rolex watches to impress their families back home.

Outside the clothes stores, Ibrahim notices stupid Desert Storm T-shirts hanging on rails and in a rack outside the International Bookshop, comic postcards making fun of Arabs and the war. He glances round but can't see the *muttawa*, the religious police, who usually patrol this area to enforce prayer time and correct dress. There's a rumour they've been sent to another part of the country so they won't annoy Western soldiers and depress this thriving tourist business. Confident that the war's as good as over, the Saudi shopkeepers have also returned to sit behind their cash registers. They look disappointed with the Saudi *riyals* Ibrahim uses to pay for his small homecoming gifts, and clearly prefer the Crusaders' fresh, green US dollars on which they can charge commission.

In the narrow streets of the gold and silver *souk*, soldiers cluster at the shop windows admiring gold necklaces, chains of pearls, and diamond earrings destined for their wives and girlfriends. He avoids these gangs of young men and in one of the quieter gold shops buys a chain with *Allah* engraved on the pendant, a gift Muna can wear close to her heart. The grey-bearded Saudi shopkeeper is respectful, indicating that these uniformed barbarians talking loudly and laughing as they peer into his jewellery cabinets are not the customers he wants. Ibrahim's tempted to respond and criticize the ignorant invaders and this loosening of righteous order, but decides it's too risky on the eve of his and Saeed's great plan. He trusts the shopkeeper, but his smart Pakistani shop assistant wearing a college T-shirt and jeans might talk to his friends about a Sudanese troublemaker.

Ibrahim walks on to the Shula shopping centre and as he passes through the entrance doors, he's sickened, almost overwhelmed, by the stink of fried chicken from the corner cafe. Through the open doorway he can see two young Filipino nurses in their hospital whites sitting with their legs showing beside Western soldiers who are obviously not their husbands or brothers. If the *muttawa* were here, this would not be allowed. It should not be allowed in this holy land and he averts his gaze, hurrying past the Western clothes stores towards the far side of the shopping centre. This stinking place has become grossly American with its takeaway fast food, loose women and pagan music that even Saudi young men are buying and listening to.

Now he can hear what sounds like Madonna, an obscene prostitute with revealing dresses, screaming out from the reopened House of Music. He feels sorry for the Christians enduring such gross obscenity. A religion that's grown so weak that it allows the mother of its prophet to be mocked and defiled by a degenerate young woman stripping off her clothes and screaming for sex. Truly, as the martyred Sayyid Qutb said, these Americans know only lust and money.

Ibrahim hurries past the House of Music and down the next corridor to find the market stalls that some small traders have set up. He haggles briefly to buy traditional Eid gifts – boxes of luscious Al Hasa dates, Eid sweets and nuts, and Muna's favourite *baklava* made with pistachios and in a beautiful decorative box.

Finally, relieved to escape from the shrieking of Madonna and the pagan *jahiliyya* of the shopping centre, Ibrahim strolls through the quiet back streets towards Safeway to make his international call home. It's easier to use Majid's phone in the apartment, but he suspects that security are listening in on calls to countries like Sudan, which support Iraq. Instead, he'll use one of the pay phones outside Safeway – one that poor Asian labourers use to speak to their families and which is unlikely to be listened into by the *mabahith*. Who wants to listen to labourers' problems?

But he has to queue with Indian shop assistants and grimy Korean labourers for nearly an hour before he reaches a booth and gets through to Khartoum. His father mentions Majid but Ibrahim avoids discussing his elder brother, who deserted the battlefield for home and the comfort of his wife and children. Although his father doesn't criticize Majid, he praises Ibrahim for staying at work and sending money home to the family. In return Ibrahim promises that soon they will pray at the blessed Mahdi's tomb together.

At last he speaks to Muna and she and the baby she's carrying are well. When Ibrahim says he's returning soon he's warmed by her excitement and promises that they'll visit the local photographer's for Eid family portraits. He doesn't tell her about the Eid gifts but feels sure the gold chain and Allah pendant will be perfect for a righteous young mother.

Outside Safeway he boards the Greyhound bus and pretends not to see the treacherous Egyptian teacher clutching his glossy bags from Western clothes and sports stores. Instead he sits with the moustachioed Palestinian who works in Krieger's group. Before the war, he had a heart operation and only returned to the company to complete his ten years' service and pay for his son's house.

'*Inshallah*, only three months and I'll be free of these Western devils,' the Palestinian says, his face grey with illness and anxiety. Ibrahim sympathizes when he complains about Saudis like Aziz insulting him and avoids mentioning this war or the attacks on Palestinians in Kuwait. It's too painful for an old man who's already suffered too much.

As the Shoppers Bus drives back up the hill towards the main gate, Ibrahim realizes he's forgotten about the ID check. Before the war, it was casual, with the guard asking everyone to hold up their card and wave it to him. But now every ID is examined. If Rob or Krieger have told security about him, the guards could drag him off the bus. The Greyhound slows at the gate, pulls into the parking area, and the door clatters open for a young Saudi guard to climb aboard.

Ibrahim takes out his ID card and glances down at it, his younger face peering back. After tomorrow, like a freed slave, he can cut up this card and forget about his employee ID number. But now the guard's walking slowly down the aisle, looking at faces and checking individual IDs. Ibrahim offers his card and the young *bedu* peers at it, then looks into his face.

'You Sudani,' he says. 'You don't live on this camp.'

'I'm staying here with my brother.'

'You go for checking,' the young *bedu* demands, keeping hold of the ID card.

'Why?' Ibrahim's shocked. Should he resist? But then he'd be arrested and their plans would collapse. He must follow this young *bedu*'s command and stand up with his shopping bag of Eid gifts.

But the old Palestinian intervenes. The guard was a student in his class at the training centre and they exchange warm handshakes and greetings. The Palestinian teacher congratulates his student on his success and refers to

Ibrahim as a fellow *muallim*, a good teacher and friend who's visiting him. The guard hands back Ibrahim's ID and moves on to two young Filipinos who he orders off the bus for questioning.

Alhamdullilah. Relieved, Ibrahim chats with his Palestinian friend. After all, this will be the last time he sees this old man who's saved their divine mission for tomorrow. When they step off the bus at the ball field, Ibrahim points towards the white Arabian Pioneers banner hanging over the entrance to the community centre.

'What do you think of that?' he asks. 'These American cowboys think they are pioneers and Arabia is like their Wild West. *Inshallah*, we will soon send these infidels home.'

'*Inshallah.*' The old Palestinian laughs and they shake hands on that.

27

Desert Storm

26 February 1991 / 12 Sha'ban 1411   20.05

'Inside you, there's an artist you don't know yet,' June tells her students at their first class. 'We're going to discover your inner artist.' She loves that inspirational bit. But tonight it's the grunt work she's enjoying almost as much – making sure the work's displayed to its best effect.

Past eight o'clock and wearing her Show Coordinator badge, she stands in a side-room at the community centre supervising the Art Show set-up. It's got to be finished by ten when the centre closes. Rob said he might come by but when is Rick returning?

So what's she going to do after this war's over? Maybe she should see the travel agent and book a flight home. But will Rick let her go? The company holds everybody's passports so she needs to persuade him to apply and get her passport. Danny and Kate are the key and convincing him they need to see her. But tonight she must focus on the show and hang her pictures. Maha's too, of course, and that won't be easy if she plays the *prima donna* like at the last show.

'This OK, ma'am?' She watches the Indian head janitor reverentially placing *The Ancients*, her Anasazi painting, in the centre of the back wall – the first thing people will see as they enter this room – and nods her approval. The view is from inside a dark cave, looking out as if from the womb to an elegant black-on-white vase bathed in a halo of sunlight at the cave entrance. Beyond it lies the bright blue of the Chaco Canyon sky.

'Great art is permanent. Everything else is transitory – including us'. That's another thing she tells her students and gives as an example this simple black-on-white pot, discovered flawless and unbroken by archaeologists exploring New Mexico. The Ancient Ones, the Anasazi, left this elegant pot, this signifier of their civilization, as a guardian of the cave or farewell gift to be found hundreds of years after they mysteriously fled the canyon. June's not sure whether this whole story's true. She read it somewhere in one of her art magazines. But it feels artistically true and impresses students with her sensitivity and Native American heritage.

'Very beautiful, ma'am,' the janitor says. That's more than he said about her *Desert Storm* picture on the other wall. 'You want more help?'

'That's fine for now,' she says and heads for the foyer to grab another black coffee from the machine.

The show's opening tomorrow when a new Saudi General Manager is visiting with Maha, his artistic daughter. A lot of people are bound to show up and she's still worried about her lip. Rob noticed it immediately last night. Yet gradually Rick's mark is disappearing. She could see that in the mirror this morning as she tried to cover up, the effort making her even angrier.

But now the war's almost over, she must get away. On the front page of the *Arab News* there was a report about an anti-war protest in San Francisco. Kate's probably marching with the other students, just as she herself marched against Vietnam in the glorious spring and summer of '68. Of course Danny will be marching to a different drum at that uptight military college where Rick sent him to become an officer and a gentleman. But she'll visit the kids separately.

She takes her coffee from the machine and waves across the foyer to DJ Jerry in his Deadhead T-shirt setting up a video about the Arabian Pioneers, the first American oilmen to come to Saudi. She glances round at the black and white prints lining the walls. Bearded geologists wearing Arab robes pose with their Saudi guides and interpreters. They rest under mosquito nets in their dusty wooden bunk house, probably not far from here, and drive Model T Fords out into the desert to survey the land and search for oil. How crazy was that? The men look handsome in their robes and have that lean hungry look like old Henry Fonda in *The Grapes of Wrath*. It's the same 1930s Dustbowl period – the same hardy pioneer spirit. Back in the US and wearing ordinary clothes, they'd just be regular guys at the office, watching the ball game and mowing the lawn at weekends. But here they were exploring uncharted desert, learning about Bedouin customs and this stern medieval religion. She has to admit it –these guys were heroes to come out to Arabia and discover oil in this bleak Old Testament world.

Rick's parents were the next, less heroic, generation. She remembers meeting them, his mother a dry stick of a woman who sat sewing clothes and country quilts through the long dreary Arabian evenings and hanging on for the company's retirement package. His father was a shut-in disciplinarian, straight-backed and taciturn, who spent his free time in the camp workshop making useful things out of wood and metal. Saving money was so ingrained they'd eventually retired to a miserable bungalow near Las Vegas so they could take advantage of cheap food and transportation provided by hotels and casinos. Not that they left Rick much money in the end. From something his mother said, June suspects that, after a lifetime of thrift, the old woman got addicted to stupid fruit machines.

She peers at a photo of three tents pitched in desert scrubland. Seems it was taken near here in the mid-Thirties. And like Bill said, this is what it would still look like if the Americans hadn't come to search for oil and drill the first wells. The tough old Bedouin were dirt poor, skinny and living off goat's meat, camel milk and dates before their grandchildren became oil rich and started to drive luxury cars and grow fat on hamburgers and Pepsi.

'June'. Startled, she turns before embracing Maha, her dear Saudi friend and artistic protégé.

'You look wonderful, Maha,' she tells the General Manager's daughter who's wearing a silky black *abaya* with the *hijab* wrapped loosely round her head to reveal glossy black hair. Her nails are varnished a girly pink and following June's suggestion she's dared a touch of red lipstick on her mouth.

'Antonio from the Arabian Gallery wants to see our work.' Maha indicates the slim Filipino in white T-shirt and powder blue jeans standing beside her, and June acknowledges this gay pain in the butt who hasn't asked to exhibit *her* work yet. Behind him Maha's chauffeur is carrying two bubble wrapped pictures that the head janitor is anxious to take care of.

'June! What happened?' Maha's noticed it right away, her eyes widening with concern, as she raises a pale bony hand to June's face, touching the ragged mark down from her nose to her lip.

'I fell over Jackson, our dog.' She brushes aside her protégé's concern. 'An accident,' she says, hating the lie and the man who's humiliated her. In Arab families the man's king and can do what he likes, but isn't she a feminist, a liberated American woman? Once this war's over, she'll leave Rick, leave him for good and be what she's always wanted – a full-time artist.

But now she's Show Coordinator and must be bubbly, bright-eyed and bushy tailed.

'Let's look at the artwork.' She gaily links arms with her girlfriend.

'But these are lovely, June.' Maha delays her teacher to admire two colourful country quilts displayed in glass cabinets – one with a green floral pattern and the other featuring a white Texan Lone Star on a sky-blue background.

'They're American country quilts,' June says. 'Housewives make them.'

'Beautiful.' Maha peers through the glass. 'Are they for sale?'

'Looks like it. But let's hang your paintings, Maha. I've reserved space for you.'

She leads the General Manager's daughter and her entourage to the first side room where paintings are stacked ready for hanging up on the freshly painted cream walls. The head janitor unwraps Maha's pictures and under June and Maha's direction carefully positions them on the walls. The artists and Antonio, the gallery manager, stand back to appreciate the two watercolour paintings. *Hidden Beauty* reveals Maha's garden in the Golden Ghetto – red flowering bougainvillea and hibiscus plants with yellow trumpet-shaped blooms stretch across whitewashed garden walls. Next to it, the *Fruits of Arabia* shows a brown wooden bowl containing richly coloured fruit and dates, with a Bedouin dagger in its jewelled scabbard and a belt decorated with coloured beads. Too boring and conventional, June thinks, but Antonio is full of praise for his newly discovered Saudi artist, the General Manager's daughter.

'Antonio's gallery wants to show my pictures,' Maha says. 'Do you think I should advertise them for sale, June?'

'Don't you want to become an independent artist?' This is the question June always asks and her protégé enjoys agonizing over. Could Maha ever become an Artist? What would her father, the General Manager, and her highly respectable family say?

'I don't know what to do,' Maha says, looking to her mentor.

But June knows. Why should this spoiled little rich girl give up dabbling to her heart's content and going on fine art and shopping trips to Europe and the US? Even she, a Fine Arts graduate and teacher, must summon up all her courage to leave Rick for the insecurity of the 'real world' outside.

'Maha, let's think about it,' June says as usual, and they embrace each other as fellow artists, battling to survive in this philistine world.

'Now I want to see your war painting,' Maha says.

June leads her protégé and Antonio into the next room where she's hung *Desert Storm* and *The Ancients*. Her pictures dominate the room, making others' conventional paintings of Bedouin carpets, Arabian coffee pots, mosques and minarets diminish into insignificance. But looking at *Desert Storm*, this dark confusion of colours and surreal images, Maha seems uncertain of what to say.

'It's very good, June,' she says at last.

'Very good,' Antonio agrees but there's no critical or buying enthusiasm in his voice.

'I'm trying to capture the bloodshed and darkness, the violence and confusion, the chaos of war.' June moves closer to her picture and explains how she used real oil, desert sand and gravel, even her own blood for the colours and texture. She indicates the windblown Bedouin tents, a studded Arabian shield, the square hood of a white NBC suit looming out of the gloom, and a black Apache helicopter like a malevolent spider hovering over the scene.

But the more she explains, the angrier she becomes at their lack of appreciation – the 'very nice' Maha keeps repeating and Antonio's indifference as he turns to survey other pictures. It's too dark and abstract for them, she realizes, determined to keep smiling. No way now she'll let her work be shown in Antonio's precious gallery of Arabian *kitsch*.

'I need to learn more about surrealism, June,' Maha says.

'You should visit the Guggenheim and Museum of Modern Art when you're in New York,' June says. 'Maybe we can visit together.'

But Maha has noticed another picture. 'That's very good.' She's pointing to a mosque and minaret illuminated by the setting sun. 'My father would like that. I wonder how much it costs.'

June hands her protégé the price list and refuses to comment, despite her exasperation. More mosques and minarets. She'll be glad to get away from Muslims trying to convert you and Bible belt evangelicals being born again. According to Rick, being reborn and joining the Republican Party would guarantee his job. Sure, Rick, she'd said, but why not turn Muslim and collect the Ramadan bonus as well?

Now Maha's surveying the room and the other pictures, wondering whether her work is in the right place, especially with her father and his friends coming tomorrow. She suggests that her paintings might be moved to a more prominent position and Antonio agrees. June says she'll look into it, but irritated by this last-minute dissatisfaction she escapes to the Ladies' restroom.

Walking back through the foyer, she's surprised to see Rob talking to DJ Jerry. They are watching the opening of the Pioneers video with grainy black-and-white film of Model T Fords chugging along desert tracks, first to the sound of cheerful hillbilly music and then as they meet the sand dunes, the wailing of Arabian instruments. The American voice-over describes 'this ancient land encountering the Western world for the first time, with Saudis and Americans forming a creative partnership to exploit the kingdom's natural wealth.'

'More corporate bullshit,' June says, greeting the two men.

'Sure,' says Rob. 'But you've got to admit these guys were brave. No airport, no four-wheel drives, no phone calls home.' His voice is louder than usual and she guesses he's been drinking.

'And no Scuds,' DJ Jerry says. 'Rob was telling me about the Souks bombing. He's sure lucky to survive.'

They stay silent, watching film of the pioneer camp's wooden bunkhouses through the dust of a *shamal*. A heavily bearded geologist is chipping at a rock with his hammer and beaming towards the camera.

'I'd better get back to setting up this show,' says June. 'Want to see the pictures, Rob?'

'Hey, I've finished recording my Gulf War tape,' DJ Jerry tells them. 'You guys want copies, souvenirs?'

'Sure,' Rob says as he follows June through the foyer towards the library.

'So, ET, did you phone home?' she asks.

'Had a call from Chris, my son, and then from my sister-in-law. Fiona's ill and they want me to come home.'

'What a surprise.' She feels the irritation and bite in her voice. 'So everybody wants you to come home now.'

'Chris has to go back to university. And my sister-in-law can't stop work to look after Fiona.' He seems to be talking to himself, instead of her, and trying to reach some decision. Like it's an afterthought, he asks, 'So where are your pictures?'

As she leads him to the side room, June realizes she's angry with him and *Desert Storm* is becoming a test – not just of her picture but of this man. How much does he care for her?

'So what do you think?' she asks, as they stand in front of her painting. He's seen it before, but after Maha and Antonio's rejection, she needs him to enthuse and support her. Instead, he looks uncertain and moves up closer to the picture. He's peering at the pale outline of the NBC hood hovering like a ghost over the windswept Bedouin tents, a part of the painting she's had problems with.

'You don't like it.' She vents the frustration repressed earlier. 'I know it's not obvious or beautiful. It's not desert scenery, pretty mosques or minarets. Is that the problem?'

'I'm not sure,' he says with a stupid drinker's smile. His mind's elsewhere, probably thinking of his neurotic wife, while she's standing here, wanting him to appreciate her work and tell her that *Desert Storm* is striking with its imagery of modern warfare.

'Sounds like you're not sure of much, Rob,' she says. 'So what do you think of my other painting?'

She indicates the elegant vase standing in a halo of sunlight at the cave entrance. 'It's called *The Ancients* after the Anasazi Indians who lived in Chaco Canyon, New Mexico. This pot was discovered hundreds of years after the Anasazi fled from the canyon.'

She wants a response, but her words feel like pearls dropping before swine.

'It looks great, June.' He's trying to compensate for his previous blundering.

'So what's great about it, sweetheart?'

Put on the spot, he's struggling. 'I like the colours. And the atmosphere.'

'OK. Let's go outside and talk. Maybe you want to tell me something.'

She leads him through the late evening melancholy of the camp library. A few men close to retirement sit studying the stock prices in the *Wall Street Journal*, while a bunch of Junior High School kids are whispering round a table, hurrying to finish their homework. She opens the glass fire door at the back and, stepping out into the chill smoky evening, they look across a near-empty parking lot towards the old row houses.

'Rick's coming back tonight,' she says, forestalling another night together.

'OK.' He doesn't seem concerned. 'Tomorrow, I've got to get up early for this emergency exercise at headquarters. I'm playing one of the casualties. An injured or dead man.'

'That figures,' she says, and he laughs with her, but then realizes she isn't joking.

She continues, looking for his reaction. 'I've decided to leave and fly back to the States, to see the kids.'

'OK. So when are you going?' He asks like it's a polite inquiry, and nothing to do with their making love this morning or planning to go to Santorini together.

'As soon as flights start up again. I'll go see Kate in San Francisco.'

'Good idea.' He sounds relieved, as if that's settled and he can concentrate on his neurotic wife back in the UK.

'So what's wrong with Fiona now?' she asks.

'The doctor says it's bronchitis and maybe all this stress.'

'Stress?' She realizes she's shouting and lowers her voice. 'You came back for this war and I stayed here with Rick. Doesn't your wife know it's stressful *here*, with Scuds flying round and people being killed? *You* were nearly killed. Did you tell her? And she's staying at home, a fucking housewife...'

'I promised her I'd leave after ten years,' he says, like he's reminding himself. 'The ten years are almost up.' As if she's interested, he starts talking about mortgages, pensions and jobs back in the UK. But she doesn't want to listen to his financial sense. It reminds her of the 'big bucks' and retirement package Rick's always talking about. No other sense, physical or emotional, seems to matter in these men's lives.

A knock on the glass fire door and she turns to see the Filipino gallery manager with the head janitor trying to catch her attention. They probably want to move Maha's precious paintings to a more prominent position, more suitable for the General Manager's daughter. She has to go back in.

'You'd better leave then,' she says. 'Get ready to fly back to your wife.'

'When can I see you?' he asks.

But she's already closing the door, going back inside to attend to Maha's precious pictures. She doesn't need all this hassle, but the Art Show opens tomorrow and she's determined it's going to be great.

28

Judgement Day

27 February 1991 / 13 Sha'ban 1411   03.35

War never sleeps, and Ibrahim remains stubbornly awake. TV images of injured women and children and fears for Muna and his baby keep returning with this continuous droning of planes above. Another wave of bombers rises up to inflict death and destruction on teenage Iraqi conscripts entrenched in Kuwait, women and children trying to shelter from the bombing in Baghdad and Basra.

His illuminated *adhan* clock marks four in the morning and still two hours before they leave. But his head won't settle on the pillow, his body can't lose consciousness and free itself from this relentless drone of planes taking off and landing. Exhausted, he twists and turns in bed, the wisdom of Sheikh Azzam resounding through his head – *one hour of jihad is worth more than seventy years of praying*, and *martyrs are the true building blocks of Muslim nations*. The Scud falling on the Crusaders' barracks and last night's talk with his father about the noble Mahdi have stimulated him, signifying the time for vengeance. If he and Saeed wait any longer, this *Mother of All Battles* will be lost and the Western Crusaders victorious. Instead of joining the struggle, they would have stood by ignobly, too cowardly to strike.

Ibrahim's used to safety and maintenance checklists and to calm himself, he runs through this list in his mind.

The Transit van. Repaired and serviced by Saeed's Filipino mechanic. They've driven it around camp and finished preparing it, curtaining the back windows so nobody can see inside and hanging a thick grey Bedouin blanket behind the front seats. The blanket hides the tube assembly they've bolted to the floor and the steel framework from the junkyard they welded together at a firing angle of forty-five degrees. He's cut away a section of the roof for firing the mortar and covered it with a large sheet of cardboard – white like the van, for camouflage.

The oxygen cylinders. Recovered from the junkyard behind the camp garage and used for launch tubes. How much explosive pressure can these rusty cylinders withstand? Enough, Saeed reckons. This should be simple compared to the Stinger, and firing doesn't need special training.

The mortar bombs. Saeed and a brother who works at the agricultural research station filled them with ANNIE, an explosive mixture of ammonium nitrate and nitrobenzene. The Irish fighters' mortar attack in London showed how to do it. Simple, like the Brighton bomb that almost killed the British iron woman, Mrs Thatcher. One powerful blow, just one successful strike, could destroy the Crusaders' famous IT Centre.

Ignition. Saeed talks about the batteries and timers he learned about in the Sheikh's training camp. But despite his boasting, how much real experience does he have? He was a charity worker and it's over two years since he returned from the Afghan *jihad*. After the Stinger failure, they'll keep things simple and use an ordinary fuse long enough to give them time to escape.

Parking. The van should be positioned as close as possible to the IT Centre. Too far away and the mortar bombs will fall short onto the headquarters concourse, the explosions weakened by paving stones and palm trees.

Hitting the IT Centre and the technicians at their morning shift change should halt oil and gas production and slow down the Crusader war machine for weeks. That's ideal. But even if they only hit something close like the IRA did in London and appear on the BBC and CNN *Headline News*, they'll strike fear into the enemy and rouse the faithful to action.

Saeed talked about booby-trapping the van to destroy any evidence, but Ibrahim's heard that the Irish were sometimes killed by their own booby traps, priming the explosive before they reached their destination and the van's movement setting off an explosion. The van will probably explode anyway so there'll be no evidence left when they escape in Saeed's sports car.

Ibrahim tries to think calmly. Anything they've missed? Anything they'll regret or realize later was obvious? This relentless drone of planes is making his head ache, but in a few hours he and Saeed will strike back. Muslims are used to heavy blows—punishment from the Zionists and Christians— but these Crusaders, despite their superfast computers and smart technology, can be shattered with just a few well-aimed strikes. He remembers the Beirut bombings, when two blessed martyrs exploded truck bombs and killed three hundred American and French marines in their barracks. That day Reagan's cowboys were scattered like cockroaches when the kitchen light's switched on, and fled to the safety of their aircraft carriers in the Mediterranean. They never dared return to Beirut. *Alhamdullilah.* This so-called 'superpower' has a weak will and no stomach for sacrifice.

He turns over to his illuminated *adhan* clock ticking down the minutes and ready to ring out soon. He's delayed long enough and throwing off the sheet, he can hear Saeed starting his martial exercises and smell the fresh coffee for their last day on camp.

One hour of jihad is worth more than years of praying, Ibrahim repeats, as he hangs his ebony prayer beads around the rear view mirror and pushes the key into the Transit van's ignition. One turn and the engine putters into life, an innocent purring from the Filipino mechanic's servicing. He feels the relief, the tension easing from his neck and shoulders, the day's excitement and adrenaline beginning to pump through his body. He shivers, thinking about the power of the explosives lurking at his back, behind the thick grey blanket, shifting so gently now, caressing the back of his head and shoulders.

With Saeed's red Camaro following, he sets off, driving slowly out of the parking lot into the early morning mist darkened by smoke from Kuwait. The lights are on along the road, illuminating the brown edge of the spray fields, the sandy curb still wet from last night's sprinkling. No vehicles are moving yet through the sleeping camp and it feels as if only he and Saeed are alive on this day of judgement. He's approaching the traffic lights onto the main road, but with this explosive power behind him, he's fearful of stopping and having to start up again. Nothing coming, and ignoring the red light he turns left, driving past the brightly coloured BMX ramps under floodlights and the ghostly shapes of sandstone *jebels* bordering the golf course.

The traffic lights at Golf Course Road are red, but the road's deserted and turning right in the van, he glides gently through the intersection. Saeed's still following in his sports car, like a wealthy but faithful disciple, as they drive slowly up past the oiled fairways where in a few hours, fat middle-aged Americans will be trundling round in golf carts, and boasting about their victory in Kuwait. Shifting into third gear, Ibrahim passes the club house and the deserted driving range by the filling station.

Now he can hear through his half-open window the voice of the muezzin calling *Come to success, come to success* and he can see before him the stained glass windows of the new mosque, the illuminated towers of Houston East looming behind it. Slipping down into second gear, he eases the van over the speed bumps, turns into the mosque's near empty parking lot and heads for a space by the fence closest to and opposite the IT Centre. Slowly he reverses back into a parking space so the mortar is facing the Centre. He brakes very gently to a halt, pulls on the handbrake, switches off the engine, and, relieved, gets down from the driver's seat. Looking over the barrier of concrete blocks topped by green fencing and towards the IT Centre he realizes that the first step's completed, the Transit van and mortar are ready and in position. At seven o'clock, after prayers and when the Centre's technicians are meeting for their shift change, they will strike.

29

Rick's ID

27 February 1991 / 13 Sha'ban 1411   04.30

Gateway to Safety. Rick gazes up towards the white printed lettering on the green archway above the main gate. He's standing outside, beside the road, watching the guards check vehicle stickers and passenger IDs as cars and trucks drive slowly through. He needs to get back onto camp, into Houston East. But where's his ID? Where's the laminated card with his mugshot, the C for Senior Staff, his badge number, blood group and 'All Areas' security clearance?

It's not in its usual place, hanging in a plastic holder clipped to his shirt. He feels for the card in his jeans' pockets but nothing there. Panicking, he peers down to the sandy ground around his feet, in case he's dropped it. But there's no ID lying beside the camp's high chain-link fence. He steps forward to peer through the fence towards the Big House beside the main gate.

But no one he knows is standing outside on the steps. No Al smoking one of his cigarillos or the Chief in his white *thawb*, standing with arms folded, pretending to be the master of all he surveys. Several guards walk out with gun holsters on their belts but Rick doesn't recognize them and they don't seem to notice when he waves towards them.

Maybe he can walk up to the gate, speak to the guys in the guardhouse and show he's American, maybe phone somebody to sign him in. He remembers an ID number—182372—and there's another number, too, he dimly recalls. But isn't that the old one? His dad's badge number – the one Rick used when he'd fly back from college as a returning student? In those days he needed a dependent's ID to get into the snack bar and swimming pool, to hang out with his Junior High buddies through the vacation, showing off to the girls and diving and splashing around to those good, good, good vibrations, the Beach Boys' surfing sounds echoing over the speakers all summer long. It felt like being in carefree California as he sat up high in the lifeguard's chair overseeing the pool. 'Wouldn't It Be Nice', 'Sloop John B' and 'California Girls' on a loop. And wasn't there some weird religious argument with mom about 'God Only Knows?'

But where's his ID now? A terrible suspicion's dawning on him. For some dumb reason he's abandoned Mother, landed in Houston and enlisted in the Marines heading for boot camp at Parris Island and onto Vietnam. No, he's not going back through *that* door…

Somehow he's lost Mother's ID and taken the big bird back to a chaotic world of druggies and draft dodgers, a world where there's no respect or place for men like him. Can he get his ID back? He looks towards the gate where other men—Americans and Arabs—are driving past the guards without a problem and heading towards the towers of Houston East. Gazing across at company headquarters he knows now – he needs to get through the main gate to rescue these people in the towers, to save them from disaster. But first he needs his ID.

Fully awake now and panicking, he sits up on the couch, dishevelled and uncomfortable from sleeping in his uniform. What time is it? He peers at his TAG Heuer service award. It's almost five o'clock. Three hours before the Emergency Response exercise. Faint light is slipping in around the sitting room blinds, and through the gloom he can see his glass with its sweet black residue of *sid* and Pepsi. June's art magazines are piled up on the coffee table and her wooden easel's empty, without that *Desert Storm* picture. Now he remembers the Art Show. She'll have taken her painting across to the community centre ready for the opening. He relaxes back on the couch, relieved to find himself safely returned to Mother, to February 1991 and in his bungalow on Main Camp. Thankfully, he closes his eyes.

Later, when Rick sits up again, his ID's safe in its plastic holder, lying on the floor beside the couch. He must have dropped it when he returned after midnight from his inspection tour along the coast – checking security at the oil refinery, the old gas plant and the off-shore supply base. In Khafji, he sat on a wall outside the abandoned Beach Hotel, strolled along the rubbish-strewn sands to see a grimy sea awash with oil, and watched Saudi National Guards clambering over a broken-down T55 Russian tank and posing for their buddies to take photos. But now he's home and reassured, he glances at his watch – just after six. Almost two hours before the Emergency Response exercise.

Jackson's lying across the room on June's couch. Usually he jumps up as soon as it's light, bugging Rick for a walk, but after turning his head to check his master's not moving, he lies back to doze again. Recently, he's been lethargic, moping on the couch or lying out on the patio in the back garden. Did June take him to the vet's like he told her? More money, but he'll pay the price for his dog, like he's paying for Danny and even Kate, June's peacenik daughter. He's proud to have always paid the price for what's needed. That's being a real man, despite what these crazy feminists say.

Finding the remote, he switches on CNN and is shocked to find the war's almost over. The bombing dragged on for weeks but this ground war's moving fast and feels like it's ending soon. Over twenty thousand prisoners taken, most of them eager to surrender, and there's film of Iraqi soldiers straggling along with their hands in the air, being shepherded by Apache helicopter gunships flying overhead. The Marines are fighting for control of the airport outside Kuwait City and the Iraqis are fleeing north towards Basra. Shit. Vietnam should have been this easy.

But then, like a sick afterthought, there's bad news – a Scud dropping on an army barracks near the Souks. There's film of smoking rubble cordoned off with police cars blocking the road. Thirty dead and over a hundred injured. So close. That Scud could easily have dropped here on camp. And wasn't Bill moving into a place near the Souks? All this shouting about victory and liberating Kuwait, but nobody's talking about the poor grunts killed and wounded in that barracks. And why weren't the Patriots fired?

He hauls himself up, pads through to the phone in the kitchen and calls Bill's number. Nothing, but also he realizes probably nothing to worry about. Bill always escapes, home free. Wasn't he one of the first guys out of Da Nang, before the whole joint went belly-up? And that AWACS flight over the Gulf he keeps boasting about was another BS triumph for his CV. Different story, though, if that Stinger some terrorists fired had shot up his backside. Afghan Saudis, the Chief said. Seems the *mabahith* have caught some crazies from Riyadh. But they're keeping these guys under wraps. Don't want the world to know there's trouble in paradise.

But he needs to get ready for this Emergency exercise. Sounds dumb with the war almost over but Mother always follows the Plan and that Scud could have carried chemicals or nerve gas. Still no sound from June's bedroom as he passes and he showers in the bathroom, with her face and body stuff all over the place. A few weeks since the desert trip and him losing it – splitting her lip with blood running down and June scratching his face, yelling and screaming. He'd driven her to the clinic to get the lip stitched. Thank God she told the Arab doctor she'd fallen over Jackson. But the way that guy looked at him and the long tell-tale scratch on his face… It wasn't his fault. It was her and that Brit playing him for a fool. And the kicking he gave the guy showed he wasn't going to be jerked around.

Before leaving the bathroom, he needs to take his blood pressure pills. He opens the medicine cabinet to find them surrounded by more of June's tubes, boxes and bottles of lotion. That's why his blood pressure's so high. Because of her fooling around, as well as all the BS he has to put up with at work. One blue tablet, one yellow, one white and one orange, plus a garlic pill for his heart. He swallows them down with a tumbler of water and catches sight of his face in the mirror. Tired, older, but still handsome. He could find another woman from someplace where they've never heard of feminism. A cute Filipino or a Vietnamese girl. But they're always shopping and spending money. Does he want more hassle at his age?

Once dressed, he puts Jackson on the lead and pulls the poor mutt to his feet. Did June take him to the vet's? He'll wake the bitch and find out when he gets back.

Outside, the sky's gun-metal grey, the atmosphere tart with smoke from burning oil wells. But it's nowhere near as bad as up north where the sky was near black and he'd looked out at a grimy tide swilling in to dump gobbets of oil along the beach. Relieved to be back home, marking out his territory, Rick glances round the ball field, but nobody's about yet. Looking up towards the ballfield apartments, he remembers Maria, the Chief's secretary. A missed opportunity but maybe she'll come back now the war's almost over. He adjusts to Jackson's plodding pace, leading him past the bleachers and through the empty parking lot behind the snack bar and movie theatre.

The poor mutt's dragging on his lead and Rick halts on the grass verge in front of the old row houses where they lived in the Sixties. The long wooden veranda in front of the houses reminds him of the family sitting out in the cool of the evening to watch the sunset. No air conditioning then, only electric fans and keeping the windows open to catch the slightest breeze. He looks to Jackson but he's showing no interest in the fallen dates round the palm trees, and has to sit down to pee in the grass. God, the poor mutt looks like he's on his last legs.

Leading his dog home, Rick glances across towards the community centre, the Arabian Pioneers banner fluttering over the entrance. June will be there all day playing the Great Artist and maybe he'll pass by this afternoon, score some brownie points when the Saudi General Manager visits. Entering the bungalow, he listens for sounds of movement, of June in the bathroom or getting dressed. The lazy bitch should be up by now. He feeds Jackson and fills the dog's water bowl, watching him slop round and flop down again on the couch. He'd like to do that himself after the long journey home and only a few hours' sleep…

But it's time to get ready for duty. He straps on his Beretta in its neat button-down holster and feels the weight and authority of the gun against his hip. He'd worn it on his trip north and the security guards had been impressed, eager to be equipped and trained for action. He takes a last glance in the bathroom mirror. Good to go, but still no sound of movement, of that bitch getting up. Suddenly anxious, he pushes open the bedroom door and peers into the gloom. June's lying under a sheet, motionless and seeming dead to the world.

He stamps his feet stepping into the bedroom but June's still motionless, lying on her side with her back to him. He can't see whether she's breathing or not. Walking over to the bed, he leans over, peering into her face. The ragged scar running from nose to lip looks almost healed. She seems to be breathing. Maybe she's taken too many pills and mixed them with *sid*. Her olive-skinned shoulder is exposed outside the sheet and he strokes the skin with his fingers, hoping she'll move. But then, worried, he shakes her shoulder until she opens her eyes.

'Wake up!' He's furious, but breathing in her languorous odour of scent and perspiration, and with her naked body close and sprawling under the sheet, he gets this crazy desire to strip off and slip in beside her. To burrow in, warming and refreshing himself with her body. But he steps back, a big man in his Security uniform and with the Beretta in its button-down holster. Is he frightened of her, of what she might do? If he just took out this gun, it would all be over. He steps back to a safer distance for both of them.

'Jackson's sick,' he tells her. 'Did you take him to the vet's?'

'Sure. I did what you told me.' She leans up on one elbow, on her side looking at him. 'So we're playing happy families now?'

'What's the vet say?'

'Jackson's tired and depressed like the rest of us. No high temperature, so the vet gave me some more tablets for his joints and multi-vitamins.'

'Vitamins! He needs more than fucking vitamins – he's sick.' The phone's ringing in the kitchen but he let it ring. 'You hear about this Souks bombing? Bill Eliot said he was moving to a place over there.'

'No worries, Rick. Your best buddy's OK. He called to let us know.'

At least she's talking sensibly so he tells her the big news. 'The Iraqis are retreating, dragging their tails out of Kuwait. Looks like this war's going to be over soon.'

'Good. So I can leave and go see the kids.' She turns her back on him, the sheet slipping down over her bare shoulders.

'Sure, bitch, be my guest.' Sounds tough, but then he's almost overwhelmed by a surge of self-pity. He's just got back from this long trip through the war zone but had to sleep on the couch because of her craziness. She'd threatened to knife him when he tried to make up to her. But he could use some warmth and consolation instead of this constant aggro and threatening to leave.

'You can't leave this country without my permission,' he tells her.

She turns back, levering herself up on her elbows, the sheet slipping from round her breasts. He steps forward, tempted to smack her face or pull the whole sheet off but the phone's ringing again. Maybe it's Al and the exercise has been cancelled.

But instead, when he picks up the receiver, it's Bill telling him he's OK after the Scud bombing. He's moved onto the Base, making sure the Iraqis get what they deserve. 'It's personal now,' he says.

That's Bill and this war. It's personal and justifies his whole life. Rick puts down the receiver and can hear sounds of June showering in the bathroom. She's got her painting and pottery. Why can't she just shut up and settle down like other wives? Like his mother in that old row house with no air conditioning? Needlework and fancy embroidery, that's what *she* did most nights, and made beautiful country quilts like the ones in the community centre.

But, no excuses. He knew June was trouble when he met her. Only then it had seemed a challenge, an adventure he could handle.

At the bathroom door, he shouts through. 'Anybody calls, I'm heading over to headquarters for the Emergency exercise.'

Yet then, on a hunch, an ugly suspicion – did he see something on the bedroom floor? He doesn't leave. Instead, he forces himself to walk back into the bedroom. The window blind's still down and he puts on the lights so he can see better. As usual, she's not made the bed – an Indian blanket and pillows lie where they've been flung on the floor. Rick bends down, and almost hidden by the blanket is a white towelling wristband with blood on it. He'll kill the bitch and that Brit.

30

The Building Blocks of Nations

27 February 1991 / 13 Sha'ban 1411   06.10

'Master of the Day of Judgement. Guide us to the straight way.' The words resound in Ibrahim's head as he prays in the *musallah*, wanting to be possessed by this guiding spirit. Yet as he leaves, the fever in his mind returns. He waits for Saeed on the steps of the mosque, fingering his prayer beads, as he gazes across towards the grey concrete blocks and steel fence protecting the high temples of the Crusaders. The smoke-rimmed sun is rising up over the towers, glinting off rows of still undamaged plate-glass windows. No Muslims are working today inside the IT Centre and only a skeleton staff of *kuffar* technicians are monitoring the supercomputers that control the country's oil and gas. In less than an hour, the technicians' turnover and shift change begins.

But this Gulf war is ending in disaster, heading towards a humiliating defeat with the Crusaders raining down bombs on thousands of Iraqi conscripts fleeing Kuwait. The Zionists and Christians are already celebrating victory and preparing to impose their New World Order. The Scud that fell on the American barracks briefly silenced and subdued them, but stronger blows are needed to regain the pride and honour of Muslims all over the world.

He glances round for Saeed, impatient with the young Saudi talking to Dr Eissa and Kamal, the Egyptian manager. It's getting late and Saeed should be preparing to fire the mortar. The young man's chatter is annoying but still Ibrahim envies how he wins over people and makes himself popular. Maybe it's because his father's a senior manager, but his charm seems to make it easier for him to deceive his American boss and colleagues, even the women secretaries in his department. How can someone so friendly and so modern in his love of new technology be hiding something? How could *he* attack their IT Centre with its advanced supercomputers?

At last, Saeed, accompanied by Kamal and Dr Eissa the sweet-voiced imam, join him on the steps of the mosque.

'My son, Hashim, sends his good wishes,' Kamal says, shaking Ibrahim's hand. 'He's marching in the anti-war demonstrations in London.'

He seems to expect praise and congratulations for his son going on a student march but Ibrahim just nods. These talkers think they're so important and are changing the world, but only holy warriors prepared to be martyrs can defeat the Crusaders and expel them from Muslim lands.

'I'm returning to my country,' Ibrahim tells them. '*Inshallah*, I will celebrate Ramadan and Eid with my wife and new baby son.'

Dr Eissa, blessed with four sons, congratulates him. 'It's good that Saeed is travelling with you. Many of our brothers visit Sudan these days. Dr al-Turabi gives blessed sanctuary to the faithful and is guiding the new Sudanese leaders. I hear the Sheikh will also be travelling there for his company to build a new airport.'

Ibrahim glances at his watch and looks towards Saeed.

'I fear this war is ending very badly for our brothers,' Dr Eissa continues. 'All we hear about are smart bombs and video film from these Crusader jets, while thousands of our brothers and sisters are being killed. Yet Allah does not give us more than we can bear.'

The other men agree but, impatient with such fatalism, Ibrahim turns to Saeed. 'It's almost time. We must go.'

'We pray for your success,' the imam assures them and, secure in his ignorance, embraces his young disciples.

'Saeed.' Kamal takes the young man's arm. 'I have a message from Hashim.'

'I'm going to the van Saeed,' Ibrahim says. 'I'll see you there.'

'A minute and I'll come.' Saeed turns to the Egyptian.

Leaving the two men, Ibrahim hurries down the steps and across the small courtyard. He turns the corner of the mosque.

But a security car has pulled up beside the Transit van. A slight figure in Western clothes, the Saudi Texan he recognizes from the camp gates, and a heavily built young man are standing there. The Saudi Texan is peering through the van's windscreen at the thick grey blanket hanging behind the seats and concealing the mortar assembly.

'This your van?' the Texan demands. 'You must go. We have emergency exercise this morning.'

'What emergency?' Ibrahim asks but the heavy young man, built like a wrestler, moves forward to assert his authority.

'We are internal security.' He places his hand on a leather holster, and Ibrahim is shocked to realize these men are carrying guns. 'You drive away, my friend, and leave this place.'

Ibrahim looks round to see that other security guards have appeared and are hurrying along the departing worshippers, cordoning off the parking area with cones and red-and-white tape. He has to leave – any more argument and these men will search the van. And now they have guns to enforce their orders. The Texan is examining the Transit van's vehicle sticker on the windscreen and writing in his notebook.

'Your camp sticker's out of date, my friend. You must replace it at security office.'

'Yes, sir.' Ibrahim forces himself to be humble. 'Tomorrow, *inshallah*.'

'OK. You leave now.' The Texan is glancing over towards the head-quarters entrance. The emergency exercise seems to be starting with the guards opening up the steel gates for patrol cars, ambulances and what looks like an armoured truck to drive through and onto the paved concourse.

'Go quickly now,' the heavy young Saudi repeats, fingering the holster of his gun.

'*Assalamu alikum.* What's the problem my friends?' Saeed's arrived, standing beside Ibrahim. There's an exclamation from the young security man and Ibrahim's surprised to see him and Saeed embracing each other.

'Faisal, my dear cousin,' Saeed tells Ibrahim. So this man, built like a wrestler, must be his contact in Security.

'OK. But you leave now,' the Saudi Texan insists, glancing over towards the ambulances and patrol cars parked around the Red Crescent Portakabin. 'The emergency exercise is starting.'

Ibrahim looks to Saeed. How can they refuse to leave? What can they do now?

'*Yalla.* Let's go,' Saeed says. 'I'll take my car and follow you.'

'OK. See you later.' Ibrahim struggles to keep his voice calm as he opens the van door and climbs up onto the driver's seat. 'Just follow me, Saeed.'

He watches the young Saudi and his security cousin embrace once more and whisper in each other's ear. What are they saying? Saeed strolls back to his sports car while the two security men turn their attention to more vehicles driving onto the concourse. Medics in hospital whites are gathering by the ambulances and several figures wearing white NBC suits are clambering out of the armoured truck to unload their equipment.

Saeed's got into his sports car and Ibrahim starts up the Transit van, listening to the reassuring putter of the engine. He reverses carefully and drives slowly away, trying not to disturb the mortar explosives as he drives through the parking lot, scrupulously following the exit signs in case the Saudi Texan is watching and wants to stop him again. Whatever happens, he mustn't attract their suspicions or bump over something with these explosives. But he needs to control this trembling that's started in his hands, the fear threatening to take hold. He thinks back to their plan, the steps he's rehearsed in his head. But everything's disrupted now. Where can he go? Saeed needs to help him fire the mortar, so where can they meet?

The gates to the headquarters buildings are still wide open. If he turns sharp left and charges through the entrance, he could drive straight across the concourse and head straight for the IT Centre. The guards would be caught by surprise – there'd be nothing to stop him ramming the entrance doors and exploding the van. But that would be martyrdom, with no chance of escape. He picks up speed towards the turning, and glancing left towards the open gates, his body tenses for battle. Yet now the steel gates are swinging closed, the opportunity disappearing, and his body eases back into the driving seat. He brakes, slowing down, takes a right turn and drives out onto the road in front of the mosque. He checks in the rear view mirror and is relieved to see Saeed following in his sports car. So where can they park and fire the mortar? It must be within range of the IT Centre.

He's passing the mail centre, driving down by the Communications building with its tall aerials and satellite dishes perched on the roof. At the bottom of the hill, he turns left through the traffic lights and passes the hospital with its line of ambulances parked outside. He's picking up speed and, conscious of the explosive power behind this blanket shifting against his back, he feels drops of sweat dripping under his armpits and into his shirt. He turns left again, round the back of the headquarters buildings but then, in his rear view mirror, he sees the Security car following.

They suspect something. The Saudi Texan's in the passenger seat with Saeed's cousin driving. Just behind them, he can see Saeed in his red sports car. They need to talk, to decide what to do next. But how can they talk now?

Motherfucker! Rick sees the Brit sitting outside the Red Crescent Portakabin with his arm in a sling. He's talking to some Arab, another of the walking wounded with a bandage round his head. Thinking about that sweaty wristband, the blood on it, lying on their bedroom floor, Rick fingers the button on his holster. The bitch has done it again – betrayed him while he was on duty up north near the Kuwaiti border. He unbuttons the leather holster and walks over towards the Brit. An accidental shooting? The Beretta just going off?

But there's no way he'd get away with it. There'd be witnesses, an investigation. The Brit seems to be talking to the Arab about quitting and leaving the country. Like that bitch June this morning. Is that it? They're planning to leave together, June abandoning him here?

'Are your guys ready?' the Emergency Coordinator demands, walking up to him.

Rick realizes he's been staring over towards the Brit and his Arab buddy and this big exercise is starting soon.

The Coordinator glances at his watch. 'Almost seven. We'll be kicking off in eight minutes.' He heads over towards the armoured truck, and the guys in white NBC suits checking their equipment.

Rick looks round for Al and Faisal, but they're not by the guard house at the main gates or on the concourse. Have they gone into the mosque? Prayer time finished a while ago, when the guards cleared away the worshippers and their cars, and cordoned off the area. Al and Faisal were around then, but they should be here now when the exercise starts. So where the hell are they?

Ibrahim sees the drop-off space at the IT Centre's rear entrance gate. He signals to pull in there, hoping the security car drives on and he can speak to Saeed. But the patrol car's turning in behind him, stopping, and in the wing mirror he sees the Saudi Texan opening the passenger door. He'll ask more questions, probably demand to look inside the van.

Ibrahim can't stay, and starts the van again, his hands shaking, his foot slipping on the clutch. The van jerks forward and he feels the thick blanket swishing against his back and shoulders. He forces his way out into the stream of cars and trucks, his eyes darting to the rear view mirror, the men in the patrol car pursuing him. But where's Saeed? He can't see the sports car. He leans forward to peer through the mirror again, then the wing mirror, but Saeed's gone. He's abandoned him again, like he did on the wasteland by the airbase. He's on his own – so what can he do?

Where can he go? If he keeps driving along this road, he'll be stopped at the main gate. The Saudi Texan and the wrestler will catch up and search the van. Somehow, he has to turn back and escape.

This early morning traffic is still light and the opposite lane nearly empty with a wide gap between cars. But if he makes a U-turn and hits the opposite curb, the mortar bombs will explode. Any shock will be the end and he slows down, veering left towards the inside curb, then wrenches the steering wheel round, making a screeching U-turn in the road, the thick blanket swaying against his head and shoulders, the patrol car blaring its horn behind him. Narrowly he avoids hitting the pavement on the other side and righting the van, accelerates away, back down towards the hospital. Security know for sure now. The patrol car's siren is shrieking as he races back, through the traffic lights as they switch to red, and up the hill towards headquarters.

The siren's warning everybody and some white uniformed medics crossing from the mail centre turn to stare and jump out of the way. The security men are closing up behind him as he heads back towards the mosque where only a short time ago he'd prayed and was at peace.

Where to? He has nowhere else to go as the headquarters gates are opening wide for another ambulance to drive through. Grabbing this last chance, he forces his foot down on the accelerator, hurtling towards the gates.

He's close behind the ambulance, past the guardhouse and through the steel gates, racing across the concourse towards the IT Centre. A bunch of men in NBC suits are gathered round the armoured van and start shouting when they see him. Medics and men wearing slings and bandages round their heads are scattering like cockroaches before him and he's delighted, lightheaded with this power in his hands and at his back. He wrenches the wheel round, avoiding a palm tree, and pulls round again to right the van as he heads for the IT Centre, with all the Crusaders fleeing before him.

But a tall security man has stepped out, standing alone and pointing a gun towards him. A wave of images is surging through his mind – of himself as a boy taking scholarship exams in the school hall; standing with his father on the Prophet's birthday outside the Mahdi's tomb; sitting for an Eid family portrait with Muna and his family. Strengthened by this righteous spirit and proving himself to Allah and his father, he charges on until the windscreen shatters in his face.

The van swerves out of control and crashes into a palm tree. A moment of excruciating pain, of sacrifice and martyrdom, before everything explodes into his day of judgement and the glorious Paradise to come.

31

The Turkey Shoot

28 February 1991 / 14 Sha'ban 1411   21.40

So what now, Rob wonders. He's still shocked by yesterday's attack just as he and Tony were sitting by the Red Crescent Portakabin. All at once, people were yelling, medics scattering, and Rob glimpsed the Transit van careering across the concourse. Then Rick stepped out in front of the van and it exploded into flames. Another explosion and Rob covered his head with his arms as fragments of the van flew all over the area. Then a few moments of stunned silence as they watched the burning debris, before an uproar of voices and sirens broke in. Rob watched the flaming skeleton of the van and Rick in his uniform holding a gun and surrounded by security guards congratulating him.

It felt like a last act, a blazing conclusion. And now the Gulf War is suddenly over, suspended as George Bush announced a ceasefire and the Iraqis accepted all the UN resolutions. Bill Eliot phoned before Rob left on patrol and was furious about Bush and Powell, the Chief of Staff, ending the war too soon, after only one hundred hours of the ground offensive. Bill wanted to march onto Baghdad and execute Saddam, but it seems the

State Department are afraid of Iran increasing its power and Iraq splitting into three parts – the north for the Kurds, the centre for the Sunni, and the south for the Shia. Bill's indignant but Kuwait's been liberated and Rob feels satisfied with this peace as he lights his ritual Marlboro cigarette and stands once more on the bluff overlooking the airbase. No planes seem to be taking off or landing and the hardened shelters and barracks lie wrapped in silence as if, like him, they're wondering what to do next.

CNN have been showing film of the Iraqi army's rout – long distance black-and-white shots of what journalists are calling the Highway of Death. As the soldiers fled along the road from Kuwait City, driving luxury limousines, stolen police cars, fire engines and anything else they could steal, they'd been caught in the open. American jets had blocked the convoy by dropping mines in front and behind, and attacked with cluster bombs and rockets. Trapped bumper to bumper, the Iraqi convoy had shuddered to a halt, stranded in a four-mile traffic jam that the planes and helicopter gunships kept attacking. Thousands of burned out and abandoned vehicles were scattered over and around the highway, along with the plunder the troops had looted from Kuwaiti stores and houses. Video recorders and stereo systems intended for soldiers' homes in Iraq, jewellery and cosmetics for their wives and girlfriends, and toys for children they'd never see again, all spilled across the highway and littered the surrounding desert. Corpses, charred beyond identification, lay in and around the burned out vehicles. 'It's a turkey shoot,' Bill had crowed over the phone.

Now the danger's passed, Rob's brought Cilla along to celebrate his last patrol. He shines his flashlight down the bluff to see her wandering around the shallow crater where the flaming Scud and Patriot pieces fell early in the war. If he'd stayed here longer that night, maybe for a second cigarette, he'd have been incinerated. Not that he recognized it at the time – he was too tired and preoccupied with June. And later, if the Scud had dropped on Bill's apartment block, he wouldn't be here to taste this cigarette and blow smoke rings into the night air. Blind chance and good luck had determined whether he lived or died.

He looks up to what people used to call the heavens, but the smog blowing south from the Kuwaiti oil wells still shrouds the moon and stars. Another drag of his Marlboro. Should he continue this treat after the war? But will it taste the same without the excitement and danger? He'd tried one of Derek's Silk Cut when he called round earlier to see him but the taste lacked this drama.

'So who's going to be the new Liverpool manager?' Derek had asked. And next weekend with no more night patrols and alert sirens, Rob can listen in peace to the World Service commentary on the Reds' crucial game against Arsenal. These long hours of patrolling the perimeter fence, sudden alerts and missiles flaming through the sky have ended, to be replaced by nights of uninterrupted sleep and the steady hum of life plodding forward. Yet he still has to decide – go home and look after Fiona like everybody seems to want, or stay here?

For a moment, he savours the pleasure of thinking about June: the joy and relief of making love after escaping the Scud attack, the sigh of satisfaction as she turned over naked beside him. Poor Jackson scratching at the kitchen door had to wait.

But at the Art Show, he'd stupidly failed to admire her paintings and when she talked about leaving Rick, he'd said nothing. Maybe he could make it up to her. But he'd have to do it soon.

Nearly ten o'clock, and tossing his cigarette, he walks down to the patrol car to check in with the Big House.

'Your last patrol, *sideeki*.' Al sounds cheerful. 'Tomorrow you can sleep all night.'

'Looking forward to it, Al. Any news on that suicide bomber?'

'We were chasing the van before it exploded. I saw an African guy, but there wasn't much of him left for the medics. I don't know whether they found the head. But God willing, we're lucky to escape, my friend.'

'I didn't see anything about it on tonight's news.'

'No, you won't see it on CNN. They've decided to keep it quiet – low profile. Who wants to encourage these *jihadis*? We were lucky, my friend.'

They're silent for a few moments, appreciating their good fortune. There were minor cuts and bruises among the medics and security guards, but the ambulances and nurses were already there.

'So what are you going to do now?' Rob asks.

'I've been transferred to a new area. This place in the desert where they've discovered a new oil field. My assistant, Faisal's taking over here. He's wanted my job for a long time, so he's got it now.'

'What about your family?'

'They can stay at home and I'll fly back every few weeks. I'm going to be like you guys – a visiting father. But the extra money for working in a remote area will help.'

'Is the new job a promotion?'

'*Inshallah*. If I please everybody. Maybe now the war's over and the Shia have proved their loyalty. There's some talk about reform, a *shura* council to advise the King. But what about you, *sideeki?*'

'I've got to decide some things as well.' At last Rob asks the question he's kept thinking about since parting from June. 'So, is Rick around?'

'No, my friend. He's the big hero now. I think he's gone north with the company CEO, who specially wanted to thank him. All the big men go north these days, to Kuwait City for the victory celebrations. Do you want to congratulate Rick as well? They're talking about a gold Kuwait Liberation Medal and some big reward for him.'

'Good.' But Rob's thinking about June. Maybe he'll phone and try to make up for their stupid argument. Maybe he could still go to Santorini on that Easter trip – show some courage and change his life after all.

'*Ma'assalama*, my friend,' Al concludes. 'And you stay careful out there.'

Rob gets out of the patrol car and opens the back door so Cilla can scramble onto the yellow carpet over the seat. He'll drop her at home and phone June, see if she's OK and can speak to him. The war's over and why shouldn't he take a break on his last patrol?

But as he turns to get back in the driver's seat, he notices a truck driving down past the camp garage and the agricultural station. Now it should turn the bend, heading for the lights of the bachelor housing block. But instead, the truck's headlights are beaming on, bumping along the rough track by the perimeter fence. It looks like a Land Cruiser. Maybe June's coming to see him and make up after their argument. Maybe they'll get together tonight.

But then, as it comes closer, he realizes – it's Rick and when he last saw him he was holding a gun. No time to call for help and Rob starts the patrol car, driving along the track, through the mounds of dirt and rubble, and towards the electricity substation. The Land Cruiser's following and in the rear view mirror, he can see it closing up on him. He's driving too carefully and presses down on the accelerator, bouncing in the seat as he bangs over bumps and potholes. Cilla's standing on the back seat barking and swaying on her yellow carpet. Desperately, he glances round at the dirt mounds on either side looking for a way out. Can he turn somewhere, head back to the main road, and reach safety?

He's passing the chain-link fence round the substation and looks to turn along a track towards the road. But that way's blocked by rubble and he has to bump and bang further along towards the trees and thickets round the lake. Now the Land Cruiser's so close – its headlights in the rear view mirror blinding him. He tries to fix his gaze on the track ahead, ignoring the bangs and scraping against the car's floor.

He reaches the clearing before the trees where he usually parks, but Rick's close and could run him down. He ploughs forward, forcing his way through long grass and scrub, until the trees stop him driving on. He jumps out, the engine still running, and Cilla scrambles over from the back and out of the car. But Rick's close behind and the Land Cruiser's almost on top of them, its headlights illuminating their escape.

With Cilla racing in front, he starts running down the jogging track, brushing past the thickets and trees on one side, the reeds bordering the black waters on the other. A truck door slams, then all he hears is his heart pounding as he tries to run faster, his body gasping for breath.

A shot cracks out. Shocked, he staggers, nearly falls, but then scrambles forward glancing round for somewhere to hide. Terrified, Cilla's racing ahead, leaving him behind. He wants to turn and see where Rick is, but there's no time – he's too close and will shoot again.

At the end of the lake, there's a gap in the thickets and Cilla leaps through onto the flat, open spray fields, the lights of bachelor housing shining in the distance. He chases after his dog but trips over, jarring his knees, scrabbling on the ground and crawling into the long grass and prickly thorn bushes.

He can see Cilla running free across the spray fields but she's caught in a sudden stream of light. A shot, and with a yelp she stumbles, captured in the beam of Rick's flashlight.

Rob crouches with his head down in the thicket, panting heavily and pushing away thorns from his face to see what's happening. Out of reach on the spray field, Cilla's yelping in pain, crying for his help but he must steel himself to resist and stay hidden. Rick's light beam shifts, surveying the jogging track and bushes, searching for him. Slowly, the light skirts above his hiding place, lingers a few moments, and moves on. Cringing in this hedge while his dog lies out there wounded, he remains rooted with fear, hiding in these thorn bushes.

Rick's flashlight beam returns to Cilla yelping and whimpering in pain and Rob watches the tall uniformed figure advancing across the wasteland towards his dog. At that moment his whole world feels struck dumb. He can't believe what's happening, and doesn't want to believe it. Rick's gun is against Cilla's head. A shot and she's silenced.

There's a growing hiss from somewhere and he realizes it's under the ground. The sprinklers around the spray field start up, gently showering the earth and Cilla's body lying out there.

'You can hide, motherfucker,' Rick calls out from nearby. 'But you're next.'

Through the steady showering of the sprinklers, Rob listens. Where's Rick now? Cramped in the bushes where he's kneeling, he has to move, easing his body into a new position, his face away from the thorns. He hears muffled steps along the jogging track, the flashlight beam advancing towards him, then halting as Rick searches for his enemy.

He can still hardly believe it – Cilla's lying out there, dead. And he's hiding here like a coward, feeling powerless again. But not this time – instead of retreating further back into the thicket, Rob crawls forward to the edge of the sandy track. His face is clear of the thorn bushes and he can see now that Rick's moved past and is standing with his back to him, the flashlight trained on a clump of trees. Stealthily, Rob raises himself free from the sheltering bushes and lurches forward, hitting Rick in the back and knocking him to his knees. Summoning all his strength, he kicks him in the ribs. Rick shouts out, struggling to get up and Rob kicks him again – then again. Beside Rick's flashlight, the gun's lying on the ground and Rob grabs it, pointing it towards his enemy crawling away. 'Run, you bastard. Run!'

But Rick's still on his knees, cursing and massaging his side. Afraid he'll recover, Rob steps forward and kicks him hard again in the side. 'Run, you bastard!'

Rick staggers up, hobbling down the track while Rob peers through the gun sight, calmly holding the weapon with one hand and aiming it at Cilla's murderer. He squeezes the trigger and fires, the recoil knocking back his arm and shoulder. But Rick's still moving away, a figure now stumbling back down the jogging track. He's missed the bastard.

He waits, recovering himself, until the truck door slams, the Land Cruiser's engine erupts and headlights flood the trees as Rick drives away towards the perimeter fence.

Rob throws the gun into a thicket, grabs Rick's flashlight and hurries across the spray field through the sprinklers and towards Cilla's body, curled up as if for protection. Illuminated by the distant lights from the road, he bends over his dog, his companion all through this Gulf War. Desperate to do something for her, he takes off his windbreaker and presses it down on Cilla's side to staunch the blood still trickling out, mixing with water and pooling round her body. But there's no sound or movement left, no way he can revive Cilla to run again.

Soaked through and recognizing his impotence, Rob stands up, feeling the chill of the night through his body. Standing alone amidst the deathly silence, he feels utterly bereft and lost in this desert wasteland. All he can do now is go back for the yellow carpet from the patrol car, wrap Cilla up in it, and drive back home to bury her in the garden. Tonight their Gulf War and their finest hours together have ended.

Tomorrow he'll have to call Fiona and Chris, tell them that Cilla died in an accident and mourn her loss with them. He'll let them know he's resigning and coming home after all – maybe leaving on the same flight as Derek. No consolation for Cilla's death but maybe a fresh beginning for them all.

32

Cutting the Gordian Knot

Kuwait. Twelve Years Later

09 April 2003 / 07 Safar 1424   17.00

Shut your eyes and you can see better, said frisky old Gauguin before opening them again to paint all those ripe bare-breasted Polynesian girls. June closes her eyes, trying to blank out this hotel swimming pool, the civilian contractors and soldiers lounging round as they wait to cross into Iraq. In her mind's eye, she tries to see where Danny is. What's he doing now, at this moment, somewhere in Iraq, as she swims across this hotel pool? Stretching into her stroke, kicking her legs, breathing and gliding through the lukewarm water, she touches the poolside, turns in a pleasing wriggle of her hips, pushes off with both legs and is heading back. Another length completed, her arms lift her through the water and she's delighted to be swimming again in this Arabian spring sunshine.

Since last week when she flew into Kuwait, she's swum every day to clear her head and savour this body while she's still alive, and so many others she knows are dead. Dead like her disappointed alcoholic father and Christian doormat of a mother, like Rick's miserable parents in Las Vegas, and Geno, Kate's Deadbeat Dad, following his rock 'n' roll heroes into oblivion. But no famous Paris cemetery or memorial stone for him. Who'd be crazy enough to pay for that?

Death, the end of even this body, as she slides through the all-embracing water. Returning to the warm Arabian Gulf, she remembers Desert Storm, when Rick was the great hero who shot a suicide bomber and saved Mother's precious IT Centre. That guaranteed his job, made sure Danny's school fees were paid, and beefed up his retirement pension. But that suicide bombing so close to headquarters had felt like a premonition, when ten years later, on the morning of 9/11, Rick yelled for her to leave the studio and they watched the Twin Towers fall.

It felt like an assault from this alien yet familiar world of *muttawa* and *jihadis* following them from Saudi and catching up with them. It was hard to believe, like the *Towering Inferno* movie, until people started jumping from the Towers, even from Windows on the World where after the Gulf war, Bill took Rick and her for a celebration dinner. That night she'd sat in a window seat with her feet against the ledge, looking down from the 107th floor to the twinkling lights across New York Harbour and Liberty Island – Manhattan lying literally at her feet.

Now the Towers had gone, all one hundred and seven floors with almost three thousand people dead and thousands more injured.

Yet life shrinks or expands in proportion to your courage. She must be brave and enjoy this body while she's still got it, and can warm to the memory of Rob loving her on the night when the Scud fell. A sweet guy, but after the war, he'd wimped out and hightailed it back to his neurotic wife. Like a Sunday school teacher, he'd talked to her about responsibilities, and with her and the whole wide world before him, he'd skedaddled back to Liverpool and that stupid football club. Christ, even the Beatles got out of there ASAP.

This invasion's triggering memories, though. Last week, he emailed her through Friends Reunited and talked about coming over to Kuwait as a safety consultant. He said he'd recently got divorced – as if that would interest her. She might email him back sometime, but in this life you need to keep going forward, like swimming on to your last lap.

Rob hadn't liked her *Desert Storm* painting, probably didn't understand it. Where is it now? Somewhere in her studio and maybe she'll show it again when she gets back to the States. Maybe this War on Terror might awaken interest. First time she showed it in Denver, people had already lost interest in the Gulf War. After all the build-up and months of hype, the fighting had been over too quickly. Like Rick said one time when they were arguing, her picture had finished up like the war – a dark confusing mess. She'd had too many different ideas, mixing her blood with oil and using desert sand. Some of the surreal imagery worked, but maybe she'll paint over some of it and look at the picture again when she gets home, see if it can be resurrected. Maybe she can make it about this War on Terror, this never ending battle for Western civilization and the oil and gas that keep the whole show on the road.

One more length done and suddenly tired, she turns over on her back to rest, looking up into the clear blue sky to enjoy the spring sunshine, to absorb all that healthy Vitamin D and feel-good serotonin entering her body.

It seems like a long time ago now, but what was the last Gulf War about? Freedom for Kuwait? At least freedom from Saddam and the Iraqis. It was the end of the Vietnam complex, like Bill said, so the military could have their tickertape parade down Broadway with heads up high, and good old boys like Rick and Bill could play patriotic hard-asses round the barbecue on 4 July. They'd called it a great victory but there'd been no clear conclusion, just a mess with Saddam still controlling Iraq and Bin Laden's *jihadis* trying to drive the US out of Saudi. They'd even bombed the Khobar Towers where Bill used to live. Instead of an end, the Gulf war had proved just the start of what Bush calls the War on Terror.

So what's this Iraq invasion about? Getting rid of Saddam and his Weapons of Mass Destruction? Freedom and democracy for Iraq? Creating a new Middle East and New World Order? Sure, there's million dollar contracts as well for companies like Bill and Rick's that have taken over this hotel near the Iraqi border. And there's the oil, of course – the dirty black stuff that even protesters like Kate use in their cars, to heat their homes and depend on for all kinds of cool stuff. Nobody wants to get their hands dirty, like Bill says, but everybody sure wants the product.

She's flown over to see Danny but like Rick warned her, his division had already headed north by the time she arrived. They say there aren't many casualties so far, but only a few soldiers died or were wounded last time, compared to the thousands struck down with Gulf War Syndrome. So what was this mysterious Syndrome? Was it physical or mental, or both? Some said it was the crazy anthrax vaccinations and pills the GIs were given, or maybe depleted uranium from missiles and shells. Strange, but the Iraqis seem less lethal to soldiers than guys like Cheney, Rummy and the Pentagon top brass. So what about this new war under the same Republican mismanagement? For Danny's sake, she hopes the Texas cowboys have learned something.

She turns at the pool wall and, feeling rested, kicks off again. Rick and Bill are sitting together at a table under a green umbrella, with Bill reading that clash of civilizations book he carries round and quotes from, like it's the Bible. It's written by some Harvard professor with a name that sounds like a disease and old Henry Kissinger's praising it on the front cover. According to this Bible, the 1991 Gulf War was the first war of civilizations, and Bill says this War on Terror is the second. He's supposed to have retired from the battle and be sitting in an armchair somewhere, but retreads like him never seem to retire. They keep answering the call and screwing with stuff until they disappear someplace or fall off the stage. They reckon the military can't do without them.

Rick's watching the poolside TV but where's Clive, the Brit reporter she met in '91 and sat next to on the plane coming over to Kuwait? She slows her stroke to glance round but it looks like he's skedaddled. After lunch, he was sitting by himself beside the pool writing in his notebook. She'd said hello as she passed, sat down beside him to be sociable, and in hushed tones they'd critiqued this latest war. They joked about George W Bush, that dumb cowboy, and Deputy Blair, and Clive praised some big Stop the War march in London – the kind of protest Kate's still getting into in San Francisco and that Rick and Bill call treachery. She and Clive had been getting along fine, reliving the old Vietnam War protests and him saying she was still a good-looking woman in her swimsuit. But then Bill showed up, shouting that journalists should be downtown at the Marriott, not sniffing round here, and the company took over this hotel exclusively for its offices and employees. Bill wanted to know how Clive got in through security and called his British newspaper 'Commie propaganda'. Disappointed, she'd left them to argue and now Clive's disappeared. Pity. The clash of puffed-up male egos was always fun to watch.

The hotel gym faces onto the swimming pool and when she looks up she can see these cocky crew-cut GIs on the other side of the plate glass, lifting weights, pounding the treadmills, determined to build up their bodies for the coming battles in Iraq. Some of their T-shirts are weird, pledging vengeance for 9/11. Has nobody told them? Most of the hijackers were Saudis. There were no Iraqis. And anyway, Osama bin Laden and Saddam hate each other. She feels sorry for these poor kids spending hours in the gym, believing only more muscle and brute force can save them – they can charge into Iraq like Rambo and knock some sense into these ragheads. A few words of Arabic would be more useful, and she's sent Lieutenant Danny a phrase book, hoping to God he'll use it.

A bunch of young officers are sitting under an umbrella at the poolside, sunning themselves and lathering sun-cream over their muscular tanned bodies. She senses their eyes following her through the water and feels proud of this body surging towards them, firmer now after she's lost ten pounds since the New Year.

'Hey, June.' Rick's voice and shadow loom over her. 'Come and look at what's happening.'

But she's determined to finish her ten lengths and there's only one more left. Leg kick against the wall, breathe, and she's gliding away from him through the warm water, the spring sunshine beaming down on her body surging through the pool. She doesn't want to leave yet, lift herself out and step back into the irritations of listening to grumpy old Rick, Bill, and their good old boy contractor buddies. If she's not careful she'll grow like them and be spouting the same Republican bullshit.

Last night, Fahad, Bill's Kuwaiti boyfriend, joined them in the executive lounge. He swept in wearing gorgeous Kuwaiti robes and was going with Bill to meet some local businessmen about re-opening Basra port. She'd been thinking of visiting Danny sometime when things settled down in Iraq – got some idea she'd like to see the archaeological sites and ancient pottery before the tourist parties started coming. So while Rick and Bill were at the seafood buffet, loading their plates, she asked Fahad about visiting Babylon and if there was anything left of the Hanging Gardens. But 'Don't go there,' he warned her. 'The Kuwaiti are like babies. Soft and gentle. But the Iraqi are brutal. Saddam made them worse. My cousin never came back when they took him in '91. Sure June, oil makes us rich but curses us as well.'

As she finally touches the pool wall, there's clapping and cheering spreading round the poolside with guys standing up to applaud. For a crazy moment she thinks it's a joke and they're clapping her, but...

'June, it's happening. It's over.'

Rick's elated, his bulk overshadowing her as she stands against the wall, breathing heavily but happy at completing her distance. Too tired to haul herself out, she paddles over to the pool steps, water streaming and dripping from her black swimsuit as she climbs out.

Excited voices are blaring out from TVs positioned around the pool. CNN are reporting the drama of Operation Iraqi Freedom, the world coming together to watch another shock-and-awe Pentagon spectacular in the Middle East. The old Masters of War are at it again and conquering all before them.

Brushing the hair from her eyes, she follows Rick, wearing his Hawaiian shirt and old khaki shorts, in padding back to their table. One last payday before retiring, he'd promised her, and he wants to make sure it's a big one so they can all live happily ever after. So he says!

Old Bill, who must be on his last overseas assignment, heading for some prison outside Baghdad, is already celebrating. He raises his Pepsi bottle in the air towards the big TV screen showing Paradise Square in the centre of Baghdad – a GI is climbing up and covering the face of Saddam's statue with the Stars and Stripes.

As June wraps herself in a big hotel towel and sits down, Bill turns from the TV.

'We're making history today, folks,' he announces. 'Like Alexander the Great, we've cut the Gordian knot. The peaceniks said it was too complicated, too difficult. But we've cut through all the crap and are remaking the Middle East.'

For a few moments, the great dictator's head is draped in Old Glory but slowly the flag's slipping off. An officer, probably trained in PR, takes over and replaces Old Glory with a red, white and black flag – presumably the flag of Free Iraq once the politicians have got their act together. 'Boy Scout,' Rick mutters, but the Iraqis yelling and screaming round the base of the statue want more than a new flag. They want to drag their failed Saladin down into the dust. They're fixing a rope round the giant statue, this colossus which until now had been untouchable. They heave mightily on the rope but despite all their efforts need help. Obligingly, a US tank grinds forward and now Saddam Hussein's great statue in the heart of Baghdad, the symbol of his unrelenting grip is leaning sideways, being hauled down. The great dictator—author of at least quarter of a million Iraqi dead, one million Iranians killed and wounded, and millions of other stunted lives— is toppling slowly and inexorably towards the dust. His arm, raised to the heavens in triumph and defiance of his enemies, is pointing now towards the ground and tumbling to earth. Twenty-five years of brutal dictatorship are collapsing into a heap of worthless scrap metal, concrete and cement rubble. Furious Iraqis jump on the statue, battering it with their flip-flops as they yell their contempt and celebrate their liberation.

June glances across to the long windows of the hotel gym where the GIs chosen to remake the Middle East have broken off from their muscle-building to yell and cheer at the TVs showing the scene from Baghdad.

'Should have done this in '91,' Bill crows. 'Finished the job like I said.

The Ayatollahs in Tehran will be watching this and crapping themselves. Well, buddy, your turn next. Get ready for some more good old American shock and awe.'

'Sure, but let's finish this first,' Rick says. 'We've still gotta get the real Saddam.'

'Wanted dead or alive.' Bill raises his glass. '*Mafi muskallah*. No problem, amigo. Hey, let's go to the Iranian restaurant tonight, get used to eating *chelow kabab* again. Next year in Tehran, my dear friends.'

June smiles to please the poor deluded guy. But is he really so deluded? If Iraq can fall so quickly, why not Tehran? American shock and awe seems to rule the world now the old Soviets and their empire have collapsed. Globalization, the Internet and mobile technology are the new things and America's charging ahead with this New World Order.

In CNN's studio, the armchair generals and gung-ho reporters are wetting themselves at the fall of Saddam's statue and this new Middle East. June wonders if Rob's watching. Maybe he's somewhere in England, observing this from some dull company office or sitting with his neurotic wife in some suburban bungalow. He hadn't cared enough for her. Say what you liked about Rick, he cared and was still prepared to pay for Kate and the twins in San Francisco. Ready to pay for her as well, so that her life is still changing and exciting with the joy of flying here, and being alive. She feels buoyed up by the fall of Saddam's statue and the celebrations all around her. Maybe she'll visit Lieutenant Danny when things settle down, she decides, dismissing a fleeting sense of fragility – that somewhere a door might be closing, accidentally locking, while she's sitting here celebrating by this hotel swimming pool.

Lightning Source UK Ltd.
Milton Keynes UK
UKHW011846190120
357228UK00001B/44